TRACKS

TRACKS

J. T. GODDARD

First published by Underhill Books in print and electronic editions.

ISBN: 978-1-988908-54-0 (first trade paperback edition)

ISBN: 978-1-988908-58-8 (first electronic edition)

The characters and events in this book are fictitious. Any similarity to real persons, living or dead, is coincidental and not intended by the author.

To the 158 members of the Canadian Armed Forces who did not return from Afghanistan

And the 40,000 who did

Thank you for your service

Chapter 1

Sergeant Gavin Rashford of the North-West Mounted Police scuffed his shoe at a small pebble on the sidewalk. It flew for a couple of feet before bouncing off the column of a parking meter and ricocheting into a shop doorway. Rashford raised his arm in celebration, exclaiming 'goal!' under his breath, then quickly bent his elbow so he could scratch the side of his head as he received a strange look from the lady exiting the store.

He continued down Twentieth Street, past the charity clothing stores and the pawn shops, heading towards the hospital. He was early for his dinner date and had decided to take the long way around to the restaurant. The shops gave way to some rundown houses, built for returning veterans after the Second World War and barely renovated since.

The houses each had a small front garden, narrow boxes of dirt or grass between building and street. Some still had the descendent of an original hedge, but most now sported a chain wire or wooden picket fence.

As he walked along, he could feel the late afternoon sun on his neck. Peering over a fence, he was pleased to see a few late crocus flowers, yellow and mauve against the grey dirt. In another garden he saw a row of yellow daffodils, nodding on the warm breeze and imperiously ignoring the old cigarette packet, fast food wrappers, and a used condom, all blown around their stems.

The warmth of the sun and the colour of the flowers reminded him that here in Saskatoon it was early spring, not the late winter he had left behind. In the north the snow was just starting to melt, revealing the detritus of communities without garbage collection or a waste recycling program. He remembered driving his snowmobile along a lane just outside a small, isolated village, the walls of waste on each side acting like boundary markers. 'Diaper alley', one of his colleagues had called it, a name that had stuck in their heads and even found its way into reports.

He crossed the road at a traffic light and reversed his course. A couple of men squatting on the sidewalk hurriedly returned small bottles to their pockets and looked down at the pavement as he walked by. Even in civilian clothes, the aura of a police officer emanated from his very pores. He returned to the main road and turned left, then was soon approaching the restaurant where he was to meet his date.

"You froze your dog?"

"Yes."

"Why?"

"Well, um, he was dead."

Gavin Rashford looked across the table. He could sense that this dinner date was going the same way as the last one he had had, that is, nowhere. The woman sitting across was staring at him, her mouth open, tendrils of linguini trembling from the fork she held halfway to her mouth.

"Dead?"

At least her mouth remained closed after she spoke. The marinara sauce had made her teeth look like she was a vampire.

Her eyes never left his as she slowly returned her fork to the plate. Then she reached out with her hand until she felt the napkin and lifted that to dab at her lips. She put the napkin down.

"I think I'll go now," she said, standing up. "Thank you for the dinner invitation but I am afraid I am suddenly not feeling very well."

Rashford quickly put down his fork and stood as well.

"I'm sorry to hear that," he said. "Well, if you want to try again some time, when you're feeling better, you have my number."

"Yes. Yes, I think I do," she said, then moved past him. They were sitting in one of the two window booths, so she had to step down and make her way through the tables as she walked out of the restaurant. Rashford sat down again and reached for his beer, then turned his attention back to his Chicken Parmigiana with fries.

He had thought it all out this time and was surprised at how unsurprised he was with the outcome. They had sat next to each other on the plane down, and he had learned she was a government lawyer who specialized in resource extraction cases. When he had said that he was a police officer, she had seemed interested in his work.

She had recommended the restaurant, an Italian place located in a building constructed to appear like a pair of railway carriages. She had told him she would get a cab and meet him there. The walk from his hotel had taken nearly forty minutes, including his detour, and he was hungry. He had thought that after dinner they could walk through town then over the bridge to Bud's, which had a reputation for great live music. It looked like he was now going to be going on his own. He went to take another drink then realized his glass was empty, so looked around for the waiter.

It was early evening, and the restaurant was nearly empty. A family of four were arguing in a lighthearted way about who would get the last calamari. A couple in the corner were picking at the lasagna they were sharing, and the woman who had been sitting at a table in the other window booth when he arrived had still had not ordered her food. Rashford waved his glass in the air and a waiter over by the bar nodded.

The woman at the next table held up her own empty glass and called over to him.

"Can you get me one as well, please?" she said. "He's been ignoring me."

Rashford looked at her, then waved at the waiter again, this time holding up two fingers. The waiter nodded again.

"It's coming," said Rashford. "I hope Original 16 will be okay?"

"That's the local one, right?"

"Yup. Brewed here in Saskatoon."

"That's fine. I was drinking Coors Light but hey, you only live once, right?"

The waiter arrived carrying two glasses, both of which he placed in front of Rashford.

"No, one is for the lady," he said, gesturing to the next booth. The waiter looked at him, then carried it over and placed it on her table.

"Would madam like to order now?" he said, his tone implying that she had sat in a prime seat long enough.

"Yes, I think so," she said. "I'll have Spinach Salad please, the one with cranberries and goat cheese. Thank you."

He nodded, then took away the two menus which had been on the table.

"This as well, please," said Rashford, and the waiter removed the plate of seafood linguine marinara. The woman smiled.

"At least your date met you before standing you up," she said, raising her glass in a mock toast. Rashford raised his back.

"I suppose you're right," he said. "Cheers." He took another bite of his chicken and swallowed, then took the chance.

"If you've been stood up as well," he said, "would you like to join me for dinner?"

She looked at him for a moment.

"Sure," she said, "that would be nice. Thank you."

She stood up, picked her purse off the back of her chair, and held her glass in the other hand. As she crossed over to Rashford's table the waiter rushed across and quickly moved new cutlery into place.

Rashford looked at her. She looked like she was in her early thirties, wearing a lightweight tartan jacket over a pale blue blouse and a medium length skirt. He noted that she was about five and a half feet tall, with curly red hair dropping to her shoulders. Her cheekbones protruded a little, rounding out her face, and she wore drop earrings that looked like silver feathers.

She was not heroin thin like a model, but neither was she what he personally thought of as 'clumpy.' Rather, she had a solid look to her, curved in all the correct places. She was wearing black knee-high leather boots,

"Please, keep eating," she said. "Mine is only a salad, it won't be long."

Before she had finished the sentence, the waiter reappeared, this time carrying a salad bowl which he placed in front of her. He stepped away, then returned holding a huge pepper grinder in his hands.

"Would madam like some pepper?" he said.

"What a big grinder you've got," she said, giggling. Rashford tried to hide a smile, but the waiter kept a straight face; he had no doubt heard that one before. The woman blushed a little.

"No, this is fine, thank you," she said. He nodded, then turned and walked back over to the bar.

The woman looked at Rashford, then raised her glass again.

"This is actually pretty good. Thank you for suggesting it. My name is Roxanne, by the way."

"I'm Gavin," said Rashford. "Pleased to meet you."

"Ditto."

They both ate quietly for a few minutes. Rashford finished his chicken and picked at a few remaining fries.

"May I have one?" said Roxanne. "I try to be healthy in my diet, but I do like fries, I'm afraid!"

"So, if you don't order them, then they don't have calories?" said Rashford.

"Something like that," she said, laughing, and reached across to spear two fries with her fork. She ate them slowly, as if savouring every morsel, and Rashford could not help but smile. When she had finished, she took another drink of her beer, then looked straight at him.

"May I ask a question?" she said.

"Of course," he said. "Go for it."

"Well," she said, "I know it was rude of me, but I couldn't help eavesdropping on your conversation with your date. And I have to ask this, because I'm dying to know. Why did you freeze your dead dog?"

Roxanne was still laughing as they left the restaurant and made their way across the busy street at the traffic light.

"Thank you for making me laugh," she said. "That was brilliant."

Rashford smiled as well. The frozen dog story had not been particularly funny, it was simply a matter of reality, what happened when you lived in an isolated northern community. Snafu had been almost eleven years old, seventy-seven in human terms, and so when he passed it had not been too much of a surprise. But there were no vets in Black Rapids, the small fly-in community where Rashford had been posted for the past eighteen months. He had had Snafu since before he went to the training program in Regina, and so far, his name had mirrored Rashford's career.

"You know, SNAFU, it's old army slang, situation normal, all effed up," he had said, ordering them both a third beer. "I'm a police officer, a Mountie, and I'd messed up on a case, let the prime suspect get away, and so I got sent to the north as a penance. When Snafu died, it was winter, and the ground was frozen. I didn't want to just throw him out in the garbage, or in the bush, so I put him in a plastic bag and put that in the freezer."

"Next to your food?"

"Well, yes. But that was all in packets as well. And it wasn't like he was going to eat any of it."

She snorted into her drink, and he looked aggrieved.

"I really don't see what the problem is here."

"No problem," she said, holding up a hand. "It's just not, you know, what most people might call normal."

"It made perfect sense to me," he said. "Anyway, I kept him there until I could come south, which officially was today. I was lucky to get on an earlier flight, there was a last-minute cancellation, and I was on a stand-by ticket, so I snagged it. But I wasn't able to check a bag, the freight hold was full of frozen caribou or fish or something, so I wrapped Snafu in a blanket to keep him frozen, then another bag in case the first one leaked or anything, then put him in my carry-on."

"Wasn't there a problem at security?"

"What, in Black Rapids? No, I could probably carry a frozen human on through there, they never look at the x-ray machine, they're always too busy gossiping. Anyway, I had put the bag in the overhead rack thing and when we landed, the lady next to me accidently knocked it down when she was getting out her bag. She'd picked it up and given it to me and made some comment that it was heavy. Then, when we met for dinner tonight, she reminded me of that, and asked me what was in the bag."

"And the rest is history?"

"Indeed," he said.

"So, why is it called Black Rapids? That sounds a bit gruesome."

"It's a good story," said Rashford. "Apparently one of the early explorers, perhaps Samuel Hearne, was travelling in the area, back in the late 1700s. He had with him a Dene guide, whose name is lost to history. Not Matonabbee, that was later, he guided the big expedition to the Coppermine River. This was an older guy, and he brought with him his grandson.

"Anyway, they were canoeing down the river from Stony Lake when they hit the rapids and their canoe capsized. They lost everything. Their gun, food, spare clothes, powder, ammunition. It all got swept away. In fact, they only just escaped with their lives. Luckily the guide had managed to keep a hold on the canoe, and was able to swim it to shore, so they had that at least. They portaged down to the bottom of the rapids and tried to figure out what to do next. They were cold, wet, hungry, and miserable, and had no matches to light a fire even if they could find something to eat.

"The grandson saw an eagle's nest up in a tree, so he climbed up and snatched the eaglet that was there. When he got back to the group they wrung the neck of the bird, then pulled off the feathers and devoured the flesh. There was a lot of thick yellow fat, apparently, and both the boy and Hearne ate that as well. The old man just took one slice of meat from the leg of the bird and chewed on that slowly.

"According to Hearne, and I read this in his diaries, that night they slept well, until about three in the morning. Then both Hearne and the boy started vomiting, and had uncontrollable dysentery, something that continued for two full days. On the third day they were recovered enough that the guide could help them get into the canoe.

"'How was it you did not get sick,' said Hearne to the old man.

"'I did not eat the baby eagle,' he said. 'All the people know that to do this will make you sick.'

"Dene means 'the People' in their language," said Rashford, as an aside. "Anyway, to continue."

"Hearne was pretty mad at learning this information. 'Well, if you knew that, why did you let us eat the bird?' he said.

"'Well,' said the old man, 'the boy had to learn it on his own, not by me telling him. He has now learned this lesson. So that was good. And you, you are an old man, nearly as old as me, I thought you would already know about this truth. But then I saw you eat the bird, and I thought you must have some kind of great whiteman's magic to keep you safe from the sickness. I could not argue against your strength.'

"Hearne recorded the story in his diary and decided that Black Rapids was an appropriate name for the place where he had nearly lost his life not once but twice."

"Two days of dysentery and vomiting," she said. "That is gruesome enough for me."

"Yes," he said. "Too much information, I guess. My boss is always telling me off for that. 'Just the facts, Rashford', that's what she says. She doesn't like background and context."

"But that makes it a story," she said.

"Well, she would say that it was all supposition and speculation. We don't know how long after it happened that the explorer wrote it down, so he may not have remembered everything correctly. Was it really Hearne who had this experience, or had he heard it from someone else? If it was him, then he was only one of three people involved, so would the other two agree with his version of events? Those are the kind of things my boss would ask me."

"How would she tell it, then? Your boss. What would she say?"

"Probably something like, 'Black Rapids was named, possibly by Samuel Hearne, to mark what might have been the location where his canoe capsized, and where he nearly died.'"

"That's it?"

"Just the facts, Ma'am."

"Boring!"

"Indeed. But that's how I am supposed to write my reports."

There was a pause. They both sipped their beer.

"So, tell me, what is it that you do, exactly, in Black Rapids?" she said.

"Exactly?" he said.

She waited, expectantly.

"Well, not a lot, really. Usually, it's just driving around and letting people know you're there. There are two communities, Black Rapids and a small Dene village called Stony Lake, but there are only three officers posted there. So, you each basically do five or six 12-hour shifts a week, unless someone is on holiday or whatever, then you do more. There is an airport at Black Rapids, and a gravel road that gets you the fifteen klicks to Stony Lake. That's about it."

"But what kind of crimes do you have?"

"Just normal stuff. Checking that hunters have the right tags. Helping the conservation officers when the fishermen get lost. There might be petty theft from one of the tourist lodges. Drunks, fights. Sometimes there's a domestic situation that you have to calm down. Just normal life stuff."

She looked disappointed that there were no more scintillating stories, so he took a deep breath.

"The reason I'm here, today, is that I'm on my way to Regina. I have a meeting on Monday morning, so I took a couple of days leave and came down early. I thought I'd get some rest and relaxation in before I get my bollocking. This might be my last weekend as a Mountie."

Now she looked interested.

"Really? Why, what did you do?"

"Nothing, actually. That's partly the problem. That plus a local bigwig who's pissed off at me."

He signalled the waiter again, who arrived with two more beers and took away their empty plates. Rashford looked across the table.

"Are you sure you want me to bore you with this?"

"Yes. Please."

"Well, it was like this. I got posted to Black Rapids a year ago last October, just over a year and a half ago. Like I said earlier, I had messed up on a case and let a suspect get away. And he beat me up as he was doing it.

"When I arrived up north there was one other southern officer there, plus a special constable, a Dene guy. The people at the Rapids are all mixed, there's whites and Dene and new Canadians and everything, even a few Cree, but the largest group are Métis, and they tend to run things. Stony Lake is pretty much all Dene, except for a few teachers and nurses from southern Canada, and a priest who's been there for years but was originally from France.

"Things were fine at first. The three of us got on well, and we got into a routine. The local folk go trapping for furs in the winter, and hunting for tourists in the summer. Sorry. Bad joke."

She nodded, but he did see a bit of a smile, so he continued.

"The first year went well. I got on with most people except for this one Métis guy, Sammy Samson, who I didn't like much. He drove taxi and was making a fortune from scamming the system. If they had to be flown south for treatment, all the Treaty people at Stony Lake got chits from the nurses. These covered the taxi to the Rapids and back, plus the flight south. Samson used to load his taxi with seven or eight people, and take the chit from each of them, so for a twenty dollar ride he was collecting a hundred and fifty or more. And we couldn't stop it, because it wasn't really illegal.

"Anyway, he was also bootlegging, although we couldn't pin that on him either. He was too clever. Everyone in Black Rapids is allowed enough booze for private consumption, of course, but you're not supposed to sell it, and anyway Stony Lake was officially a dry community. We didn't know how he was getting it in, maybe by the summer barge or else he was having it sent to him by parcel post. We just didn't know.

"Late last fall, once we had freeze-up then a lot of people were out on their traplines. There was lots of snow to cover up the garbage and stuff left around the communities, the lakes were mostly frozen, but we could still fish in the shallow parts of the rivers, where the current was fast. It was a nice time of year, and I was enjoying myself.

"I would drive out on my skidoo in the evenings, watch the light crystals reflecting from the branches, stop and try to call the northern lights with the zipper on my parka. I had been on leave in the south over the previous Christmas and New Year, so it was all new to me. People were happy, chatting to each other, hunting caribou and ptarmigan and getting ready for the holidays. Things were quiet around town as we got into the middle part of December, even though we were expecting Christmas to be busy.

"Then one day we got a tip off. Apparently, Sammy was in La Ronge, the biggest little town in the north, and had spent an awful lot of money on booze. Cases and cases of it. Rye, vodka, rum, you name it. And he was taking it to the airport there, where he had chartered a plane. I don't know why but the young lad working at the liquor store called it in, and the La Ronge detachment called us. They said they had applied for a search warrant, and please would we have a look at the plane, when he landed.

"So, we got a copy of the warrant and then Charlie Toutsaint and I went out to the airport and waited. Charlie was the special constable I mentioned, a real big guy. He was quiet, but funny in a laid-back kind of way. We were sitting there in our car, a big old four by four, drinking coffee, and Charlie said, 'someone's gunna tell him.' 'Tell who?' I asked. 'Samson,' he said. 'Look.'

"He pointed over to one of the hangers, where a guy was standing. He was leaning against the door frame, holding a phone in his hand, and was clearly staring straight at us. 'That's one of his brothers,' said Charlie. 'Ah well,' I said, 'what's he going to do? He's in a plane, he can't just stop somewhere and drop it off. No, we've got him.'

"Charlie shrugged but didn't say anything. We waited. Eventually we saw the plane come up over the trees, circle the airstrip to make sure that the runway was clear, then come in for a clean and steady landing. The pilot decelerated as he passed the hangers, then when he was almost stopped, he turned and taxied slowly back. As he came up onto the tarmac apron we got out of the cruiser and walked towards the plane.

"It was a little Cessna, just a single engine, with room for five passengers and the pilot. The pilot was busy writing notes on his clipboard, but the offside door opened, and Sammy Samson stepped down. He ignored me and spoke to Charlie.

"'Officer Toutsaint,' he said. 'To what do I owe this pleasure?'

"'We hear you've been buying your Christmas booze, Sammy,' said Charlie. 'We have a warrant to search the plane.'

"'I'm allowed enough for family and personal entertainment,' said Samson. 'And as you know, I've got a big family.'

"There was an outburst of laughter, and I realized that nine or ten men had gathered around us. More of his brothers, I guessed, and some of the guys who did odd jobs around the airstrip. It was hard to say who was who, exactly, as they were all bundled up in their winter coats, toques, and scarves.

"'Yes, well, we need to have a look inside,' said Charlie.

"Samson turned and looked at me.

"'This is on you, isn't it?' he said. 'Ever since you got here you've been on my case. You screw up down south and they send you up here, and you think we're all just going to roll over and let you tickle our bellies. Well screw you. This is racial profiling, this is. Just 'cos I'm Métis and you're a southern prick. I'm gunna lodge a complaint.'

"'We still need to have a look," said Charlie, mildly. Samson spat on the ground between us, then stepped back and joined the others in the crowd.

"'Go ahead,' he said. 'But you break anything, you pay for it.'

"Charlie and I walked forward and climbed into the plane. The four seats in the area behind the pilot had been taken out, to provide cargo space, and sitting in the middle of the floor was a large cardboard box. Charlie looked at me and, when I nodded, took out his knife and cut the seal, then opened the flap. We both peered inside, where we could see twelve bottles.

"'Rum, rye, scotch, vodka, bourbon, and brandy,' shouted Samson from outside. 'Two of each. Now what the fuck's wrong with that?'

"'Panels off,' I said to the pilot.

"He sighed, then climbed out of his seat and rummaged around for a tool kit. Charlie and I watched as he undid each of the screws holding the inner panels to the fuselage, carefully lifting off the panel to reveal the wiring underneath. When he had finished, we made him take off the panels on each of the wings, and at the back under the tail fin, where the emergency beacon was kept. There was nothing there, nothing anywhere. Charlie and I looked at each other.

"Samson was still standing there. He only had two or three of his brothers still with him, the others had got bored and walked away.

"'You finished now?' he said. 'I'm going to make a formal complaint. Harassment, that's what this is. Any idiot could see there was nothing here. You've just wasted nearly an hour of my time. And it's fucking freezing. If I get pneumonia and can't drive my taxi, I'm gunna sue you for lost earnings as well.'

"He turned around and stomped off. I told the pilot he was free to go, drove Charlie back to the detachment, then went to my apartment and made myself a stiff drink. I could not figure out how Sammy Samson had tricked us, but I knew he had, somehow.

"Christmas went OK. There seemed to be quite a bit of drinking going on around town, a bit more than usual, but I figured that was just down to the holiday, people had come in from their traplines and sold furs, there was money around. Samson wasn't anywhere to be seen, though, and I heard that he had gone to another community for Christmas.

"On New Year's Eve I got the shock of my life. I spent it over at Stony Lake and at midnight all this gunfire broke out, rifles and shotguns and who knows what else, it was an awful racket. I was actually off-duty that night and was spending the evening with one of the nurses from the community clinic. I leapt up and got dressed, then raced out to see what was happening. People were outside their houses, firing up into the sky. I could hear the shotgun pellets skittering on the roofs as they returned to earth, and for a moment wondered what would happen to the 30-30 bullets. But the guys with rifles seemed to be smart and firing away from town, into the bush.

"Susie the nurse came out and grabbed my arm. She was French, from Quebec somewhere. 'Ooh, it's so romantic,' she said, leaning into me. 'They fire one round for every person in their house. Just to celebrate life, n'est-pas?'

"She pulled on my arm. 'Come back inside, I only had time to pull on this robe and I'm freezing. Warm me up.' So, we did, and I did.

"It was about a month later that Charlie told me what had happened, and why Samson had left town. We were driving back from Stony Lake after taking statements from a family. Some young kids had been playing cowboys and Indians and had taken their dad's 22. The seven-year-old had been in the outhouse when the 10-year-old took aim from outside. He shot him in the buttock. Susie assured me that the younger boy was fine, it was just a minor wound, but we still had to do the paperwork.

"As we drove along, Charlie said, 'Remember Sammy Samson?' I did, of course, but mentioned that I hadn't seen him around for ages, not since we'd searched his plane.

"'I hear he's in Flin Flon now,' he said, 'driving taxi there. He takes fishermen out to what he calls secret fishing holes along the Hanson Lake Road, then charges them double to pick them up later. I heard he quit drinking as well.'

"I was surprised. 'Really? Why?'

"'Remember I told you that someone would tell him about us? Well, they did. That phone call was to the flight tower in Prince Albert, and they persuaded the air traffic guy to radio a message to Samson that the Mounties would meet him at Black Rapids as arranged. But Samson knew he hadn't arranged anything, of course, so he figured that out pretty quickly.

"'Just south of Black Rapids there are all those small lakes. They were well frozen just before Christmas, and the snow had drifted up along the edges. Sammy got the pilot to fly really low and slow along the outer rims, and he pushed all his cases of booze out into the snowdrifts. Except for the one we found.

"'He had to wait until we were finished with the search, but as soon as he could he rushed home, got his skidoo and sled, then drove out to the lakes to get his cargo. But the problem was, it wasn't there. Someone had seen the plane doing these slow circuits and had figured out what was happening and had told all his mates in town. By the time Sammy got there, all that was left was a bunch of snowmobile tracks. And of course, he couldn't complain to us, because officially he hadn't been carrying anything to lose.

"'He got a new nickname that day, people started to call him Snowdrop, and to laugh at him. After about a month he figured that they were never going to stop, so he decided it would be easier all round if he just left town. Which he did.'"

Rashford stopped talking and had another sip of his beer. Roxanne was staring at him, shaking, tears running down her cheeks.

"That is so funny," she said. "Snowdrop! I love it. What a great story."

Once they finished their beers, Rashford paid the bill, dismissing Roxanne's requests to contribute.

"You can get the next ones," he said.

"Where will I do that," said Roxanne as they made the safety of the other side of the busy street. "What's your next idea?"

"I was going to go to Bud's to listen to some music," he said. "It's a bar up on Broadway, across the river. Are you interested in that?"

"Sure," she said. "Lead on."

They walked down the shopping street that runs next to the mall, passing groups of teenagers standing around and looking cool, the whiff of marijuana smoke sharp on the air.

"I still can't get used to it being legal," said Roxanne. "It kind of takes all the fun away."

On the pavement outside the main entrance to the mall someone had laid an old green blanket on the sidewalk and was busily putting the finishing touches to a sand sculpture of a dog.

"Look, it's Snafu," said Roxanne, clapping her hands delightedly. Rashford just shook his head.

"Too big," he said, but he threw a five-dollar bill into the guy's jar anyway.

The street artist looked at him in amazement.

"Awesome," he said. "Thanks, man."

They made their way down to the river and then walked over the old traffic bridge, so named to differentiate it from the railway bridge. It had been lovingly restored, with wide sidewalks for pedestrians, and every few minutes they had to step aside for cyclists or skateboarders and, once, for what looked like a grandmother on a push scooter. On the other side they puffed to the top of the hill and snagged an ice cream from the famous Homestead dairy bar, lining up outside before fighting their way to the counter. They ambled along Main, chatting about nothing in between taking bites from their waffle cones, and ended up at Bud's just after eight.

It was busy inside, the normal press of bodies squeezed together. People were drinking, office workers in suits standing shoulder to shoulder with leather jacketed bikers, shop assistants in pastel pink skirts next to kohl-eyed goths with green hair, everyone eating peanuts and throwing the shells on the floor, the noise a constant throb until suddenly it stopped. The band came out for their second set, and within seconds the crowd were all swaying as the music blasted into the room. It was a blues band, one nobody had ever heard of, but they made up in passion and volume what they lacked in skill and finesse.

Roxanne passed Rashford a twenty and he grabbed beers from the bar. There was a two-hour Happy Hour for domestic beers from seven to nine, so they stuck with Labatt's Blue, but Roxanne didn't seem to mind. They couldn't speak because of the noise, just drank and ate peanuts and sometimes caught each others eye, one of them looking at the other. As the set ended, she grabbed his arm and pulled him outside.

They stood on the sidewalk, admiring all the Harley Davidson's parked in a neat chromatic row, and she told him that she had now had enough fun for the evening. She thanked him, and kissed his cheek, and asked if she could get her cab to drop him off somewhere. Rashford said sure, and when the taxi came, they sat together in the back. He leaned over into the front seat. 'Senator Hotel first, please,' he said to the driver.

The taxi drove down Broadway and over the wider bridge, passing lots of couples walking along arm in arm and waving at the tourists on the Prairie Lily, an old paddle steamer that does circuits along the river and under the famous bridges of Saskatoon, a city Leonard Cohen once called the Paris of the Prairies.

When the cab pulled up outside his hotel and Rashford opened the door to get out, Roxanne leaned across to look up at the building.

"I've heard of this place," she said. "It's supposed to be really old and ornate, with big ceilings. Is it still like that?"

"Yes, it is," he said. "Built in nineteen oh eight or something. It's like something out of old Europe. Big oil paintings on panelled wood walls, that sort of thing."

Rashford paused on the sidewalk and looked down at her.

"Do you have time to come in and look?"

"Sure," she said, "I'll get another cab in a minute."

She got out, he paid the driver, and they went inside, stopping to admire the overstuffed armchairs in the lobby and the red telephone box in the corner. Rashford stopped at the front desk and picked up the room key from the man standing behind the counter.

"Another old European tradition?" she said, as they proceeded up the wide marble staircase.

"Yes, they ask you to leave it when you go out. I'm not sure whether they're scared you might get mugged and someone would come back and rob your room, or they don't want to pay for new keys, or what. But it's what you do. Ah, here we are."

He opened the door and let her enter the room ahead of him. She paused on the threshold and looked around.

"Where's Snafu?"

"Oh, I left him in the main kitchen, they've got a walk-in freezer."

"Of course, they do," she said, and walked further into the room.

It was a large and well-proportioned space, with two double beds separated by a narrow passage. A door at one end led into the bathroom and shower, and the windows along the wall looked out onto the pedestrian precinct. The walls were covered in a creamy wallpaper, a design of roses intertwining.

"It is just as I imagined," she said, turning to him. He opened his arms and she walked into his embrace.

The phone alarm woke them both up with a start.

"What the heck time is it?" Roxanne said.

Rashford looked at his phone.

"Five thirty," he said. "Sorry, I forgot to turn off my alarm."

"You get up at five thirty every morning?"

"Yes, then go for a run, before it gets too busy on the roads. I like it when it's quiet."

"Even after such a late night?"

Rashford laughed. They had made love at passionate speed, then lain in bed talking for hours. He had told her about following Claude Dallas across Alsama, eventually catching up with him at the Ontario border. She had sympathized with his anger at losing his captive, and the unfairness of him being posted to a far-northern community as a consequence.

At some point he had dressed and gone down to the bar, buying a bottle of red wine and borrowing two large glasses, and a corkscrew, from the taciturn bartender. He had taken these back to the room, and they had drunk wine as Roxanne talked about growing up as the only daughter of an older couple.

"They treated me like I was made of precious metal," she said, "and tried to keep me bubble wrapped against the world. I left home as soon as I could, and went to Toronto, to make my fortune."

"How's that going for you?" said Rashford.

"Nearly there," said Roxanne, laughing. Then they had put down their wineglasses and made love again.

After turning off the alarm, Rashford got out of bed. Roxanne stretched, extravagantly, then demurely pulled the sheet up over her breasts.

"Well off you go, then. How long will you be?"

"I usually do about 5 kilometres, so half an hour or so. Plus, some time for before and after stretches. So perhaps forty-five minutes. I'll leave the key here and you can let me in."

"Well, you do that, and I shall doze for a bit longer. Then when you come back, you can give me my own personal cardiovascular workout. OK?"

"OK," he said, kissing her forehead. She pulled the sheet up over her head. Rashford quickly got dressed, and then quietly slipped out of the room.

He did his stretches in the lobby, the clerk on the counter never looking up from his phone. Once he felt limbered up, he went out, and jogged slowly down to the river. He turned left and headed up towards the university, running along the riverside trails. It was a cool crisp morning, the type that turns hot later in the day.

Rashford made good time and was soon past the weir and at the old CPR bridge, now a pedestrian walkway to the campus. He turned around there and jogged back the way he had come. The pelicans at the weir bobbed around in the current, every so often dipping their heads under to catch a fish. Red-winged blackbirds chattered at him from the reeds, and the Prairie Lily looked magnificent at her mooring next to what was once the Mendel Art Gallery, probably the best art gallery in the prairies during its prime and now a science centre for children.

As he came round the bend he could see its successor, the Remai Modern, the glass and concrete monstrosity that had replaced it, peering up behind the multi-towered Bessborough Hotel like some malevolent spirit. He sprinted the last couple of hundred metres and then walked up from the river, cooling down as he returned to the pedestrian area. Rashford walked back into the Senator and nodded at the desk clerk, then started up the stairs.

"Your key, sir," said the clerk.

Rashford stopped, then turned and went to the desk. The clerk handed him the room key.

"Oh, and the lady said, don't forget your dog." He looked troubled. "You know we don't allow pets, sir."

"I know," shouted Rashford, and ran up the stairs and down the corridor. He fumbled the key but made it work and burst in. The room was empty. The bed was made. His shirt and pants had been picked up from the floor and folded neatly on the second bed. His jacket was hanging in the closet.

He walked over, knowing what he would find. Nothing. The wallet was empty, all his cash gone. The north is still pretty much a cash economy, and he had been carrying about three hundred and fifty dollars. 'At least my cards and ID are still there,' he thought. He opened his suitcase; it appeared untouched, so it didn't seem like she had had time to do a proper search.

"Shit, shit, shit."

Rashford banged his fist on the bedside table in frustration, then went into the bathroom to have a shower.

Chapter 2

On Monday morning at eight o'clock, Rashford was standing at attention in front of Chief Superintendent Tracey Pollard. She was just under five feet four inches tall and weighed about a hundred and twenty pounds. Her blonde hair was shoulder length but pulled back in a tight ponytail. Rashford was six foot five and weighed two hundred and fifty-eight pounds. He had a shaved head. She terrified him.

"Sergeant Rashford," she said. "What are we to do with you?"

"Ma'am?"

"Rhetorical, Rashford, rhetorical. You don't have to respond to everything."

This time he kept quiet.

"Do you?"

"No, Ma'am."

She smiled her barracuda smile, the one where you could sort of see her teeth, but she didn't actually move her lips at all. The teeth just appeared, then disappeared again.

"Mr. Samuel Augustine Samson. Remember him, Sergeant?"

"Yes, Ma'am."

"He's lodged an official complaint. Apparently, you harassed and racially profiled him, because he is Métis. You made his life such a misery, he had to leave his community. This is a serious accusation, Sergeant."

"Yes, Ma'am."

"So, tell me about it. Is this something to which I can respond, with an explanatory letter to Mr. Samson, or do I need to get the Civilian Review and Complaints Commission involved?"

"I think that would be unnecessary, Ma'am."

"I'm sure you do. Come on. What happened?"

Rashford told the story and the Chief Superintendent listened, now and then jotting a note on her iPad. When he had finished, she looked at him.

"Do I understand, then, that the complaint was initiated by La Ronge, and you responded by obtaining a search warrant and then executing that search?"

"No, Ma'am. They got the warrant as well and sent it up to us."

"And did you know about the detour taken by the plane?"

"No, Ma'am. At least, not until early this year, when Special Constable Toutsaint told me what had happened."

"Were you involved in any way in the process that led to the community deciding to call Mr. Samson 'Snowdrop'?"

"No, Ma'am."

"Well then, I think I can write a response to the complaint and assure Mr. Samson that we have investigated it thoroughly but have determined that no further action is required at this time."

"Thank you, Ma'am."

"Of course, if he continues to kick up a fuss, or gets the media involved, then that position might have to change. But we'll wait and see on that score."

She paused and drummed the fingers of her right hand lightly on the desk. She cleared her throat.

"Now, changing the subject, what's this I hear about Saskatoon? And don't look so surprised. When one of my officers goes to the local police and reports a robbery, from his hotel room no less, then of course I get informed. What happened?"

Rashford explained, the Superintendent never taking her eyes off his face. When he had finished, there was silence for a few moments.

"Well, it seems to me, Sergeant, that you got her cheap. From the reports I see cross this desk, girls like her can go for between three and five hundred an hour. You spent just over that for a night."

"I don't think she was a professional, Ma'am."

"No? She took you for dinner, dessert, drinks, a taxi, and a hotel room, as well as your cash. Sounds like a pretty gifted amateur. What was that, Sergeant? Don't mumble!"

"I said, she paid for the drinks, Ma'am."

"Ah, right. I forgot. So, you spent about six hundred and she spent twenty? Yup, that makes you about equal, obviously. Just call it quits, will you?"

This time Rashford had the sense to stay silent.

"You're a good detective, Rashford. You proved that when you tracked that Dallas fellow across Alsama. But you're getting a reputation for making silly mistakes, for not being quite as detail focused as you might be. Dare I say it, for being a bit cavalier?"

Rashford stared straight ahead, focused on a point on the wall, a metre above her head and about the same behind her.

"How is your FILTER going?" she said, abruptly changing the subject.

FILTER, the Focused Indigenous Language Training for Emergency Responders, had been a key part of the agreement which had maintained neutrality from the various western Indigenous peoples when Alsama had been formed, nearly two years previously. Prior to what was now referred to as the supportive intervention of the US forces, the Alsama government had secretly negotiated with the various Treaty nations and agreed that all government employees, including the police and other emergency responders, would have to learn at least one of the Indigenous languages of the western prairies within two years, or they would lose their jobs.

"I tried to learn Dene when I was in Black Rapids," said Rashford, "but it's a very hard language. Some linguists apparently say it's the third hardest in the world, to learn."

"What are the other two?"

"I have no idea. I guess that *klick* language of the Kalahari people would be one of them. After that, I don't know ... perhaps Mandarin, or Arabic?"

"No matter. How did you get on with Dene?"

"I didn't get much beyond '?edlanet'e, edza.'"

"What does that mean? 'Hello, how are you?'"

"No, Ma'am. It means, 'Hello, it's cold!'"

"Yes, I can see that being useful up there," she said, almost laughing. "Maybe you should focus on Cree while you're down here."

"I'm staying here, Ma'am? At headquarters?"

"Well, yes, in a way. You see, we are professionals, not bureaucrats or politicians, so we cannot reward incompetence. At least, we cannot be seen to reward it. You've had three strikes, two and a half if I accept that you were off duty in Saskatoon. But losing your suspect, and then alienating an Indigenous community member, those are big black marks on your dossier. So yes, I want to keep you near, when I can keep an eye on you.

"But, and it's a big but," she said, "truly, one more cock-up and you're out. Comprenez vous?"

"Oui, madam."

"God, I'm so glad I don't have to speak French anymore. Give me an Indigenous language any day, you don't get any of that 'poor me' political garbage with it. How do you say, 'I understand' in Cree, Sergeant?"

"I don't know, Ma'am."

"Well, you've got less than six months to find out and pass the test, Sergeant. There'll be lots of time to study where you're going."

This turned out to be the community of Maple Creek, where Rashford was posted to cover the south-west corner of Saskatchewan. The detachment was based in a long low-slung building made of dun-coloured bricks and topped with a brown metal roof. A clipped hedge provided a break in the otherwise beige monotony, with spruce, poplar and mountain ash trees providing some shade.

On one side of the detachment there was a small bungalow where he was supposed to live, but an ant infestation meant he spent the first three weeks living on the other side of the building, in the Aspen Motor Inn. His room was comfortable enough, and there was free WiFi, but he missed the ability to cook his own meals and wander around at his own convenience. Some evenings he would go for a drink at the Jasper Hotel, but he noticed how quiet everything went whenever he walked into the bar, and how some people seemed to go off to the washroom and then not return.

Once the ants had been exterminated, Rashford was able to settle into the bungalow. It had a spare bedroom which he converted into a personal office space, although he knew if another officer got posted to Maple Creek, then they would no doubt have to share the house, and he would lose the office. In the interim he put out a large duvet to cover the guest bed and used the surface as another desk.

He spoke with Howard at the Bakery, which was three buildings down from the detachment office, and arranged to walk over and collect two hot bagels each morning at six thirty, once he got back from his run. It was an hour earlier than the shop would normally open but the baker was glad to do a favour for the local police officer.

Rashford found that soon his life settled into a routine. Every two weeks he would go across the street to the barber shop and get his head shaved, 'the famous number one cut' as Raymond the barber called it. On the third Thursday of each month, he would drive into Swift Current for a meeting with the other regional officers, those based in Shaunavon and Leader as well as those responsible for the rural and urban areas of Swift Current itself. They would share information about what was happening in each of their regions and let each other know of any disturbing trends that seemed to be evolving. In truth, though, Rashford seldom had much to offer in those conversations. Not much happened in his corner of the province.

He had soon determined that there were two main sections of his sub-division where he needed to maintain high visibility. One was on the Trans-Canada Highway, which ran from west to east a few kilometres north of Maple Creek. The second area of focus was to the south, the Cypress Hills Inter-Provincial Park, especially the campgrounds, where over 600 sites meant that more than two thousand people could be in the area on a busy weekend. However, the other sections of the sub-division could not be ignored, and so he plotted out four routes which, with variations as circumstances dictated, became the routine of his working day.

For the eastern region, he would first take the Trans-Canada and then turn south on the road to Eastend, checking in to the village of Piapot and other communities along the way. At Eastend he would grab a coffee at Café Terra or Jack's, perhaps a sandwich as well, then keep driving down to Loomis, the prairie vast and empty around him. From Loomis he would head west along highway 18, through the ghost towns of Claydon and Robsart, the ramshackle buildings grey and dusty under the sun. Rashford would then cruise north through the Cypress Hills, detouring through the park if he had time, and return back to Maple Creek on highway 21 in time to complete any necessary paperwork before retiring to his residence for a quiet beer.

On another day, he would head south to the provincial park, providing an early morning presence, before continuing south through Vidora and Consul to spend half an hour visiting with the Canadian border agents at Willow Creek, who were always glad of some company. What had historically been the fourth lowest by volume crossing between Canada and the United States was now the lowest by volume between Alsama and the US, a record which looked unlikely to be challenged anytime soon. A few local residents would cross back and forth, and sometimes an intrepid tourist heading into or out of Montana, but most days were very quiet, and if he timed it right, he could join the agents for lunch and snag a free meal from their canteen.

The northern zone was sparsely populated, so Rashford would pick a quiet day and then drift north, stopping to chat anytime he saw a rancher out on the pasture, keeping a wary lookout for pronghorn antelope as he drove through Fox Valley. He would cruise into Richmound, wondering as always what Kirby Maier was doing these days. According to the big sign at the edge of the village, she had been Miss Rodeo Maple Creek in 2006, but that was a long time ago now. 'One day I should look her up on Facebook,' he often thought, but he never had. He would drive past the mural which graced the auto shop on the corner of Main and Railway, then pull into the Richmound Hotel for a burger and to chat with whichever locals were propping up the midday bar. After lunch he would drop down past the hamlet of Golden Prairie and the ghost town of Hatton and spend the rest of the afternoon cruising up and down the Trans-Canada highway to the Alberta border and back.

For his fourth loop he would head west on the 724, a gravelled road which led him to the Alberta border and then north to the TCH. He would spend the day on the highway, driving east to where the Shaunavon sub-division started, where the divided highway began again just past Piapot, and then heading back west. Rare was the day when he did not stop six or seven cars for speeding, the long straight roads and the wide flat landscape seemingly putting people into a sort of automotive trance. Sometimes he would use his rear-view mirror to watch them, apparently oblivious to his presence as they approached. They would race past, and he could see their heads jerk up in surprise when he turned on his lights and siren. At other times they would be on the other side of the road, heading towards him, triggering his radar scanner, and he would turn on his lights before pulling down and across the meridian and then hit the siren as he began the pursuit.

His social life was non-existent. He went for a five-kilometre run every morning, had a shower and his breakfast, then went to work. He would get back from driving and spend an hour or more completing all the reports and other administrative duties which were required. If the weather cooperated, he would go for an evening run, then make himself a simple supper and watch some television before going to bed. He didn't even have many friends on social media, and soon got bored of their photographs of evenings out at dance clubs and bars.

One day he was surprised to get a letter from the Chief Superintendent's office in Regina. Inside was an envelope, addressed in neat handwriting to 'Sergeant Gavin, NWMP, Regina,' together with a note saying 'this arrived, and I think it's for you, TP.' He opened the envelope and found seven new fifty-dollar bills folded inside a sheet of photocopier paper. He opened the paper to read the note.

'Sorry for borrowing this without asking but I needed bus fare to go and see my cousin. R.'

Rashford put the bills in his wallet, then took the note over to his desk and laid it on the rest of the papers piled there.

Twice a week, on Tuesday and Thursday evening, he walked for fifteen minutes through the community, past the town office and the campground, to a small house on a well treed corner lot. Built just after the Second World War, the house was immaculately maintained, with creamy yellow vinyl siding and grey trimmed windows. He would walk up the narrow cement path, brushing past the well-trimmed lilac bushes, and up onto the concrete step by the front door.

As soon as he knocked, the Doberman pretending to be asleep under the covered dog kennel in the large, fenced back yard would drop all pretence and start barking furiously. The door would open, and a tall woman would step out, nod at Rashford, and then utter a short, three-word command. The dog would immediately lie down and be quiet. Rashford had never figured out what the words were, she spoke so softly and rapidly, but he was always glad of the ensuing silence.

The woman was obviously Cree. Her long black hair was usually either braided or tied back in a ponytail. She wore silver earrings, each a small silver teardrop shape with a greenish blue stone, that he assumed to be turquoise, at the end. She would often be wearing a black shirt, with sewn on beads or sequins glittering, and a pair of stone washed denim blue jeans. Rashford always smiled and nodded at the woman but she seldom reciprocated, instead stepping back inside and calling out to the back of the house.

"*Nôhkum, kêsiskam.*" Grandmother, he is here.

Rashford would follow her as she walked into the small front room. He knew that there were two bedrooms at the back, and the shuffling of slippers on the vinyl tiled floor indicated that someone was leaving the bathroom. He stood and waited until the old woman appeared. She was stooped in the shoulders, but her eyes were clear, and she wore her greying hair in a long braid. The younger woman guided her to one of the armchairs and she sat down with a sigh. She indicated that Rashford should take the other chair, which he did, and the younger woman walked out of the room and into the back of the house. Rashford was never sure what she did during his visit.

"*Tansi,*" said the old woman.

"*M'on ana'tow*," said Rashford. "*Kitha maka?*"

"*Kiya. Kiya maka*," she said, and Rashford cursed to himself. He knew that. It was a simple greeting, the only Cree he had learned in the north, but the Cree spoken in Black Rapids was the *th* dialect of the Woods Cree, not the *y* dialect of the Plains Cree.

"*Kiya maka*," he said, with a smile.

And so began his twice-weekly Cree language lesson, an hour of conversation with Mrs. Roberta Christine Buffalocalf, more commonly known to all as Kôhkum Christine. An elder from the Nekaneet Cree Nation, she had grown up in the Cyprus Hills. Now in her eighties, she had spent the first third of her life as a stateless person, for it was not until 1968 that the Canadian Government had recognized the treaty rights of the Nekaneet people.

In 1874 they had signed Treaty Four, along with the other Cree, Saulteaux and Assiniboine bands of southern Saskatchewan, but in 1882 the Nekaneet were punished when they refused to relocate out of Cypress Hills. The government wanted to move all the Indigenous peoples on to reserve land set aside on the prairies, but the Nekaneet had a fine life on their traditional land of forest and rolling hills and did not want to leave. A reserve was eventually created in the Cypress Hills in 1913, and fenced a year later, but it was not until 1955 that the children of Nekaneet were allowed to attend the local schools.

Kôhkum Christine told Rashford stories about the early years in her community. Her grandparents raised her, as was the tradition, and her grandfather told her stories of the Lebret Residential School. 'He knew of bad things that happened there,' she said, and so when the authorities came to collect the children of the community, to attend school, he hid his grandchildren in the bush until the outsiders had gone. In 1968 the Canadian government recognized the Nekaneet as Treaty Indians, and thirty years later agreed to pay a claim for compensation requested as being part of outstanding lawful obligations. 'That's legal talk which means, what they owed us,' she said.

Rashford was always amazed at how matter of fact and gracious Kôhkum Christine was about her history. She was serene about the fact that she had never attended school. 'I was a nosy child,' she said. 'I was the first born to my parents and I have eight brothers and sisters. When people came to visit my parents or grandparents, I would say, I can look after the baby, because there was always one around. That meant I could stay in the corner of the room, and listen to the talk, and that way I learned a lot. And when I got older, and my children were in school, I went back and got my grade 10. My *nôsisim* was very proud, eh.'

"Weren't you," she shouted, and a patient voice from the bedroom called back, "*êhe, nôhkom.*"

As the summer progressed, Rashford became more proficient in Cree, and started to speak with more confidence. He even entered into conversation with people whom he met when he drove through the reserve, although he soon realized that not many of the young people knew much of their language. One Saturday he drove all the way into Regina and went to the big university bookstore. He found a Cree dictionary and a standard phrasebook, both in Standard Roman Orthography rather than syllabics, and some children's story books in the same language.

He took these home and tried to spend an hour each evening practicing his reading and writing. Online he found some YouTube videos which were fun to watch, and the Cree Literacy Network carried occasional blogs and podcasts, most of which he found interesting.

In his work he explored the small side roads which branched out from his main loops and got to know some of the ranchers and homesteaders by name. Now, when he walked into the Jasper Hotel people would nod at him, and some would even say hello.

One Tuesday afternoon in the middle of August he was driving back from an afternoon cruising the Trans-Canada Highway when he realized that he was looking forward to getting home to Maple Creek. It had taken a few months, but he was starting to feel that he was becoming an accepted part of the community. That evening he walked over to the small yellow house and knocked on the door. When the young lady who answered had quietened the dog, and beckoned him in, he did not move.

"Excuse me," he said.

She stopped in the doorway and turned back to look at him, a questioning look on her face.

"Who are you?" he said. "I mean, I know that you are the granddaughter of Kôhkum Christine, but that is all. I have been coming to this house for nearly four months, and I don't even know your name, or what you do."

"Why does this interest you?"

"I would like to be polite. I would like to greet you properly when I arrive, to treat you like a real person, not just a door opener."

She looked at him steadily.

"I don't want a boyfriend," she said.

"No, no, that's not what I meant," he said, his voice rising, the words tumbling over each other.

"It would just be good to say, '*tansi*, Susan', or whatever your name is, instead of us treating each other like we are invisible."

"Alright, then," she said. "My name is Bettina Blackeagle."

"I'm pleased to meet you, Ms. Blackeagle," he said.

"*Doctor* Blackeagle, please. My PhD is in gender, race, sexuality and social justice, from the University of British Columbia."

"Oh," said Rashford.

"No, I did not deal drugs or sell my body in order to pay for my education. I had a four-year doctoral fellowship from UBC and then won an eighty-thousand-dollar SSHRC doctoral fellowship as well."

"I never thought ... What's SSHRC?" said Rashford.

"The Social Sciences and Humanities Research Council of Canada. I am a professor in Indigenous Health and Restorative Justice at the University of Regina, but I do my work at the college in Swift Current. I teach students in the first year of their programs in education, social work, and pre-nursing. My research takes the form of post structural feminist narrative inquiry into the experiences of Indigenous peoples, especially Indigenous women, in their interactions with the criminal justice system."

"Oh," said Rashford.

"It used to be that people did research on us," she said. "Then research was done for us. Then it was done with us. Now it's done by us, and we are starting to reveal the truth."

"Oh," said Rashford.

"You are a police officer, I think?"

"Um, yes, yes I am."

"Therefore of course you understand the institutionalized racism and systemic discrimination faced daily by Indigenous people, peoples of colour, racialized and sexualized communities, and other minority class and cultural groups, don't you? In fact, as a member of the oppressive racist patriarchy, you probably participate in it."

"Well, hang on, it's ..."

"It's what? 'Not as bad as all that?' See what my namesake, Helen Betty Osborne, might think of that. Or any of the many women, and men, in the fifty plus years since she was abducted and killed. Ask what Neil Stonechild and Nadine Machiskinic might say, or Brooklyn Moose and Colten Boushie."

She turned on her heel and strode into the front room.

"*Nôhkum, kêsiskam,*" she said, but this time did not wait with him until her grandmother appeared.

The next day Rashford decided to do the long drive to Willow Creek. There were very few places to stop once he got past the Cypress Hills campground and he made good time. He was fortunate that the border crossing was having a quiet day, even by their own lax standards, and so he was able to sit and visit without feeling that he was interrupting work.

He had spent a restless night thinking over what Bettina Blackeagle had told him. He knew that some people did not like the police, but he had never thought of himself as being part of an oppressive racist patriarchy, whatever that meant. He was just trying to do his job.

As he cruised through the short grass prairie landscape, he tried to see things from her perspective. He had heard vaguely of Helen Betty Osborne; the fiftieth anniversary of her death had happened when he was a young constable. He knew of Neil Stonechild and the Starlight Tours, of course, made infamous in Saskatoon but sadly common in many jurisdictions, but that had been in back in the last century. Nadine

Machiskinic was more recent, he remembered that in January 2015 she had somehow fallen 10 storeys down a laundry chute at a Regina Hotel.

To his chagrin he had had to go onto the internet to refresh his memory of Brooklyn Moose, a young woman whose body had been found later that same year, in the attic of a Regina home. The whole country knew of Colten Boushie, shot dead in his car by a white farmer who was subsequently acquitted of both murder and manslaughter charges. But surely, he thought, she can't blame the whole system for a few poor decisions.

He felt a bit better after lunch with the border agents and was still laughing at some of their corny jokes as he drove back along the Red Coat Trail. One of the male officers had asked a female colleague if she could help him with a question that he could not answer. She had agreed, albeit a bit reluctantly. Rashford thought perhaps she had heard some of these before.

"Tell me, if a man makes a statement about something, and his wife isn't there to hear it, is he still wrong?" said the border agent.

The other agents had laughed, especially when the female officer slapped the questioner on the back of his head and knocked his cap flying. Rashford chuckled at the memory. There had been no reference at all to institutionalized sexism or workplace assault, he thought. Just a group of colleagues having fun. He wondered, though, how a post structural feminist narrative inquiry might describe the encounter.

As he approached Consul, he noticed that the sky to the west had started to darken. A storm coming, he thought, turning on the radio news as he drove into the small village. The breathless weather reporter spoke of thunderstorm warnings and a tornado watch from Milk River to Climax and down into Montana, running along the Medicine Line, which was what locals still called the United States border. Just where I am driving now, he thought.

The railway ran parallel to road, and he passed the slate grey grain elevator with its attendant grain cars lined up alongside. As the road left the community the grain cars gave way to stock pens and auto repair shops, and soon he was back on the open prairie.

The storm was getting closer and at the next intersection he pulled over to watch. A narrow gravel road bisected the highway at this point, the burned grass in the ditch marking the edges of an irrigation canal. He stopped at the edge of the ditch and, on a whim, walked out to the middle of the crossroads. Turning in a circle, he was mesmerized by the sheer vastness of scale. Each of the four roads disappeared to a vanishing point, the only structure breaking the horizon being the grain elevator at Consul. If he looked back the way he came, by moving a step to one side the grain elevator was right at the vanishing point of the main road.

The blackness to the west now filled the sky, but there was a sharp line along the bottom of the cloud. The strip between the prairie and the black was bright, pulsing with light, and he thought he could see funnel clouds dropping down from the base of the cloud. He could not see whether they actually formed into a tornado, though. He could hear thunder now, and the light was changing. There was a purple-pink hue to everything, and he fancied he could not only hear the crackle of static electricity but actually taste the ozone in the air. A huge flash of lightning seemed to erupt from the grasses a hundred metres away, followed by a loud crash of thunder that made him jump. He had just got back into his car when the heavens opened, and rain poured down with an intensity he had seldom seen before.

As suddenly as it had started, the rain stopped, the steam rising from the road surface. The black clouds had moved away to the east, leaving clear sky above, and behind him the rays of the sun illuminated the Consul grain elevator as though it were a religious icon. He got out of his car again and started walking towards where he had seen the lightning strike. He could hear the water running into the irrigation ditch, and when he peered over the fence he could see a small burnt patch of grass, but any flames had been extinguished by the sudden downpour. Relieved, he returned to his vehicle.

He had just started the engine when suddenly a red pickup truck raced past him from behind, skidding a little as the driver slammed on the brakes. Rashford got out of his car again as the truck reversed at speed, stopping inches from his own vehicle. He unholstered his sidearm as he cautiously walked around the back and walked towards the driver's window, which wound down as he approached.

“Thank god I found you,” a high pitched and panicky female voice said. “You have to help me. I’m being chased.”

“Calm down, please,” said Rashford. “Step out of the car, please, and can I see your driver’s licence.”

“Yes, of course,” she said, opening the door and climbing down from what Rashford now realized was a big Ford F-150 with a crew cab. She was fumbling in her purse for her ID and so Rashford looked over her shoulder to check that she was alone. She was, and the cab was indeed empty. When he looked back at her, she was standing there staring at him.

“Oh shit,” she said.

“Roxanne?” said Rashford.

Chapter 3

"I can explain," she said, but Rashford waved at her to be quiet. He opened her wallet and took out her driver's licence.

"It says here that your name is Anne," he said.

She nodded.

"Anne Sylliboy Gaudet, to be technical about it," he said.

"Goody," she said.

He looked at her blankly. She stared back.

"That's how you say it."

"Say what?"

"My name. Goody."

"It's not how you spell it," he said.

"I'm from Prince Edward Island," she said. "It's an old Acadian name, one of the first settler families, along with the Gallants of course. You pronounce it Goody. Not Gored Ette."

"Prince Edward Island?"

"Yes. And yes, my parents had a sense of humour. That's why they called their red-haired daughter Anne. With an E."

"Ah, I see. So where did Roxanne come from?"

"From school. There were about seven Anne's in my class, so we all got nicknames. In physical education class it turned out that I was good at curling, so I got called Rocks. That's what you throw, at curling."

"Yes, I do know what curling is," he said.

"Well, Anne Rocks soon became Roxanne, you know. But I never changed it officially."

"OK. And what about your middle name. Sylliboy?"

"That's my mom's family name. She's Mi'kmaq, from Eskasoni."

She saw the incomprehension on his face.

"It's on Cape Breton. Mom used to say she ran away from home to see the world, and only got as far as the next island along."

They both stood and looked at each other for a few minutes, neither saying anything. Roxanne broke the silence.

"So, are you going to arrest me?"

"For what?"

"Well, robbery, I guess. Saskatoon. Stealing your money. Although I tried to repay you. Did you get my letter?"

"I'm thinking about it," said Rashford, ignoring the question. "First, tell me about who is chasing you."

"He's a scary guy," she said. "Can we go somewhere off this road?"

She was trembling with fear, Rashford noticed, He thought for a moment, then nodded.

"Head straight along this road the way you were going," he said. "Just past the next village, Vidora, you'll see that highway 21 heads north, to your left. Take that and keep going all the way up to Maple Creek. I'll be right behind you so no speeding."

"Can you help me get rid of these damn grasshoppers first?" she said. "I drove through a huge swarm of them just after Milk River, when I was near to that Writing on Stone provincial park. There were so many that I couldn't see, but when I turned on the windshield wipers, they just got smooshed and smeared everywhere. I had to get out and scrape them off with the snow scraper. It was disgusting.

"A couple of them hitched a ride for miles, they were clinging on to the wiper blade like those daredevils who used to walk on the wings of aeroplanes. And then, just after that storm made me pull off the road, one of them came crawling out of the air vent. Inside the car!"

Rashford inhaled sharply.

"What?" he said.

"A grasshopper came inside the car!"

Rashford shook his head, slowly.

"I might have to arrest you for that," he said. "It's illegal to transport herbivorous chewing pests over provincial borders without a permit."

She stepped back a pace and put her hands on her hips, looking at him in amazement.

"Seriously?"

He tried hard to keep a straight face, but he couldn't help himself, he just laughed.

"No, just joking. Come on, they won't hurt you. Drive ahead and I'll follow you, just in case someone comes along chasing you like you said."

It took them almost an hour to get to Maple Creek, Roxanne scrupulously following the 80 kilometres per hour speed limit and slowing down even further whenever she saw a 'beware of deer' sign. Rashford did not think he had ever driven so slowly in his life. He was pretty confident that there was nobody following her, not then at any rate, for otherwise they would certainly have caught up to them.

As they approached the outskirts of Maple Creek he put on his lights and blipped the siren a couple of times. She slowed down even further, and he pulled up alongside, waving at her that she was now to follow him. He turned off the lights and drove into town, pulling up outside the detachment and staying in his car until she had parked behind him.

He waited while she clambered down from the truck, then escorted her into the detachment office. It was simply furnished, with two chairs in a small waiting area. There was a long counter serving as a barrier to the back part of the room, where there was a large desk, two grey four door filing cabinets, and a gun safe flush to the wall. At the back corner was a door, which stood open. It led to a narrow corridor.

"Washroom and cells down there," said Rashford, pointing at the corridor. "Should you need either of those facilities, that is."

"Maybe the washroom," she said, and walked past the counter.

"On the right," he said.

Rashford waited patiently, and then less patiently. He was about to go and see if she had simply walked out of the back door when she reappeared, looking a bit less stressed.

"You didn't do a line of coke or take some pills in there, did you?"

"Don't ask don't tell," she said, sitting demurely on one of the visitor chairs. "Seriously, are you going to arrest me for taking your money?"

"I don't think I have jurisdiction," Rashford said. "That was reported in Saskatoon, to the local police, not out here in Consul. There's not a warrant out for you or anything, so let's just leave that for the minute. And, yes, I did get your note, thank you. And the money back. That still doesn't change the fact that it was stolen first, though. Anyway, leave that for now. Instead, tell me about this man who might be chasing you."

Roxanne sat quietly for a few moments, looking down at her hands. Then she took a deep breath and faced him again.

"I'm glad I met you, again," she said. "I'm really scared."

"Why? What happened?"

"I'll tell you in a minute. But, first, do you have a place I can stay tonight?"

"Well, I have a spare room, yes. Why?"

"I don't want to be outside right now. I'm worried he will be driving around, looking for me."

"What does this fellow want with you?"

"And the truck," she said, ignoring the question. "I think we should get the truck off the street as quick as we can. It stands out a bit, you know. Not just the Alberta plates but also the go-fast stripes. You don't see many rigged out like that. Even if he doesn't see it, someone else might, and then they'll tell him. He's got lots of friends. Bikers."

Her voice was getting louder, her words starting to run together.

"Okay, okay, calm down," he said. "I'll move it. But I can't leave you here in the detachment alone. Do you have a bag?"

"Not really. I do have my purse, though. It's in the truck."

"Go and get it, I'll think of something."

She went outside and was back a few minutes later. He saw her on the security camera and buzzed her in before she had a chance to knock. She was carrying a small purple clutch bag, with shiny stones embroidered into the fabric.

"That looks like you're about to walk a red carpet somewhere," he said. "Come on, in here."

He ushered her down the hall again and this time to the left, into a small cell.

"You wait here," he said. "Give me the keys and I'll move the truck. I'll be right back."

"What if you have a heart attack or get run over or something? Will I be stuck in here?"

"Someone will find you eventually."

He took the truck keys from her. There were two of them, a large one for the ignition and a smaller one which looked like it fit into a padlock. They were on a keyring with a shiny green metal square attached. On the square was a stylized drawing of a lake surrounded by mountains, with the text, 'Waterton Lakes National Park'.

Rashford left the detachment building and drove the truck to the end of the street, where he pulled in behind Alf's Car Service, an auto-repair shop on the corner. He went inside and asked if he could leave the truck there for a day or so, perhaps longer, where it was out of sight from the road. The grizzled mechanic looked at him but did not say anything. He just nodded. Like Howard the baker, Alf was happy to have the local Mountie owe him a favour.

They walked outside and Alf unlocked a large padlock, then pulled open the gate to his yard. Rashford drove the truck inside and parked it nose-in against the back fence, trying not to crunch over the various slats and nets that were piled in the corner. He shook hands with Alf and then went back out onto the street.

Rashford walked back to the detachment building, then sidetracked and went into the police house. He quickly picked up a beer bottle that was on the floor next to the couch and tidied away his Cree books into a drawer. In the spare bedroom cum office, he collected all the reports and other official papers he could find and put them into a large reusable grocery bag. He took that with him as he walked back to the detachment.

He entered his code, then went into the office and put the bag full of papers in the top drawer of the filing cabinet, which he relocked. Only then did he go down the hall and open the cell. Roxanne came out and sat back in the chair, taking the truck keys from him and putting them back in her purse. Rashford pulled the other chair out in front of her and turned it around, then sat down facing her. He rested his arms on the back of the chair, his legs sticking out to each side, and looked straight at her.

"Right, then," he said. "Tell me a story."

"Where shall I start?"

"Why don't you start on April seventeenth, in Saskatoon, the morning after you left the Senator Hotel. I know what happened just before that, so that would be a good place to start."

"Well, your alarm woke me up early, if you remember. Woke us up, I should say. Then you went off running or whatever, and I just couldn't be there when you got back. We'd had such a lovely evening, and night, and I liked you. But I was scared, scared that you would find out who I really was, what I really was like, and then you wouldn't like me. So, I wanted to leave you still thinking I was a good person."

"Right," said Rashford. "And stealing my money was the best way to make that happen?"

"It was early. I'm not a morning person. I wasn't thinking straight."

"Sure. What kind of person did you think I would find out about?"

"Well, I hadn't been on the street or anything, I wasn't a sex trader or a druggie or whatever. But I had been living rough. I had left the Island to see the world, I thought I'd make my fortune in Toronto. Streets of gold and all that. But it didn't happen.

"I got dead-end jobs in retail, minimum wage gig economy stuff where they only pay you for shifts worked. I couldn't afford my own place, so I was couch-surfing, staying with friends and friends of friends. Islanders are good like that, they're very supportive."

"Uh-huh," said Rashford, just to show that he was listening.

"Anyway, it all got boring pretty quick, and I had a miserable winter. Then one day in early spring I was sitting in the food court at the mall, having my lunch break, and this guy hit on me. We chatted and I let him buy me lunch. Then I went back to work.

"Nothing had happened, but he had given me an idea. After that, every week or so I would dress up and go to a restaurant or a café and pretend that I was being stood up. Usually, some guy would come along and ask me to join him, and I would let him buy me dinner."

"Yes. I remember that strategy," said Rashford.

"Well, no, you don't, not really," she said. "I always had a reason to leave, I would say thank you and get a taxi back to my sick sister or whatever. All I ever gave anyone was company, and all they ever gave me was lunch or dinner."

"OK, I believe you. Please, continue."

"One day I heard from my mom. She phoned to see how I was doing, I guess she had heard stories. I just cried at her for twenty minutes. Then she told me about Jenny, my cousin, who was living in Calgary.

"Mom said I should leave Toronto or else I would find myself in a bad space. She said that had happened to her once, between leaving home and getting to the Island.

"Mom told me to go out west. I had enough money for a ticket to Saskatoon, so I went there. Three days on the bus, I never knew Canada was so big. Well, Canada and Alsama, I guess."

"Did you have any trouble at the border?"

"No, that was easy. I just had to show my PEI driver's licence and give them my cousin's contact information. The border guards took my photograph and gave me what they called the Alsama Pass, it's like a small identification card, and then I was through. I have it in my purse here, somewhere, if you want to see it."

"No, that's OK," said Rashford. "Alright, so you got to Saskatoon, then snared me at the restaurant, and then ..."

"I didn't know you would be there! After I left the bus depot, it was the first place I saw that looked halfway decent. I had been sitting there for over half an hour when you showed up. I was pretty sure the waiter was about to throw me out, so when your date left you, I thought I'd see if I could get you to notice me."

"Which I obviously did. So, we had dinner, and went to the bar, and back to the hotel, and then you left. What happened then, that morning?"

"I took your money because I was broke. I am so sorry about that. Then I remembered what you had said about the key, so I left it with the guy at the desk. I went into town, down the other side of the mall, and back to the bus depot.

"I got lucky, there was a bus leaving for Calgary, so I bought a ticket and got on. I was worried you would come around looking for me, so I sort of huddled down in my seat and started muttering to myself, just gibberish. I was trying to make myself look scary, you know? Some of the people who travel by bus are kind of weird."

"Uh-uh," he said, nodding his head in amusement.

"What? I'm not weird! Am I?"

"No, not at all. Please, carry on."

"So, I got to Calgary that evening and called Jenny, my cousin, she lives down in Bowness. She told me that mom had called her as well, and she was expecting me to come over and stay with her, so that's what I did.

"It was great. I got a job in a store at the Shaganappi Mall, selling fancy clothes to the daughters of rich ranchers and oilmen, and we had a nice quiet life. And as soon as I saved enough money, I sent you back what I'd taken. I really only borrowed it you know."

"I know," said Rashford, "and thank you for returning it to me."

"You're welcome. It was Jenny who suggested the extra sheet of paper, so that nobody at the post office would see it was cash and manage to 'lose' the envelope."

"Yes, that was a good idea," said Rashford, smiling.

"Well, Jenny and I get on well together. I'd get the transit to the mall and work my shift, then go home and we'd have dinner together. I was still doing the food court thing, so I'd tell her about the people who bought me lunch. She works as a waitress in the restaurant on the top of the Calgary Tower, the revolving one, and she had some great stories about the people who used to eat there."

"You kept doing that, looking lost in the food court?"

Roxanne shrugged, defensively.

"Well, there was no harm to it. I only ever had one issue, a guy who really glommed on to me. The same day, every week, he came and tried to get me go for a walk with him. He was old and fat and ugly, yeuck."

"What did you do?"

"When I figured his pattern, I stopped going for lunch on Fridays. I never saw him again. I guessed he must come into town once a week for business or something. Then yesterday," she said, then paused. "Today's Wednesday, right?"

"All day," he said.

"Yes. So yesterday, Tuesday, it was the birthday of a friend of my cousin. We decided to go out dancing, six of us girls, at one of the clubs in town. It's a country and western place, it calls itself the Barrel Races and tries to pretend it's full of cowboys, but they're really just posers and wanna-be's. Still, they have good music. I've been there a couple of times with my cousin, on Ladies Night.

"So, like I said, Tuesday is Ladies Night, so we didn't have to pay a cover charge or anything, and drinks are half-price for women. Not that we were planning on having a lot, we all had to work the next morning, and anyway one of the girls is pregnant so she wasn't drinking.

"A group of guys started eyeing us up, you could see they were interested, and one came over to my cousin and asked her to dance. She agreed, and went off with him to the dance floor, and then the others came over. The one who picked me was a big dude, kind of heavy but fit with it. He walked like a boxer, light on his feet, and he was a good dancer. I thought I had maybe seen him before, but I hadn't talked to him.

"We danced for a bit then went back to the table and he bought me a drink. We chatted, and the others would come and go, have a rest then go back to the floor. When I stood up to go back dancing, though, I felt kind of dizzy and light-headed. My new friend said I needed some air and so he helped me to get outside. As soon as we got into the car park he pushed me into the back seat of a car, I was really disoriented, I couldn't stop him."

Roxanne paused and looked across at Rashford.

"Do you have any coffee? Instant would be OK."

He got up and turned on the electric kettle, then spooned some Tasters' Choice into a cup. He brought a bowl of sugar and a spoon to the table, then a carton of two percent milk. The kettle boiled and he made the coffee, then brought it over to her. She nodded her thanks and resumed her story.

"Anyway, I was in the back of the car, and he got in the front and turned on the ignition, then I heard the locks click. Nothing happened for a few minutes, then he wound down his window and said something. I couldn't see exactly who he was talking to, but it looked like one of the other guys from the group. I started to pass out again, and when I woke up, we were driving.

"I still felt awful and thought I must have been drugged, so I put my finger down my throat and made myself throw up. I figured that might get some of it out of my system. The driver yelled at me and called me a dirty bitch but didn't stop. I decided it was best just to lay there and pretend I was still unconscious.

"I don't know how long we were driving but then we pulled over to the side of the road. The guy came around and dragged me out of the car, I kept all limp and useless. He just let me fall to the ground. I kept my eyes more or less closed but looked through the lids as much as I could.

"There were three guys now, the one who had taken me and two others, they had obviously followed us on their motorbikes, which were parked behind the car. 'Is this the right place?' one of them said. 'Yeah, he'll be here in a minute,' said another. I could see a picnic table and some trees, and there was a bit of moonlight, but otherwise it was all quiet. Then another car arrived, and a new guy got out, he was a lot smaller than the other three.

"This new guy came across and stood over me. I could see his boots, they were cowboy boots made of snakeskin or something, really fancy. He pushed me with his boot, and I groaned.

"'This is her,' he said. 'She's filthy.'

"'She threw up in the car,' said my driver. 'Made a real mess.'

"'That'll be the roofie,' said the new fellow. 'That, or your driving.'

"'Har di har,' said my driver. The others chuckled loudly.

"'Five grand, right?' said the guy with the boots.

"'Six,' said the driver, 'I'm gunna have to get the car cleaned and detailed now.'

"'Five is a lot for her,' said Boots. 'She's a right fucking mess. I'll give you four.'

One of the other guys, the bikers, spoke up.

"'Five is good,' he said. 'She does five guys a night at a hundred a pop and you'll have your investment back in under two weeks.'

"There was silence, a kind of scary silence, and I could sense the three of them were coming closer, more threatening. Then Boots spoke again.

"'OK, five it is. Here.'

"He must have given them the money, because then he said, 'put her in my car.' Someone picked up my feet and someone else grabbed me under my arms, then they slung me into the back of a pick-up truck. Not the tray, but the back of the cab, the second row of seats."

"The crew cab," said Rashford, nodding.

"I pretended I was still unconscious and just lay there. One of the guys must have picked up my purse because he threw it in on top of me. Boots got into the truck, and we drove out of the rest stop area and back onto the highway. He didn't drive fast, just steady, and never said a word until he pulled into a gas station. Then he came out and opened my door and put his hand on my neck. He must have been feeling for my pulse.

"'At least you're still alive,' he said, then closed the door. He filled up the truck with gas, then opened the front door and took out his wallet. I heard him walk away and decided to see if I could figure out where we were. I sat up and looked out and saw him walking across the forecourt.

"He was a short guy, and slim, but he walked like someone who spent time in the gym. He sort of rolled on his feet, you know? As he crossed in front of the pumps, I saw that he was wearing a leather jacket, a brown one, and a baseball hat. Oh, and he had a ponytail, a long grey one. He went inside the store, and through the window I saw that he didn't go and pay, he went first towards the toilets.

"I was going to run away and then I saw that he'd left the keys in the ignition. I slid across the seat and opened the door on the side away from the store, got out and kind of rolled to the ground. Then I opened the driver's door, climbed into the front seat, and turned the ignition. It started immediately, and I drove away.

"That's it, really. I got on the highway and went as fast as I could, hoping I'd get stopped for speeding, but there's never a policeman around when you need one."

They both laughed at that, Roxanne a little more loudly than Rashford would have preferred.

"I just kept going, I wasn't looking at the signs or anything, I just kept driving. I know that I went past Lethbridge, I saw the lights. After about an hour or so I calmed down and decided I should probably get off the highway. Then I saw a sign saying that I was heading to Coutts and the American border, so I took the next road, through a place called Milk River, and just kept driving.

"When I got to the provincial park I pulled into the campground and parked in an empty lot, under some trees. I tried to phone my cousin, but my phone was dead. I think I cried a bit at that point. Then I slept for a few hours, I was exhausted.

"When I woke up it was morning. I had no idea where I was. Well, I knew I was probably in southern Alberta but that was it. And I didn't know that for sure, not really. I still had lots of gas, so I decided to just keep going. I knew that Fancy Boots or his biker friends would be out looking for me and I was scared.

"And it kept getting scarier. First there were all those damned grasshoppers, then that huge storm. Then I saw you parked at the side of the road. And here I am."

"And here you are," he said.

"Do you have any idea who this guy might be?" said Rashford.

"No," she said.

"Would you recognize him again?"

"I'd recognize his boots, but not his face. I never looked at him, except from the back."

Rashford nodded.

"OK, well let's just hold onto that for a bit, and see if you remember anything else. I've got to do some work as I have a few reports to finish. You can drink your coffee in the house."

He stood up from the table and then paused, one hand on the back of his chair.

"That is, if you're OK with that. Are you hungry?" he said. "I'm not sure what's there but you can dig around in the freezer and find something."

Roxanne looked at him.

"I won't find Snafu or his cousin, will I?"

"No," said Rashford, laughing. "Everything in there is edible, honest. Except the out-of-date stuff, of course."

"Of course," she said. "So basically, you want me to have dinner with you, but I have to cook it?"

"That would be great," he said. "Then I can finish this work."

"Right," she said, waving her hand at him. "Show me where to go and I'll get on it right away."

He gestured to her to pick up her purse and walked out of the office. Roxanne followed him along the narrow path, the lilac leaves brushing against her thighs. He opened the door to the small bungalow, and she walked into the large living room. He pointed to the various areas. Kitchen, bathroom, spare room slash office, his room. She nodded along with him, walking over to look into the spare room. There were some old newspapers on the bed, and a folded down laptop computer on the desk.

"I'll move that stuff later and make up the bed," said Rashford.

"One question," she said, looking at him.

"Yes, what's that?"

"If I stay here, do you have a spare toothbrush? I don't have any stuff with me."

"Actually, yes. I had a check-up last week and the hygienist gave me a spare one, plus some floss. You can have those. You'll have to share my toothpaste, though, I only have one kind."

"I can do that," she said, laughing.

Rashford left the room and Roxanne sat quietly for a few minutes, sipping her coffee. She was surprised that she was still shaking from having told her story. Each time she thought of being taken from the nightclub, of being sold on to that strange man with the expensive boots, she started to hyperventilate. And yet, here she was, feeling respected and, in a strange way, trusted. She knew the sex had been good, but she thought it was more than that. At least, she hoped so. Eventually, she stood up from the table, and went into the kitchen.

Rashford spent the next hour at his desk in the detachment office, completing most of his regular daily reports. He decided to only make a vague reference to Roxanne, noting simply that he had been stopped by a woman in a pick-up truck who had reported being chased by someone. He wrote that he had escorted her to Maple Creek but had seen no evidence of anyone being in pursuit. He left it at that, not mentioning that she was currently in his house and was about to make him dinner. Nor did he mention that she was a woman of whom he had prior knowledge.

Even as he wrote out the sparse details, he knew he was probably setting himself up for trouble. But he couldn't help himself. He was infatuated with her, with her smile, with her body. He had known other women, many of them, but with Roxanne he felt immediately at ease. They seemed to be able to predict each other's wants and likes, and to move together as one. He didn't want to jeopardize that, not for anything.

And especially not for this Fancy Boots character. Every time he thought of the man, the red mist of anger descended, like it did whenever he thought of Claude Dallas. He could not think straight. He wanted, no he needed, payback. Then he had wanted payback for being sucker punched at the border, after chasing the man halfway across the country. Now he wanted it for the fear this man had put into Roxanne. And he wanted payback in advance for the damage that his career had suffered, and would no doubt suffer if, or more likely when, his subterfuge with the report was discovered.

He shook his head rapidly from side to side, trying to clear the foggy thoughts that were swirling around his brain. Finishing the report, he saved it, then opened up the secure e-mail link and added the attachment. Taking a deep breath, he paused, then pressed send.

When he returned to the house he was struck immediately by the smell of food. Normally there was nothing but house smells, but right away he could identify tomatoes and onions. Roxanne was standing in the kitchen, holding a wooden spoon over a saucepan.

"I made meatballs," she said. "There was some ground beef which I microwaved to defrost it, then I found some onions and a tin of crushed tomatoes. It's pretty simple but I'm not really a cook."

"It smells delicious," he said. "And I'm starving."

He went to the cupboards and got some bowls, cutlery, and glasses.

"Water or wine?" he said.

"Just water, please," replied Roxanne. "I'm still not sure what was put into my drink last night and anyway, I don't usually drink alcohol during the week."

Rashford opened the fridge and took out a large glass jug with a stopper inserted in the mouth.

"The water here can be a bit musty, sometimes," he said, "so I use this filter thing."

He poured them both a glass of water, then opened a small wooden case on the counter and took out a loaf of bread.

"It's a day-old baguette from the bakery," he said. "It should still be good for dunking, though."

She served the food into the bowls and carried them to the table. After they had both sat down, he cut a few slices of bread and passed two to her, then lifted his glass.

"Cheers," he said.

"Cheers," she said, reaching forward and clinking her glass against his. "It is good to see you again."

He nodded, then busily spooned some sauce into his mouth.

"That's fantastic," he said, and they both ate hungrily, not talking except to comment on the food. Once they had finished, he took the bowls and cutlery into the kitchen and quickly washed them under the tap, returning everything to its proper place.

"Bachelor habits," she said, laughing.

"I guess," he said, then went into his small home office. After a few minutes he called her to join him.

"You can stay here," he said, showing her the guest bed. He had tidied up the bed by moving all the newspapers into the top drawer and folded the cover quilt so that it looked like it was available for a cold evening. The laptop was now in its case and slung over his shoulder. He had found a pair of old socks on the floor and had hurriedly stuffed these into his trouser pocket.

"This looks great, thank you," she said. "And I am tired, it's been a long day."

"Right," said Rashford. "Well, I'll leave you to it, then. I have one more report to finish but you can use the bathroom and stuff while I'm next door. I put the toothbrush next to the sink."

He left and went back into the detachment. Forty minutes later he returned to the house and was not surprised to see the door to the guest bedroom closed.

"Good night," he called, but there was no response. He shrugged off his jacket and hung it up, then put his sidearm into the gun safe. He turned the television on but kept it at a low volume, then drank a beer while watching Jeopardy. He always liked to impress himself by knowing some of the answers, but he was sure he would freeze up if he had to come up with the answer on the actual show. The Final Jeopardy question asked which Canadian lake crossed the Alberta and Saskatchewan borders. What is Cold Lake, he called out, laughing when the given answer was Lake Athabasca. 'That's just the biggest!' he shouted, shaking his fist at the television, but in his mind he was happy. He knew the judges would have to rule in his favour and that he had just won eighteen thousand American dollars. Then he went to bed.

He heard Roxanne once in the night, woken when she got up to use the bathroom, but otherwise he slept well. The next morning, he woke up, got dressed quietly, then went for his normal run. He had a five-kilometer loop that took him round Maple Creek, ending up with a cool down walk along his street to the bakery. Here Howard gave him a paper bag with two bagels, and he returned to the residence.

He let himself in quietly and was surprised to see that the door to the guest bedroom was open. He looked inside and saw that the bed was neatly made, but the room was empty. He stepped back into the main room and walked over to the counter, on which he had left his wallet. He opened it and saw that the four red fifty dollar bills he had placed inside were gone. Instead, there was a small, folded piece of paper.

He extracted it and opened it to read. 'Thanks for the bus fare,' it said, written in a neat and legible hand. He put the paper on the counter next to the wallet and looked up at the ceiling for a few moments. Not getting any insight or inspiration there, he walked over to the bathroom, shedding his clothes as he went, and stepped into the shower.

He ran the water hot and then almost painfully cold, shaking his head at the ache of the spray. Stepping out of the shower he dried himself, then looped the towel around his waist. He walked into his bedroom to get dressed.

The first thing he noticed was a pile of neatly folded clothes on the side table next to the bed, the lamp pushed back almost to the wall. Then he saw Roxanne, lying in his bed, her head on the pillow and the sheet pulled up to her chin. She was looking directly at him.

"I thought I might get a later bus," she said, "if that's OK with you."

He nodded at her, unable to articulate any words.

"And anyway," she said, "you owe me a cardiovascular workout."

She raised one arm, holding the sheet away from her naked body. He flipped the hooked-over end of the towel with his thumb, and it pooled on the floor around his feet. Then he got into the bed.

Chapter 4

"If we're going to have that much exercise every morning," she said, "we're going to need more than two bagels."

"I'll talk to Howard," he said, reaching forward to wipe a smear of butter from her lip. "So, what are you going to do today?"

"I'm not sure," she said. "Maybe I'll just wander around town here, see what's happening. I need to buy a few things, some clothes and stuff. I can't wear these same old things all the time. I should also call my cousin and let her know I'm safe. What about you?"

"Today I have to go to Swift Current," he said. "It's our monthly coordination meeting. I'll be back around five or six but then I have to go out again, my Cree lesson is from seven to eight. I'll give you the key to this place and you can come and go as you like."

"Thank you for trusting me," she said. "Why are you doing this?"

Rashford looked at her.

"I like you," he said, simply. "You're fun to be with, and I think we're good together. And if you are in any danger, real danger, then this is probably the best place in town to be right now."

Roxanne looked at him.

"PWB?" she said.

Rashford was confused.

"I don't know what that means," he said.

"Prisoner With Benefits," she said, not really smiling.

"No, no," he said. "You can leave anytime. You can leave now if you want. Really, it's no problem ..."

Roxanne walked over to him and put her finger on his lips. He saw that she had tears pricking at the side of her eyes. She reached in with her other arm and embraced him tightly.

"I like you too," she said. "Maybe that's good enough for now.

They stood quietly for a moment, then she stepped back and looked up at him.

"So, is there a bank with an ATM somewhere?"

"Yes, at the CIBC. It's just a block over, on the corner of First and Jasper. There's a Bank of Montreal kitty corner to it as well. Just down the street is the Daily Grind, that's a really nice coffee shop, and there are a couple of shops on Jasper that sell women's clothes. So, you should be able to keep busy. If I give you some money, can you pick up something for dinner tonight as well? The Co-Op is the best bet, it's about a ten-minute walk down First Avenue from here."

"No problem," she said.

He went to his jacket, pulled out some bills from an inside pocket, and gave her a fifty-dollar bill.

"Keep that bus fare safe," he said, then dodged out of the way as she threw a punch towards him. Laughing, he grabbed his jacket and went to the gun safe for his side arm, then walked to the door.

"Right, see you later, probably just after five," he said. "Oh, and here's the house key."

He took the key out of the drawer and laid it on the counter.

"Don't lose it," he said, "it's the only spare I've got."

"Thanks. Oh, and is there a charger somewhere, for my phone?"

"There's one on the side, here," he said, pointing to the socket. "As long as it's an iPhone?"

"Yes, that should work," she said, walking over and plugging her phone into the end of the cable. "That's great, thanks. I think I'll call my cousin first, before she goes to work, and then I'll go for a walk."

Roxanne reached up and kissed his cheek, but he turned and embraced her.

"Are you OK with me telling her where I am," she said, looking up at him. "I can ask her to put a bag of my stuff on the bus."

He kissed her hair.

"Of course, you can tell her where you are," he said. "Tell her to put your name and care of RCMP Maple Creek on the label, that will get here."

"Thank you," she said, resting her cheek on his chest.

"You're welcome. I'm glad you found me," he said.

"I'm glad as well," she said, holding him tightly. "Every time I think of what that guy was going to do to me, or make me do for him, I start to feel sick."

"That's understandable," said Rashford. "Don't worry, you should be OK here. He probably hopes you're still running, not that you've told anyone about him. See you tonight."

He released her from his arms and walked out to his cruiser. Roxanne watched him drive away, then went to the counter and picked up the phone to see if there was enough charge for a call.

Rashford found himself whistling as he drove down the TransCanada Highway towards Swift Current. The sun was high enough that it wasn't shining directly in his eyes, but low enough that he had to pay close attention to the road. A group of pronghorn antelope caught his eye as they loped along inside the fence that lined the highway. 'Stay over your side,' he thought, mesmerized as always by the sun gleaming on their golden flanks.

He arrived at the detachment without incident, parked in the yard and went inside, nodding at the civilian desk worker as he passed through the public reception area.

"Morning, Evie," he called, and she waved back at him in reply, holding up her phone to show she was already engaged in conversation. He went up the short flight of steps and into the meeting room on the second floor. There were seven or eight officers already there, standing in pairs or small groups and chatting. He went to the silver urn on a side table and poured himself a cup of strong black coffee, then wandered over to a couple he knew quite well.

"Good drive over?" asked Staff Sergeant Paul Miller, a gruff veteran with nearly thirty years service to the RCMP and now the NWMP.

"Pretty quiet. I saw some pronghorn, but no speeders, no accidents, nothing interesting."

"There was no wrecks and nobody drown'ded, fact nothing to laugh at, at all" chuckled Constable Gayle Morgan, who had recently emigrated to Alsama from England and still spoke with a broad Mancunian accent. She had told them that she has served in the local police in Preston, a small town in Lancashire, and had met a Saskatchewan farmer who was on holiday in England.

After a whirlwind romance they had corresponded for a few months, then she had come over to Canada to meet his family. Alsama had been created while she was visiting and they had got married, primarily so that she could stay with him. She had moved into his house on the prairie near Osage, a small-town southeast of Regina abutting on the Wellington Community Pasture, but she had soon got bored of looking at nothing all day. She steadfastly refused to sit on a tractor for eight hours 'going in straight lines', as she put it. 'Not even circles!' she would exclaim.

When she had enquired at the local detachment about opportunities in the NWMP, she had been encouraged to apply, and to her surprise and delight was immediately offered a position at the Carlyle detachment, which was about an hour further east from the farm. It did not take long, however, until she started hearing rumours about her husband, and one afternoon she came home early to find him *in flagrante* with a neighbour's daughter. She had left him immediately, and transferred to Leader, the detachment north of Rashford's area of responsibility.

Morgan and Rashford were about the same age, and were both new to the southern prairies, so it was not surprising that they had gone on a few dates together. They went for drinks in Swift Current once, after a late meeting, and to a movie in Regina, then booked a room in a Medicine Hat hotel for some anonymity. No sparks had flown, however, and when they lay in bed together after their third date, she had stroked his cheek pensively.

"It were just a comfort cuddle, luv," she said, "mekking sure that all the bits still worked. No harm no foul, as you lot say over here."

He had driven her back to her small ground floor apartment in Leader, then drifted slowly south through the rainbow palette of a prairie dawn. They had stayed friends as well as colleagues, and she teased him unmercifully. Now she looked at him carefully, and a grin appeared on her face.

"You're looking pretty chipper this morning, Rashford," she said. "Did you get laid or something?"

Rashford did not reply. He went to his usual seat at the table and focused on making his notebook sit straight on the desk in front of him, but he could feel the blush start to spread across his cheeks.

"You did!" she said, delightedly. "Who was it? Was it that Cree professor you're always on about? Did she show you the power of a decolonized matriarchy in action? Was it all I can I Kant or did she just say sweet Foucault?"

She always managed that, thought Rashford. No matter the topic, Morgan always dropped a reminder that, before she had joined the police, she had studied philosophy at the University of Manchester. He didn't mind her sharp mind and sharper tongue, but some of her female colleagues found her overpowering at times.

After the first regional meeting following their tryst in Medicine Hat, Rashford heard a rumour that Morgan was rubbishing another officer. According to the story, gleefully recounted to him by a young constable, Morgan had been in the washroom with two other women officers. She had told them all about an evening she'd had with a male officer and concluded that 'I'd only give him a six, like,' before pausing, then adding 'with a following wind, if you get my drift.' Apparently, she had laughed loudly before going back into the meeting room.

"'Knives like that on her tongue, it's good she didn't give him a blow job,'" the constable reported as the response of one of the other women, adding, "I guess they're calling her Cutknife Morgan now." Rashford had laughed at the story, grateful that he wasn't mentioned by name, and told the young constable not to listen to station gossip. Privately, he thought he warranted at least an eight.

He had noticed this latest verbal probe, however, and was trying to put together the words to deny the accusation. His thoughts were all mixed up, though, and he could not articulate his emotions. Morgan kept grinning at him, waiting for a response, and he kept his eyes focused firmly on his notebook. Luckily just then the Staff Sergeant called the meeting to order.

The meeting following the usual routine, with each officer giving a basic summary of the past month and then a more detailed reporting on any unusual occurrences. The sequence of reports varied but this time went west to east, so Rashford started. As usual, his report was simply a litany of speeders and common assaults, this month with the addition of two trespassing incidents and one domestic violence case. He mentioned Roxanne in passing, focusing most of the attention on the storm. Then he waited for questions, but none were forthcoming, and he sat back while Morgan gave a similar report.

Her detachment covered a large rural area that was popular with tourists, coming to visit the Great Sandhills Park or the Smith Barn. She could understand the attraction of the Sandhills, 'like Blackpool without the Tower', but was amazed that people would travel to see what was, basically, the foundation of what had apparently been, and remained, the largest barn ever built in North America. Constructed in 1914, it had been dismantled in 1921, and only the concrete foundation remained. 'It's like looking at a Roman ruin', she used to say. 'You get a few bricks in the dust and you have to imagine the rest.'

Corporal John Smithson from the Swift Current Rural Detachment was next. After he had recited his list of arrests and incidents, he looked across at Rashford.

"There was one weird thing," he said. "Actually, I thought you might have been the one to report this, Gavin."

Rashford sat up straighter in his chair and looked attentive.

"What's that?" he said.

"Yesterday, I stopped this car, he was doing a hundred and thirty-seven on the highway. I thought you might have seen him, earlier."

"No, yesterday I was down to Willow Creek and Consul, I didn't go on the TCH. Sorry."

"Oh, right, that makes sense. Well, anyway, he was really moving. I pulled him over and there were three guys in there, two big dudes in the front and this little thin guy in the back. I made the driver get out and show me his ID, of course, and I'm sure he was a biker. He had all these tattoos and was a big guy. I ran the plates, and the car was his, no problem there, so I started to write up a ticket. Then the guy in the back seat pipes up."

"'It's my fault, officer,' he says. 'We're trying to find my truck. It was stolen and I think the thief came this way.'

"'Who are you?' I said, and he started to open the door and get out of the car.

"'Please stay in the vehicle, sir,' I said, and he did, leaving the door open.

"This little fellow, he said, 'my name is Justin Bourque, but I can't prove that I'm afraid. My wallet and all my ID is in my truck. That's why we're trying to catch it.'

"'Can you spell that, please. Your name,' I said, and he did.

"'What's the truck look like?' I said.

"'It's a red crew cab with white racing stripes on it,' he said. 'You can't miss it.'

"'I haven't seen it,' I said, 'but I'll keep an eye out. Have you reported it stolen?'

"'Yes, but back in Lethbridge, Alberta,' he said, 'to the local police.'

"Anyway, I wrote the ticket and served the driver, and told him to slow down in future or he'd lose the car, then they went on their way. But here's the interesting thing. Something seemed a bit off, so when I got back to the office I called Lethbridge, a guy I went through Basic Training with is posted there. He said there was no report of a truck being stolen. I looked up Justin Bourque in our system, and the only reference is to that guy who shot the Mounties in Moncton a few years back. And he's still in jail."

"Interesting indeed," said the Staff Sergeant. "What else can you tell us about Mr. Bourque, other than he was a 'little thin guy.'"

"Not a lot, sir, sorry. He was wearing a leather jacket, a brown one I think, a Saskatchewan Roughriders baseball cap, and a cowboy tie, you know, those long stringy ones with a green stone clip. His hair was grey, almost white, and he had it tied back in a ponytail. Oh, and when he tried to get out of the car, before I stopped him, he had already put his feet out and I saw his boots. He had the most amazing snakeskin cowboy boots that I've seen in a long time."

"And the third man, Corporal?"

"I didn't pay him much attention, sir," said Smithson. "He stayed in his seat so I just kind of kept him in my peripheral vision, you know? I was more worried about the one outside the car."

"Fair enough," said the Staff Sergeant. "OK, you've all heard the Corporal. What can we do with the information he's just given us?"

Rashford looked down at his notes. His mind was racing but he did not want anyone to know what he was thinking, not yet. He wanted to check a few things out first.

"Anybody?" said the Staff Sergeant.

"Look out for a red crew cab with Alberta plates and white racing stripes, sir," said Smithson.

"And?" said the Staff Sergeant.

Smithson looked confused.

"And try to find the car you stopped, John," said Morgan, nodding. "To have another chat with the snake boots guy."

"Indeed," said the Staff Sergeant. "Details, please, Corporal. As much as you can remember."

As soon as he was back in Maple Creek, Rashford went into the police house. Roxanne was sitting in the living room, reading the local newspaper.

"What's new in the News-Times?" he said.

"The pickleball club is having a tournament," she said. "What's pickleball?"

"It's like badminton played with ping pong paddles on a tennis court," he said. "Exercise for old people."

"Oh," she said. "Did you have a good day?"

"It was an interesting meeting," he said. "Where are the keys for your truck?"

"The keys? They're still in my purse, I think. Why?"

"I need to just go and have a quick look at something," he said. "Could I have them, please."

"Sure."

Roxanne shrugged and got up from the couch, then walked over to where her purse was sitting on a small side table. She reached in and felt around, then brought out the truck keys.

"Here you go," she said. "Do you want me to come with you?"

"No, you stay here, I'll just be a minute. Can you make some coffee? The stuff they have in Speedy Creek is awful."

She nodded and walked into the kitchen as he left the house.

Rashford walked quickly up the street and let himself into Alf's yard by the back gate. As he expected, Alf was sitting in a sunny corner of the yard, his battered baseball cap pulled down low over his eyes. He was on a flimsy looking metal chair, which had a pale blue fabric stretched across the seat and back. He held a cigarette in one hand and a chipped cup in the other.

As Rashford entered Alf struggled himself more upright, taking a long drag on his smoke as he did so. He was a portly man, probably in his early seventies, and both drank and smoked too much. Rashford knew that the battered old cup probably did not contain coffee. He nodded a greeting and received the same back.

"Afternoon, Alf," he said. "How's business? Keeping busy?"

"Busy as I want to be, I guess," said Alf, taking a healthy swallow of his drink. "Young Brian is helping out in the shop so when it's quiet I just come out here."

Rashford looked around the yard. In addition to the red crew-cab with racing stripes, which was parked in the corner furthest from the gate, there were three motorcycles, the front half of red Mustang convertible, a snowmobile, two all terrain vehicles, and the main body of an old yellow school bus that needed wheels before it could move again.

Two large poplar trees stood guard over the motley collection, and an old black Labrador wheezed quietly under their shade, but Alf had carefully placed his chair to avoid that interference.

"What do you do out here?" asked Rashford.

Alf stood up, took a long drag on his cigarette, then another swallow of his drink. Only then, to Rashford's amazement, did he let the smoke dribble out from his nose and mouth. He looked around.

"Well, sometimes I sits and thinks, and sometimes I just sits," he said, eventually. Rashford could not help but smile. He waved the keys in the air.

"I just need to look in the truck," he said.

"Your truck, your business," said Alf. "Anyways, I'd best be back to see what young Brian is doing."

Alf nodded at Rashford and walked to the grey wooden door in the back wall of the garage building. The dog thumped its tail as he passed but did not move. Rashford knew that Alf believed the dog was as good a guard as he needed, for nothing he owned was worth stealing.

One day Rashford had asked, "What happened to that Mustang?" Alf had paused, taken a drag of his cigarette, and shaken his head.

"Well, it's the damnedest thing," he said. "The fellow was a young lawyer or something, out of Calgary, trying to impress his girlfriend. He slammed on the brakes when a gopher ran into the road, so he wouldn't hurt the poor little thing." He spat on the ground. "Apparently the girlfriend was a vegan."

"Luckily, he had real good brakes and stopped right quick, so the gopher was fine. Unluckily, the brakes on the semi behind him weren't so good, and the guy rode his rig right up onto their back seat and pushed them along for a quarter mile. How they both got out of there without a scratch I have no idea. I heard she took the bus back to Calgary, though."

Rashford smiled at the story. Alf paused at the door, stubbed out the cigarette under the heel of his boot, and disappeared inside. Rashford went across the yard and looked at the truck.

He now realized that the truck had a cover of some sort, one that folded out from behind the cab. He dropped the tailgate of the truck and reached underneath for the catches which held the cover in place.

They popped open easily and he folded back the frame. Welded onto the bed of the truck he saw a large metal trunk that appeared to be locked with a padlock.

Rashford climbed into the tray of the truck and tried the small key, which as he had hoped turned with a subtle click. He lifted the clasp out from the bracket and placed the lock on the floor of the truck bed. Then he eased open the latch and slowly lifted the lid.

He was surprised to see that the trunk was nearly empty. In addition to a length of yellow construction rope, a plasticky fibre wound in a tight braid, there was a transparent bag of white cable ties, each fourteen inches long, and a torn-up t-shirt that was stained with oil. Rashford closed and relocked the trunk, then climbed down and went to the cab.

He opened the passenger door first and climbed inside, then reached forward and opened the glove compartment. Most of the space was filled with two copies of the user manual, one in English and one in French.

'Old habits die hard,' thought Rashford, putting the books onto the seat. Beneath them, he saw a small black wallet. He opened it to find truck registration papers and what the police called a PAL certificate, a firearms Possession and Acquisition Licence. The name Alvin Karpis was on the registration papers and that of Joseph Kelley on the PAL certificate, but both had the same Alberta address.

He put the wallet next to the manuals, then felt around to see if there was anything else stuck in the corner of the compartment. There was nothing. He conducted a similar search of the console between the two seats, and of the pocket area on the inside of the passenger door, both of which were empty of anything.

Going round to the driver side of the truck, he repeated his search in the door pocket, and also slid both front seats backwards to see if anything had been hidden, or mislaid, underneath them. The floor was clear, however, so he stepped back and thought for a moment. Then he opened the door to the crew cab.

These seats were fixed and did not slide forward, and he could see that the base of the seats was flush with the floor of the cab. He checked the seat pockets on both doors, and inside the small rear consul which extended out towards the back seat, providing a resting place for two cups. There was nothing there.

Rashford ran his hand along the ledge behind the seats, a narrow defile between the seatback and the rear window, but that was empty as well. As he lifted out his hand, one of his fingernails snagged on a piece of fabric or wire that seemed to run from the headrest down to the back of the seat. He looked more closely and realized that it was a fine filament fishing line, almost invisible, which was tied to the metal catch that could be used for a baby carrier or a child safety seat belt.

Carefully, Rashford tugged the on the line. It came out from the seat back enough to give him some purchase, and he found that he could hold the line between his finger and thumb. He pulled gently on the line, trying to keep it vertical, and heard a soft click. The seatback on one side fell forward. He scrambled out of the way and let it fall completely, so that it lay flat on the seat cushion, and then peered behind.

He could see the back wall of the truck cab, but the light was poor, so he pulled out his phone and switched on the emergency light. Immediately he saw that the back wall ended just below the height of the cushion, leaving a narrow ledge that was hidden behind the back seat. It was a perfect secret compartment. He shone his light down and realized that he was looking at a a metre long tube made of some sort of cardboard, and at a rifle.

Carefully he extracted the rifle, checking to make sure it was unloaded. It was, and the safety catch was engaged. It was painted a metallic grey and looked like the weapons carried by soldiers, but Rashford knew that it was an AR-style deer rifle, rather than the AR-15 issued to the military. Underneath it was a cardboard box of Winchester 350 Legend ammunition.

Next, he picked up the cardboard tube. It was light but, when he shook it gently, he heard something rattling inside. Carefully he placed that on the seat next to the rifle, then checked to make sure he hadn't missed anything. The compartment was empty.

Rashford pushed the seatback upright and heard it click back into position. He looped the fishing line back around the metal clasp, pushed it out of sight, and then backed out of the truck. He returned to the front seat and placed the black wallet and the instruction manuals back into the glove compartment.

Straightening up and looking around, he saw that he was alone. Quickly he put the rifle under his jacket and clamped it to his side with his right arm, picked up the tube in his left, closed and locked the truck doors, then walked out of Alf's yard and tried to be nonchalant as he returned to the detachment building.

Chapter 5

Once he was back in the detachment office, Rashford locked the rifle into the gun cabinet. He placed the cardboard tube on the desk and looked at it for a moment, then went outside and round to the house. Roxanne was in what had quickly become 'her' chair, reading a magazine. She gestured towards the table.

"Coffee is on the side."

"Thank you," he said, going over and pouring some. He then came around and sat in the other chair, taking a sip from his cup.

"Mmmmm. Good, as always. Thanks."

They sat quietly for a moment. Roxanne looked at him.

"But?" she said.

"But what?" he said, startled.

"But whatever is on your mind. I can tell, you know!"

He smiled.

"Well, I have to go back to the office for a few minutes, then off to my Cree class, but I do have a quick question for you, yes."

She looked at him.

"Can you just tell me again about what happened, when you took this guy's truck?"

"Sure. I was in the back of the cab, pretending to still be unconscious. He went inside to pay for the gas, and I got out, got back in the driver's side, and drove away."

"And did he take anything with him to the gas station?"

"Just his jacket, and his wallet of course, to pay."

"You're sure about the wallet?"

"Yes. The jacket must have been on the back seat, with me, because he pulled it out from under me after he checked my pulse. Then he reached in and got his wallet from that little storage space between the front seats. Then he left the truck."

"OK, that makes sense. Thanks."

He drank some more coffee, then looked across at her again.

"So, I thought we might grab a late supper from the takeaway. Is that alright with you?"

"Yes, that's fine. Do you want me to order?"

"Sure, you call it in for us and I'll pick it up on my way home, just after eight. Two thirty-six eighty-four."

"Is that their phone number?"

"No, that's what I want to eat. Spring roll, beef with black bean sauce, vegetable fried rice."

"You know their menu that well?"

"Not really. I always order those. I like them."

"Haven't you tried anything else?"

"Why would I? I like those."

"But what about General Tsao's chicken, or tofu, or wonton soup?"

"What about them?"

"I know, you like the others. Right. Well, I might branch out a bit, is that alright with you?"

"Go for it. Their phone number is on the wall, it's the Bel-Air. And you can ask, but I don't think they do General Tsao's chicken."

"Really? What kind of Chinese restaurant doesn't make General Tsao's chicken?"

"I don't know. I've never asked for it."

"Right. You know what you like and that's good enough for you. I'll have a look and pick something, then phone them up."

"Right, and I shall go back to the office, then out to class. Thanks for making the coffee."

He took his cup and walked back around the path to the detachment, then closed the door behind him and sat at the desk. He put his coffee cup down and lifted up the cardboard tube. The contents rattled softly.

"I wonder what we have here," he said under his breath, opening the desk drawer and bringing out a pair of scissors. Carefully he cut around the lid, then popped it off and placed it next to his coffee cup.

Turning the tube upside down, he gently shook out the contents onto the desk. Then he sat back in his chair, stunned.

In front of him, spread out in an arc, he saw a receipt from ArtsChic in the Shaganappi Mall, a horseshoe, a thimble, a red and cream striped pebble, an old napkin with a phone number on it, a bus ticket, and a yellow fishing lure.

He reached into the drawer again and took out a packet of cigarettes, a lighter, and a small glass ashtray. He tapped a cigarette out, then lit it, exhaling slowly. Smoking was not allowed in the detachment, of course, but at certain times the rule had to be broken.

"Well, well, well," he said. "Claude Dallas rides again."

Rashford sat quietly for nearly twenty minutes, smoking three cigarettes, turning things over in his mind. Eventually he came to a decision and stood up.

He carefully returned all the items to the tube, and replaced the lid, then put the tube in the gun closet next to the rifle. He dumped the ashtray into his waste basket, then opened two of the windows a little so that the smoke would clear away. Then he walked out of the detachment.

First, he walked up the street to the mechanic, arriving just as Alf was locking the front door. Rashford called out his name, so he stood and waited until the policeman arrived. They nodded at each other.

"I wonder if you could do me a favour, Alf," said Rashford.

"Another one?" said Alf, raising his eyebrows.

"Yes. Tomorrow morning, when you come to open up, can you please give me a call and report that there is a strange red pick-up truck in your yard."

"A red pick-up truck with white racing stripes?"

"Yup."

"And Alberta plates?"

"If that's what it has, sure."

"Tomorrow morning?"

"Yes."

"OK, I can do that. If I find that a red pick-up truck with white racing stripes and Alberta plates suddenly arrived in my yard tonight, I'll let you know first thing in the morning."

"Thank you. I appreciate that."

Rashford started across the street, then stopped and turned back. He smiled when he saw that Alf was already going to the big double gate.

"I figured I'd probably not set the lock properly, if a truck drove in tonight," Alf said, stepping on his cigarette as he fiddled with the big padlock. "Nothing too easy, mind, just off the latch a little."

Rashford nodded at him in appreciation, then turned and walked across town to Kôhkum Christine's house. He knocked on the door, greeted Bettina Blackeagle politely, and then sat on his regular chair. The old lady came in and sat down opposite to him. She looked at him.

"You seem troubled today, Sergeant. Do you want to talk about it?"

"Yes," he said. "What do you know about the Mi'kmaq?"

"Ah, the People of the Dawn. They are from the east, from the coastal lands. They had a great hero, Glooscap I think was his name, but I do not know much about him or their stories. Why?"

"Oh, I was just wondering."

"Ah. So, this is nothing to do with the young lady who you are keeping in the police house?"

Rashford stared at her. He realized that his mouth was open, so he closed it.

"What, you think this is a secret? Everyone in town with eyes has seen her going to the coffee shop. Everyone with ears knows she is not from around here."

"And everyone who is First Nation knows that she is also Indigenous, but she is not one of our people."

Rashford jerked around. Bettina Blackeagle had come silently to the door and was leaning against the frame.

"I spoke with her this morning, this Roxanne," she said. "We were at the Daily Grind together. We had a good conversation. I like her. I have been invited round to the police house for tea, tomorrow morning, while you are at work. Do you mind?"

Rashford shook his head, trying to clear it.

"It is a small town," said Bettina, gently. "Do not concern yourself."

"It just amazes me, how quickly word spreads around," said Rashford.

"Well, remember," said the old lady, her eyes gleaming. "Not everyone has eyes and ears. There are many who do not know."

"Mostly *môniyâw*, the white people," said Bettina, laughing, then walking away as silently as she had appeared.

"Now, where were we. Ah, yes. Tell me the seasons. Start with *mīyoskamik.*"

"*Êhe. Mīyoskamik,* spring. *Nīpon,* summer. *Tagwākin,* fall. *Pipon,* winter."

"*Mīwāsin.* Now, pass me the computer."

Rashford reached over and took the laptop off the table. He opened it, and she instructed him carefully.

"Go to Google and write, 'Small Number counts to one hundred.' *Êhe. Mīwāsin.* Now click on the one that says it is in Cree, not the Blackfoot language."

Rashford did as she asked, and the page opened.

"That is the one. '*Apsch Akichikiwan akichikeet isko mitatomitano.*' Now, read it to me."

Kôhkum Christine leaned back in her chair, folded her arms in her lap, and closed her eyes. She sat there quietly while Rashford read the story about the little boy who was always getting into trouble, smiling when the black cat with a white stripe turned out to be a skunk. When he had finished, she looked up at him.

"Sometimes you can find a short cut to the answer, but you need to know what you are trying to find."

Then she stood up, wheezing, and walked off into the back of the house, her cane tapping on the floor. Rashford waited until she had gone, then stood, and quietly left the house. He walked down to the Bel-Air and picked up their food order, wondering what Roxanne has ordered as he paid three times his normal amount. He carried the brown paper bag down the street to the police house, stopping only to double check that the detachment was locked.

When he entered the house, he saw that plates and cutlery were already on the table, along with some glasses. Roxanne walked in with a can of beer, and carefully poured half into each glass.

"I'm starving," she said, opening the bag and arranging the small Styrofoam dishes on the table. "So, what do we have here?"

"I have no idea," said Rashford, truthfully, "but I admit that it does smell good."

"Well, we have rice and noodles," said Roxanne. "Beef and chicken. Vegetables and tofu. Spring rolls and deep-fried wontons. So, we can mix and match, and if there is too much, I can have the rest for lunch tomorrow."

"If you still have room, after your tea with Bettina," he said.

"Oh, she told you. Good. You don't mind, do you? She seems such a nice lady. We met when the barista got mixed up with our orders this morning, I guess he's never had to make two different lattes at the same time before. She says she will bring me some Bannock that her grandmother makes, and we can have it with our tea. Wow, this chicken is amazing. And it is General Tsao, look. See the red sauce. I just asked and they said they would make it special for us."

Rashford smiled and listened to her talk. He picked at the various dishes, finishing the beef in black bean sauce but at least trying everything else. As he ate, he thought about the cardboard tube and its contents, and tried to figure out what he should do next.

The following morning, they were still eating their bagels when the phone rang. Rashford answered it.

"Maple Creek Detachment, good morning. Oh yes. Hello, Alf," he said, then listened for a few moments. "Really? Thank you. I'll be right over."

He finished his coffee with a quick swallow, then returned the cup to the table and kissed Roxanne on the top of her head.

"I just have to go out for a minute," he said. "I'll try and get back here before I go out for the day."

"Have fun," said Roxanne. "I'll clean up here. I don't want Bettina to think you're a total slob."

"Yes dear," muttered Rashford, walking across to the door. He had his back to Roxanne and did not see her big smile, something she hid as soon as he turned and waved back at her.

"Later," he called, and left.

Rashford walked up the street and crossed over at the intersection. Alf was standing outside the big double gate, a cigarette dangling from his lip. The two men nodded at each other.

"So, what's this about, Alf?" said Rashford, taking out his notebook. Alf straightened his back, took a drag of the cigarette and then dropped the butt to the pavement. He put his hands by his sides, almost looking like he was standing at attention, and cleared his throat.

"Well, erm, I came to work this morning and went to open up the yard, like, and I see'd that the gate was already open. Nothin' broke, like, I must have not latched it properly last night."

He leaned forward and pointed at the open clasp on the padlock. Rashford nodded and kept writing his notes.

"So, then what happened?" he said.

"Well, I went in to see if anything had got stolen, I've got some valuable tools in here you know."

Rashford stopped writing and looked at the old man.

"Really?"

"Oh, aye, so you keep writing them down, 'cos I'm going to need your report, for the insurance."

They looked at each other for a moment. Alf did not say anything, but he never looked away and maintained his steady stare.

Rashford shook his head, then started to write again. Alf smiled, pulled out a cigarette, lit it, and then opened the gate with his other hand.

"So, I came inside, right, and straightaway I see my chainsaw is gone.

It was my new one, a Husqvarna 455 Rancher, 20-inch blade, seven hundred bucks plus tax from Canadian Tire. That's H U ..."

"Yes, I can spell Husqvarna," said Rashford. "And you have your receipt for this new chainsaw that got stolen, do you?"

"Well, here's the thing, see. It was so new, it was still in the box, I just never got to bring it inside the shop yet, and the receipt was taped on the side, so they took that as well. But it's OK, they'll remember me at the shop. It was my nephew's girlfriend's brother who served me."

"That will be helpful," said Rashford, "especially if the insurance adjuster doesn't try to unravel your genealogical tree."

"Come again?"

"Never mind. So, you come inside, see that the chainsaw is missing, then what?"

"Then I start towards the shop, towards the back door there, and I suddenly realize that this 'ere truck is in my yard."

Alf pointed dramatically towards the back corner, where the red pick-up was parked.

"Like I said on the phone, it's got Alberta plates," he said. "Not from around here."

They walked over to the truck and stood looking at it.

"Nice rig," said Alf. "Racing stripes and everything."

"Is it locked?" said Rashford.

"Yup," said Alf, then looked across at the policeman.

"What? I checked it, that's all. There might have been a body or something in there."

"That's OK," said Rashford. "So, if you left a good truck somewhere, and were planning to come back for it, where would you leave a spare key?"

"Magnetic clip inside the front driver's side wheel well, up front toward the bumper," said Alf, without hesitation.

Rashford walked over and knelt down next to the front wheel, keeping his left side toward Alf and his right arm tight against the truck.

"Just check the other side, would you?" he asked, and Alf ambled off around the front of the cab. Rashford quickly brought the keys and a small magnetic clip out from his front pocket and felt around under the wheel well. He brought his hand out empty.

"Well, I can't find it," he said, grumpily. "Are you sure this is where it would be?"

Alf looked at him across the hood.

"Normally, yes. I'll try this side though."

He ducked down and was out of sight for a few minutes, then re-emerged.

"Nope, nothing here."

"Well, you try this side, will you? Maybe I'm not reaching into the right places."

"Maybe," muttered Alf, coming back around the truck and kneeling by the wheel. He reached inside, then brought his hand out and stood up, smiling.

"Here you go," he said. "I'm not surprised you missed them, you have to go to the chassis beam, then feel over the top to the side that's out of sight. That chassis beam is the only thing that's magnetic these days, everything else is fibre glass. Oh, look at that, will ya?"

He pointed towards the corner of the fence, where some broken sticks and bits of ripped fabric were caught up on an old nail.

"Look, the bastards went and broke my grandkids' hockey net as well. Sherwood Proform Regulation, hundred and eighty bucks plus tax. Write that down."

Rashford did, then took the key and walked towards the driver's door.

"Thank you for your help, Alf. I think I'll drive this truck down to the detachment for a proper examination, and safe keeping."

Alf looked disappointed that he was not going to see the vehicle being searched but nodded.

"Just make sure those notes of yours are legible," he said. "I'm going inside to phone my insurance."

He walked away across the yard. Rashford climbed into the cab, adjusted the front seat so that his legs would fit under the console, and slowly backed out of the yard. He left the truck running while he went back and closed the big double gates, then drove slowly down the street and into the parking lot next to the detachment office. Taking the small wallet from the glove compartment, he locked up the vehicle and walked into the office.

Once inside, Rashford closed and locked the door behind him. He opened the wallet and saw that the truck was registered to an address in Mountain View, Alberta. A quick online search showed him that this was a small community in the southern part of the province, on the edge of the Waterton National Park.

The name on the firearms possession licence was Joseph Erving Kelley. There was no record of any such person in the data base, and Rashford was not surprised when another online search turned up a link to the 'outlaw cave dweller of the Big Muddy' story. More usually known as Sam Kelley, it seemed, or by his alias Red Nelson, Kelley was originally from the Cape Breton region of Nova Scotia.

A tall man with a bright red beard, he had arrived in the west in the late eighteen eighties and had joined an American criminal in what became known as the Nelson-Jones gang. They were so successful in terrorizing ranchers in the area that the North-West Mounted Police set up its first detachment in the Big Muddy valley. He was never caught, though, for whenever the police came by a lookout posted on Peake's Butte would signal, and the gang would cross the border into Montana.

Rashford reached into his drawer for another cigarette. He lit it and pondered on what he knew. The evidence was still only circumstantial, but it seemed that he had once again crossed tracks with the person he knew as Claude Dallas. The physical description of a short, wiry man that Roxanne had provided sounded similar to the man he had encountered in Manitoba two years earlier. The items in the cardboard tube matched his recollection of those in the medicine bundle that Dallas had been carrying.

There was also the question of who Dallas really was. So far, he had been identified as Claude Dallas, Albert Johnson, Peter Smythe, Justin Bourque, and now Alvin Karpis and perhaps Joseph Kelley, or possibly Red Nelson. For whatever reason, and except for the Peter Smythe reference, Dallas liked to use the names of different outlaws as an alias, which suggested he knew a good deal of history. His real name could be any of those, or none of them.

At that point, Rashford was stumped. He could not figure out why Dallas had paid five thousand dollars to some bikers for Roxanne. Was she singled out specifically, or was she just a coincidental connection? If she had been targeted, then what was the link between her and Fancy Boots, as she called him? Rashford did not see how it could be anything to do with the night he had spent with Roxanne in Saskatoon, but at the moment he was grasping for any link, no matter how tenuous.

He did recognize what he had to do next, though. With a trembling hand, he reached for the telephone.

At two o'clock that afternoon, the meeting room on the second floor was crowded. Rashford sat at one end of the table, his notebook in front of him. His colleagues sat along both sides of the table, talking quietly but studiously ignoring him. The other end of the table was empty.

The door opened and Chief Superintendent Tracey Pollard walked in, Staff Sergeant Miller a step behind her like a giant bodyguard. She went to the empty seat at the head of the table, and he placed a manilla file in front of her. Then Miller went and sat on a chair by the wall. There was silence in the room.

The Chief Superintendent opened the file and skimmed through the first few pages, even though everyone knew this was just her being dramatic. Rashford sat straight-backed, staring ahead. Eventually, she closed the file, then looked up. She leaned forward, rested her elbows on the desk, steepled her fingers, and stared straight at Rashford.

"In your own words, Sergeant," she said. "What kind of cluster fuck have you got into now?"

Morgan snorted but quickly recovered, nobody else moved. Rashford found it uncanny that they could stand at attention while sitting down. He paused for a few moments, then began to speak.

"Thank you, Ma'am. I think we have a link between two active cases. First, the Claude Dallas case, and now the Snake Boots case."

"I see. Alright, one at a time then, for anyone who is not up to speed."

"Claude Dallas is probably an alias, Ma'am, but he was the fellow I tracked all across Alsama a couple of years ago. He was a prime suspect in a number of theft, physical assault, sexual assault and poisoning charges, all the way from Calgary to Manitoba. We caught him at the border with Ontario, but unfortunately he got away."

"Indeed, he did, Sergeant, and we don't need to revisit the circumstances of his escape. Now what do you see as the link between him and this Snake Boots character?"

"Well, Ma'am, there are a couple of things. First, I started to wonder after our last regional meeting, when Corporal Smithson talked about the car he stopped for speeding, and the passenger with the snakeskin boots. You see, as I reported then, I hadn't been on the TransCanada that day. I had been down to the Medicine Line, to the American border.

"But this morning a mechanic in Maple Creek, he phoned to report a truck had been left in his yard. And it fit the description of the one the fellow Corporal Smithson had stopped was looking for. It was red with white racing stripes and had Alberta plates. So, I went and saw it, we found a spare key under the front wheel, and I drove it back to the detachment.

"I looked in the truck and found a wallet in the glove box which said the truck was registered to a fellow in Mountain View, Alberta. Name of Alvin Karpis but there's nobody of that name on the system. There was also a firearms possession certificate in the name of Jospeh Kelley, with the same address as Karpis. Then I found a sort of secret compartment behind the back seat of the crew cab. In there I found a hunting rifle, some shells, and this."

Rashford brought the rifle, box of Winchester 350 ammunition and the cardboard tube up from the bag he had placed on the floor next to his desk. He popped the lid off the tube and shook out the contents.

"You see, Ma'am, I recognize these. They are the things that Claude

Dallas was carrying when we questioned him on the border. He called them his medicine bundle."

"Are you sure?" said the Chief Superintendent.

"Yes, Ma'am, because he was very careful with each of them. That got me thinking, so I did a general Google search for Alvin Karpis, and it turns out he was from Montreal, part of the Ma Barker gang back in the depression years. I did a search for Joseph Kelley as well, he was a criminal from Nova Scotia, who was in southern Alberta at the turn of the twentieth century.

"So, more aliases. But it has to be the same guy, these are his things."

"Are they all exactly the same?"

"Exactly, Ma'am. Except these two pieces."

Rashford pointed at the bus ticket and the shop receipt.

"The bus ticket is from Calgary to Pincher Creek," he said. "I don't know its relevance. But this is interesting."

He used his forefinger to push the shop receipt to the front.

"This is new," he said, "but I think it provides another link."

"And what might that be?" said the Chief Superintendent, showing interest for the first time.

Rashford took a deep breath.

"Well, Ma'am, there was one other thing, which I didn't actually report. Yet."

Pollard sat back in her chair. She folded her arms and raised one eyebrow.

"Go on."

"Well, you might remember Roxanne, Ma'am, the, umm, lady whom I met in Saskatoon?"

"Indeed, I do, Sergeant. What of her?"

"She's in Maple Creek, Ma'am."

"Is she now? And how is that relevant?"

Rashford could feel his cheeks blushing furiously. He sensed his colleagues turning towards him, with questions in their eyes. He felt the silent laughter emanating in waves from Gayle Morgan. He stared straight ahead.

"Well, Ma'am, she's, umm, she's staying with me, Ma'am."

"I see. And you reported this, of course, so that your rent can be adjusted from single to double occupancy?"

"No, Ma'am. Not yet, Ma'am."

"Probably not something we need to worry about right now," said Pollard. "Carry on, Sergeant. Why is your personal life relevant here?"

This was the part where Rashford knew he was crossing a line, when the truth was couched with unspoken caveats and evasions. He kept his face straight, did not take another deep breath. He just kept talking.

"When I met up with Roxanne again, Ma'am, she told me that she was running away from somebody. She didn't know who he was, but he had fancy snakeskin boots."

"And how had she met this person, if she didn't know him?"

"She was sold to him, Ma'am. By some bikers who drugged her drink at a Calgary club and then kidnapped her."

Now he had everyone's attention, he knew, and hopefully nobody would circle back to the 'how did you meet with her again' part of his story.

"After she left Saskatoon, Ma'am, she went to Calgary and stayed with her cousin. One evening they went to a birthday party. They were in a bar called the Barrel Races and this guy who danced with her a couple of times, he spiked her drink. He and some friends took her out of the club and drove her down the highway to a rest stop area. Then the snakeskin boots guy turned up and paid them five thousand dollars for her."

"What, was he going to use her as a hooker?" asked Morgan, earning herself a stern glance from the Chief Superintendent.

"She didn't know," said Rashford. "She was able to escape before anything happened."

Morgan kept speaking.

"Five grand. Whew. She must be pretty good. What do you think?" she said, coyly glancing over at Rashford.

"Corporal Morgan, enough," said the Chief Superintendent.

"Sorry, Ma'am," said Morgan, settling back into her seat.

"But here's the thing, Ma'am," said Rashford, trying to ignore the comments. "This new addition to the medicine bundle, this receipt."

He pushed the slip of paper out to the front of his desk.

"This is from a place called ArtsChic, it's a small and rather exclusive clothing boutique in the Shaganappi Mall in Calgary. Before I left Maple Creek this morning, I asked Roxanne where she worked when she was staying with her cousin."

He paused, and looked around the room, making eye contact with each of his colleagues, including Corporal Gayle Morgan. His gaze ended up focused on the Chief Superintendent.

"She worked at ArtsChic, Ma'am. I think he targeted her."

Chapter 6

Gayle Morgan was the first to break the silence.

"Whoa!" she said, shaking her head. "That's a bit of a stretch."

"I know it seems weird," said Rashford, "but what else can it be? She was the only one in her group who got drugged. She thought she'd seen the guy before. When the snakeskin boots guy turned up, at the meet, he said 'this is her'. Not, 'is this her?' Like he knew who to expect."

"What's the connection between them?" said the Chief Superintendent.

"I don't know yet, Ma'am," said Rashford. "I'm hoping that you will let me find out."

"And how will I help you do that?"

"I'm not sure, Ma'am," said Rashford. "But in the first case, I think I should be seconded to go to Alberta and join the team that checks out this address in Mountain View."

Tracey Pollard said nothing. She gathered her papers together and then stood up, handing them to Staff Sergeant Miller, who had materialized at her side. When she spoke, it was directly to him.

"I'll let you know what I decide, Paul," she said, quietly. "Until then, just have everyone doing the same as always. You've got them well organized down here."

"Thank you, Ma'am," said the Staff Sergeant, proudly. "I'll see you out."

He opened the door and followed her out of the room. As soon as they left, chatter broke out as people left their seats and gathered around Rashford. He stayed in his chair, trying to calm his heart rate through steady breathing exercises. Then he looked up.

"Sorry to have had you all dragged in here for another coordination meeting," he said. "Two days in a row. But it doesn't look like there's going to be anything to coordinate."

Morgan's voice cut through the general noise, and he looked over towards her. She was standing at the side of the room, a cup of coffee in hand, leaning her hip against the edge of the table.

"You think he saw her before, at the club," she said, "and then sent the biker guys to cut her from the crowd?"

"That's what I am thinking, yes." Said Rashford.

"Have you asked her? Did she see him before? Does she have any idea why he might have targeted her?"

"Other than to use as a sex slave, you mean?" said Rashford. "No. No, she doesn't remember ever seeing him before. No, she has no idea why he might have targeted her. No, she has no idea what he was going to do with her. She was working in a shop, selling clothes. She went to a club with some friends. Someone spiked her drink, and her life went sideways."

"No, not at the club," said Morgan. "Did she remember him from the shop? He has the receipt from there, it must have a date and time on it. Can she remember anything unusual?"

"That's the thing. It was timed for lunch time, when she was usually having a sandwich in the food court. She can't remember exactly but she doesn't think she will even have been in the shop at the time he made the purchase."

"What did he buy?"

Rashford looked at the receipt.

"Well, he, or else someone who later gave him this receipt, bought a silk scarf. An expensive one, nearly two hundred bucks."

"That sort of sale can't be common," said Morgan. "Did you ask the other shop assistants? Maybe one of them remembered something."

"No, I've not been to Alberta, remember. That's a good point, though. If the Chief Superintendent lets me join the team over there, I'll make sure someone checks that out."

Just then the Staff Sergeant came back into the room.

"OK, boys and girls," he said, clapping his hands together. "Let's not waste this opportunity. We'll use this time for reports, tell us what's been going on in your world. Things you didn't have time to report yesterday. Rashford, I think we've heard enough from you for a bit. Morgan, you're up."

Everyone took their seats, and Gayle Morgan stood up. She opened her notebook and started her report.

"I have heard something interesting, actually," she said. "It's not from my detachment, not really, but I was called to deal with it."

"And why was that?" asked the Staff Sergeant.

"It was from a colleague where I used to work, in Carlyle," she said. "Apparently they were called to an unusual case at the hospital. Someone had turned up at the Emergency Department, covered in blood and with his face all bashed in. That's obviously not too unusual, not in Saskatchewan, but when the nurse asked him what had happened, he said that he had been hit by a flying dog."

Everyone chuckled, even the Staff Sergeant.

"So, anyway, my colleague, or rather ex-colleague, he spoke to this fellow and it turned out that he had been at a party organized by one of my ex-husband's brothers. His name is Doug, but people call him Dougie, and he's had his run-ins with the law before.

"He isn't usually very cooperative, but we got on alright, so my ex-colleague asked if I could give him, my ex-brother-in-law not my ex-colleague, a call and see what had happened. The guy with the broken face wasn't making much sense."

Morgan paused, and looked around the room, making sure of her audience.

"Wi' me so far?"

Various people nodded, some murmured assent.

"Right, then. So, I called up Dougie and said I'd heard he'd had a party, and there'd been a spot of trouble, and what had happened, like. He told me, yeah, he had a party, but there were no trouble. I said there was a fellow ended up in Emergency, that must have been summat, and he just roared with laughter.

"'That was just an accident,' he said, 'that's why they call it Accident and Emergency.' Smart arse.

"OK, I said. Tell me what happened, then. And he says, sure, anything to help the Constabulary, even if you're not Royal anymore. So, this is his story, more or less verbatim.

"'I had a party, right,' he said, 'out at the house. You know I live a fair way from town, half-way to the reserve. So, lots of people came, from both places, and we had a good time. About two hours in, this big guy arrives with a fuckin' big dog, some sort of Rottweiler Alsatian mix. Big black fucker with blue eyes. Proper scary, it was. I didn't know the guy, but he told me that Phyllis from the butcher shop had invited him along.'

"'I said, look, you can come in, but leave the dog tied up outside somewhere. He chuntered a bit, but everyone was backing me up, so he went out and came back in without the dog.'

"'The party continued. Around eleven o'clock we had nearly run out of beer, so my mate Phil said he'd go to the pub and get some more, before the bar closed. We had a whip round, he took the money and went outside, then came back and said his truck was blocked in, but there was an old pink and white Dodge Ram on the outside and could he use that. Some girls from town said it was their truck and threw him the keys, and off he went.'

"'Half an hour later there is this banging on the door. I opened it and this guy is standing there, covered in blood. It's Byron from the farm up by the crossroads. 'What the fuck happened to you?' I said.

"'He said, 'I got hit by a flying dog.'

"'By now there were a bunch of people at the door with me, crowding around. Someone got a cold towel and tried to wipe the blood away from his eyes.

"'No, really,' I said, 'what the fuck happened?'

"'I just told you,' he says. 'I was walking here, and a big pink truck come screaming past me. I was on the side of the road, so I knew he'd seen me. I was just up on the bend by the cottonwood trees.'

"'I interrupted him. 'That'd be Phil,' I said, 'he was going to get more beer.'

"'Well anyways,' says Byron. 'The truck came past and then wham, there was a fucking dog flying along behind it, it just hit me in the head.'

"Suddenly this big feller pushes by us and out the door. 'What you done to my dog?' he shouts, 'I tied him up to a bumper like you told me.'"

"Well, we all just sorta looked at each other. Just then there's headlights in the drive, then they're turned off, and Phil comes in with a coupla' two-fours. He sees us all looking at him.

"'What?' he says, and then can't understand why we all crack up.

"'The big fellow goes running off to behind the truck, and then starts screaming and yelling, so we get Phil inside and lock the door. Then we drink the beer, and when the big buddy had taken off, taking what was left of his dog with him, someone drove Byron to the hospital.'

"'So, that's what happened, no trouble at all.'

Morgan closed her notebook and sat down. The rest of the team just stared at her. Suddenly she began to laugh.

"This is why I love Canada," she said, shaking her head. "A flying dog. You can't make this stuff up!"

Rashford was not surprised to see Morgan's squad car in his mirror all the way back to Maple Creek. They arrived at the detachment, and she pulled in on the other side of the red truck. Getting out of her vehicle, she stretched, then walked around the Ford.

"Nice rig," she said, nodding approvingly. Then she pressed the button on her collar, next to the epaulette, and spoke into her microphone.

"Yes, Staff, it's sitting here, as reported," she said.

Rashford couldn't hear the reply, which went straight to her earpiece, but when she held out her hand, he knew enough to pass over the keys.

"I have them," she said, pressing the collar button once again. "Yes, Staff, I'll tell him."

She turned to Rashford.

"Sorry, Gavin," she said, "but Miller has ordered me to tell you that you're to stand down for a few days. Paid leave. Don't leave town and all that. He'll be in touch once the Chief gives him instructions."

"Do you want my badge?" said Rashford.

"C'mon, don't shoot the messenger. That's all he said."

"Sorry," said Rashford, looking at the pavement and scuffing his shoes.

"Listen, for what it's worth, most of us think you're on to something. Your report was tight and logical and drew clear lines between the evidence. Circumstantial evidence, mind, but still. I can see things happening the way you described it. I think that the Chief agreed as well. She said now't about it being a load of bollocks, did she?"

Rashford thought back to the meeting. The Chief Superintendent had listened, asked some questions, and then left. But she had not denied him, not once. He nodded.

"On t'other side, of course, you've no proof. They could be two completely different people. Even if the trophies belong to this Dallas guy, it doesn't mean he had them in the truck. Fancy Boots could have got them from anybody. Shit, they could have been left in the truck by the previous owner, right? Somehow we've gonna have to sort that all out."

Rashford started to protest but then spluttered to a stop.

"You're right. It is all circumstantial. There's got to be proof somewhere, though."

"Maybe," said Morgan, "but right now, let the rest of us worry about that. I reckon you and this Roxanne can have a few days honeymoon now, get to know each other a bit, then you'll be nice and relaxed when the Chief calls you."

She looked around at the detachment building.

"Talking of, do I get to meet the lovely lady?"

Not waiting for an answer, she bleeped the lock on her car and then set off round the sidewalk along the edge of the detachment. Rashford sighed, locked his own vehicle, and followed.

He caught up with her in time to reach ahead and open the door, calling out as he did so.

"Roxanne, we've got company," he said, just hoping that she wasn't lying in bed waiting for him. Morgan must have been thinking the same thing, for she pulled a face.

"Spoilsport," she said, in an undertone, then in a normal voice added, "good afternoon."

Roxanne called back.

"Hello, I'm just in the kitchen."

She appeared around the corner, wiping her hands on a tea towel, and reached up to kiss Rashford on the cheek.

"Hello, honey," she drawled, "did you have a good day? The kettle's on for tea. Or would you prefer coffee?"

This last comment was directed at Morgan, who stood slightly behind Rashford and so did not see the look of amazement on his face. Morgan stepped forward.

"Tea is fine, thank you. Milk and two sugars, please. I'm Gayle, Gayle Morgan."

Roxanne took the outstretched hand.

"Roxanne. Roxanne Gaudet," she said.

"Goody? That's an unusual name," said Morgan.

"It's Acadian," said Rashford and Roxanne, simultaneously.

Morgan looked from one to the other, a slight smile on her lips.

"Well, when you two have finished playing happy families, perhaps we can talk about things?"

Roxanne returned to the kitchen while Rashford showed Morgan to a chair at the table. They sat down, not speaking.

Roxanne came in with a tray on which she had placed three mugs, a glass preserves jar half filled with sugar, three small teaspoons, a small jug of milk, and a plate which held seven or eight chocolate digestive biscuits. She left the tray on the table and returned to the kitchen.

Rashford carefully moved everything to the table and propped the empty tray up against the table leg nearest to his foot. Roxanne returned with a large brown teapot, which gently steamed from the spout. She sat down at the third chair and folded her hands across her lap.

There was silence.

Eventually, Rashford leaned forward and picked up the teapot. He lifted it over the mug in front of Morgan and was about to pour when she stopped him. She had a horrified look on her face.

"Not yet," she said. "You have to put the milk in first."

"Says who?" said Rashford, looking puzzled.

"Says everybody!" said Morgan. "Everybody who knows anything about tea, that is."

"Why?" said Rashford.

"In the old days, if the milk was bad, it would curdle when the hot tea hit it," said Roxanne, nodding. "Then you could throw it out and get some new milk, but you wouldn't have to make a new pot of tea, because you would only have wasted a little bit. If you put the milk in last, and it has gone off, then you've lost a whole cup of tea."

"Where did you learn that?" said Rashford.

"According to my mom, it's an old Cape Breton habit," said Roxanne.

"It's an old English habit, originally," said Morgan. "From when they were first bringing the tea back from India and didn't know whether the milk on the ship had soured. I guess the first settlers who came to Canada brought the idea with them."

Rashford sighed and put the teapot back on the table. He lifted the milk jug and poured some into everybody's mug.

"How do I know how much milk to put in, then?" he said.

Morgan sighed, theatrically.

"You put in a bit first," she said, "then we can each add more if we think we need it."

"Absolute madness," said Rashford, but he did what he was told. Once everyone had their tea in front of them, with milk and sugar added to taste, and everyone had refused a biscuit, Morgan spoke.

"Right, you two, here's the situation. Roxanne, if I may call you that ..."

Roxanne nodded.

"Right, well then, Roxanne, Rashford here has told us all about your horrible experience at the Barrel Races in Calgary, and what happened after the guy who drugged you sold you on to this stranger with the fancy boots. Then he told us about what he found in the truck.

"I must say that I, personally, was a bit unclear about the part between you running away and ending up here, or the coincidence of the truck turning up a day later, but the boss didn't ask any questions, so I won't."

Rashford looked across at her, gratefully. She nodded, indicating that she expected the full story later.

"So, the situation now is that Rashford has been suspended from duty for a few days, with pay. He is not supposed to leave Maple Creek without permission, and while he is here, he has to wear civilian clothes, not uniform. If he needs to go anywhere in town, he either walks or takes a cab, not the cruiser. Is that clear?"

They both nodded.

"I've been asked to cover the Maple Creek area for the next couple of days but obviously I still have my own area to look after as well. Before I go, I'll forward the phone in the office so that it rings directly to my detachment. If anyone drops by and knocks at the door, can you just get their information and pass it on, please? Other than that, I'll lock everything up and then head out."

Rashford cleared his throat.

"Umm, you're going to lock up the office?" he said.

"Yes, those were my instructions. Is that a problem?"

"No, not at all. Can I go in and pick up a couple of personal items from the desk?"

"Yes. As long as they are not evidential."

"Right."

Rashford and Roxanne stood up at the same time.

"Can I get you more tea?" she said, standing next to Morgan as Rashford left the room.

"No, I'm fine, thank you," said Morgan, pushing her chair back from the table.

Roxanne stood her ground.

"How long have you been a police officer?" she said. "And where are you from, you don't sound like the people round here."

Morgan paused, her hand on the back of the chair.

"Listen luv, the doe-eyed look might work on Gavin, it won't work on me. So, stop trying to keep me chatting and let me go and make sure he only gets what he's supposed to get. OK?"

She strode past Roxanne and followed Rashford towards the detachment. When she got there, he was already inside the office, the desk drawer open. He looked up at her.

"It's not here," he admitted. "I thought I'd left the receipt here, from the shop in Calgary, but it was in the tube with the other stuff, that I had to leave in Speedy Creek."

"Why would you want that?" she said.

"Oh, I thought I'd get Roxanne to phone her cousin, to go and ask around the girls at the store, see if they remembered the silk scarf sale."

"Not a good idea, Gav," she said, gently touching his shoulder. "I know you're all upset about this, and want this guy pretty bad, but right now, don't stir the pot. The Chief hasn't given you a bollocking, so don't go looking for one. Just spend some time with Hiawatha in there and enjoy a few days of holiday. When this goes down, it will go down hard and fast, believe me."

"Hiawatha was a guy, a warrior chief," said Rashford.

"Whatever," said Morgan. "C'mon, get what you want and then we're out of here. I have to drive up to Leader yet and see what's been happening on my patch. So, let's get a move on, right?"

"Right," said Rashford. He didn't think she had seen him pocket the cigarettes, lighter, and ashtray, so he hoped that small transgression was still safe. He closed the desk drawer, watching as Morgan put the truck keys in the centre of the desk.

"They'll be there when we need them," she said.

Rashford reached out and picked his heavy coat off the hook by the door to the cells, checked that the gun safe was locked and bolted, and then followed Morgan across to the door.

When Morgan had left, silence descended on the police house. Rashford went over to his chair, in front of the television, and sat down. Roxanne stood at the table, watching him. Eventually, she spoke.

"What?"

He looked at her.

"What? 'Hello, honey.' Tea and biscuits? That's what!"

She walked over, flicked him with the tea towel, and sat on the arm of his chair.

"Well, I saw both your cars pull in and when a woman got out, I figured that she was the famous Gayle Morgan. And I'm sure she'd like to get her claws into you, if she hasn't already, so I thought I'd get my revenge in first."

"Why do you think she would want to get her claws into me?" he said.

"Because there can't be that many eligible bachelors around here, not ones who would date a policewoman anyway, and from what you've said about her you quite like her."

Rashford couldn't actually remember saying anything about Morgan, at least not to Roxanne, but he decided that wasn't something he really wanted to know anyway. After all, she was correct, he did like Morgan, and found her interesting in her own way. And Medicine Hat had been fun, although only a short romance. But he did not want to have that discussion either, not yet at least.

"How was your tea with Bettina?" he said, hoping to change the subject.

"It was good. She is fun to talk to, and she brought her dog with her."

"Really? That vicious thing?"

"She's not vicious, she's a lovely dog. She likes having her tummy rubbed."

"Like someone else I know," he said, putting his arm around Roxanne's waist and pulling her down onto his lap. She laughed as he kissed her, putting her arms around his neck as she kissed him back. Breaking their embrace, he looked up into her eyes.

"So," he said. "It's looks like I've got a few days of unexpected holiday time. Would you have any ideas as to what we should do to fill the hours?"

She got to her feet and reached out her hand. He held hers, and she pulled him up. Leading him by the hand, she walked across the room towards the bedroom door.

"I'm sure we can think of something," she said.

The next day was Saturday, and they soon established a routine that extended into the beginning of the following week. Rashford would get up early and go for his run, then Roxanne made coffee while he showered, and they ate their breakfast together.

After clearing up, each morning before it got too hot, they took a different road from the police house and walked to the edge of town, circled to their right until they reached the next major road, then walked back into the town centre and back to the detachment. Depending on which roads they were on, some mornings they choked on fumes from big diesel trucks and on others were blasted the incessant dust funneled down the streets by the prairie winds.

When they got back to detachment it would be time for lunch, so they would make sandwiches and sit outside in the small garden. A tall poplar tree provided shade from the afternoon sun, and the ever-present prairie breeze rustled the leaves as well as Roxanne's hair. Rashford would make a second pot of coffee, and they would lounge around, Roxanne scrolling through the social media accounts on her phone and Rashford reading his Cree books until it was time to start making dinner.

After eating and then cleaning up they played crib, keeping score and each delighting in victory over the other with taunts and jeers, until it was time for Jeopardy, where their rivalry continued. They sometimes stayed up to watch the news at ten o'clock, but more often called it a night and went to bed shortly after nine.

On Monday afternoon they walked the ten minutes down First Street to the Maple Creek Bus Depot, where they waited for twenty minutes until the bus from Calgary arrived. Once the passengers had taken their bags and departed, Roxanne showed her driver's licence to the clerk and received a large suitcase in return. Rashford wheeled it down the street back to the detachment.

"What on earth is in here?" he said.

"Cousin Jenny said she'd send me all my clothes," said Roxanne, laughing, "plus some emergency supplies."

"What kind of emergency supplies?"

"I have no idea."

When they got to the police house, Roxanne shooed Rashford away from the bedroom.

"Let me unpack in peace," she said. "There might be secret things in here."

Rashford went back into the kitchen and saw it was nearly six o'clock, so he opened a beer and turned on the television to watch the news.

On Tuesday evening he went to his Cree class and this time Roxanne came with him. Bettina met them at the door, quieted the dog, and then led them inside.

Kôhkum Christine was already sitting in her chair. She lifted her head with a sideways jerk and made a 'tcch' sound through her teeth as she pointed with her lips, silently instructing Rashford to sit in his normal place, opposite her, which he did. She then nodded to Bettina, who disappeared. Roxanne stood silently.

Bettina returned with a small chair she had pulled from the kitchen. She placed it on one side of the room, then returned to her usual place, leaning against the door frame.

Kôhkum Christine looked at Roxanne.

"Sit there, you," she said.

Roxanne walked over and sat on the chair, her hands folded in front of her.

"Tell me about your Glooscap," instructed Kôhkum Christine. "Tell me how he made your world."

Roxanne nodded. She sat quietly for a moment, then began to speak.

She recounted the story of how Glooscap created the world for the Mi'kmaq, painting the world into existence. How then, dipping his brush into a mix of all the colours that were left, he created Prince

Edward Island, which he called *Abegweit,* which means "Cradled on the Waves." She spoke of how when he slept his bed was Nova Scotia and he used Prince Edward Island as a pillow. She told of him fighting the Frog Monster and rescuing all the animals who had been swallowed. She told of how Glooscap had taught the Mi'kmaq about good and evil, fire, tobacco, fishing nets, and canoes. As she spoke, Kôhkum Christine smiled and nodded.

When she had finished her stories, there was silence. After a few moments, Bettina spoke.

"Come with me," she said. "We shall leave them to their class."

Roxanne walked with Bettina into the back of the house. Kôhkum Christine turned to Rashford.

"Now you know her story," she said. "This is important for you to remember."

Rashford nodded.

"But now, you will learn our stories," said the old woman, and began speaking in Cree. She spoke of how the Creator had made all things, and then told Wîsahkecâhk to teach them how to live. But Wîsahkecâhk, the Trickster, did not obey, and the people quarreled and disagreed, hurting each other and arguing all the time.

The Creator was angry at this and sent a great flood. Only four things survived the flood – Otter, Beaver, Muskrat, and Wîsahkecâhk. They obviously needed somewhere to live, so Wîsahkecâhk asked them each to dive down and bring up some mud from the bottom of the flood.

Each one of them tried to do this, but only Muskrat was successful. He stayed under the water for a very long time and when he came back to surface, he had earth in his paws. He gave the mud to Wîsahkecâhk and he, using the powers given to him by the Creator, blew on the mud until it expanded and became an Island on which they could live.

"So that is how the world was really created," concluded Kôhkum Christine. "Now you can teach that truth to the People of the Dawn."

She laughed, happily, then pulled herself out of the chair and walked down the hallway, calling out to her granddaughter as she went.

"*Êhe, nôhkom*," said Bettina, appearing at one of the doorways. She came into the main room, Roxanne a pace behind her, and then showed them both to the door. Rashford noted how the two women exchanged a slight hug, not really touching, and parted without words.

That night, when they got back to the police house, there was a message waiting on the telephone answering machine.

Chapter 7

Rashford listened to the message, then pressed nine to save it and hung up the phone. He went into the kitchen and reached under the sink, pulling out a dark green bottle.

"Join me?" he said.

Roxanne looked from him to the bottle.

"What is it?" she said.

"Scotch. A single malt, to be precise. Ardbeg. Ten years old, from the Isle of Islay."

"Eyre-la? Where's that?"

"Islay, spelt I S L A Y. It's in Scotland. Your island isn't the only with funny pronunciations, Ms. Gaudet," he said, ducking out of the way as she threw a seat cushion at his head.

"Careful, this stuff is expensive! Look, you can smell the seaweed, and the smoke from the peat fires they use when they're mixing the batch."

He carefully unplugged the stopper and held out the bottle. Roxanne leaned forward and inhaled, then stepped back coughing.

"Seaweed? More like old socks!" she said.

"Peasant," Rashford sent, going over to the kitchen sink. "Do you want some or not?"

"Just a very small one," she said. "What are we celebrating?"

He poured a small amount of the scotch into a glass, then passed it to her. He poured himself a healthier slug.

"Now just take a very small sip," he said.

She did so, then pulled a face.

"It burns," she said.

"Yes, now try this."

He took her glass and went to the sink, turning on the tap and letting two drops of cold water drip into the scotch. He returned the glass to her.

"See, you can see the essential oils on the surface. Look."

She looked down and saw a smear of colour across the top of the drink.

"It looks like there's been an industrial accident," she said.

"Taste it again."

She did.

"Can you taste the difference?"

"Yes. It's a bit sweeter now."

"That's right. And that's the trick with any good single malt. Just a small drop of water."

"No ice?"

"God no. No ice, and no ginger ale or coke or any of that polluting garbage."

He sipped his drink, nodding appreciatively.

"What happens if someone was over and asked for scotch with ice and coke?" she said.

Rashford turned back to the kitchen sink and pulled out a smaller, clear glass bottle, with the drawing of some kind of bird on the label.

"Then they get this," he said. "It's a blend. They never even know the Ardbeg exists."

Roxanne shook her head, smiling.

"OK, then, so what are we celebrating?" she said, holding her glass out in front of her in the classic position of making a toast.

Rashford raised his glass and clinked it against hers.

"That phone call," he said. "It was from Regina."

"What did they say?"

"Two things. First, a date has been set for my FILTER exam, I've got to go in three weeks. I'm going to have spend a lot more time with Kôhkum Christine over the next little while.

"Second, the Chief Superintendent wants me to call her in the morning. They've made a decision about me joining the Alberta team when they go looking for Fancy Boots."

"Are they letting you go?"

"I think so. They didn't say anything, but if it was a no then they'd have just told me that on the phone. I think the fact she wants me to call her means that I'm going. So, that's what we're celebrating."

"Oh," she said, and her face fell.

"What? Have I missed something?" said Rashford.

"I thought you were being all romantic and celebrating that tomorrow will be one week since we met out on the highway," she said.

Roxanne looked at him, her lower lip quivering, her eyes misting slowly. Rashford felt his stomach start to ache. Then, after what seemed like a very long moment, she burst into laughter.

"It's OK, silly," she said. "I'm just teasing you. But now you have no excuse for not being romantic tomorrow."

Rashford wisely said nothing. He just raised his glass and drank.

The next morning, he ushered Roxanne out to go and have coffee with Bettina, then sat at the table with a notepad and his phone. At nine-thirty, he dialed the direct line number for the Chief Superintendent. Her administrative assistant answered.

"It's Rashford," he said. "I'm expected."

"Yes, Sergeant. I'll put you through."

"Pollard," she said, answering on the first ring.

"Good morning, Ma'am. This is Sergeant Rashford."

"Yes. Did you get the notification for your FILTER examination?"

"Yes, Ma'am. It's in three weeks."

"Don't screw it up."

"No, Ma'am."

"I mean it. You pass, or you're out of the Force. Understand?"

"Yes, Ma'am."

"*Tansi isi kīsikāk?*"

Rashford looked out of the window.

"*Wāsēkwan anohc*," he said.

"Good. Well done."

Pollard paused and Rashford could imagine her sorting through the file on her desk, fanning out the pages as though she needed to make one last confirmation before speaking. He kept silent.

"I have spoken to our colleagues in Alberta," said the Chief Superintendent. "They have clarified a few things for me and opened questions about a few other things. Let me tell you what I have learned.

"First, Dr. Peter Smythe and his wife, from Calgary. Remember them?"

"Weren't they ones who went missing, from the house where Dallas was supposedly living?"

"Yes. It turns out that was true. Dr. Smythe is a professor at the University, and his wife used to be one of his students, apparently much younger. Anyway, he came back from vacation and found the Calgary police had left a card on his door, so he phoned them.

"He told them that his wife had met a veteran who lived on the street and used to collect their empty bottles, to get the recycling money. She befriended this guy. When they decided to go away on holiday for a couple of weeks, she suggested that this fellow look after their house."

"What name was he using?" said Rashford.

"Smythe said the veteran was called Johnson, Albert Johnson."

"Well, that fits," said Rashford.

"Indeed. It seems the Smythes were having marital problems and went away for a few weeks' holiday, some kind of boat trip around Haida Gwaii. While they were there, Mrs. Smythe 'became infatuated' with one of the guides, according to Professor Smythe. It sounds like she traded him in for a younger, sleeker model, and decided to stay and enjoy island life.

"He made his way home, which reading between the lines was a journey with a few alcohol-friendly interludes in Victoria and Vancouver, then he got back to find the police note. He also found his freezer was full of squirrels."

"Squirrels?"

"Yes. And a magpie. It seems that Mr. Johnson was running a trapline in suburban Calgary. He hadn't eaten any of the food in the fridge."

"Right. So, he was not all there, then?"

"I'm not sure. According to the professor, Johnson had served at least two tours in Afghanistan, maybe three. He had come back affected by what he'd seen there, and things had gone downhill for him. He'd either left his wife and kids, or they'd left him, and he'd lost the job he had managed to find.

"Smythe said that his wife spent a lot of time talking to Johnson and got him to see a doctor. He was prescribed some medications and they seemed to work, to calm him down. That's why they thought he'd be OK looking after the house while they were away.

"Of course, nobody had expected an American invasion or the breakaway of Alsama. Smythe had trouble getting through the border up by Lake Louise, he had only been on holiday, so he didn't have a lot of identification papers with him, but he got through eventually.

"He told the police that in addition to losing his wife, and gaining a load of frozen squirrels, he had also lost his electric bike. So that part fits with the story you heard, as well."

"Yes, it does. Did this Smythe guy speak to his wife's parents, in the Soo?"

"I asked that, and it seems that he hadn't, he thought they would just ridicule him, and anyway they were her parents so she could tell them."

"Has anyone checked that she is actually still alive, out on Haida Gwaii?"

"Yes, that was followed up as well. She is living in Charlotte, in a little house by the water, with a fellow who works the tour boats when he can and is a fisher at other times. He is only a couple of years older than her, and she is already pregnant. Someone from the local force in Sault Ste Marie contacted her parents just to tell them she was alive. They can figure out the rest themselves."

"And Professor Smythe?"

"I have no idea and don't really care. He is irrelevant now. So, that's item one."

Pollard paused, and Rashford could hear her moving some of the papers on her desk. He sat patiently until she spoke again.

"Item two. The Calgary police had a brainwave and went to the Military Family Resource Centre there, to see if they had a veteran known by the name Albert Johnson. They hadn't heard of anyone. The police also asked if they knew of any veterans who might have disappeared over the past couple of years, people who had been around but who nobody had seen recently. There were a few of those.

"Unfortunately, that might not mean a lot. As the Co-ordinator at the Centre said, by definition, homeless people are a fairly transient population. A lot of them migrate out to Vancouver or back east to Toronto, they don't always stay around in one place.

"In addition, the person we are looking for might not even have registered at the Centre. Not everyone does, it isn't compulsory or anything. The Co-ordinator also checked with the Homes for Heroes Village, to see if anyone had graduated from there, but they didn't think so."

"Home for Heroes Village? What's that?" said Rashford.

"It's a small group of mini-houses, all arranged in a block around a regular house," said Pollard. "It's almost like a compound. Veterans who want to get off the street can apply to live there. They just have to show that they are not addicts, that they've given up booze or pills or whatever it was they were using.

"Each house is named after a fallen hero from the Canadian military. You get to live in it for two years and then you graduate to the real world. It's a sort of transition place. They have a full-time counsellor who lives in the regular house, and on the main floor is an activity room and social centre. The idea is to make it a safe and secure place for people who want to leave the street."

"Sounds like a great idea," said Rashford.

"It is," said Pollard, "but unfortunately they don't know of any missing veterans. So, we're no further ahead there. Moving on, item three. The registration papers you found in the truck. As you surmised, there is nobody of that name recorded as living in Alberta, not by any of the government agencies. So, we can assume it's another alias. Same for the firearm certificate. But the address does exist.

"It is a house near Mountain View, a small community on the edge of Waterton National Park, south of Pincher Creek. It's a pretty isolated place, an acreage with a big fence all around it. The local police have driven past a couple of times, and even put a drone up in the area, but they haven't seen any activity. If someone is there, they are staying inside.

"The detachment at Pincher Creek has applied for a search warrant and it has just been granted. They are going to go in tomorrow. If you are still interested, I have asked if you can join the team, and they have agreed."

"Yes, Ma'am, I am very much still interested. Thank you very much, Ma'am," said Rashford.

Pollard sighed.

"Stop gabbling," she said.

"Yes, Ma'am."

"Here is the cell number of the Inspector who is in charge of the operation," said Pollard, reading out the numbers. Rashford quickly wrote them down in his notebook.

"Does the Inspector have a name?" he said.

"Yes. Whitehead. Inspector Ian Whitehead."

Rashford wrote the name into his book as well.

"Get yourself organized and drive over today," said the Chief Superintendent. "We've booked you into the Country View Inn, in Cardston. It's not the Hilton but it's within budget. When you get there, give Inspector Whitehead a call and he'll fill you in on the details."

"Yes, Ma'am. Thank you, Ma'am."

"I've told you before, Sergeant. No gabbling."

Pollard hung up the phone. At his end, Rashford put the phone down slowly, then leapt to his feet with a shout, punching the air.

"Yes!" he said.

It took Rashford nearly an hour to get ready.

He called Gayle Morgan, to let her know the news. She was out on patrol but said that she would note the call in her log, so nobody would accuse him of 'slipping the leash', as she put it.

He walked over to the bakery and picked up two fresh cinnamon buns, both smothered in white icing, and left them on the kitchen table. Next to them he put a piece of paper, on which he had written "Happy One Week Anniversary" and drawn a picture of a grasshopper sitting underneath a rainbow. He collected his side arm from the gun safe and took it apart, oiling each component as he rebuilt the weapon.

He made sure that it was loaded, and the safety catch was on, and then put an extra two boxes of bullets into his bag. There they sat on top of two ironed and folded uniform shirts, spare underwear, and his washbag. He took the bag out to his cruiser and locked it into the trunk.

At eleven o'clock Roxanne returned from her visit with Bettina. Her face lit up when she came into the room and saw the cinnamon buns on the table. She laughed with delight and plumped herself down on his lap, her arms around his neck.

"Aw, you remembered! How sweet," she said, nuzzling his neck. He squeezed her waist and then spoke softly.

"I have some news," he said.

Roxanne leaned back and looked at him.

"And what would that be?"

"I spoke with the Chief Superintendent. They have decided to act on my report. There is a team going to go into the address that was on the registration papers of the truck. They have agreed that I can be part of the team."

"That's wonderful," said Roxanne. She looked at him again.

"That's what you wanted, isn't it? You look sad."

"Well, the thing is, I shall have to go to Alberta. I don't know for how long, but I might be gone for a couple of days. Perhaps more. I know I won't be back until the weekend at the earliest. I will drive over this afternoon, we have the operation planned for tomorrow, and even if it all goes one hundred per cent then I won't be able to come back until Friday. I don't like leaving you alone."

Roxanne stood up and slapped his arm.

"Don't be silly. I'm a big girl. I'll be just fine here. If I get bored, I will go and visit with Bettina or Kôhkum Christine. You never know, Gayle Morgan might drop in for some girl-talk as well. You just get on and do your job."

She walked away a few steps, then stopped, and turned around.

"I want you to catch this guy," she said. "That's the most important thing right now."

Rashford stood up and held her again.

"I know, and I will," he said, kissing the top of her head.

"Right, then," she said, pushing him away with a laugh. "Off you go. If you stay here, we shall only get distracted."

"Well, I said I'd leave after lunch," said Rashford. "So, we've got an hour or so ..."

Rashford pulled away from the detachment just after one in the afternoon. He drove along the TransCanada Highway, keeping a steady five kilometres above the limit. He noticed how most of the oncoming traffic slowed down as they saw him approach, and just past Irvine he was surprised when one car passed him at speed.

Rashford turned on his lights and siren, and saw the driver jerk their head up and look into the mirror. The bright yellow Volkswagen Beetle slowed down immediately, indicated, and pulled off to the side of the road. Rashford came up and parked a few metres behind.

He entered the number plate into his computer and saw that the car was registered in Thompson, Manitoba, and the owner was a Cicily Steele. He got out of his car and approached the driver's side window. As he came closer the window was powered down. A young woman with bright blue streaks in her hair looked up at him.

"Sorry, officer, I must have been day-dreaming," she said.

"Could I see your licence, please," he said, and took the document she passed through the window. Sure enough, the licence was in the name Cicily Steele. He handed it back to her.

"The limit on the TCH is a hundred and ten kilometres an hour," he said. "You were driving at a much faster speed. That can be very dangerous."

"Yes, officer. Sorry, officer," she said. "I was just driving and thinking of other things."

"Please pay better attention to the road in future, and slow down," said Rashford. "I am going to let you off with a warning this time."

The woman tried her best not to smile.

"Thank you, officer," she said. "I will certainly pay attention now."

"If you are travelling a long way, it is a good idea to take a break every few hours," he said. "I think you'll find that will help you to maintain concentration."

"Yes, I know. Yesterday I drove ten hours and got as far as Saskatoon. Today I've done five and a half already, so I must be nearly there."

"Where's there, if I may ask?"

"Sure. It's Maple Creek. That's where I'm going."

"Maple Creek? I'm sorry, ma'am, but I have to tell you that you've already been there."

"Excuse me?"

"Maple Creek is about forty-five minutes back that way," said Rashford, pointing past his own cruiser and trying not to laugh.

The woman stared at him.

"You're kidding me, right?"

"Sorry, no, I'm not. You're going to have to turn around and go back. Luckily this bit of road has not been twinned into a four-lane highway yet, so you can do a U-turn when it is safe to do so."

"I don't believe this," she said, banging on her steering wheel in frustration. "My friend Betty is never going to let me forget this."

"Maybe you just don't tell her," said Rashford. "Say you slept in at the hotel or something."

"Nah, I already texted her to say I was on my way. Gosh, she'll think I've been in an accident."

"Well, you might be if you don't slow down," said Rashford. "Look, I'll see you safely across the road, but don't speed on your way back. Some of my colleagues are out this morning as well, one of them will probably catch you on their radar."

"No, I'll stay to the limit, I promise," she said. "Thank you again."

"You're welcome," said Rashford, returning to his cruiser. He took a large hand-held flash bar out from the trunk and switched it on. It immediately emitted a very bright strobe light that he thought, with his own flashing blue and red lights, ought to slow traffic down.

He turned off the light, then walked back to Ms. Steel's bright yellow Volkswagen Beetle and leaned in her window.

"OK, when I wave at you, pull out and turn across the highway, then head back that way. It's not far, forty-five minutes at the most. You have to turn off to Maple Creek at the highway 21 junction. You'll see an Esso gas station on the corner."

"Oh, I thought the town was right on the highway."

"No, it's about ten kilometres south from the highway to the town, maybe a little less."

"That's really helpful. *Chi meegwetch*."

Rashford switched on the lightbar and walked into the road. Cars immediately began slowing down. When there was a gap in the traffic, he nodded at her and waved to indicate she could leave. Then he walked back to his car, smiling to himself. That had been so much easier than it could have been. If he had written her a ticket, he would have had to complete countless forms to explain why he was stopping motorists outside his jurisdiction. He would have prevailed in the end, but it would have been a lot of work. Plus, it had stopped her from driving to Medicine Hat, or wherever she would have next paid attention.

Back in his cruiser, he checked his mirror. The yellow Volkswagen was already out of sight down the busy highway. He turned off his light bar, signalled, and pulled back into the flow of traffic.

At Medicine Hat he turned onto Highway 3, the Crowsnest Trail, driving past the airport and then onto the long straight highway which cut across the prairie. At Taber the huge fields of ripening corn made him realize that he was hungry, and he turned off, stopping at a coffee shop he had heard about. The heat of the summer afternoon hit him as soon as he got out of the air-conditioned car. He ordered a sandwich, which was ready when he returned from the restroom, and then bought a coffee to go.

He left the Crowsnest Highway at Lethbridge and drove south of the city, then out along the edge of the Blackfoot lands at Stand Off. In the late afternoon he saw the Mormon Temple at Cardston rise into view in front of him. Following his GPS to the hotel, he realized that the Country View Inn was only going to be a few minutes walk from the Temple. He pulled into the forecourt and checked in to his room, then phoned the number he had been given.

The Inspector arrived about twenty minutes later. He was short and moderately rotund man, dressed in civilian clothes, and with a sun weathered face. He met Rashford in the lobby.

"Sergeant Rashford, I presume? Hi, I'm Ian," he said, shaking hands. "Hope your room is OK? This place has seen better days but it's still one of the best hotels in town, I'm sad to say."

"It's fine," said Rashford. "I'm not sure where to get coffee, though."

"Sorry, but there's no restaurant here. You can use the perc in your room. For now, let's go to Sauce, it's just up the street."

They walked up to the small restaurant, which seemed to serve mainly Italian food. Rashford adjusted his pace to match that of the Inspector, whom he noticed had a slight limp.

"Tonight, for dinner, I'd recommend you come here and have the calzone," said Whitehead. "People say it's the best they've ever eaten."

"People?" said Rashford. "What about you? What do you say about it?"

"Touché," said Whitehead, patting his stomach. "Nah, I'm on a diet, I'm afraid. Doctor's orders. I usually have the Tree Hugger Salad."

"How's that working for you?"

Whitehead laughed.

"Police life, right? If you're not sitting around having a coffee and a bite, then you're just sitting waiting for something to happen."

It had taken them just over five minutes to walk to the restaurant, a small operation which stood out because of its façade of river rocks attached to the front wall.

"That was cutting edge art, back in the day," mused Whitehead.

Once inside he greeted the server with an easy familiarity, and they were shown to the table in front of the plate glass window.

"I hope espresso is alright for you," said the Inspector. "Because that's what we're getting."

Rashford looked around, noting all the specials written on the blackboards that surrounded the serving hatch.

"I don't see a drinks menu," he said.

"No, there isn't one. They serve pop and filter coffee, basically. This is a food place. Most people get take-out and eat at home, or in their hotel room."

"So, how come the espresso?" said Rashford.

"Oh, I helped them out once, some trouble with some local yahoos. It got sorted. The owner has a personal espresso machine in the back, and some of it flows to me."

Just then a young woman came out, carrying a tray on which were two small espresso cups, each full of a steaming black liquid, a glass shot glass full of brown sugar twists, two teaspoons, and two cut glasses of what turned out to be ice cold water.

"Thank you, Maria," said Whitehead, and the young woman bobbed her head in response. She gave a shy smile to Rashford.

"Will you be eating?" she said.

"Perhaps later," he said. She nodded and walked away.

Whitehead tore the top off two of the paper twists and emptied the sugar into his cup. He stirred the coffee around to dissolve the sugar, then took a small sip, his eyes closing in pleasure.

"Nectar," he said. "Pure nectar. I could live in this place."

Rashford sipped his own coffee, which was hot and strong, a slight edge of bitterness giving the espresso a bite. He waited for the Inspector to come to the point. After another sip of his drink, Whitehead started to speak.

"First, welcome to the team. Your Chief Super seems to think a lot of you, so hopefully we will benefit from your expertise."

He paused, waiting for Rashford to respond, but Rashford was reeling at the idea that Pollard had paid him a compliment. He sat silently.

"Well, anyway," Whitehead continued, "we have identified the location named on the registration and firearm papers. It is a fancy place out on the prairie, just south of the community of Mountain View. It's a newly built house, all timber frame and big glass windows. I'm guessing it was architect-designed and custom built."

"So, this fellow has some money, then?"

"It would seem so. Quite a lot, if he actually owns this place. Of course, he might just be renting it."

"What, like an Air BnB or something?"

"I guess. Stranger things happen. Anyway, there is the main house and then a couple of other buildings. One looks like it was originally a workshop, but now we think is recreational. From the drone footage we could see through the windows, it looks like there is a pool table and a table tennis table set up. There's also what might be a guest house of some sort, or perhaps an artist's studio. That one looks pretty fancy to just be an outbuilding."

"Any vehicles?"

"Not that we can see, but there are three attached double garages so those could be stuffed full of cars and trucks."

"Three?"

"Yup. We don't build small in Alberta, you know."

"What about landscaping?'

"There doesn't seem to be any. There's just bare grass, acres of it, leading out to the fence. The fencing is basic wire mesh, except along the roadside, where it seems to be some sort of darker mesh or fabric."

Rashford thought for a moment.

"Is the house on a hill?" he said.

"Well, not a hill exactly, but it is up on a small ridge, yes. So, from the road you are looking up towards the buildings. From the house itself, I expect you're looking out over the landscape towards the Park."

"Waterton?"

"Yes. He'll be able to see the mountains from there, easy."

"He's got a good defensive position as well, doesn't he?" said Rashford.

"What do you mean? He's in the middle of nowhere, totally exposed."

"True. But he has clear lines of sight in all directions, and he would be looking down on anyone who was approaching. You're not going to be able to surprise him, are you?"

"We were thinking of going in very early, before dawn."

"If he is there, and I'm not convinced that he is, but if he is there then he will have warning bells set up. There will be trip wires or laser beams or something. He'll know we're coming."

"He's one guy," said Whitehead. "We'll have him surrounded. He might hold out for a day or two, but we'll get him in the end. No problem."

"If you say so," said Rashford, but he was not convinced.

Chapter 8

At five thirty the next morning, Rashford met up with Inspector Whitehead and the other four members of the team. Their rendezvous was outside the Mountain View Motel, in the small hamlet of the same name, about half-way between Cardston and Waterton National Park. There were four cars between them, as two cars had driven down from Pincher Creek, each carrying a pair of officers. The eastern sky had begun to lighten, that period called nautical twilight, but it was still dark on the forecourt. Inspector Whitehead used a red screened flashlight to illuminate the map spread out on the hood of his car.

"We're here," he said, pointing at the map, "and the house is about five minutes away, straight down highway 5 towards the park. We'll go down in two cars, driving really slowly and without lights. The dawn will let us see the road. Look out for elk and bear, even if you're in the second car, they can just come up out of the ditch, without warning.

"As we get to the house, you'll see the fence has this sort of dark mesh on it, to hide the view of the house from the cars, I guess. We go past there to this little dirt road, on the right, you'll see it's got one of those cute cowboy ranch gates with the big frame. We go up there for about twenty metres then turn right again, another dirt road that runs straight to the main gate of the house.

"Any questions?"

"Are we going right up to the house gate," said Rashford. "Won't he see us?"

"It's not even sunrise until six forty-five," said Whitehead. "He'll still be asleep."

"If the fence goes all the way around, then he can't get out anyway, even if he sees us," said one of the Pincher Creek constables, a large, fresh faced young man who was wearing a traditional Stetson. The others from that detachment nodded sagely.

"This guy's not stupid," said Rashford. "We can't just go waltzing in there and expect him to give up without a fight."

"Maybe not in Saskatchewan," said Whitehead, smiling at his colleagues. "But here in Alberta, that's what we do. We go in, all six of us, and of course he'll give up, what's he gunna do? Fight all of us?"

The other constables laughed. Rashford started to say something, then closed his mouth. He simply nodded, then asked which car he would be in.

"You come with me," said Whitehead. "Then you can see how it's done. Sergeant Hamill, you drive the other car. MacNeill and Matheson, you go with him. Larsen, you come with me."

Everyone checked their sidearms, then moved to the appropriate vehicle. As they pulled out of the small parking lot in front of the Motel, Whitehead smiled across at Rashford.

"Just teasing you there, Sergeant," he said. "We've got carbines in the trunk of both vehicles, and flak jackets, plus a few whizz-bang grenades. Larsen here is the star pitcher with the Pincher Creek softball team, he can put one of those beauties on a pin up to seventy feet away. Don't worry, we'll get this guy."

They eased slowly down the road with the second car some twenty metres behind. To the left, directly south of the road, the bulk of Chief Mountain emerged from the gloom, its eastern flank starting to be picked out by the first haze of morning twilight. Ahead, a mauve tinge stained the crest of the mountains behind Maskinonge Lake, then slowly started to creep down the flanks. The still water of the swampy pond reflected the mountains and the stars with uncanny accuracy.

The cars rolled slowly past the long grey mesh of the fence, and it was only as they turned under the gate that Rashford saw the house. It had a steep peaked roof, like a Swiss chalet, and a large wrap-around deck. A second privacy screen was now visible, extending along the roadside of the building. As they came parallel, they saw that this second mesh screen cut back towards the lane along which their cars were now creeping. It was only as they turned onto the final approach that they had a clear view of the house.

"And he of us," said Rashford to himself.

"What's that, Sergeant?" said Whitehead. "Your Chief Super said you sometimes mumbled. Out with it, lad, if you have something to say."

"I don't think he'll be there, sir," said Rashford. "I think he'll have gone."

"Well, we shall see about that, shan't we. Would you like to put a pint on that belief of yours?"

"Sir?"

"A wager, man. A small bet. If he's not there, I buy you a pint at the pub tonight. When he is there, you buy one for me."

"Ummm ..."

"Actually, let's make it a round. Alright, Sergeant? Tonight, after we've caught this fellow, you buy a round for the whole team. How does that sound, Larsen?"

"It sounds very good, sir," said Larsen. "The lads will appreciate the generosity."

"Indeed, they will," said Whitehead. "Well, Sergeant, are you game?"

"Yes, sir," said Rashford, wondering how much six pints would cost in a southern Alberta tavern. Just then, the Inspector pulled up to the main gate leading into the compound.

When they had quietly exited the police cruisers, Rashford looked around. The drive continued past the gate, running in a straight gravelled line up to the house. This was perched on the crest of the small rise, the lawns stretching down and away to the front and the sides. Rashford assumed that there was a similar slope at the rear of the building.

He saw now that the lawns were not the shorn grass of golf clubs or suburbia but, rather, a mass of wildflowers and grasses. The early light was now starting to reach down to the house, and small masses of spider webs glistened with dew.

The entrance in front of them had a pair of traditional three bar split rail gates, with side posts that hinged to two large pillars, each about six feet high. The top horizontal rail was about three feet off the ground, and a diagonal pole ran from the base of the central vertical strut to the top of each pillar. At the central strut was a large padlock.

"Manchester gate," said one of the constables, the one Rashford thought was called MacNeill. His tone was dismissive.

"He means it's a designer gate, best used for acreages and fancy houses like this," said Whitehead. "Not a proper ranch gate, right, constable?"

MacNeill sniffed in agreement, not bothering to waste words on the obvious.

"Not sure why he's put a padlock there," said Sergeant Hamill. "Even Matheson here could climb over that gate."

The largest and youngest constable tipped the front of his Stetson.

"Yes, sir," he said, and moved towards the gate.

"Wait," said Rashford.

The group stopped and looked at him.

"What now?" said Whitehead. "Do you want to go first?"

"No, sir," said Rashford. ""But I agree with Sergeant Hamill. Why is there a padlock there? That's not normal for a ranch gate, is it? Especially one which anyone could climb over."

"It's just city folk stupidity," said Constable MacNeill. "They think that if they make a place look secure, then it is secure."

"This guy is not 'just city folk', constable," said Rashford. "He's lived off the land. He's travelled across Alsama by canoe. I think he's probably an Afghan war veteran. He paid five thousand dollars to some bikers for a woman. He doesn't do things for no reason."

Inspector Whitehead looked at him, this time with a thoughtful expression.

"Fair enough, Sergeant," he said. "What do you suggest?"

Rashford turned to him.

"Let's not just rush in, sir," he said. "Let's look at this situation carefully before we send someone climbing over the gate."

He stepped forward and stood in front of the padlock, then dropped down into a squatting position. He took a ballpoint pen out of his pocket.

"Look," he said, pointing the pen. "There is a trip wire here."

The others crowded in. Whitehead nodded.

"It looks like a thin filament fishing line," he said. "Hard to see in this light. Well spotted, Sergeant."

"Where does it go?" said Constable Larsen, reaching out to pull the wire.

"Don't touch it!" said Rashford.

Larsen pulled his hand back quickly.

"Sorry, but it might trigger something. Let's just use our eyes for now."

The wire ran from the padlock down the inside of the central support post, then seemed to disappear into the dirt.

"It looks like there might be something under the ground," said Whitehead. "When you move the padlock, it might pull the trigger."

"What, like an IED?" said Sergeant Hamill. "In Mountain View? I can't see it. Where would he get the explosives?"

"What's an IED?" said Matheson.

"Improvised Explosive Device," said Whitehead. "Something you rig up to go bang and hurt people. You say he was in Afghanistan? I remember, they were used a lot there."

"Lots of explosives on ranches around here," said Larsen. "They use them to blast out big rocks, or to clear deadfall when you can't get close with a chain saw."

"Or, it could be a bluff," said Rashford. "Why would he rig an explosive device where anyone could trigger it? What if someone came selling encyclopedias or something?"

"Or the JWs," said Hamill, smirking a little.

"That I would understand," laughed MacNeill, "Watchtowers shredded all over the landscape."

The Inspector stood back, his hands on his hips, and looked around. Eventually he turned to Rashford.

"Alright, Sergeant, you found it. What would you suggest?"

"Do you have any wire clippers in the car, sir?"

"Yes, I believe so. Why?"

"I think I'd like to cut the wire, sir," said Rashford. "If there is an IED, then without the wire it is disabled. And if it is just a bluff, then cutting the wire won't matter."

"What if it's a double bluff?" said Hamill. "There is an IED and cutting the wire breaks the circuit, and that makes it go off?"

"We can over-think this," said Rashford. "All we're doing is wasting time. I think this is a delay tactic, nothing else, and it's working. Please sir, let me just cut the wire."

The Inspector nodded.

"Sure," he said. "I'll get the clippers. Everyone else, get behind the second car."

Whitehead went to the trunk of his car and came back with the wire clippers, plus a Kevlar jacket.

"Put this on as well," he said. "It might give you a bit of protection, if you're wrong."

Rashford nodded and shrugged into the jacket. Then he walked to the gate and knelt down.

"Everyone under cover," he said, looking over his shoulder to check.

"Yes, we're fine. Good luck," said the Inspector, who with the rest of the team was crouched behind the second cruiser.

Rashford took a deep breath, leaned forward, and with one snip cut through the wire.

"Well, that was a bit anti-climatic," said Sergeant Hamill.

The five Albertan police officers stood in a semi-circle around Rashford. He had cut the wire, then leaned back with relief. Reaching forward again, still on his knees, he had carefully brushed away the sand and gravel at the foot of the gate posts, around the wire. The wire popped loose; the end not connected to anything.

"Nothing to laugh at, at all," muttered Rashford to himself, remembering the spoken poem Gayle Morgan loved to recite.

He stood up.

"As I was saying," he said. "He knows we are here. And if he didn't before, he does now."

The rising sun had cleared the top of the rolling hills to the east, and their shadows were long in front of them, reaching up the slope towards the house.

"Perhaps," said Whitehead. "But we're going in anyway, and we're going in prepared. With me, Larsen."

They walked back to the cars and opened the trunks, Whitehead handing out carbines and Kevlar flak jackets to Larsen, who carried them to his colleagues. Whitehead put on his own flak jacket, then stepped forward to check that everyone was fully equipped. Only then did he hand out what looked like grip weights. About six inches long, with a large hexagonal nut at the base and a bulbous head, the metal bodies were round, with three rows of holes visible. A safety handle ran parallel to the body.

"M84 stun grenades," said Whitehead, unnecessarily. The whole team knew what these were and had used them in exercises at the training school in Regina. Nobody had ever thrown one in a real operation, though.

"Hold the safety bar while you pull the pin," said the Inspector. "Remember, the round loop is the primary pin, this triangular one is the back up. As soon as you pull the pin, throw the grenade. Any questions?"

There were none.

"Hamill, you and Larsen take these smoke grenades as well," said Whitehead, giving both of them two similar sized grenades with a solid pale green body, each encircled by a white band about three quarters of the way down.

"Don't throw the smokers unless you absolutely need to," said Whitehead. "We don't have breathing units either, so let's not get ourselves in trouble."

The group looked at each other.

"Right, let's go. Over the gate and up the drive but walk on the grass so you don't make any noise on that damned gravel. Hamill, you take Matheson and go left, round the side and then to the back. Leave someone on the flank side. Larsen, you and MacNeill go to the right flank and make sure that any exit there is covered. Rashford, you and I will go to the front door and knock politely. Saddle up, gentlemen."

Inspector Whitehead climbed over the gate first, then the rest of his team. Two of them slipped and fell heavily onto the gravel, muttering curses. Matheson went over fifth, gingerly balancing his weight on the split rails, but they held, and he made it safely to the other side.

Rashford was the last. On a whim, he put his hand on the shackle of the padlock. It was not secured, so he quietly unclasped it from the hasp, then opened the gate and walked through.

"Close the damn thing behind you," said Whitehead, his face reddening. Rashford did so, hanging the open padlock back on the hasp, then turned and followed the group up the drive.

As they approached the house, carefully walking on the grass to the edge of the gravel, the low rise became more apparent. From the slope behind the compound, three large ducks suddenly rose up and flew directly over their heads.

"Mallard," said Whitehead, authoritatively.

"Shovelers," said Larsen, giving them the swift practised glance of an avid duck hunter. "The beak is too big for mallard. And listen."

A distinctive 'took took, took took' call came from the birds as they went overhead.

"Mallard don't sound like that," said Larsen. "There must be a slough back there."

"Yes," said Whitehead, more sure of himself now. "The real estate notes said that the property has a good-sized pond which could be used for irrigation or fishing."

At the front of the house, they came to a large, gravelled area, obviously constructed for parking or to facilitate the turning of cars. The Inspector gestured and the gaggle of officers split into their three groups, two of which then moved off round to each the side of the building.

Whitehead and Rashford walked up to the door.

"Shall I ring the bell?" said Rashford, indicating the small plastic panel set into the frame.

Whitehead ignored him. He pulled his sidearm from the holster and held it vertically by his shoulder.

"Hammer on the door," he said.

Rashford did so and immediately the Inspector yelled as loudly as possible.

"Police! Open up," he said.

Nothing happened. There was no sound of movement, no twitching of curtains.

Whitehead aimed his gun at the door lock.

"Stand back," he said.

"Wait," said Rashford, and reached forward. He turned the handle, and with a soft click the door opened. Rashford pushed it wider and stood back, loosening the flap on his holster as well.

There was no response.

"Police! We're coming in," said Whitehead in a loud voice.

He stepped inside, both arms outstretched and holding his gun before him. With each step he jerked his gaze from side to side, the weapon following a moment later. Once he was fully inside the building, he stopped.

"Clear," he said. "Come on, Sergeant."

Rashford walked through the door and found himself in a large entry hall, with a high cathedral ceiling. There were two doors to the right, and a third to the left. Between the doors, a wide staircase rose to the second floor. Behind it, a corridor led towards the back of the house.

At a hand signal from the Inspector, Rashford opened the two doors on the right. One revealed itself to be a mud room and coat closet, with boots lining the edge of the space. The second contained a toilet and small hand sink, with a mirror over the taps and a yellow towel hanging from a hook on the wall.

He walked to the left-hand door, which opened to a large room. The floor to ceiling windows framed a view of the mountains surrounding Waterton National Park. In the near distance, the grassy swathe surrounding the house ran down to a fence line. A dark smear nearly two thirds of the way might be the pond, thought Rashford.

Beyond, in the middle distance, was another large chalet-style house, almost a kilometre away but evidently the nearest neighbour. Beyond the second house the landscape was covered with a thin haze of morning fog, from which the mountains emerged. The sun was high enough now to give a rose-coloured tint to the rock faces, which were starkly etched against the clear sky.

The Inspector came back from his walk down the corridor.

"Two rooms down there, a kitchen and a dining room area," he said. "And a door to the outside."

Matheson and MacNeill walked into the room behind him.

"No one came out, sir," said MacNeill. "The others are watching the outside anyway."

"Good. Well, there's nobody down here," said Whitehead. "Let's check upstairs."

The four of them moved cautiously up the staircase, sidearms in hand. At the top there was a landing, with a railing that looked back down into the hall. There were two doors, each with a brass number. Rashford stood to the side. Whitehead leaned back against the railing and folded his arms.

"Matheson, door 1," he said. "MacNeill, door 2. On my mark."

The two of them moved to their respective door and, in unison, turned the handles as Whitehead counted down to 'now!'

"Wow," said MacNeill and Matheson, simultaneously. Whitehead and Rashford looked in through the open doors.

Each of these opened onto a large room. It was apparent that the house had been designed with two bedrooms, each with a large king-sized bed in the four-poster style. In each room, a glass chandelier hung from a large decorative hook in the centre of the ceiling. The walls were clear glass, providing views over the mountains and the foothills. There were two wing-backed armchairs, each with a small side table, and high on the wall a heat pump to provide either warmth or cool, depending on the season.

As they walked around, they realized that each room also had two walk-in closets and an en-suite bathroom. The latter each contained a claw-legged bath and a large glassed in rainforest shower. There was another door at the far end of each bedroom.

"You do the honours here, Sergeant," said Whitehead.

Rashford opened the door and stepped into another bright room, this one with a direct view of the Rockies. The room contained a large whirlpool style bath. There was a second door to his right.

"An indoor hot-tub," said Matheson, stepping in behind him. "I've always wanted one of those."

Rashford opened the other door and found himself face-to-face with MacNeill, who was still exploring the second bedroom.

"You'd have to share, then," he said. "It looks like there's only one of them."

Whitehead came into the bathroom and stood next to the hot tub.

"Fair play," he said, nodding at Rashford. "You're right, he's not here. If he ever was."

"Oh, he was," said Rashford, moving closer to the window, "Look."

He pointed down to the lawn which extended outward from the house. A clear line was visible where something had moved through the dew-covered stalks, leaving a precise trail.

"It goes down by the pond," said Rashford. "At least, I think that is what that dark area might be. That must have been what scared up the ducks."

"You mean he was here before then?" said Whitehead.

"Yes, sir. I think he was watching us to see what we were going to do at the gate. Then when he saw us coming up the drive, he left."

"Well, then," said Whitehead. "If you're right, he can't have got too far. Come on."

Once they got outside and were gathered on the gravel forecourt, Whitehead paused.

"Before we go running off chasing shadows, let's do our due diligence. Where are those outbuildings that were in the report?"

"They're around the back, sir," said Hamill. "We didn't go inside or anything."

"Let's just make sure there's nobody there, then."

They walked around the side of the house, following Hamill's lead, and saw the two smaller buildings. Whitehead and Rashford stood outside while the other officers entered. The Inspector looked around.

"Well, I could live here, couldn't you, Sergeant?"

Rashford did a slow turn, taking in the rolling foothills to the east and the mountains to the west, the vast expanse of sky, the distant neighbouring house.

"It would sure suit someone who wanted a quiet life, away from prying eyes," he said.

"Cynic," said Whitehead, but he nodded in agreement. Then he gestured to the two outbuildings.

"What do you think of this set-up, then?"

"He was probably living in the guest house," said Rashford. "There was no sign of any day-to-day stuff in the big house, it was almost sterile, like a hotel."

Whitehead nodded.

"Yes, the kitchen was spotless, all polished copperware, it looked like something from a magazine. Ah, here we go. Yes, Sergeant?"

Hamill walked over from the guest house.

"There are three bedrooms, sir, one has an ensuite and the other two share a bathroom, they have one of those Jill and John set-ups where there is a door from each side into the shared bathroom. There is also a kitchen and living room. The larger of the rooms looks like someone is living there. The bed is made and there are clothes in the closet, shaving supplies in the ensuite, personal things like that. All from a male.

"The other rooms look like someone might have been living there until recently, at least in one of them. There are some women's hygiene products on a shelf in the bathroom, and some tissues in the basket, but no clothes in the closets and the beds are both stripped, there are no sheets or anything.

"But here's the thing, sir. Those last two bedrooms, they've both got big heavy padlocks on the doors. On the outside. Luckily each one had a key left in it."

Whitehead looked at him.

"Padlocks?"

"Yes, sir. As though someone was kept prisoner, sir."

"I've read stories about people being kept in dungeons and things, used as sex slaves for perverted people, but they were in Britain or the States. Not Alberta."

"It's not impossible, sir," said Rashford. "We're just as weird as the rest of the world."

"True, Sergeant. Very true. Ah, Matheson, what did you and Larsen find?"

"Nothing, sir," said the constable. "The doors are unlocked and there's some games equipment inside, but it's all dusty. The only thing that looks like it's been used at all is one of those home gym set-ups."

Whitehead turned away and thought for a moment. Then he looked back to the group.

"Sergeant Hamill, you and Constable Matheson stay here and secure the scene. Call the situation in to Pincher Creek and ask for the Forensic team to come down and search this place. Full speed ahead, please. There must be traces of him somewhere."

Hamill nodded, then walked over to the nearest car and took two rolls of yellow crime scene tape out of the trunk. He passed one roll to Matheson, then reached back into the car and brought out a staple gun.

"Good to go, boss," he said. Whitehead gave him a thumbs up gesture, then turned to the others.

"MacNeill, you and Larsen get the cars and drive over to that next house. Wait for us there. Rashford and I will follow his trail and see if he left any clues along the way."

He moved off without saying anything further, so the two constables went over to the cruisers. Rashford hurried after the Inspector, who had walked off around the side of the house. He caught up with him just at the point the trail through the grass became visible.

"Hang on, sir," he said. "How did he get to here, to start walking?"

"What?"

"There's no door here, sir. Where did he come from?"

Whitehead looked around. The wall of the house was almost entirely made of windows, on both floors. There were no doors on the side facing the two officers.

Rashford looked at the ground.

"It's like he just appeared here, sir," he said. "There are no tracks coming together here. The grass and the gravel are both clear, untouched. Then he starts walking."

"Well, he's not an apparition, Sergeant. He didn't just fly in."

Rashford had a sudden memory of Morgan's flying dog story. A dog on a rope. He looked up at the wall of windows again. Then he saw it.

"There, sir," he said, pointing up at the eave of the gable roof. "Just inside the vee made by the roof beams, sir. You can see a small opening."

Whitehead shaded his eyes with the palm of his hand, although to what purpose Rashford wasn't sure because the early morning sun was behind them. He peered up at the top of the wall.

"Right, now I see it. What, you think he jumped?"

"No, sir. I think he had a rope, sir, and climbed or abseiled down the wall. There must be an attic or something up there as well, even though we didn't see it."

"Let's see if you're correct again," said Whitehead. He pulled a small radio from his pocket.

"Hamill? Listen, when you've cordoned off the place, you and Matheson go upstairs. See if you can find a trapdoor or something, it should lead to a small attic. You're looking to see if there's a place this joker might have attached a climbing rope."

There was a response of crackle and static, then he clicked off the radio and turned to Rashford.

"He'll let us know if they find something. When they find something," he said, ruefully. "You've been right so far, Sergeant, why not again now?"

"I'm not sure, sir," said Rashford. "Chickens and eggs, eggs and chickens, I think."

Whitehead laughed.

"Fair enough," he said. "Alright. You go first."

Rashford led the way across the field. The sun had risen enough that the dew had started to burn away, and some of the grass stems were already returning to the upright position. By following the line of sight, however, he could see the faint trace left when the track itself had disappeared.

After about ten minutes they came up to the reed fringed water of the slough. The ground was softer here, and Rashford was pleased to see the clear imprint of a shoe, etched onto a small patch of mud. Whitehead did not need any encouragement.

"Tell Forensics they should bring a cast set down here to the slough," he said, after reaching Hamill on the radio. "I'm going to mark it with my jacket."

He listened for a few moments.

"Right, thanks. Okay, tell the Forensics guys to go there first and process that as soon as they can. It could be vital. Then they can come down here."

Whitehead turned to Rashford.

"You were correct. They found a little box attic room, with a new grab bar on the wall. He must have tied his rope off there, using something like a highwayman's hitch to make it secure. Then when he made the ground, he quick-released the rope and took it with him. Clever bastard."

Rashford looked at him, impressed.

"Do you climb, sir?"

"Used to, Sergeant, used to. Then I got my knee blown out. We were doing a vehicle stop and one of the bastards pulled a gun. My team got him, but not before he got me. Reconstructive surgery means I can walk but I don't fancy risking it popping when I'm up a mountain."

"Ah, yes. I had noticed you have a slight limp, sir."

"Yes, it's normally okay though. Usually, I have to go into Calgary on a Friday, for a couple of injections, but then I'm alright for another week. It is what it is."

"Yes, sir."

"Anyway, back to this situation. The other thing Hamill and Matheson found, even more interesting. A water glass and a half-eaten sandwich. He must have been having breakfast when we arrived. I'll ask Forensics to do a rush analysis, see if there's any way we can identify this fellow with anyone already in the system."

Rashford stared at him.

"That's brilliant, sir," he said. "This could be the proof I need."

"There's no I in team, Sergeant," said Whitehead. "You'd do well to remember that."

"Yes sir. Sorry sir."

Whitehead took off his jacket, transferred the radio to his trouser pocket, and folded over a half-dozen reeds so the stems were about sixty centimetres off the ground. He left the jacket draped over the impromptu clothes horse and gestured Rashford forward again.

"Keep going," he said. "And yes, I recognize that he must have scared up those ducks when he came past. Like Larsen said, they will have been feeding in the shallows here."

Rashford did not say anything, he just kept walking. Soon they came to the fence and, looking down, could see where the mesh had been cleanly cut alongside a post and horizontally along the ground. A piece of a fallen branch had been used to peg the mesh at the corner, but once this was removed the flap opened up easily. The two men bent over and were able to walk through under the top strand of wire.

On the outside of the fence the grass continued but had been more closely cut. The footsteps were harder to see but Rashford took the chance that they would continue in a straight line. They walked across the field, and he noticed that they were heading straight for the second chalet. To his left, the two cruisers were now visible, turning onto the neighbouring drive.

The police cars pulled up outside the door to the house at the same time as the two men climbed over a small retaining wall and came across a neatly tended flower garden. They then crossed the gravel in front of a two-car garage attached to the house itself. One of the garage doors had a blue sweater pinned underneath the entrance.

As the group came together, the front door of the house opened. A large red-faced man in a white dressing gown looked out at them. There was a crest on the pocket of the dressing gown, TSX with an arched line running across and through the X.

"Can I help you?" he said.

"Possibly, sir," said Whitehead. "We are police officers, as you can see, and we would like a quick word. May we come in please?"

"In the house?"

"Yes, sir. It would be easier than talking out here."

"You'll have to take your boots off," said the man. "And Carolyn will probably kill you if you walked on any of her perennials. Oh, and I should probably see some identification, please."

"Are the police cars not enough?" said Whitehead, sharply.

"They weren't in Portapique," said the man, his tone equally sharp.

Rashford stepped forward, his hand outstretched, placatingly.

"That's quite right sir, you can't be too careful. Here is my warrant card. Gentlemen, please."

He offered his wallet with the card in its clear pouch, gesturing to MacNeill and Larsen to do the same. They looked across at Whitehead and he nodded, taking out his wallet at the same time.

The man looked at all the warrant cards then nodded.

"Thank you," he said. "My name is Toews. Henry Toews. Please, come in. But do take off your footwear."

He turned and went inside.

"Stay here," said Whitehead, talking to the two constables. "Stay with the cars."

Whitehead and Rashford followed the man inside the house, pausing in the foyer to remove their boots. They padded after him down a long wooden-floored corridor, and then into a large living room. This too faced the Rockies, although the amount of glass was less than in the previous house. A tall thin woman wearing track pants and a tight-fitting t-shirt stood behind an armchair. She had dyed blonde hair and was at least twenty years younger than her partner.

"My wife, Carolyn," said Toews, waving his hand in her general direction.

"May I offer you coffee?" she said.

"You may," said Whitehead, pompously, "but we would have to decline. We have some important questions to ask."

"What could be more important than coffee?" said her facial expression, but she just nodded and sat on the arm of the chair. Henry Toews sank down into a well-cushioned settee.

"Out with it, then," he said.

Whitehead stood in front of them with his arms behind his back. Rashford wandered around the periphery of the room, reaching up now and again to stroke the back of a bone china figurine, or to lift and flip through a book. He listened to the questions, and their jumbled answers.

No, they had never met their neighbour. They thought he had been there about a year, perhaps fourteen months. He drove a very sensible car, one of those hybrid ones. They had never seen motorbikes come to visit, but he did have rich friends.

"They drove some pretty fancy cars," said Carolyn. They did not think he had a girlfriend, at least not a regular one.

"There was seldom the same car there twice," said Carolyn.

Whitehead was writing the responses down in his notebook. Rashford stepped forward.

"Do you play the stock market, sir?" he said.

Toews and Whitehead both looked at him in surprise.

"Yes, I do, actually," said Toews. "Although I don't 'play' it as such. I mean, it's my job, not a game."

"Yes, sorry. And you do well, it seems," said Rashford, gesturing around.

"Thank you," said Toews. "I try to keep on top of things."

Inspector Whitehead looked puzzled.

"The TMX on his gown, sir," said Rashford. "It stands for Toronto Stock Exchange, the venture capital market. It used to be known as CDMX, the Canadian Venture Exchange, and, before that, as the Alberta Stock Exchange."

Whitehead stared at him.

"My dad lost a lot of money on Bre-X, sir," said Rashford. "It was a gold company that collapsed in the late nineties, due to a massive fraud scheme. I've kind of had a lay-man's interest in the market ever since."

Henry Toews nodded his approval.

"Yes, that was a black-eye for everyone concerned," he said. "Even for those of us who got out in time, it was very close."

"Very interesting," said Whitehead, "but we're not here as part of a fraud investigation."

"Yes, sir," said Rashford. "But I was wondering, sir, where do you do your trades?"

"From my office. In the back of the house," said the man, gesturing behind him.

"And where have you been for the last hour or so, sir?"

"There. In my office. I have to get up early and work Toronto hours."

"That's what I thought, sir. Thank you. And you, madam. Where have you been for the past hour?

"In the gym. I usually get up shortly after Henry and I do my workout and yoga while he is making money, then we rendezvous for coffee and to plan the day. Why do you ask? Are we suspects or something?"

"Yes, why do you ask, Sergeant?" said Whitehead. "No madam, you are not suspects," he continued.

"I ask because I wanted to confirm my theory. And you have just done that."

"What theory, Sergeant?" said the Inspector.

"Mister and Missus Toews here have been incommunicado for the past hour, sir. The gentleman probably wears headphones to keep up with what is going on, and the lady no doubt plays music during her workout."

They both nodded.

"I would like you to come and describe the vehicle that was stolen, please," he said.

They looked at each other.

"Stolen? What vehicle?" said the woman.

"The one that was parked in the second of the garages, please," said Rashford.

"That would be mine," she said. "But who stole it."

"Please, one thing at a time. Let us just confirm the theft, can we."

The four of them went outside, Rashford and Whitehead pulling on their boots while Henry slipped into a pair of casual deck shoes and Carolyn into a pair of flip flops. They walked over to the garage.

"What is my sweater doing here," said Carolyn, bending down to pick it up. She tugged but it was stuck by the weight of the door. Henry went to the side of the garage and pressed a switch that had been camouflaged as part of the bass relief on the pillar. The door opened smoothly and silently.

Carolyn picked up the sweater than looked inside the garage.

"My car has gone," she said.

She turned to Rashford.

"How did you know that?"

"Well, we've been following a man, what you might call a person of interest, and it seemed like he had disappeared. I saw the sweater and recognized it was an expensive one, probably cashmere?

"Yes, it's an Alexander Wang design," she said.

He nodded.

"I didn't think anyone would leave something like that on the floor, especially not pinned down by a greasy garage door. Then I thought if he had stolen a vehicle, and found a sweater on the seat, he might have thrown that away as he left the garage. It was just his bad luck that it didn't fall inside the garage."

"I see. But why did you want to know where we had been and what we had been doing?"

"Because that would explain why you didn't hear anything," he said. "When we arrived, neither of you was upset or flustered, or asking us if we here to find your car. That's because you didn't know it had been stolen."

He walked inside. On the other side of the garage was a large sports utility vehicle, light grey in colour, with the swept back design and predatory front grill of a European import. The alloy wheels bore a capital B logo on the centre bore, with the same symbol on the front hood.

"Is that a Bentley?" Rashford said.

Henry Toews nodded his head vigorously, his voice proud.

"Yes sir. Betayga V8, 2022 model."

"What's that cost, two hundred and fifty k?"

Toews laughed.

"Only if you were buying used," he said.

"Right," said Rashford. "Very nice. A bit outside my paygrade, though. What about you, madam. Where is your car?"

"My car is obviously not here, officer," she said, firmly. "If it was, you would see that it is an Audi R8 Spyder, a convertible. It is green. British Racing Green, to be exact."

"That car is also above my paygrade, madam, but very distinctive. Thank you. What is the licence plate number, please?"

"CT 40," she said, looking straight at him. "It was a birthday present."

"Your husband was planning ahead, was he?" said Rashford.

Carolyn Toews burst into laughter, her face suddenly looking much more relaxed.

"Oh, very good, Sergeant. You are going to go far in the force."

"Thank you, Ma'am," he said, smiling back.

Whitehead looked from one to the other, puzzled, then turned back to Henry Toews.

"Are both of you planning to be at home today?" he said. "We might need to talk to you again later."

"Yes, I'm in for the duration," Toews said. "It's nearly the end of the month so lots of trades to track, hey? What about you, dear?"

"I have no plans to go out, except for brunch with friends at the Prince of Wales," said Carolyn. "I'll use the Bentley."

"Do you like cars. Ma'am?" said Rashford.

Henry Toews guffawed.

"Carolyn? She's a right petrol head!"

Rashford looked directly at Carolyn Toews.

"Is that how you knew they were expensive, the cars visiting the house?"

"Yes," she said, colouring slightly. "Assisted by my field glasses, of course. But Porsche and Alfa Romeo and Saab, they have some pretty distinctive profiles. I even saw a Rolls once, one of the older ones. A Phantom 3, I believe, but I'm not sure which year. Probably 1937 or 1938. It's got the long hood with the spare tire mounted on the side in front of the passenger door, and that classic swept back design. He only came once, that I saw."

Whitehead stared at her with his mouth open.

"He?" said Rashford.

"It was definitely a man," she said. "They generally are, the people who visit there. I have good field glasses, I use them for wildlife watching in the park."

"Did you ever see a red pick-up, a crew cab?"

“A few times, yes. I thought perhaps that was the maintenance guy or something.”

“Thank you, again,” said Rashford, nodding. “I think we can leave this good couple to their morning coffee, sir,” he said to Whitehead.

“Indeed,” said the Inspector. “Let’s go and chat with our colleagues.”

He nodded again to the couple, and then waved his arm as Carolyn started to rise off the chair.

“It’s OK, madam, we can see ourselves out,” he said.

Once outside in the yard, Inspector Whitehead gathered the group around him.

“We are looking for a late model Audi convertible,” he said. “An R8 Spyder to be exact, English Racing Green in colour.”

MacNeill whistled.

“Wow, very nice. That would cost a fair bit.”

“You should see the back up,” muttered Whitehead. “Anyway, for the Spyder. The licence plate number is CT 40. I’ll call it in and then we’ll go back to the other chalet and see if Forensics have turned up yet. Any questions?”

He looked around.

“No? OK, then, saddle up.”

He got into the car with MacNeill, indicating that Rashford should join Larsen, and they turned around before heading back down the drive.

Chapter 9

As they approached the chalet, they saw that another police vehicle was already at the scene.

"That was quick," said Rashford. "I figured it would take them at least an hour to get here."

"Normally would, yes," said Larsen. "But the Inspector called them in earlier. When we were getting the carbines from the cars, after you cut the trip wire, that's when he called for Forensics. The second call was just a hurry up to them."

"Interesting."

"Yes. He might come across as a bit of a country bumpkin, huntin' and fishin' and drinkin' coffee all day with the locals, but he's actually quite a smart copper. He says that he learned how to read men when he was in the army."

"He was in the army?"

"Yes, before he became a copper. He drove a tank or something, but he doesn't like to talk about it. That's where this 'saddle up' garbage comes from."

"Really? I thought maybe he was in the Ride."

Larsen laughed.

"Really? I can't see him in the Ride, can you?"

"I suppose not," said Rashford.

There was a silence as they each considered the image that had been evoked, of a short round rider amidst the hand-picked and photogenic Praetorian Guard of the Musical Ride.

Larsen shook his head.

"Anyway, he respects your judgement," he said.

"Really?"

"Yeah. He was quite impressed by what your Chief Superintendent said about you, but he said he wanted to see you prove you were as good as she said. I guess you've done that, now."

"What do you mean?"

"Well, he's letting you ride in here, instead of with him, where he can keep an eye on you. It shows he trusts you now."

Rashford thought back over the morning and realized that Larsen was correct. This was the first time since they had left the Mountain View Motel that he had not felt the presence of Inspector Whitehead at his shoulder. He smiled quietly to himself.

"I reckon we might even get two rounds out of him tonight," said Larsen, with a grin. "You've well and truly scuppered him today."

Rashford laughed out loud at that, and they were both still chuckling as they drove onto the large gravel forecourt by the chalet house. The other car had already arrived. Whitehead stepped forward to meet them.

"We've had a sighting," he said, looking very pleased with the way things were developing.

"What, already?" said Rashford.

"Yes. The thing with distinctive cars, you see, is that everybody knows them. One of the local guys was coming up from the border crossing at Chief Mountain and saw the Spyder cross in front of him, heading into the park. The local police say hers is the only car anything like that around here."

"Is he at the hotel?" said Rashford.

"I have no idea," said Whitehead. "The officer saw the car about forty-five minutes ago, but only reported it after we put out the call. He didn't know it was missing. He had thought it was Mrs. Toews, she often goes to the Prince of Wales Hotel to use their spa, or to have lunch with some friends."

"The good news, then," said Sergeant Hamill, "is that there is only one road in and out of the park. So, he if doesn't drive out, he'll have to climb or hike."

"Or swim," said Matheson.

"Swim?" said Rashford.

"Yeah, there's a lake, Cameron Lake, that goes across the border. You could swim across the Medicine Line and be in the States."

"Or you could take the tourist boat down the lake," said Larsen. "Then don't get back on, just keep walking when you get to the other end."

"He'd need to have his passport, though," said Matheson. "They won't let you off the boat unless you have positive ID. And why would he risk that? I think he'd just swim past the boundary markers."

"All good possibilities," said Whitehead, "but let's get to the park first and debate those ideas later."

They went back to their original seating placements, with Rashford and Larsen joining the Inspector and Matheson and MacNeill going in the other car with Hamill. Whitehead turned on his lights, but not the siren.

"No need to spook him," he said.

At the gate to the park, they pulled onto the small area marked with cross-hashed lines, which Whitehead felt were being reserved for official vehicles. He and Rashford walked up to the nearest of the two small cottages that served as the entry booths.

A young woman looked out of the window at them, only glancing at Whitehead's warrant card.

"Hello bonjour, may I help you," she said, in a strong accent.

"We're looking for a green sports car," said Whitehead.

"Ah yes, Missus Toews?" said the girl. "Try the hotel. She drove through nearly an hour ago."

"Did you speak with her?" asked Rashford.

"No, we were busy. About six camper trailers came at the same time. But she has a pass, so she drove straight through in the express lane."

"But you know it was her car?" said Whitehead.

"Mais oui, she is the only person with a car like that."

"So, you have met her?"

"Yes, sometimes she brings us here, from the dorm, if she is leaving the hotel and we are walking up the hill. She is very kind."

"It is very important that we speak to her," said Rashford. "Is there a way you can get a message to the park wardens? We need them to call us if they see her car."

"Is she in trouble?"

"No, not herself. But it might not be her in the car, so they must not approach her. They just need to report the car."

"OK, I will call the le garde en chef du parc. Just wait une moment, s'ils vous plait."

The girl turned away and picked up a telephone. Rashford looked at Whitehead.

"Do they still have to be bilingual French in the Park?" he said. "What about the Indigenous language rules?"

"I'm not sure," said Whitehead. "I seem to remember something about Canada agreeing to keep funding some of the Park activities, as long as Alsama let Francophone bilingual employees keep their jobs if they wanted to stay. The others have to do that FILTER training thing."

"Yes, so do we, in Saskatchewan. Don't you?"

"I guess. But I'm nearly retired, so I'm not bothering. I've got enough to do without learning Indian."

Whitehead looked at Rashford, as if he were seeking a confrontation, but Rashford stayed silent. The girl reappeared at the window, holding an old-fashioned telephone on a long lead.

"Here, you tell him," she said. "C'est plus facilement. Pardon. That will be easier."

Whitehead took the phone and listened for a moment as the other person introduced themselves. He then explained who he was, and why he was looking for the Audi Spyder that belonged to Mrs. Toews, who was obviously well known to the Park's employees. He then listened intently. After a few minutes, he recited his cell phone number, then handed the phone back to the young woman.

"Thank you," he said, then walked back to the cars. Rashford followed him.

"Right, here's the plan," said the Inspector, once they were all together again.

"We're going to drive down to the Prince of Wales hotel and get a coffee in the foyer. The dining room should be open, and the Warden says that they will serve us. He is going to put out a call to all the field people and will let us know as soon as he hears anything. He did say that it is a big park, and there are lots of roads and parking areas, so it might take some time. Any questions? Nope? Right, let's go."

Rashford had never been to Waterton before and found the drive in from the gate to be awe-inspiring. There was a lake to their left, slowly getting wider as they drove along the bank, with mountains behind, and a stand of dead willows to their right. The road continued along the edge of the lake for some time, the mountains slowly appearing closer. They passed signs to the Hay Barn picnic area, and to Red Rock Canyon, both of which sounded interesting, then drove over a bridge across a shallow and fast-flowing river.

"The water is that grey-green colour because it comes from the glaciers," said Larsen.

The road rose up over a crest, the sides closing in with heavier vegetation, then they turned left onto a smaller road. This wove through the trees before leading them out onto a gravel parking area, at the edge of which was a large building with a green copper roof. The walls were salmon pink, with balconies edged in white trim. The effect was like looking at a grounded cruise ship.

After they had parked, Whitehead led them through the door and into the hotel entry hall. He kept walking past the gift shop to the main lobby. Tourists milled about, looking at the paintings and clothing in the gift shop, chattering together in a babel of languages. Some sat in the high-backed wing chairs that were scattered in small groups across the heavy carpet. Others peered up at the walls and balconies, which appeared to be made of teak or oak beams, dark with age. At the far side of the lobby a large group were clustered in front of floor to ceiling windows, nine huge vertical panels in a metal frame.

Rashford walked across to the windows and edged his way through the crowd, which parted easily at the sight of his uniform. He stood open-mouthed before the vista that opened up before him. The lake extended down the centre of the landscape, a necklace of mountains framing the view. In the foreground, to the right, he could see the buildings which made up Waterton village itself. To the left, ranks of trees marched down to the water. It was a picture-perfect view, one enhanced by the hotel's location on a high bluff, and the constant clicking of cameras and cell phones soon became irritating. Whitehead joined him.

"Pretty spectacular, eh?"

"It is indeed. Beautiful."

"You know you're going to be in lots of holiday slide shows?"

"Sorry?"

"A Mountie in front of this classic view, priceless."

Rashford turned around and realized that many of the tourists were including him in the composition of their photographs. He decided to ignore them and turned back to face the lake.

"Well, you enjoy the view. I'll order coffees. How would you like yours?"

"Just black, please. I want to keep it pure, like this view."

Whitehead barked with laughter.

"Right, well, we'll be sitting over there when you care to join us."

He left Rashford standing in front of the windows.

They had nearly finished their coffee when Whitehead's phone rang. He picked it up from the table in front of him, then nodded as he listened.

"Just a second," he said, snapping his fingers at the group around the table. "Paper, please."

Sergeant Hamill passed him a small coil-wire notebook, opened to a blank page, and a pen. Whitehead scribbled notes as the caller continued to speak. After three or four minutes, he nodded briskly.

"That's great, thank you. We'll talk later."

He clicked off the phone and sat back in his chair, studying the notes he had just made.

"Well, then," he said. "That's very interesting."

The group waited expectantly.

"The Warden says that his staff have checked all the major car parks, and there is no sign of the Spyder. That likely means that he parked it off-road somewhere. There are over fifty kilometres of official roadways in the park, plus the maintenance roads that are supposedly only used by Parks staff, plus all the streets in the townsite. So, it's going to take a while to find him.

"But as Sergeant Hamill said, earlier, there is only one road in and out of the Park. So, we know the car is here somewhere."

"Do we just wait, sir?" said MacNeill.

"Yes and no," said Whitehead. "Here's the plan. Sergeant Hamill, it's your car that we drove here, correct?"

"Yes, sir."

"Whose was the car we left in Mountain View?"

"Mine, sir," said Larsen. "Matheson and me drove down in it."

"Matheson and I, Sergeant," said the Inspector.

"No, it was me," said Larsen, looking to the others for help.

"Never mind," said Whitehead, shaking his head. He looked around the group.

"To start with, I shall drive Larsen and Rashford back to Mountain View, to get their cars. Matheson, you stay here at the hotel. The Warden will call the front desk if anything comes up, so make sure the clerk there knows where you are.

"Sergeant Hamill, you and MacNeill go back to the Park gate and set up a roadblock. Check every car that comes out. You're looking for a thin fellow, late thirties or early forties, narrow face. I don't think you'll actually see him but look out for any car where the numbers seem wrong – a couple plus an extra guy, that sort of thing.

"Oh, one other thing. Sergeant, take a formal statement from that French girl at the kiosk. Get her to tell you about the block of camper vans that came through at the same time as the Spyder. I wonder how he managed to organize that little trick.

"Is that clear to everyone?"

Everybody nodded and murmured assent, so Whitehead stood up from his chair.

"Right then, we'll rendezvous back at the Park Gate. Rashford, Larsen, come with me. We'll go and get your cars then drive back here.

That way everyone will be independent. Plus, I don't like leaving police vehicles unattended, even in a little place like Mountain View."

The three of them strode out of the hotel, followed at a more leisurely pace by Hamill and MacNeill. Matheson made his way over to the dark-haired young man standing behind the large mahogany check-in desk, then swerved to his left and lifted his hat as a young woman came out from behind the partition.

"I wonder if you could help me, miss," he said, "I'm in need of assistance."

"Always happy to do what I can to help a man in uniform," she said, laughing, and brushed her hair away from her cheek as she leaned in to speak with him.

It was nearly two hours later that the team reassembled at the main gate to the National Park. Rashford and Whitehead had parked on the edge of the road, across from where Hamill's cruiser was parked crossways, blocking both exit lanes. Larsen continued down to the hotel and collected Matheson before driving back up and joining the group, parking on the side of the road next to Hamill.

"Anything to report?" said the Inspector, looking around.

"No, sir," said MacNeill. "No strange or unusual people in any of the cars we've checked so far."

"I spoke with Josee Onlange, in the kiosk," said Hamill. "She told me that one of the camper van drivers reported a blockage on the road just before the last bend. He said there were three or four tree branches across the road, big ones, they looked like they had fallen off a lorry. He had thought maybe Parks had been clearing some of the deadwood from that big fire they had a couple of years ago."

"How was it cleared?"

"The driver told her that he couldn't get past, but he couldn't move the wood by himself, so he waited until the other camper vans came. Then they all pulled the branches to the side and carried on. He was telling her so she could arrange for them to be removed. Plus, he thought maybe he and the others should get a discount, but she wouldn't agree to that."

Whitehead looked up at the sky for a moment.

"Interesting," he said. "My theory is that our boy blocks the road, then drives back the other way a bit. He knows that nobody would notice him, they are all busy looking at the scenery. He gives them enough time to clear the blockage, then he turns around and follows the group to the Gate. While Ms. Onlange is busy with them, he drives through, knowing she will just recognize the car and not be worried about him."

"How would he know that the Spyder is known in the Park?" said Matheson.

"By the Park Pass," said Rashford. "If she is a regular visitor, she will have bought an annual pass and hung it from her rear-view mirror. Dallas will have seen that when he got in her car, it probably gave him the idea of going to the Park."

"Yes, and either he forgot there is only the one road in and out, or he has another plan to escape," said Whitehead.

"I think the latter," said Rashford. "This guy doesn't forget things like that."

"Let's hold that idea for now, until we get some actual evidence," said Whitehead. "It's likely correct, though. Matheson, what about you?"

"Well, sir, Darlene, I'm sorry, I didn't get her last name, Darlene was very helpful, sir," said Matheson.

"I'm sure she was, always happy to help a big country boy like you, was she?" said Hamill, laughing.

"Yes, sarge," said Matheson, blushing.

"Well, come on then, what did she say?" said the Inspector.

"She gave me a cranberry soda and let me sit by the window without buying any food, sir, while I waited for the Warden to call."

"Right. And did he call?"

"No, sir, he did not."

"Did Darlene sit with you while you waited, constable."

"Yes, sir."

"And did you talk about Missus Toews or her easily identifiable car at all?"

"Not really, sir. She has seen it, of course, and knows Missus Toews because she comes to the spa every two weeks, but that was all."

"Do I want to know what you did talk about, constable, you and the delectable Darlene?"

"Not really, sir," said Matheson, blushing again.

"Well, then, what is said in Waterton, stays in Waterton. Moving on, I got a call from the Warden as I was driving back just now. They still haven't found the car, and he suggests we call it a day. Even if they find it in the next hour, it's going to be too dark to do any searching.

"I'm going to suggest that we all go home for the night, no need to run up un-necessary bills. Our budget isn't that big. Rashford, your Chief Super has pre-booked your hotel in Cardston, so you go back there. The rest of us will go back to Pincher Creek. Except you, Matheson."

"Me, sir?"

"Yes, we need one person to stay here, just in case something happens during the evening or overnight. The Warden said we could have one room, it's in the worker area not the main hotel so our budget can cover it. You can stay there. Is that OK with you?"

"Yes, sir."

"Good. I'll call the Warden back and ask him if you can pick up the key at the front desk. I'm sure Darlene will show you where to find everything."

"Yes, sir," said Matheson, blushing and grinning at the same time.

"I've also asked the Warden to have two of his staff parked at the kiosk overnight. They'll stop any outgoing vehicles and warn them that there is a herd of elk out on the road. If they see the Audi, or someone who looks like out man, they'll call it in. Then you, Matheson, you will stop whatever you're doing and investigate. Understood?"

"Yes, sir."

"Right then. Okay, everyone, unless you hear anything contrary before then, we'll rendezvous in the hotel lobby at oh nine hundred hours. Clear?"

"Yes, sir," they chorused.

"I haven't forgotten our wager, Rashford," said the Inspector. "But we shall settle that once this case is finished. I don't want anyone drinking and driving tonight."

"Fair enough, sir," said Rashford. "See you in the morning."

"Yes," said Whitehead. "Larsen, I'll give you a drive home so Matheson can keep the cruiser."

They all moved to their cars. Matheson drove off down the hill towards the Prince of Wales Hotel, while the others turned and drove out in single file along the exit parkway. At the junction, Hamill and Whitehead turned left, following highway 6 towards Pincher Creek, while Rashford continued straight on highway 5. He stopped at the Barn Store in Mountain View to fill up the cruiser with gas and went into the convenience store to pay. Here he also bought himself a packet of cigarettes, together with some ginger ale and chips to snack on later, before heading back to his hotel.

That evening Rashford walked up the street to Sauce, where he got himself a bacon and chicken calzone. Maria was still working and took his order, which she relayed through to the back kitchen.

"We make everything fresh so it will take a few minutes," she said. "Would you like a drink while you wait?"

"Sure, I'll have a light beer, any kind," said Rashford, sitting at one of the empty tables.

"No, we don't sell alcohol. That's not allowed here in Cardston."

"Really? Why not? I thought the government ended prohibition some years ago."

"Well, it did, officially. In 1923 everywhere else and in 2020 here. But nobody here wants alcohol to be available in town."

"Nobody?"

"The last time they had an actual vote, back in 2014, it was about three to one. Over a thousand voted against booze and less than three hundred and fifty voted for it. I don't think that's changed much."

"Is that because of the Church?"

"Partly, I guess," said Maria. "I know the leadership doesn't want alcohol in town. But even people who aren't Mormon like the ban, they think it keeps things safer. And if anyone wants to have a drink in their own home, they can always buy booze in Lethbridge or wherever. So, it's not like it's really illegal."

"I should just have brought my own?" said Rashford.

Maria smiled at him.

"Next time," she said, shyly.

Rashford laughed, then collected his calzone and walked back to the hotel. He found it was as good as the Inspector had said, even when only washed down with a can of ginger ale.

Once he had finished his meal, he called Roxanne. She asked him about his day, and he made her laugh as he described the various events, especially the saga at the Manchester gate, and Matheson's adventure with Darlene. She was delighted that Rashford had won his bet with Whitehead but hoped that it wouldn't delay him from getting home.

"You might get as lucky as Matheson," she said, giggling.

When he asked her what had been happening in Maple Creek, she turned serious.

"Not a lot, to be honest. I don't even know if this is a thing, but I thought I should tell you. There were three bikers here today, driving big Harleys. They didn't stop or anything, but they cruised past the police station a couple of times. I think they were looking at the truck."

"Did they see you?"

"No, I stayed inside, away from the windows. It was only because of the noise they made that I even looked out at all. They went up the street towards Alf's, turned around, then came back slowly. Then they went away."

"When was this?"

"Mid-morning, around ten I think."

"And you are sure they didn't see you?"

"Yes."

Rashford thought for a moment.

"I wonder if Snake Boots guy has told people to look out for the truck, maybe offered a reward or something. I don't like you being there by yourself. Can you call Bettina to come over?"

"Look, I'll be all right. They might be interested in the truck, but they have no idea that I'm here. This is a police house, for heaven's sake. Anyway, Bettina isn't here. She has a friend over visiting, someone she hasn't seen in years, so they went over to Medicine Hat to explore the bunkers."

"Why didn't you go with them?"

"Well, first, they didn't invite me. And second, they haven't seen each other since graduate school, apparently, so I figured they could do with some time together."

"I guess," said Rashford. "Well, we can go over there one day, when I'm back. That Al Capone stuff is very interesting."

"No, not Al Capone. Those are the tunnels in Moose Jaw, aren't they? This is something to do with an emergency hospital from the Cold War."

"In Medicine Hat?"

"Yes. Bettina said that her friend works in emergency preparedness, and during her research she found out about this Civil Defense emergency hospital. It was built in the early sixties, underneath the old Post Office. It's about two stories underground from what everyone thinks is the basement, her friend says that was probably to protect it against radiation if there was a nuclear attack.

"When they demolished the old Post Office, in 2001 or 2002, they found this room filled with two hundred cots, x-ray equipment and generators, stuff like that. The city had no idea it was there! But when it became public news, people from the federal government came and took it all away. And there was a gag order so the newspapers couldn't report it anymore."

"You're joking, right? They must have been teasing you. I've never heard of that, secret cold war hospitals. That's crazy."

"Well, you never heard of it because it's secret, that's why," said Roxanne, tartly. "Bettina says that there are lots of them, even now, updated to modern times, hidden all over the country. Only a few people at Health Canada in Ottawa know where they are."

"So, how come her friend knows all this?"

"I told you, it's her work. I'm not quite sure who she works for but right now she's somewhere in northern Manitoba, attached to a company that does cold weather testing on plane engines. They're looking at adverse weather effects like ice build up, endurance in cold temperatures, that kind of thing. She does something with computers."

"How does she know Bettina?" said Rashford.

"They did their graduate studies together, at university. Well, not together, but at the same time. Bettina said they met at some student awards ceremony where they'd both won big prizes, her in humanities and her friend in sciences. They just hit it off and have been friends ever since."

"They could still have taken you with them," said Rashford. "What have you been doing all day?"

"Sitting around watching daytime television and painting my toenails. What did you think I was doing? Cooking, cleaning, and ironing your shirts?"

"No, no, I didn't mean that," said Rashford. "It's just that there's not a lot to do in Maple Creek."

"I'm fine. I read my book, I stayed in the house and watched the scary bikers. I had some lunch. This afternoon I went and did some shopping. Oh, and I talked with my mom."

"Really? How is she?"

"She is fine, but she wants to come out for a visit. She wants to meet you and see the prairies."

"Umm, fine, no problem. When would she like to come?"

"She'll be here by Monday. She was going to get the bus from Charlottetown this afternoon."

"The bus! That will take forever."

"She doesn't care. She likes riding on the bus, she says she always meets interesting people. Plus, she wants to see the country. I told you, she always said she ran away to see the world but only got to Antigonish, Nova Scotia, and then to PEI. She says that she is in no rush."

"Where will she stay?"

"I thought I'd make up your office into the spare room again, if that's OK?"

"Sure," said Rashford, shaking his head and wondering how things with Roxanne had evolved quite so quickly.

"I have to go," he said. "I need to check my notes and get some sleep. I'm not sure what tomorrow is going to look like."

"I guess you won't be home tomorrow?"

"I don't know. I'll see how it goes. What are your plans?"

"Bettina and her friend are coming over for lunch, I haven't got any further than that."

"I hope you find out interesting things about that underground hospital," he said.

"Me too. Good night. Take care, my love," said Roxanne.

"Good night."

Rashford clicked off the phone and sat thinking for a moment.

'My love'? he wondered.

Chapter 10

It was a few minutes before nine o'clock the next morning when Rashford walked into the Prince of Wales Hotel. He had woken early and driven out to the park, stopping along the shore of Lower Waterton Lake to watch the sunrise. A thin sliver of moon was setting to the west, Venus a bright pinprick of light just above the rim rock.

Standing on the rocky shore smoking a cigarette, he had turned east and watched the sky to the left of the ridge lighten. The lake was ruffled with whitecaps as the morning wind brushed the surface. The silhouette of Vimy Peak darkened, then blazed through a myriad of red and yellow hues. As the first rays of the sun came towards him, he stubbed out his cigarette with his boot, put the butt end into his pocket, and walked back up to his car.

It was not yet seven o'clock, so he decided to drive around before going to the hotel. He crossed over the ridge beneath Bear's Hump and dropped down into the townsite itself. He slowed for groups of whitetail and mule deer that wandered across the road, seeking the greener grass of a lawn on the other side of the street. A grey jay and a magpie were squabbling over the contents of a discarded fast-food wrapper, watched over imperiously by a large raven.

Rashford did the loop around the campsite, passing ranks of large trailers and motorhomes parked only metres away from each other. 'Welcome to the big outdoors,' he thought. Most of the campers were quiet, but at a few sites someone sat outside on a chair, cup of coffee in hand, either thinking great thoughts or regretting the hangover. One man waved as he drove past, so he waved back, but most people just ignored him.

He still had time, so he went out along the Akamina Parkway for the fifteen-minute drive to Cameron Lake. As he approached the sign pointing up to the jagged tooth mass of Mount Lineham he had to stop for a group of bighorn sheep that were ambling along the road. The females grazed at the shoulder grass, younger lambs bumped into each other and jostled for space, and a large ram stood on the centre line, daring him to pass. He waited until the flock moved off onto a shallow rise, followed eventually by the ram, then slowly eased past. The ram looked disdainfully over its shoulder as it effortlessly climbed up the bank.

Shortly after the sheep, a car approached him, driving in towards the town, and the driver slowed when he realized it was a police car coming towards him. Rashford nodded as he passed, and the man raised two fingers off the steering wheel in acknowledgement. Rashford saw wooden signs indicating where a trail started from the small area that had been cleared just off the road, and where cars were already starting to park, unloading hikers who were hoping to get an early start to the day.

At Cameron Lake there was a group of other early risers, clustered on the small jetty which stuck out into the lake. Rashford parked in the lot next to the other cars, then wandered down to see what they were doing. Most were holding binoculars, and a couple had set up small tripods to support a telescope. One man, who was wearing a bright neon pink fleece lined jacket, looked up at his approach.

"Good morning, officer," he said.

Some of the others turned around to see what was happening, but most remained focused on their task.

"What are you looking at?" said Rashford.

The man stepped back from his spotting scope and indicated that Rashford should look for himself.

"Far end of the lake, on that grassy bank below the scree slope. Three of them."

'Three what,' wondered Rashford, as he bent over and looked through the small lens. Immediately he saw the large yellow brown bears, with a distinctive hump at the shoulder.

"Grizzlies?" he said.

"Yup. Mum and two cubs, last year's from the size of them. They're too big to be from this spring."

"Wow. They're beautiful, not scary at all."

"From here, sure. Not so much when you get up close," said a woman standing to one side, her binoculars trained on the scene.

"Have you seen one up close?" said Rashford.

"Oh yes," she said. "Just once, mind, but it was enough."

"Sssshh," said one of the other bear watchers.

The woman looked at Rashford with a wry smile, then gestured with her head. He nodded and followed her as she walked back up towards the car park.

There were some benches outside the small visitor centre and the woman sat down on one.

"Do you mind?" she said, bringing out a package of cigarettes.

"Not at all," said Rashford. "Actually, I'm not officially on duty yet, so I might join you."

He used his lighter to light her cigarette, then took his own packet out of his pocket and lit one from there. They say quietly for a moment.

"Sorry about that," she said, nodding towards the jetty. "For some of those folks, this is like a religious event. It's not every day that you get to see the bears. They're there, of course, but it might be raining, or too hazy, or there's smoke from a fire, or they keep up close to the tree-line. Whatever. It's not every day that they're as clear as they are today."

"Do you come here every day?"

"I don't, no. For me, once a month or so is enough. But some of them do, yes."

"Is that as close as they get?"

"Usually. You might see a black bear on your way down the Parkway, but not normally a grizzly."

"You said you saw one close up, though."

"Yes, but that wasn't here."

She had finished her cigarette, so he pulled out his packet and offered her another.

"I have to be back at the Prince of Wales Hotel by nine," he said. "So, if it's not too long, what was the story?"

The woman laughed at him.

"Well, it was up on the Icefields Parkway, actually. Do you know that road? It runs between Lake Louise and Jasper."

"Yes, I've driven along there. It's one of the ten most scenic drives in the world or something."

"That's what the tourism people say, yes. And it is pretty. I was up there one spring, a couple of years back, with my daughter. We lived in Calgary at the time, so decided to do the loop up and across to Edmonton, then back down the highway. You get to see a whole bunch of pretty little towns, Banff, Lake Louise, Saskatchewan Crossing, Jasper, places like that. We had the whole weekend off and so we took a tent, to have a bit of an adventure.

"We took our time and spent part of the Friday afternoon at the eagle tracking place at Hay Meadow. Have you heard of that?"

Rashford shook his head.

"It's down in the Kananaskis valley, south from Canmore. It's about a twenty-minute drive from the main highway, you take the turnoff for Kananaskis village and the Nakiska ski resort. Just past the second turn to the village is a road on the right that is signposted for the Stoney Trailhead. You go in there for a couple of hundred metres and there's a good parking area, then you walk to where they have the scopes set up. We spent nearly two hours watching eagles and other raptors, it was brilliant."

"What, like bald eagles?"

"Mainly golden eagles, actually, although there are bald eagles as well. And northern goshawks, turkey vultures, red tailed hawks, ospreys. You name it, it probably flies over. The crazy thing is that nobody even knew the flyway existed until the early nineteen nineties. This is one of the major flyways on the continent, all the raptors going north. And coming back again in the fall, of course."

"Of course," said Rashford, a bit bemused at her passion.

"Sorry. I like watching the eagles. They are so majestic. But so are the bears. Back to my story. Anyway, my daughter and I stopped at this little campground on the Icefields Parkway, about half an hour out of Lake Louise. The camp had a simple layout. You drove into the central area, where there were the toilets and a woodpile, then the sites were on this road that looped out and back through the trees.

"It had a mix of camper trailers and tents, with the campers in closer to the electricity posts and the tents back more in the woods. We set up our tent at one of the sites, then went exploring, did a short hike up the valley on the other side of the road, that kind of thing.

"Actually, that reminds me. Are you Scottish?"

"No," said Rashford. "Not that I know of. Why?"

"Oh, just a funny thing. We were up on this hike, we'd just passed a rock pile with all these big marmots running around, when we heard bagpipes. We went around the corner and there was this fellow, standing on a rock, playing. He stopped when he saw us and came down to the trail.

"'My wife won't let me play in the house,' he said. 'I'm just learning.'"

Rashford roared with laughter, earning acrimonious looks both from the bear watchers on the jetty and also from a group who were disembarking from a minibus that had pulled up next to the visitor centre. Some were looking at the trail maps taped to the inside of the visitor centre windows, others were lifting backpacks and checking the water supply in their thermos flasks.

"Was he wearing a kilt?" he said.

"No, sadly. Just jeans and a wind jacket."

"No fair."

"Indeed. Well, my daughter and I just laughed and told him he sounded fine. So, he went back to his rock, and we continued our hike. He wasn't there when we came back, more's the pity.

"We got back to the campground and that night it rained and rained heavily. Our tent was a new one, so I was up half the night checking to see if it leaked. My daughter slept through. At dawn the rain stopped but I realized that I needed to go to the washroom. My daughter was still sleeping, so I snuck out and walked down the road.

"It was just getting light. I came round the edge of the last camper van into the clearing and there, right in front of me, was a grizzly. It was digging at the roots of a plant but as soon as I came round the corner, it stopped and looked straight at me. I counted later. It was forty-four paces away.

"That's pretty close," said Rashford. "What, thirty metres?"

"My steps are pretty small, yeah, so about that," she said.

"I was surprised at how big it was. It was big and really long, you know? I always thought they were stocky animals, but this one was long, maybe two metres. I just froze. I went into automatic threat assessment mode, like you do."

"Right," said Rashford, although privately he thought he would probably have turned and run away.

"The thing is not to scare them. So, I just stood there. Grizzlies don't have good eyesight, you know, but they have good hearing and an excellent sense of smell. There was a creek running down the side of the campground and I could hear the water rushing over the stones, so I thought maybe he wouldn't hear me. The wind was blowing across the woodpile, so it was coming from behind him, so I figured he couldn't smell me properly. So, I didn't move.

"After a couple of minutes, he put his head down and started digging again at the root of the plant. I took a single step backwards, and immediately his head came up again. He was looking right at me, moving his head from side to side. I remember his eyes looked very bright. I just froze again.

"This time I waited longer. He dug up the plant and ate it, then sniffed around and moved towards one of the camper vans. It was a pick-up truck, really, with one of those lid things on the back tray. As soon as his head was behind the truck, I stepped back behind the camper, and went back to our tent.

"There I did what was most probably the most stupid thing I've ever done in my life. I shook my daughter awake and said, 'come on, get up, come and see the grizzly.'

"She jumped out of her sleeping bag and put on her shoes, and we walked back to the camper. I looked round the corner first, then beckoned her to look. The bear had moved, it was about sixty paces away now, still sniffing around the tyres of the camper vans and trucks. We watched for maybe five or ten minutes. He was beautiful.

"I wanted a photograph, but I was worried that the bear would spook at the click. So, we went back to our tent, and I got my camera. We sat in the car, and I wound down the passenger window, then gave my daughter the camera. I told her that as soon as the car appeared, the bear would probably run away, so she would have to be quick to take a picture.

"I drove slowly down the road and then into the open area. The bear was already moving away from us. He looked over his shoulder at the car, then brought his front right leg forward in a big scooping motion, like he was throwing a ball, and as soon as his paw hit the ground he was gone. He was amazingly fast. It made me realize, if he had come at me that fast, I wouldn't have had a chance. My daughter missed him altogether, but she did get a nice photograph of the toilets."

Rashford laughed again.

"Well, thank you," he said, rising to his feet. "That was a lovely story."

"You're welcome," she said, and stood up as well. She shook hands with Rashford.

"I'd better go back to my scope," she said. "It was nice to meet you. I might see you at the hotel later, we usually stop there for a coffee and a late breakfast after we've been down here."

They stood to one side so as not to impede the people from the minibus. These were settling out into small groups of two or three, checking their maps, and then heading off down a trail that started behind the visitor centre.

"Where are they off to, I wonder," said Rashford.

The woman looked.

"Oh, that's the trail back to Waterton campsite, it brings you out at the Cameron Falls lookout. It's a full day hike, about seven hours. Maybe six if you were really fit, although there is a scree slope you've got to be careful on. It's quite a long traverse and pretty tricky."

"So, what, they get the bus here and then walk back?"

"Basically, yes. There's a company that runs the shuttle bus, so you can leave your car in town. Some people stay around here overnight, even though you're not supposed to, and get an early start so they can photograph the sun coming up behind Mount Alderson."

"What, they just set up a camp? Don't the wardens mind?"

"Like I said, you're not supposed to, but I guess if you hid in the trees until dark, nobody is going to be checking round here at night. Like, this morning, my friend and I got here at about six, we like to be set up before the bears come out.

"We were the first ones here today; the others arrived over the next half hour or so. I stepped over here to have a smoke and saw this fellow heading down to the trailhead. He came out of the trees up there."

She pointed to her left, where a line of trees stood about fifty metres back from the car park.

"So, he got a good early start, it was hardly even light out," she said.

"I watched the sunrise this morning, from Knight's Lake, over the Vimy Peak. That's what the map on my phone said, anyway. It was pretty awesome. I hope his photographs were worth it," said Rashford, heading to his car.

As he drove away, he saw that the woman was back with her friends, bent over the scope and pointing excitedly at what she was seeing. He made it back to the townsite in fifteen minutes, there were no bears or big horn sheep to slow him down and he continued up the bluff to the Prince of Wales Hotel.

As Rashford entered the lobby, he saw that he was the last to arrive. Everyone else was sitting at a table, coffee in front of them, chatting amicably.

"Good morning, Sergeant, good of you to join us," said Inspector Whitehead, smiling to take the sting out of his words. "A lot of traffic in the Mountain View rush hour, was there?"

"No, sir, I've been checking out the area. I went down to the end of the Cameron Lake Road and back."

"Did you find anything?"

"No, sir, sorry sir. Just some bear watchers and some hikers."

"Well, never mind. You can't win them all. Get a coffee then come and sit down. I've got some news."

Rashford did as instructed, nodding at the team as he joined them.

Like the rest of them, he studiously ignored the love bite visible on Matheson's neck, just above the collar. Instead, he took a sip of the scalding coffee.

"Right," said the Inspector. "This is where we are."

He looked around at the group, tapping his index finger on a neatly folded map that was on the table in front of him.

"Nowhere."

The five officers simultaneously picked up their coffee cups, trying to avoid eye contact.

"But I do have some information, although I'm not sure how relevant it might be. The Forensics team really outdid themselves. They got Calgary to process the sandwich and water glass we got from the house."

Rashford looked up.

"What, already?"

"I know. Amazing, isn't it? But yes, they did it overnight."

Whitehead paused, making sure he had everyone's attention.

"We have a name," he said. "Claude Dallas."

Rashford jumped to his feet and punched the air.

"Yes!" he said, causing a number of tourists to turn and look at their table.

"Sergeant, please control yourself," said Whitehead in a harsh voice. "Remember you're in uniform."

Rashford sat down but kept pumping his fists up and down, causing his colleagues to edge away from his flailing elbows.

Whitehead picked up his pen and tapped it on his teeth.

"Do tell us what the fuck you think you're doing," he said, slowly.

Rashford calmed down and faced the Inspector.

"Sorry, sir. It's just, I know this man. Claude Dallas. Although that's not his real name."

"That's what it says on the file."

"Yes, because that's the only name I had when we first put his DNA in the data bank, sir. This is who I thought we were chasing, based on some other indications, but it was all circumstantial. Now we've got proof that it's the same man."

"So Fancy Boots is Claude Dallas but he's really someone else?"

"Yes, sir. He has used a number of aliases, sir. I don't know which one he's using now."

"And you know of him, how, exactly?"

"He caused me a lot of trouble a couple of years ago. I ended up chasing him all across Alasama and caught him at the Canadian border. But he escaped."

"Oh, that's right, I remember hearing something about that," said Hamill, nodding. "Didn't he sucker punch a ... oh."

"Something like that, right," said Rashford, blushing.

"Wasn't he an Army vet?" said Hamill, trying to recover from his gaffe.

"Possibly. I've not been able to figure out what he called himself when he served. But, yes, I think he served in Afghanistan, maybe two tours. He's certainly got some tremendous in-country skills."

"Let's park that information for the moment," said Whitehead. "It's good that we might know who he is, or was, but it doesn't help tell us where he might be. Okay?"

The group nodded.

"Right, well, the wardens have been out since early this morning, checking the car parks. There is a drone ready to fly if we get any leads, but it's pointless sending it up when we don't know what we're looking for, or where. We need a plan."

Whitehead unfolded the map, smoothing out the creases so that it lay flat.

"This is a map of the national park. Somewhere in here, there is an English Racing Green coloured Audi R8 Spyder convertible valued at over a quarter of a million dollars. Someone must have seen it. Someone must know where it is. All we have to do is find it, and the fellow who drove it in here."

He pointed to the red lines which criss-crossed the map.

"As you can see, there are basically four roads here, plus the townsite. The Entrance Parkway comes in from the highway to the park gate, and then into town. The Bison Paddock loop is just that, a loop up off the road as you come in from Pincher Creek, and then highway six continues about eleven kilometres to the big lookoff point that gives the view back towards the park. The Red Rock Parkway goes west from the townsite, and then north a bit, about ten kilometres, and the Akamina Parkway goes west and then south, to Cameron Lake. Where you were this morning, Sergeant, and about what, fifteen or twenty klicks?"

"About that, sir, yes," said Rashford.

"So, this is what we shall do. While we're waiting, we shall not just sit here, we'll make ourselves visible. Lights but no sirens. I want you to drive up and down, keep an eye out for the Spyder of course, but mainly I want this joker to know we're in the area.

"Hamill, you take highway 6. Drive out to the bison paddock and do the loop, follow the highway to the lookoff, turn around and drive back to the paddock, repeat. Clear?"

"Yes, sir."

"What's the difference between a buffalo and a bison," said Rashford. They all looked at him.

"I don't know, Sergeant," said Whitehead, patiently. "Enlighten us, please."

"You can't wash your hands in a buffalo."

Hamill and MacNeill both laughed. Whitehead shook his head. Matheson turned to Larsen.

"I don't get it," he said.

"Ask Darlene," said Larsen.

"Moving on," said Whitehead. "MacNeill, you do circuits from the townsite to Red Rock Canyon and back. Matheson, you're on the Entrance Road, from the highway to town and back, stop in every so often at the gate and ask if they've seen anything. Rashford, you can keep doing the loop to Cameron Lake on the Akamina Highway, you already know that one.

"I'll keep cruising around the town site and up to here and back. Remember, we're after high visibility. Lights but no sirens, I don't want to scare the animals. Clear?"

"Yes, sir," they chorused.

"Right, then, saddle up. I'll call if and when I hear anything from the Warden."

Rashford had made three loops out to Cameron Lake and back before the Inspector called. It was almost ten thirty when through the static on his car radio he heard the instruction for all cars to return to the hotel. At the time he was just turning round in the small layby near the start of the Bear's Hump trail, so it was a simple matter to drive up the knoll and park outside the main entrance of the hotel. He walked inside.

Inspector Whitehead was standing with a tall man dressed in a grey short sleeved shirt, full leg cargo pants, solid looking hiking boots, and a teal green safety vest. He wore a soft tan cowboy hat and there was a sidearm on his belt, along with a baton and what looked like a can of bear spray. Emblazoned across the front of his vest was Park Warden - Garde de Parc, which gave Rashford the clue he needed.

Whitehead introduced the two men, and they all went to sit at a large round table. One of the hotel staff came over and took their orders for coffee, then left them alone. As they waited for the others to arrive, they chatted about the similarities and differences in their work. The Warden talked of having spent most of the previous day climbing all the way up the Crypt Lake trail, where he had then had to talk a tourist back down the ladder.

"Ladder?" said Rashford. "On a hike?"

"Yes," said the Warden. "It's a difficult hike. You can at least do it in a day, now, ever since they established the boat service. Before it was a multiple day event. You get the morning boat and then it's eight and a half kilometres each way, with an elevation gain of over seven hundred metres. Or, as our American friends describe it, just over ten miles in and out with a height gain of twenty-three hundred feet, give or take. It's pretty steep no matter which system you use.

"When you're nearly there, you have to go across a scree slope, it's a pretty narrow path with lots of loose rocks, they roll for ever if you kick one loose. When you get to the cliff, then you have to climb this ladder that we put in a few years ago. It's the only way up the cliff, unless you free climb, and too many people were falling off. So, you go up the ladder and then through this tunnel in the rock, it's pretty narrow and about three or four metres long, ten or twelve feet. Some people find it claustrophobic.

"Anyway, when you come out the other end, there's another narrow ledge to cross. This isn't on a scree slope, it's a drop-off, so that can be pretty scary. We put in a wire cable so that people had something to hang on to, especially if it was windy, and some wise guy put up a 'For psychological support only' sign. We left it there. As I said, it's a special hike."

"It sounds like it," said Rashford, who wasn't really that keen on heights, exposed narrow trails, or small, closed spaces. "So, what happened with this tourist?"

"Well," said the Warden, "he got up okay, and enjoyed his lunch by the lake, had a paddle, all that kind of thing. Then the group started to come back down and, of course, you have to go back the way you came. This fellow got across the cable section okay. Unfortunately, he came out of the tunnel to the top of the ladder and made the mistake of looking down. That was it. He froze. He just would not move.

"There were six people in his group, three couples. Two had already gone down the ladder, the third was at the top waiting to give a hand, but there were two people behind him, still in the tunnel. And remember, there were still other people up there, at the lake.

"This guy just would not, or could not, move. He was absolutely petrified. Apparently, they all tried to talk to him, to get him to at least move out of the way a bit. But he wouldn't. Eventually the two in the tunnel backed out, turned round, and went back over the chain section again. They talked to the other groups as they came up and explained the situation.

"Some of the other hikers were pretty mad, because you have to be back for the boat by a certain time, or you miss it. They had judged their hike without taking this kind of event into account. But what could they do?

"The fellow on the ladder went down and talked to the two women who had already gone down. They'd all tried their cell phones, of course, but there's no coverage up there. So, the two women hiked back down the mountain as fast as they could and got to the boat jetty. There they were lucky because there was another boat there, not the *International*, which is the tourist boat, but a smaller personal vessel. The owner had a satellite phone and let them use it to call us.

"I got the call and decided that there was only one thing to do. We have a small helicopter here, it's really just for emergencies, so I called in and got them to take me to Crypt Lake. Then I went along the cable and through the tunnel and, sure enough, this guy is still there. On his hands and knees, just frozen to the spot. At least his butt was far enough out that I could see around him.

"I called down to his buddy, who was still at the bottom of the ladder, and asked him to climb up. When he got to us, I told him to hold onto his friend by the shoulders. Then I slapped this guy on the ass, and I spoke to him in a really quiet voice."

The Warden dropped his voice to a whisper, and both Rashford and Whitehead had to lean in to hear him properly.

"'You've got two choices, friend,' I said to him. 'You either get up and climb down that ladder, or I'm going to shoot you in the butt with this bear tranquilizer dart.'"

"I reached over his shoulder and waved it in front of him, so he could see I wasn't bluffing. It's a big yellow dart with a syringe that's about a quarter-inch thick on the end."

"'If you're lucky,' I said, 'then your friend there will grab your shoulders, and I'll hold your legs, and we'll carry your unconscious self down that ladder. If you're not lucky, and we drop you, or if you twitch suddenly, or if you wake up earlier than I expect and struggle yourself free, then we'll try to make sure your wife has a big enough piece to identify you properly. Your call.'"

The Warden sat back in his chair and scratched his stomach. Whitehead stared at him.

"What happened?"

"Oh, nothing, really. He got up and climbed down the ladder, then I helped everyone else through the tunnel, then we all walked down to the boat. Just a normal day in the life, you know?"

The two police officers looked at each other.

"Would you really have used a tranquillizer dart on a tourist?" said Rashford, contemplating the amount of paperwork that such an act would no doubt precipitate.

"I did last time," said the Warden. "Oh, good, here are your colleagues."

He ushered everyone to the table and introduced himself. Whitehead looked at Rashford and shrugged his shoulders.

"They're crazier than we are," he said in a low voice, tilting his head towards the Warden.

"I think a pinch of salt might be helpful," said Rashford, nodding. "But there again, you never know!"

The two joined everyone else around the table.

"Right, gentlemen, we have found the Spyder," said the Warden. "It was parked on a maintenance trail, pulled off the main road and loosely hidden by some brush."

The Inspector spread out his map of the park.

"Where abouts is it?" he said.

"Here," said the Warden, stabbing his finger on to a point nearly at the end of the Akamina Parkway. "Just opposite the Akamina Trailhead."

"Where does that go?" said Matheson.

"Up to Forum Lake and Wall Lake. It's a good long loop. You go up an old logging road and then into the high country. The forested section is a bit dreary now, nothing has really recovered from the Kenow fire of 2017, but the views at the top are still magnificent."

"Are there any back-country campgrounds up there?" said Hamill.

"No, you're not allowed to overnight. Most people do one or the other, not the loop. They like to leave early in the morning, around seven, then have a late morning swim and some lunch up at the lake. It really is a magnificent setting, these huge cliffs towering over the lake. Then it's an easy hike back down and you're at your car by two o'clock, lots of time to get home for a beer."

"So, it just goes up to a couple of lakes, and some views, then you come down again?" said Rashford.

"Pretty much."

"Then he's bluffing. Why would he go up there?"

"Bluff or not, we'll have to check it out," said the Inspector. "How long is the hike?"

"Anywhere from a half to a full day, really," said the Warden. "I'd say most people would take four or five hours for Wall Lake or Forum Lake, seven or eight hours for the full loop."

"I'm sorry, I just don't see it," said Rashford. "Let me see the map. What else is close to the trailhead?"

"Nothing, really," said the Warden. "You're about a kilometre from Cameron Lake, I guess he could steal a kayak and paddle to the States, but that seems a bit crazy."

"We need to go down there and see the car," said Inspector Whitehead. "He might have left some clues around."

"And he might be up on one of the trails, waiting for us to leave," said Hamill. "Sergeant, didn't you say he was an Army vet?"

"Yes."

"So, he could probably survive up there for as long as it takes."

"He probably could," said Rashford. "But why would he? Let's think this through."

"Less thinking and more action, Sergeant," said the Inspector.

The Warden ran his hand over his chin.

"I don't know," he said. "I tend to agree with the Sergeant. Why would you drive yourself into a bottleneck?"

"How about this theory," said Rashford. "We went to his house, and he escaped. No, that's not quite true. He knew we were coming, and he walked away.

"He stole a fancy car, but that was because it was the first one that he saw. He noticed the Park Pass so he drove in through the gate, making sure he went through at the same time as a big group. He parked off the road and hid the car, but not so far off that we wouldn't find it. He's trying to point us in that direction."

"Yes," said the Warden. "And while we are looking there, he's somewhere else. Classic sleight of hand."

"But where is he, then?" said Whitehead. "Where do we look if he's not where we think he is, or was?"

"Just a minute," said Rashford, standing up quickly. "I'll be right back."

He walked rapidly away from the group and into the Royal Stewart dining room.

"Maybe he ate something?" said Matheson.

Chapter 11

When Rashford returned to the group, he was ushering in front of him a middle-aged woman with spikey blonde hair. She wore pale blue stonewashed jeans and a burnt brick coloured jacket. Her lightweight fall jacket was open, revealing a black sweater with a deep cup neck design.

"Inspector, please may I introduce Ms. Suzanne Stordy," he said. "We met this morning, and I'd like you to hear what she says. Ms. Stordy, this is Inspector Whitehead, and the Park Warden. Sorry, sir, I don't know your name?"

"Frank Giles, ma'am," said the Warden, lifting his cap as he nodded his head. "Pleased to meet you."

The Inspector pointed to the chair vacated by Rashford.

"Please, sit down," he said.

Once she was settled the other officers each introduced themselves. Rashford stood behind her chair. Whitehead looked up at him.

"Right you are, Sergeant. What's this all about."

"As I said, sir, I met Ms. Stordy this morning, when I was down at Cameron Lake. She was one of the bear watchers I mentioned, sir."

"Right. Yes. Alright, why is this useful?"

"Ms. Stordy, please could you tell the Inspector what you told me this morning?"

"Yes, of course," she said, readjusting herself in the chair and straightening her posture. She focused on the Inspector and the Warden but managed to include the whole group in her story.

"Some friends and I come to Cameron Lake once a month, for the bear watch. You'll know of that, I'm sure, Warden?"

"Indeed, I do, yes. A passionate group of animal advocates, for sure."

"Some more passionate than others, I'm afraid," she said. "My friends and I are not in the daily or even weekly category, once a month is sufficient for us. This morning happened to be our day.

"We got to the parking lot at around six o'clock and set up the spotting scope. I have my own binoculars but sometimes the scope gives you a better view. I went behind the Visitor Centre to have a quiet smoke and saw this fellow come out of the woods. He walked down and left on the Carthew trail."

"Was he a photographer?" said the Warden. "They sometimes sneak in early to take sunrise shots of Mount Alderson."

"Well, that's what I had thought, and that's what I told the officer here," she said, gesturing to Rashford.

"And I believed her, sir," said Rashford. "Then I started to wonder. Ms. Stordy has not said anything about a camera bag, or backpack, or anything like that. She had mentioned that she and her friends come here for brunch after the bear watch, sir, so I thought it worth looking to see if they were still here." He turned to look at her. "Can you tell us, what did he look like?"

"Well, he was too far away for any detail, of course. But he looked like a hiker, you know. He was slim, not too tall, and he walked quickly. Like the Sergeant said, no backpack. He wasn't wearing a hat, at least I don't remember seeing one."

"If it's alright, sir," said Rashford, "I would like to ask her to come down to the lake and show us where this fellow emerged. Let's have a look and see if we can find anything."

"That's fine with me," said the Inspector. "Ms. Stordy?"

"Can I tell my friends where I'm going?"

"Of course. And you won't be long, someone will drive you back here."

"Right. Thank you."

The woman rose to her feet and shook hands with Whitehead, who immediately started to sneeze. He covered his face with his other hand and backed away, apologizing.

"Oh, I do hope you're not allergic to me," she said, laughing, as she walked away from the table.

The Inspector recovered, blowing his nose noisily into a handkerchief he had pulled out from his pocket. He put the handkerchief back into his pocket, glanced at his watch, then looked around at his team.

"It's just after eleven," he said. "Hamill, you and Larsen go to the Park Gate and relieve those wardens. Then set up a proper roadblock. Search every car going out, you're looking for a single male. Check all of them."

"Yes, sir," they chorused.

"MacNeill, you and Matheson go down to this trailhead and examine the car. Try not to disturb anything, we might need Forensics to have a look."

"Yes, sir."

"Warden, would you be able to lead them there, and then come down to the lake and meet us?"

"Of course."

"Great. Rashford, you bring Ms. Stordy down in your car, I'll follow you. Questions, anyone?"

There were none.

"Right, saddle up," said the Inspector. "Rashford, the Warden and I will be out at the car, come out as soon as she comes back."

Rashford nodded, then walked across towards the dining room. He saw Suzanne Stordy at a table, leaning over to speak with a man and two other women. Rashford recognized the man, whose neon pink jacket hung on the back of his chair, as the one with the spotting scope down on the jetty. They all turned to look at him, then nodded at something Suzanne was saying. She left the group and walked back to Rashford.

"All good," she said. "They'll stay here drinking coffee and gossiping until we get back."

Rashford smiled.

"Excellent," he said. "Well, better not keep the Inspector waiting."

They left the hotel and walked over to Rashford's cruiser.

"I've never been in a police car," she said. "How exciting!"

"You'll have to go in the back," he said. "We're not allowed front-seat passengers. But we can talk through the wire."

"Cool," she said, opening the door and climbing in. "Am I going to be automatically locked in?"

"Yes. The doors lock when I put the car in gear," he said.

"What fun!"

She bounced up and down on her seat, reminding Rashford of one of his younger cousins, who was so perpetually excited at the prospect of going on rides at the local country fair that he sometimes peed himself. Rashford hoped that didn't happen here.

"Can you turn on the siren?" she said.

"Just for a moment," said Rashford, slowly driving past the Inspector, who was standing next to his car and talking to the Warden. Rashford blipped the siren as they exited the car park, causing Whitehead to look up with a grimace and the Warden to tip his hat. Susanne clapped her hands excitedly.

Rashford shook his head and smiled, then drove down the parkway.

They got to the visitor centre and only had to wait a few minutes until Inspector Whitehead arrived. Suzanne pointed up to the tree line and indicated where she had seen the man come out of the forest.

"Please stay here, exactly where you were before, and point us as close to the actual place as possible," said Whitehead.

She agreed and stepped back into the shade of the building.

"I was standing right here," she said, "having a smoke."

At that point she brought out her cigarettes and lit one.

"I'll shout if you go off-line," she said.

Whitehead nodded, then he and Rashford walked slowly up towards the trees.

"Sorry I was a bit late coming down," said Whitehead, in a low voice. "The Warden was telling me something interesting."

"Which was what, sir?" said Rashford.

"Well, he claimed that there is research to show that when a woman is attracted to a man, she lets off a whole bunch of something called pheromones. They're like invisible hormones which get sprayed out unconsciously."

"Unconsciously, sir?"

"Yes. She doesn't even know she's doing it."

"Yes, sir. And then what happens?"

"Well, the man reacts. Sometimes he just thinks, 'oh, that's a fine-looking woman', but other times, if there is a strong reaction, he starts to sneeze."

"Really, sir?"

"Yes."

Rashford was not quite sure what to say, so he said nothing. He kept walking. As they approached the treeline, Whitehead continued.

"I think Ms. Stordy is a fine-looking woman, don't you?"

Rashford kept walking.

"And she made me sneeze, so maybe she likes me. What do you think?"

"I think all the Warden's stories need a pinch of salt, sir," said Rashford, trying not to laugh out loud.

Whitehead grumbled something under his breath, then stopped and turned around. He waved down to Suzanne Stordy, who waved back, indicating they should move to their left. They followed her instructions for a few minutes until she suddenly held her hands above her head and clapped.

"Right there," she shouted.

Rashford looked around at the grasses and shrubs that formed the under-canopy. He noticed the broken stem of a late blooming bear grass flower, the white club-like head of florets now angled towards the ground. Letting his gaze drift further back into the stand, he saw other stems which had been snapped.

"He came here, sir, look," he said, pointing out the various breaks. "If you go around the edge, sir, I'll spot you to the last break I can see. Then we can look from there, without losing the trail."

Whitehead nodded and walked into the trees to the left of the large patch of bear grass. He circled round until Rashford told him to stop. Rashford then circled around to the right, coming up next to Whitehead but on the other side of the last broken stem he had spotted.

From this point he could see the trail clearly, leading out to the open grass, with the Visitor's Centre part way to the lake. The jetty behind was illuminated with bright sunshine, but the back of the building was still in shadow. It was only when Suzanne inhaled that Rashford saw the glowing tip of her cigarette, otherwise she blended into the dark.

He used his eyes to follow the trail up through the bear grass and half turned to see where it went next. The bear grass diminished as the woods thickened, but a stand of ferns took its place. Again, he saw some broken fronds, and then a small area where the grasses were all beaten down.

"There," he said, pointing. "That's where he slept."

The two men approached carefully. The grasses and ferns had been pushed down and formed a shallow bed, much like that formed by a deer or a moose when it lies up during the day. This was different only in its size, and in the traces of a small campfire that had been built some two metres away. Next to the ashes was a small heap of soil.

Rashford squatted next to the fire and brushed away the soil with the back of his hand, uncovering a key fob with the tell-tale four rings of power embossed upon the shaft.

"I imagine that's for the Spyder," said Whitehead, nodding. "What else has he left behind?"

Rashford carefully picked up the key fob and placed it to one side, then continued wiping the soil. After a few moments, he held up a small piece of yellow plastic, about the size of his thumb nail, with a gold square pattern on the lower quarter. The plastic was blackened and curled at the ends.

"That's a SIM card," said Whitehead. "Where's the phone?"

"It doesn't matter," said Rashford. "He either kept it, and just put in a new SIM card, or else he broke it into pieces and threw it away, it could be anywhere. This is the important bit, I bet forensics can use this."

"But he's burned it."

"It doesn't matter. They'll still be able to get data from it, you have to cook them at more than four hundred and fifty degrees before they are properly incinerated. I think he just burned this in his fire, then buried it, figuring nobody would ever find this site."

They spent the next five minutes carefully checking the area but there were no other items of interest. They walked back down to the visitor centre and met Suzanne, who was chatting to the Warden.

"What time did you see him, exactly?" said Whitehead.

"I don't know exactly. Between six and six fifteen is my best guess."

"Thank you. Warden, this is the Carthew trail, is it?

"Yes. Well, the Carthew-Alderson Traverse, to be precise."

"And where does it go?"

"It goes back to Waterton Lake townsite. It's a beautiful but pretty strenuous hike, usually seven hours or more. Some people have said it's one of the prettiest hikes in the park. You go through lots of different terrain, crossing through fir forests, sub-alpine and alpine meadows, bare scree and rock. There are some lovely little tarns or mountain lakes, lots of wildflowers, and views that will take your breath away."

"I don't think our friend is here for the scenery, Warden," said Rashford. "He's got to have another reason for being here."

"Well, I think we need to be at the trailhead to meet him, don't you?" said the Inspector. "It's a quarter to twelve. If he left here just after six, even if he hiked non-stop he won't get to town until one or later."

He thought for a moment.

"Ms. Stordy, I will drive you back to your friends. Warden, if you come behind us, then you can show me where this trail ends. I'll wait there. Sergeant Rashford, please can you go and join MacNeill and MacPherson, and see if this fob works on the car. Leave one of them with the car to wait for Forensics and bring the other back to the town. I'll radio with directions to the trailhead."

Rashford nodded, then watched with amusement as the Inspector opened the front passenger side door of his cruiser, carefully moved the files and laptop computer to the back seat, and then indicated to Suzanne Stordy that she should get in. Rashford got into his own car then laughed outright when Whitehead suddenly paused at the door, sneezed, then blew his nose loudly before climbing into the driver's seat. As he drove out onto the Parkway the Warden pulled out behind and followed.

Rashford waited patiently while MacNeill walked to the car and blipped the key fob. The lights on the Spyder flashed brightly, and there was an audible click as the doors unlocked.

"Do we look inside?" said Macpherson.

"Look but don't touch," said Rashford.

MacNeill walked around the car.

"It's pretty clean," he said. "She looks after it well. The inside looks like it's just been detailed."

"There's bits of a cell phone on the floor, under the edge of the front seat," said Matheson, opening the door carefully and peering inside.

Rashford went over and stood at his shoulder.

"Where?"

"There," said Matheson, pointing. The light was poor, and the colour of the casing matched the slate grey of the floor mat in front of the seat, but Rashford could just make out the two parts of a cell phone.

He stood back from the car, puzzled, running various recent conversations through his head. Suddenly he snapped his fingers.

"Of course," he said. "Matheson, stay here with the car. Don't let anybody touch it until Forensics get here.

"Also, make sure that you can watch the road. The cruiser is out there, keep your lights on so that everyone knows you are here. MacNeill, give him the key fob, and the keys to the cruiser. You're coming with me. Quickly now!"

Rashford had the car started and was already pulling away before MacNeill was in the front seat. He hurriedly put on his seat belt as Rashford turned on the emergency lights and siren as he accelerated up the road. He used the car radio to call Inspector Whitehead.

"Sir, we got it wrong. Please come back to the hotel, I'll meet you there. I have MacNeill with me."

"What are you talking about?" said Whitehead. "I'm in position at the trailhead. I have to stay here, or we'll miss him."

"We already missed him, sir. Please, come back to the hotel."

"On your shoulders, Sergeant," said the Inspector. "I'll be there in five minutes."

"So will we," said Rashford, swerving to avoid a group of hikers who suddenly appeared from the Rowe Creek trailhead. Startled, they ducked back into the trees behind the wooden sign that marked their exit. MacNeill grabbed hold of the safety handle, his left hand extended forward onto the dashboard.

The two cars arrived outside the Prince of Wales hotel at almost the same time. Whitehead got out and started walking towards Rashford.

"Now, what's all this about, Sergeant," he said.

"In a moment, sir," said Rashford, almost running as he strode rapidly into the hotel. Whitehead and MacNeill looked at each other, then followed.

They found Rashford in the Royal Steward dining room, standing over Suzanne Stordy and the rest of her group. Stordy was bent over the table, holding her head in her hands, while the man with the fluorescent pink jacket was nodding at something Rashford was saying. The other two women were looking surprised, one with her hand held to her mouth.

Rashford put one of his hands on Stordy's shoulder and his other on the shoulder of the man with the pink jacket. His body language showed that he was speaking to both of them, and they each nodded in confirmation. Rashford released his grip and walked back to the other officers.

"Well, Sergeant?" said the Inspector.

"I think I've figured it out, sir," said Rashford. "Can we sit down?"

"Yes, over there," said Whitehead, pointing to an empty table in front of one of the large windows. "MacNeill, get us some coffees, would you? Thanks."

Whitehead sat with his back to the window, giving Rashford the view down the lake. This strategy also kept the Inspector's face in shadow, whereas Rashford's was fully illuminated.

"Talk to me," said the Inspector.

Rashford took a deep breath.

"Two things have been puzzling me, sir. Well, three, actually. First, why come here, to Waterton Park. He could have taken that car from Mountain View and driven anywhere. If he hadn't dropped the sweater then he would have been a hundred klicks away before we realized he was gone.

"Second, once here, why stay here, overnight? And then, third, why take a one-way trail back to the town. It didn't make any sense. When we found the camp site he made, and the fob from the car, I thought he was just trying to keep things hidden, that he had thought nobody would ever find them. But I think I was wrong. I think the fob and the SIM card were left there on purpose. To misdirect us."

"How did he know we would find them?"

"Because he made himself visible. When we were up at the tree line, looking back towards the jetty, the whole back of the cabin was in shadow. The sun would have been shining right into his eyes as he came out of the woods by that bear grass. And the bear grass was white, remember, so he would have stood out even more against that background.

"Yet this guy, this experienced veteran who has probably forgotten more about camouflage than I ever knew, he walks out in full view. Why? He was trying to attract attention.

"Then I started to wonder, whose attention did he need to catch? Ms. Stordy was in the shadows, but she said she was having a cigarette, so she would have been looking in that direction. He wouldn't need to do anything clever for her to see him. Unless she wasn't just having a cigarette.

"That's what I just asked her, sir. I'm sorry, I know you like her, but she just admitted that she and Paul come here for more than the bears."

"Paul? Who is Paul?

"The fellow with the bright neon pink fleece lined jacket, sir. He and Suzanne Stordy are more than friends. They try to arrive at the car park before dawn, half an hour before the others. Then they go behind the visitor centre for a quickie before the others arrive. That's why he's got a fleece lined coat while everyone else has a light fall jacket. They put it down on the ground and lay on it while they, umm, while they're busy, sir."

"And he watched them?"

"I think so, sir. He waited until they were finished, anyway. She said that she had stood up and was pulling on her jeans when he stepped out of the woods. She tried to pull Paul back into the shadows, but she said the jacket was really bright, the fellow must have seen it. But he didn't do or say anything, he just walked across the slope and off down to the trail."

"So, what makes you think he wanted us to learn that?"

"I couldn't think, sir. Then we found the key fob for the car, and the SIM card. It was only when we used the fob to open the door, and Constable Matheson found the component parts of a mobile phone on the floor of the Spyder, under the edge of the front passenger seat, that it all started to make sense."

"Not to me, Sergeant. Please, enlighten me."

Rashford wiped his hands over his cheeks, then took a sip of the coffee that MacNeill had just placed in front of him, before going off to sit in the spare chair at the end of the table.

"I spoke with Roxanne last night, sir. She's my friend, my partner I'd guess you might say. She is living with me in Maple Creek. Yesterday morning, around ten o'clock, she saw some bikers cruise up and down the street. They seemed particularly interested in the Ford 150 pick-up that I have parked outside the detachment. That's the thing that started all this."

"A pick-up truck?"

"Yes sir, but don't worry about that just now. Other than, let's imagine that they were looking for the pick-up, what would they do, once they found it?"

"Call it in?"

"Exactly. I think they called it in to the fellow who had hired them to look for it. And that would have been mid to late yesterday, when he was driving the Spyder. So, then he went to Plan B."

"Hang on. What was Plan A?"

"I think he was going to hide the car in the brush, like he did, then steal a car from the trailhead parking lot. People leave their vehicles there while they go up to the lakes, they are gone for hours. Then he would just have driven home. But now he had new information.

"Plan B was to sit somewhere quiet and think it all through. He is a planner; he doesn't usually rush into things. So, he hid the car, then took the phone apart and kept the SIM card. Then he went and found that little nest we discovered, up behind the visitor centre. He probably stayed there all afternoon. Once it got to evening and the tourists went home, he could go down and examine all the maps, the windows of the centre are filled with them.

"He lit his little fire, maybe had something to eat, burned the SIM card, then buried it and the key fob where we were bound to find it should we get to the camp site. Then he waited.

"In the morning, after Ms. Stordy and Paul had finished their little romp, but were probably a bit distracted worrying that the rest of their friends would soon arrive, he showed himself. Did you notice, we could easily find the trail out from his nest, but we didn't see anywhere where he had gone in. He left that trail for us to find, as well."

"But he went on the hiking trail, so why aren't we there at the end of it, waiting for him?"

"No, he didn't. I think he went maybe fifty metres down the trail, until he was out of sight, then hooked back towards the main road. He would have kept in the trees and walked back up to the Akamina trail-head, where he had hidden the Spyder. Then he waited there for the first early morning hikers to arrive.

"As soon as he saw a vehicle he liked, driven by people who looked like they were going for a serious day of hiking up in the mountains, he would have waited until nobody was around, then come out of hiding and stolen the car. He knew he had at least four hours to make his getaway, even if they just took the shortest trail. By seven thirty he would have been on his way out of the park."

Rashford paused, thinking back to the car that had passed him earlier that morning, on his first drive down to Cameron Lake. He could not remember the model of car, only that it had been some kind of sporty SUV, dark blue or black in colour. The driver had been wearing a baseball cap, pulled low over his eyes, but Rashford could not remember anything else about him.

"What is it?" said the Inspector.

"No, nothing," said Rashford, shaking his head as if to clear it. "I saw a car this morning, it was going the wrong way, but perhaps it had just dropped off some hikers or bear watchers. No matter. So, anyway, our man steals a car early this morning, knowing the theft won't be discovered for hours, and heads off out of the park."

"Where does he go?" said MacNeill.

"That's the big question, yes," said the Inspector.

"Shit," said Rashford, getting to his feet so rapidly that his coffee spilled all over the table. "Maple Creek."

"Maple Creek?"

"Yes. He got the call about the truck, now he's stolen a car to go and find it. Not for the truck itself, but for the things inside it."

"Sergeant, slow down," said Whitehead. "What things?"

"His medicine bundles. Sorry, sir, I've got to go," said Rashford, snatching up his hat. "As soon as Matheson radios in with the vehicle report, please can you relay it to me?"

"What vehicle report? You're not making any sense, Sergeant."

"The stolen vehicle report, sir. When the hikers get back to the trailhead and find that their car is missing, Matheson is the first policeman they'll see so they'll report it to him. I need to know the make and licence plate, please."

Rashford strode rapidly out of the dining room and through the main atrium, not noticing the aggrieved looks of any of the tourists who he pushed out of his way, not admiring the embossed wooden panels or ornate chairs. His boots scuffed the thick carpets, his mind raced.

Outside he got into his car, turned on the lights and siren, and sped away down the wooded drive. He hardly slowed at the junction with the entrance parkway, causing a camper van to brake violently as he swung out in front of it. At the park gate he swerved around the police cruiser that had been parked across the road, Hamill and Larsen looking at each other in surprise. Then he was gone.

As he raced down Highway 5 towards Cardston, Rashford put his cell phone on hands-free and called Roxanne. The tones rang for some time, then clicked into a recorded message.

"Roxanne, please call me. It's urgent," said Rashford, then strummed the steering wheel in frustration. Cars pulled over to the side of the road as he approached, and a quick check of the instruments showed that he had plenty of fuel. He keyed his radio and called Gayle Morgan. She answered immediately.

"Where are you?" said Rashford.

"I've just looped around at Fox Valley and am heading back to Leader. Why?"

"I need you to get to Maple Creek, stat. I think Roxanne might be in trouble."

"In trouble? Why? What's happening?"

"I'll tell you the whole story later. But I think that the Snake Boots guy is on his way to the detachment, to get his truck back. His truck and all his bits."

"That stuff you showed us, in the tube?"

"Yes."

"But that's at Speedy Creek, not at the detachment."

"We know that, but he doesn't. Please get there as soon as you can. I've called Roxanne and there's no answer."

"No worries, pard'na," said Morgan. "I'm on my way. Where are you?"

"Just past Cardston. I'll there as soon as I can."

"Well, I'll be just under an hour, so I'll look after things until you get there."

"Great. Thanks."

Rashford focused on his driving. At one point he received a call from Inspector Whitehead. An angry Calgarian had accosted Matheson at the Akamina trailhead and reported that someone ruined his day. He and his girlfriend had taken the day off to go for a hike. They'd stayed overnight at the Prince of Wales Hotel, then gone for a wonderful hike up to Wall Lake, where she had accepted his marriage proposal. Then they returned to the parking lot only to find that someone had stolen his car. The Inspector provided Rashford with a description and the licence plate number.

"It sounds like you were right, again," said Whitehead.

"I wish I hadn't been," said Rashford. "I'm really worried about what I'll find when I get back."

"I'll still expect a full report, you know," said the Inspector. "I know you're this hot-shot detective, but the force lives on paperwork."

"Yes, sir," said Rashford, terminating the call. The last thing he was worried about was missing paperwork. He knew that Dallas only really wanted his keepsakes, his medicine bundle, but he also knew that that was not to be found at Maple Creek.

'And what will Dallas do then?' said Rashford to himself. Would he try and break into the police house, to see if it was in there? Would he find Roxanne? Would he recognize her? Would he try to finish whatever it was that had started at the Barrel Races bar?

Rashford had no answers to any of these questions. All he knew for certain was that he felt sick to the stomach at the thought of Roxanne being hurt, or worse. He did not hear the klaxon from the semi-trailer that he cut off, he did not see the cars pulling over to the side of the road as he approached, lights flashing, siren blaring. He just drove.

Rashford drove the three hundred and thirty kilometres to Maple Creek in just over two and a half hours. He slowed down only as he approached the outskirts of the town but was still going well over the speed limit as he pulled into the parking spaces beside the detachment.

He immediately saw that the red pick-up truck was gone. There was a dark blue Volkswagen Tiguan parked against the curb, the front wheel up on the sidewalk, and a police vehicle in the parking space next to the building. Rashford pulled up behind the SUV and jumped out of his car.

Leaving the door open, he raced up the path to the police house. The front door was open. Just then, Gayle Morgan came out of the door, a roll of yellow police tape in her hand. She put out her hand and shouted at him.

"Stop right there, Gavin. You can't come in. This is a crime scene now," she said.

He rushed up to her and she moved to block his progress, holding up both hands against his chest. He stopped, breathing heavily, looking over her shoulder.

"I mean it, Gavin. We have to let Forensics process everything first."

He saw that the frame of the door was smeared with dark stains, and there were sprays and splatters across the stoop, extending inwards across the floor. Two white plastic squares had been placed in the doorway, and it was on those that Morgan had been standing. He looked down at her, helplessly.

"But, I need, I have to go inside, I must ..."

"Not yet, Gavin," she said, more gently now. "Later."

He looked again at the bloodstains on the door frame and the floor, then sank to his knees, clutching his stomach as though in pain. He sensed Gayle Morgan guiding him down, and felt her hand on his shoulder, then everything went black.

Chapter 12

When Rashford opened his eyes, he was not sure where he was. Slowly he realized that he was in a bed, his arms strapped to his sides and an IV tube taped to the back of his hand. The sheets were tight across his chest, and the light above the bed was bright. He moved his head from side to side, squinting, and a figure slowly came into focus. She was sitting on a chair that had been placed against the wall, and when she saw his movements, she stood up and stepped towards him.

"Eyh up, sleeping beauty," said Gayle Morgan. "You've come back to join us, then? And I didn't have to kiss you or 'owt."

"What time is it? Where I am I? What happened?"

Rashford struggled to sit up but found he could not move his arms.

"Slow down, slow down," said Morgan. She looked at him, then gently wiped a cloth flannel over his forehead.

"You're in hospital," she said. "In Maple Creek, at the SIHF. You're in an acute care room at the moment, but they think you're going to be okay. It's about ten o'clock in the morning. Saturday morning."

"Saturday?"

"Yes. You collapsed and I worried you had had a coronary or something, so I called for the ambulance. The medics thought it was more likely just stress and exhaustion, but they brought you in for an assessment. The doctors here checked you out and decided to keep you overnight. You were ranting and raving, which is why they restrained you."

"I don't remember any of that."

A nurse entered the room and looked crossly at Morgan.

"You were supposed to call me as soon as he woke up," she said.

"I were going to, honest, I were just giving him the basics."

"Well just step outside for a minute while I check him, please," said the nurse. She ushered Morgan outside then turned back to Rashford.

"What happened?" he said. "Where's Roxanne?"

One of the machines at his bedside started to beep faster.

"Now then, calm down," said the nurse. "I don't know what happened out there. But I know what's happening in here. You're getting all agitated again. I'm going to give you another sedative."

"No, I'm alright," said Rashford, but she ignored him. She unwrapped a vial and attached it to a syringe, then injected him in the shoulder.

"Just sleep now," she said. "You'll be calmer in a few hours."

"No, I'm alright," said Rashford, again, then closed his eyes and drifted back to sleep.

When he woke for the second time, Rashford thought he was hallucinating. Morgan appeared to have multiplied. He saw the same hazy image of her sitting against the wall, but this time it looked like there were four of her, shimmering shapes that he observed with various degrees of clarity. They appeared diaphanous, ghost-like, as though four psychopomps had come to guide him to the afterlife.

The first Morgan stood up and came towards him.

"Back again are yer?" it said, leaning over to peer into his eyes. "Are yer going to stay with us this time, or should I bring back the nurse with the happy syringe?"

"No, I'm alright," Rashford said, but even to his ears that did not come out correctly. His mouth felt dry and crackly, as though it was full of autumn leaves. He coughed, hoping to clear his throat, then tried again.

"I'm alright. Is there some water?"

"Here you go."

Morgan held a glass to his lips, and he took a swallow.

"Not too much, now. Don't want you drowning."

"It would be something to laugh at," he said, and was relieved to see the glint of amusement in her eye.

"Aye, well, you have visitors."

Morgan looked over her shoulder and nodded. Following her glance, Rashford saw the second apparition rise to its feet and approach him.

"*Tansi*?"

"*M'on ana'tow*," said Rashford. "*Kiya maka*?"

"*Miyo achimowin*. My nôhkum will be happy to hear you are well," said Bettina Blackeagle. "Let me introduce my friend, she has also worried about you."

The third psychopomp rose to its feet and drifted over to the bed. As her face came into focus, Rashford felt a twinge of recognition, but he was not sure. Then his mind cleared.

"Yellow Volkswagen!" he said.

The woman nodded, the bright light above the bed glinting off the blue streak in her hair.

"My name is Cicily, although most people call me Cis. I am pleased you are well," she said, solemnly, reaching out and touching his chest with the palm of her hand. "The Creator has cared for you."

The three women stood for a moment, shoulder to shoulder, then simultaneously stepped back. As they did so, he realized that the fourth ghost had stood and was moving towards him. Rashford blinked his eyes rapidly, clearing his vision.

"Are you feeling better, darling?" said Roxanne, tears streaming down her face.

She leaned forward to kiss him on the forehead, wrapping her arms around his neck.

"You had me so worried," she said, clinging to him tightly.

There was silence, except for the self-conscious shuffling of feet. Then there was a quick gust of air as the door opened and someone else entered the room. Morgan coughed.

"Time to break it up, guys. The nurse is back," she said.

"Indeed, she is," said the nurse, briskly ushering them out of the way. "Come on, ladies, off you go. It's time for me to get the patient ready to see the doctor."

She guided them to the door, pausing only at the last moment to put her hand on Morgan's shoulder.

"Give me a call in about an hour," she said. "I'll be at the nurse's station. Just ask for Acute Care Ward 2 and the switchboard will put you through. Between us, I think he'll be ready to go by then, unless the doctor finds something I missed."

"That's unlikely," said Morgan with a laugh. "I'll get this mob organized and then give you a call. Cheers."

The nurse had been correct with her prediction. The doctor had started her examination of Rashford by cutting through the bandages that were restricting his arms.

"I think you've moved out of the flailing about phase," she said, smiling. She checked his blood pressure and pulse, then shone a bright pencil light into each of his eyes. As she examined him, she kept talking about the stress he was placing on his body by getting so worked up. She concluded by telling him to slow down a bit and stop getting so excited on the job.

"Give me a break, doc," he said, shaking his head. "I'm a police officer. I spend a lot of time in slow down mode, waiting for something to happen, and then when it does happen, bang, it's all adrenalin. I can't just turn it on and off."

"Well, think of your fellow officers, the ones who get old enough to retire. Are they all gung-ho types as well?"

Rashford thought for a bit.

"Not all of them, no. Actually, not most of them, if I think about it. After they had served their first twenty years, they all started to slow down and take things more patiently."

"Right. And how long have you been in the service?"

"With the NWMP for the past two years, since we were reformed after Alsama was established, and for about sixteen years with the

RCMP before that. So just over eighteen years, I guess."

"So, now it's your turn. Slow down, or else get ready to make that young woman a widow."

"Oh, we're not married, she's just a friend."

The doctor looked at him.

"If you say so," she said.

Packing away her laptop, she handed him a prescription form.

"This is for a light sedative; it will help you sleep. Other than that, I think you're good to go. But seriously, try not to get so overwrought and anxious. It really is not good for you."

"Thank you," said Rashford. "What do I do now?"

"Just stay here until the nurse comes to discharge you," said the doctor.

It was almost an hour later when Morgan led Rashford into the police house. He was relieved to see that the yellow caution tape had gone, and that someone had cleaned the bloodstains from the door and the floor. Roxanne was sitting in her chair but jumped up as he entered, running over to give him a hug and lead him to the overstuffed armchair he favoured. Bettina and Cicily were sitting at the table, coffee mugs in front of them, and Morgan went over to join them.

Roxanne fussed around until Rashford told her to stop, then she went back to her chair. Bettina had gone into the kitchen. She returned with two mugs, handing one to Morgan and the other to Rashford.

"It's from the old pot," she said. "I've put the new one on, but it will take time to drip through."

"No worries," said Morgan. "You've not had what they serve us at the meetings in Speedy Creek!"

"Where's Speedy Creek?" asked Cicily. "I don't remember seeing that name on a map."

Bettina laughed.

"It's what the locals call Swift Current," she said. "It's just a joke. They're full of things like that around here. Like, if someone invites you to see the Speedy Creek Forest, they take you out this farm that has a single tree growing on the prairie. There's not much to do in southern Saskatchewan."

Everyone laughed, then silence descended. They sipped their coffee, and Rashford looked at Morgan.

"Right, then," he said. "Who's going to tell me what happened?"

"Why don't you start?" said Morgan. "You should tell us why you came screaming in here like a banshee, lights flashing and siren wailing, having broken the speed limit all the way from the mountains. What were you expecting to find?"

Rashford explained how the Alberta team had tracked Snake Boots to a fancy house outside Mountain View, then through the national park. He described how he had suddenly put things together and realized that his quarry was going to be returning to Maple Creek for the truck.

"Well, not for the truck, not really," said Rashford. "But for some mementoes he had left in the truck, things which were important to him. And then I realized that he would probably find Roxanne here and try to finish whatever it was he had started when he had arranged for her to be abducted from the Barrel Races bar. So, I came as quick as I could."

"Not quite in time for the main event, however," said Morgan. "Ladies, what were you up to yesterday afternoon?"

"I had invited Bettina and her friend over for coffee and a late lunch," said Roxanne. We were just sitting here, chatting, when we heard a car drive up. It was going very quickly, and the tires squealed when it braked."

"I got up and looked out of the window," said Bettina. "It was a blue SUV, and this man got out. I didn't recognize him. He was wearing a leather jacket and a baseball cap. He had long white hair, tied in a ponytail. He went behind the detachment building, to the car park there. I could hear him swearing."

"I think that would have been when he realized the truck was locked," said Morgan, picking up the story. "I arrived about then, and saw the car in the road, but didn't think anything of it. I didn't see or hear him.

"I went into the detachment to make sure everything was okay before I went over to the house. I unlocked the door and went inside. The truck keys were still on the desk, where I had left them when I locked up on the day Gavin had to take leave.

"I did a quick walk through to the cells and the washrooms, just double checking that the windows were locked, that kind of thing. While I was in there, the corridor door blew closed. That's what I thought, anyway, but then when I got back to it, I realized that it had been locked. Either the latch had clicked itself or else someone had trapped me inside. I shouted and swore a lot, but there was no response."

She looked around the room.

"And yes, I did use my radio," she said. "But the Swift Current despatcher told me that there were no cars on this side of town, so it would take a while for someone to get to me."

She shook her head, ruefully.

"There's never a copper around when you need one," she said.

All of them laughed, and Cicily brought the story back to the next stage.

"Bettina had come back from the window and just sat down when suddenly this man burst in through the door," said Cicily. "He looked at the three of us and then started shouting my name. But I swear, I'd never seen him before."

"It was the guy from the SUV," said Bettina. "He is *nehiyaw*."

"He is Cree?" said Rashford, surprised.

"No, not Cree. But he is indigenous. I could tell from his eyes."

"It was Snake Boots," said Roxanne, quietly.

"Are you sure?" said Rashford.

"Certain. I'd never seen his face before, of course, but he was the right size and shape, and he was wearing those damned boots. And I remembered his ponytail, as soon as I saw him. Sorry, I forgot that before. He came in, and then he stopped just inside the door, yelling 'Cis,' 'Cis.'"

"I tell you. I have never met him before. Never ever," said Cicily, looking at everyone in turn.

"It's okay, we believe you," said Morgan, patting her arm.

"Anyway," said Roxanne, "as soon as I realized who he was, I knew we were all in trouble. He took another step towards us ..."

"And that was when Wakoshi-Mitimoye got involved," said Bettina, wiping a tear from her cheek.

"Wakoshi-Mitimoye. Who the heck is that?" said Rashford.

"Just wait, it gets better," said Morgan.

"Wakoshi-Mitimoye means Fox Woman," said Bettina. "She was a wise elder who was the guide and mentor for Ayas, the hero of the old stories. She adopted Ayas and protected him from the evil spirits."

"Is this another name for Kôhkum Christine?" said Rashford.

The four women all laughed.

"No, silly. Wakoshi-Mitimoye was my dog," said Bettina.

"Your dog?"

"Yes," said Roxanne. "Bettina always brings the old softy with her when she comes for a visit. She sits down over there, near the back door, and waits for me to give her a treat. Waited."

Roxanne wiped her cheek.

"Hang on," said Rashford. "That big Doberman you had in the back yard, that was an 'old softy'? Really? In whose universe?"

"In everyone's," laughed Bettina. "She used to bark to let me know you were at the house, but she never hurt you, did she?"

"I never gave her the chance," said Rashford. He thought for a moment.

"That's what you used to say, wasn't it? *Ayitapow* Wakoshi-Mitimoye. Sit down, Fox Woman. Now I understand."

Bettina nodded at him, smiling sadly.

"You will do well on the FILTER exam, I think," she said.

"*Ekosi*, thank you. So, how did Old Softy slash Fox Woman get involved?"

"We were sitting here," said Roxanne. "I was at the back, in the middle, Cis was next to me to my right, and Bettina was opposite, closest to the door. As soon as Snake Boots took that step towards us, Fox Woman must have thought that Bettina was being threatened.

"She just came up out of the corner and leapt at Snake Boots, grabbing him by the arm. She was biting as well, because I could see blood stains starting to come through his shirt. Then he somehow took control."

"What do you mean?" said Rashford.

"It was strange," said Cicily. "It seemed that suddenly, he was attacking the dog, instead of the other way around. He didn't shout or cry out, he didn't try to pull away or back off. Instead, he pushed his arm forward. He kind of flipped Fox Woman over onto her back and then he jumped on her, knees first. I guess he caught her throat and chest, anyway she was hurt. Then he slapped her on the side of the jaw, really hard, almost like a karate chop."

"Fox Woman had stopped moving," said Bettina. "He used his other hand to free the one from her mouth, then he pulled his arm away. Blood was coming out of his arm; it was all over the floor. He stepped back to the door and leaned on it, breathing hard. Then he looked at the three of us again."

"He had a really fixed stare," said Roxanne, "like he was sorry for us, or disappointed in us, or something. He said, 'See you later, Cis,' and then he left. We just sat here. It had only taken a minute. Then we heard the truck start up."

Cicily stood us and walked over to the window. She looked out towards the street.

"I saw him drive up there," she said, nodding towards Alf's Repair Shop. "Then I saw the police car in the lot, so I thought you were back."

She turned back to Rashford.

"I went out to find you. Bettina was on her knees next to Fox Woman. She was crying and Roxanne was trying to hold her. I went out and found the door to the detachment was open. I went inside, calling your name, and then I heard Gayle shouting from behind the inside door."

At this point, Gayle Morgan stood and joined the conversation.

"I was so glad to hear someone's voice," she said. "It felt like I'd been in there for hours. I had used my radio and called for help, but they said it would take nearly two hours before anyone could get to me. At that time, I still wasn't sure whether the door had slammed itself closed or whether someone had actually locked me in."

"The key was in the lock," said Cicily, "so I turned it and the door opened. I wasn't thinking, I should have worn gloves or used a tissue or something."

"It's okay, Cis," said Morgan, turning to Rashford.

"Forensics gave her a hard time, she smeared what might have been a good usable print from whomever locked the door."

"That's hardly fair," said Rashford. "How was she to know?"

"That's what I said. Anyhoo, so Cis opened the door and let me out. She was babbling about a guy coming in and getting attacked by the dog, then that the dog was dead, then that the guy knew her, but she didn't know him, on and on. I thought she was getting hysterical."

"I was just upset," said Cicily.

"Right. Well, I'm sorry I slapped you, but it calmed you down a bit."

She reached out and patted Cicily on the shoulder.

"Once things were quiet, I took Cis and we went to the police house. I saw all the blood everywhere, the dog on the floor, Roxanne and Bettina all upset and crying, so I decided to treat it like a crime scene. I told them all to just sit quiet for a minute, while I got some tape and floor plates from the car. I was starting to get the place cordoned off when you turned up. And then everything went sideways again."

"I think I passed out," said Rashford.

"You think?"

"Well, I saw all the blood, and I thought ... You know, I thought that Roxanne was here on her on own, and that Snake Boots had ... I ..."

"You thought it was her blood," said Morgan, gently. "Well, for once in your life, your deductions were wrong."

"And I am glad for that," said Rashford. He walked over to Roxanne and lifted her out of the chair and into his arms.

"Don't ever scare me like that again," he said.

She stepped away from him, hands on hips, staring up at him.

"Me? What did I do?"

"You're someone he cares for, darlin'," said Morgan. "So, it's always going to be your fault."

Later that afternoon, Chief Superintendent Pollard arrived at Maple Creek and congratulated Gayle Morgan on her prompt response. She told Rashford that Inspector Whitehead had been generally pleased with his work in Alberta, although somewhat perturbed at the way he had rushed off.

"There are forms you are supposed to fill in, Sergeant," she said. "You can't just go tilting at your own windmills."

"Yes, Ma'am, sorry Ma'am," said Rashford, and that seemed to mollify Pollard, who changed the subject.

"We found the truck," she said. "It was at Saskatchewan Crossing Provincial Park, left in the parking lot. He took a real chance; he must have either gone along the back roads or else right through Swift Current. He was lucky none of our people saw him, that truck was on a watch list, thanks to Corporal Morgan."

"Any sign of Snake Boots?"

"Not a thing. He had wiped the truck clean, no fingerprints or anything. The back seat was opened, he had obviously checked for the rifle and that package you brought in earlier, Rashford. We don't know if he hitched a ride, stole a vehicle, or took a canoe and went down the river. He could be anywhere."

"And we still don't know his name. Damn it," said Rashford, thumping his fist on the table in frustration. "So damned close."

"Perhaps next time, Gav," said Morgan, smiling. "Third time lucky, eh?"

"If there is to be a third time," said the Chief Inspector. "Sergeant Rashford, I know that on Monday you have to go to the hospital for another check-up. Until they clear you, you are officially on medical leave. One reason I am here is to tell you that your leave has been extended for the whole of next week."

Rashford looked at her.

"Yes, Ma'am. Might I ask why, Ma'am?"

"Certainly. You have had a pretty intense and traumatic few days. I want you to recover properly before you get back to work. I have arranged for Corporal Smithson to come down here and take over the detachment for a week. He will be staying in the hotel next door, what is it, the Aspen?"

She looked at the notes on her phone.

"Yes, that's it, the Aspen Motor Inn. He will be there, so he won't disturb you here, but he will be running the detachment. You will be on leave. *Kinisitihten?*

"Yes, Ma'am."

"Good. Also, a week from Monday is your FILTER exam, and I would like you to focus on preparing for that right now. That is going to be held in Regina, at the First Nations University. I don't know where it will be exactly, somewhere on campus, but you'll get an e-mail later in the week. The Force will give you two nights at the Holiday Inn, those details will be in the e-mail as well. The following day, on the Tuesday, I want you in my office at ten a.m. Understand?"

"Yes, Ma'am."

"Good."

The Chief Inspector turned to Roxanne.

"Ms. Gaudet," she said, pronouncing the name correctly. "I am sorry that you had to experience all this, but I am delighted that you are safe. I hope you enjoy swimming; I understand that the Holiday Inn in Regina has a nice pool."

Roxanne nodded and smiled.

"Thank you," she said.

"Doctor Blackeagle, please accept my condolences on the loss of your dog. I know this will not replace her, but there may be some insurance money to help you find and obtain a new puppy, should you want one. I shall check once I am back at my office."

"Thank you, Chief Inspector," said Bettina, standing and shaking Pollard's hand. "I look forward to hearing from you."

The Chief Inspector nodded, then turned to the other two women.

"Corporal Morgan, again, thank you for taking the situation in hand. I await your full report with interest. Doctor Steel, it has been a pleasure to meet you. I naturally have an interest in cyber security, and I've read a lot of your work, mainly the public stuff but a couple of the more classified reports as well."

Bettina grinned.

"I told you she was good," she said.

Roxanne, Morgan and Rashford all turned to Cicily Steel, who had turned a bright red.

"What? You never asked," she said.

Rashford and Roxanne spent the Sunday in a lazy fashion, slowly telling each other various parts of their story. They rented a car from one of the local car hire companies and in the afternoon drove to the provincial park, where they went for a walk along the trails at Cypress Hills.

On the Monday morning, Rashford went back to the hospital, where he was given a clean bill of health but instructed to rest for the remainder of the week. He went back to the police house and helped Roxanne clean up, again, and then they took the car and drove to the bus depot.

As they waited, Roxanne paced up and down.

"Stop being so nervous," said Rashford. "She'll be fine."

"You don't know my mom," said Roxanne. "And I've not seen her for nearly two years. People change. We all do."

"It will be fine," said Rashford. "I'm looking forward to meeting her."

"Really?"

"Really."

"And do you think she'll like dinner tonight, with Bettina and Cicily?"

"I'm sure she'll love it," said Rashford. "She will be pleased to know you have friends here."

Roxanne stopped pacing and came into his embrace.

"Instead of just a hunky lover, you mean?" she said.

"Exactly," he said, laughing.

Just then the bus drew up on the street outside the depot. There was a cloud of diesel smoke, then the pneumatic hiss of the door opening. The driver climbed down first, stretching, then turned and extended his hand. A woman came slowly down the steps. She was matronly in appearance, wearing faded blue jeans and a dark blue puffy jacket. She looked like she was in her fifties.

"Mom!" said Roxanne, dashing forward and hugging her tightly. "You made it!"

The woman closed her eyes and held her daughter back, just as tightly.

"Wouldn't miss it for the world," she said, and suddenly they were both crying. Rashford stood awkwardly to one side, then went and took a large backpack from the driver. The man nodded towards the front of his bus.

"She's been some excited to get here," he said. "Every ten minutes since we left Regina, she came to the front and said, 'how far is it now?' I had to tell her to sit down and let me drive, or we'd never have gotten here."

He spat on the ground, then closed the hatch under the bus. Nodding at Rashford, he went back up the steps and called down the aisle of the bus.

"Twenty minutes break here," he said, and walked off towards the back of the depot, pulling his cigarettes out of his pocket as he did so. Rashford turned back to the women.

"Gavin, this is my mom, Sandra," said Roxanne, wiping her tears away. "Mom, this is Gavin."

"Pleased to meet you, Missus Gaudet," said Rashford, but she shook her head.

"That's her dad's name," she said. "Mine is Sylliboy. But please, call me Sandra. Or *kôhkum*, if you get busy with my daughter!"

She roared with laughter at the look on Rashford's face.

"Sorry, Anne," she said, "I keep forgetting that white folks don't have a proper sense of humour."

"Mom!"

"C'mon, let's go. I need a mug of tea. How far is your place?"

"Two minutes," said Rashford.

"Do I get to go in a police car?"

"No, mom, that's not allowed. Anyway, Gavin is on leave this week, someone else is driving the car. We have a rental."

Rashford took the bag and the two of them escorted Sandra to the car, then drove the short distance to the police house. They entered and showed her where she would be staying. She sat on the bed and bounced up and down a few times.

"Good. It seems firm," she said. "I don't like those really soft mattresses; they make you wake up thinking someone is hugging you."

She took off her coat and then came back out to the living room. Roxanne busied herself in the kitchen, making tea, while Rashford stood against the wall as Sandra examined the various parts of the room.

"Please, sit down," he said, and Sandra did so. Rashford joined her at the table.

"Good trip?" he said.

"Not too bad," she said. "But kinda long."

"Wait," shouted Roxanne. "Don't start without me."

A few moments later she came into the room carrying the tray, which was loaded with teapot, milk, sugar, teaspoons, and mugs. She carefully put the tray on the table.

"Do you put the milk in first?" said Rashford.

"Of course," said Sandra. "Don't you?"

Rashford was saved from a response by Roxanne, who passed a mug to her mother and then stopped, staring.

"What are you looking at?" said Sandra.

"That scarf," said Roxanne. "It's beautiful. Where did you get it?"

"What, this?" said Sandra, touching the brightly coloured twist of fabric around her neck. "This is silk, this is. It was a gift."

"A gift? From whom?"

"From your brother."

Chapter 13

Roxanne froze.

"My brother? What brother?"

"Ah, well, you see, that was another reason I wanted to visit. That is one of the stories I need to tell you. But first, let's have this tea."

Her face pale with shock, Roxanne sat down heavily in the chair next to Rashford. The two of them looked across at the older woman. Rashford felt Roxanne's hand reaching out to touch his wrist. He turned his hand slightly, sideways, and she gripped it so hard he almost flinched.

Sandra sipped her drink.

"Mmmm, good tea, this. You made it well, daughter."

"Thank you."

"How do you like it out here? Isn't it too cold, in the winter?"

"Mom ..."

Rashford knew that it was probably not a good idea to get in the middle of this discussion, but he felt that he had to be polite.

"It can be very cold, yes," he said. "I only came in the spring, but people tell me that it is not uncommon to have days when it goes to minus forty."

"Minus forty! Doesn't everything freeze?"

"You just have to dress right."

"What about your car?"

"The engine can freeze, yes. That's why we have plug-ins. There's a kind of electric blanket inside the engine, at night you turn it on, and it keeps the engine from freezing."

"That's crazy."

Rashford felt that he had to defend his climate.

"There's not much snow, though."

"Why not? Is it too cold?"

"I think it's because it's too dry. The moisture all falls on the mountains. There are blizzards, here, when it's snowing and really windy and you can't see far in front of you, but not big snowstorms like you see on TV from the east cost."

"One year we had eighteen feet of snow," said Sandra, proudly. "That was a good winter."

Roxanne let go of Rashford's hand and placed both of hers on the table, palms down. She leaned forward.

"Mother, what brother?"

Sandra drank more of her tea, then reached forward with her mug. Roxanne, without moving her stare from her mother's face, lifted the pot and poured some fresh tea into the mug. She put the tea pot down carefully, without saying anything. She didn't look at Rashford, either. He reached across and took the pot, helping himself to more tea.

For a full minute, nobody said anything.

Sandra finished her tea and put down her mug. She looked up at her daughter.

"When I was a young girl, there used to be a dance club in Sydney. It was called Smooth Herman's, and every Saturday evening we'd try to go there. We would go to mass first, then rush home and get changed, then someone with a car would take a pile of us into town.

"One summer, in nineteen eighty-six, a Rolling Stones tribute band played the club. They were really good. The lead guitarist, the fellow who was supposed to be Keith Richards, he was brilliant, and really good looking. I was dancing near the front of the stage, and he winked at me. I was so excited. I was seventeen.

"A bit later, this bouncer came up and asked me if I would like to meet the band, after the show. Of course, I said yes! My friends were all jealous, and even worried. They said they would wait but I said it was alright, I'd take a taxi home later. So, when the show finished, I went to where I'd been told to wait, and the bouncer came back and took me though this door and backstage.

"The band were all in this room, sitting and talking and laughing. There were plates of food everywhere, and beer and liquor, and music in the background. There were other people as well, not just girls, but also the manager and people like that. The guitarist saw me and waved me over. He was sitting on this couch, I remember it had a red and yellow cover, and he patted the seat so I would sit down next to him.

"'You're a good dancer,' he said, 'what's your name?'

"I told him, and he said, 'you can call me Keith if you want, but my name is Jim. Really, it's James, but I go by Jim.'

"Where are you from, Jim?" I said. "Originally, that is. You've got a cool accent."

"He just laughed. 'Originally, I'm from Yorkshire, in the north of England. But I've lived in Toronto for ten years now. What about you, where are you from?'

"Eskasoni."

"'Eskasoni? Never heard of it. Where's that?'

"It's a reserve, out on Bras D'Or Lake."

"'You're Indian? Cool.'

"Yes. E'pite's."

"'Eh bee des? What's that?'

"It means Mi'kmaq woman."

"'Maybe I'll stick with Sandra, is that okay?'

"Sure.

"I laughed, and he laughed, and passed me a beer, and then the joints started being passed around, and one thing led to another, and I never did get a taxi home that night.

"The next morning, I woke up in his hotel room. Well, he woke me up by having a grope, and then we had sex again. Maybe twice, I can't remember."

"Mom!" said Roxanne, covering her mouth with her hand, her eyes wide. "TMI!"

"What does that mean?" said Sandra.

"Too much information," said Rashford, smiling despite himself.

"Oh, right. Well, anyway, the other band guys came knocking on the door and said the van was leaving, so he told me just to check out by noon and he left. I had a shower and then went home."

"And that was it?" said Roxanne.

"For about three months, yes. Then I realized that I was pregnant, we hadn't used any protection of course. I pretended I was just getting fat but my mom, your *nukumi*, she figured it out. She said that I was bringing shame to the family and would have to leave."

"I thought having children and becoming a woman were good things in our culture?"

"They are, but your *nukumi*, she had lost her culture and her language, at the residential school. She was a good Catholic now, and she said I had been sinful. She talked to one of the nuns who used to come to the community, to help with the Sunday school, and they decided that I should leave home to have the baby.

"The nun drove me to Antigonish, on the mainland, and I stayed in this little house the nuns had across from the hospital. There were two other girls there as well, one from Glace Bay and one from somewhere on the Cheticamp shore, Grand Étang or somewhere like that. She was Métis, I think. We could go out in the garden but not outside the fence. The nuns brought us food every day, and made us go to mass twice a week, and to confession.

"I didn't really meet the Glace Bay girl. She was only there for a couple of days and then left. I spent more time with Sylvie, from Cheticamp. We were both due at about the same time. I told her about Keith, and she told me her fella, a guy from Chapel Island who she'd met at a school dance. They'd only had sex once and she was pregnant. Her parents were furious, and she was upset because the Chapel Island guy had been sniffing gas or something, he was really twitchy. She worried that it might have been transmitted to her baby.

"When it was time for me to have my baby, I went over the street into the hospital. I was only there for one night. My baby was born in the morning, then in the afternoon the nuns walked me back over to the house. They told me I could stay in the house for three days, to recover, then they would drive me back to Eskasoni."

"What about your baby?" whispered Roxanne.

"They took him away from me," said Sandra, matter-of-factly. "I knew it was a boy, because they let me hold him after he was born, and the nurse told me. But I never saw him, not really. I remember telling Sylvie, when I got back to the house, and she got really upset, she didn't want to lose her baby. She wanted to keep it. I don't know if they let her, though."

"That's terrible," said Roxanne. "How cruel."

"It's the way things were, then. They had been like that for a hundred years. Young Indian girls weren't thought to be able to raise children, we were just sluts who got pregnant. The nuns thought they were doing the right thing, giving our children a better life."

"You can't think that!"

"I don't. But they did. They would even advertise, sometimes, in newspapers in the United States and even across Canada. This was in addition to the ones they took from homes on the reserve. It got really big in the nineteen sixties, children could be bought for ten thousand dollars, sometimes more."

"Bought?" said Rashford. "Surely that would be illegal? Even back then we didn't allow human trafficking."

"They didn't actually sell the children, but the nuns ran the birth house like a business. They kept records. They would ask for donations to help with their work, and then 'suggest' an appropriate gift. And people paid it. I mean, they were nuns, right?"

She raised her hands as she spoke, making air quotes around the word suggest.

"So, what happened then?" said Roxanne.

"Well," said Sandra, taking a deep breath. "They took away my baby boy and I didn't want to go home without him, and I didn't want to do a Nancy, so I ran away."

"What's a 'Nancy'?" said Rashford.

"In that song by Leonard Cohen. It was a girl from Montreal, some say she was one of his aunts, who was forced to give up her baby for adoption, and she couldn't handle the loss, so she killed herself. It seems so long ago, that was the song, and it does, mostly, although sometimes it's like it was yesterday.

"Anyway, two days later, after breakfast, I walked out of the house and down the hill into town. I went along main street, past the shops and the university, then out to the traffic light on the highway. I stuck out my arm, and soon a fellow stopped and asked me where I was going. I said, 'out west', and he said he could get me as far as Truro. So, I got in the car with him, and off we went.

"We were driving along, and he asked me what I was going to do, and I said I didn't know yet, maybe work as a waitress or something. He said I was pretty, and I would probably get good tips. Then he said he knew some people who owned a couple of bars in Halifax, why did I have to go all the way out to Montreal or Toronto. He would drive me there to meet them, if I wanted.

"I said sure, so he said great, and at Truro we turned off the Trans-Canada and went to Halifax. About halfway down there is this junction, with a bunch of gas stations and fast-food places, and he asked me if I would like some lunch. I said sure, so we turned off and he parked way over the back of the parking lot, up in a corner. He put his arm around my shoulder and kissed me on the neck.

"'First you have to pay for your lunch and the drive,' he said, then he unzipped his trousers and pulled my head down. When he'd finished, which didn't take long, he laughed and said, 'do you want fries with that?' We drove down to one of the restaurants, he bought us burgers and fries and drinks, coffee for him and coke for me, then went back on the highway.

"In Halifax he went to a bar up near the Citadel, on one of the back streets, and took me inside. The owner was this big fat guy, he was really sweaty and dirty. My driver said I would make a good waitress, and this fat fellow told me to take off my top. And my bra. He squeezed my breasts and rolled my nipples in his fingers. 'Nice tits,' he said.

"'And she gives good head,' said my driver.

"'Does she now? Maybe later,' said the fat guy. 'Do you have a place to stay?'

"I said no, and he told me the deal. I would get a room upstairs from the bar, which I would rent from him at a hundred bucks a week. I would work six nights in the bar, for fifty bucks a night plus fifty per cent of the tips. The other fifty per cent went to him, and from that he looked after the non-waitress staff. If I ate at the bar, then I got a twenty-five per cent discount off the food.

"I had to wear a t-shirt that was two sizes too small, no bra, and a skirt that showed my ass when I bent over. High heels, of course, and either knee-socks or black thigh high stockings. No panty hose. He would give me two hundred bucks to get kitted out, but I would have to repay him, with interest. When he said that, he grinned at my driver, and I could guess what the interest would be.

"I was not to take guys back to my room; the bar was not a brothel, and he didn't want the cops coming around checking for that sort of stuff. If I went with someone to a hotel or somewhere, that was my business, but it had to be outside shift hours and he was not going to provide me with security or anything. He ran a bar, end of.

"When I said that I would take the deal, at least to try it out, he said that was good. Then he told the guy who had brought me to leave, as he wanted to collect the first installment of his interest. They shook hands and my driver left, patting me on the bum as he did. 'Good luck,' he said. 'I might come by for a drink one night.'

"When he'd gone, the fat guy pulled down his sweatpants, he was so big he probably couldn't get real trousers. He told me to get on my knees and suck him off, so I did. Then he told me to grow my hair long and put it in a ponytail, I would get more tips that way. He pulled up his pants and took me upstairs to show me my room. 'Remember, I'm the only guy you fuck in here,' he said. 'No grockles.' Then he gave me some money, told me to buy shoes and clothes and stuff, and said if I ran away, he would find me and kill me. I believed him."

"What's a grockle?" said Rashford.

"It's what we call tourists, punters, regular people who don't understand the game," said Sandra, laughing for the first time. "Basically, someone who might try and pick me up in the bar. So that was my first job, and I stayed there nearly five years."

"Five years," said Roxanne. "Why did you stay so long?"

"Well, I made good money, for a start," said Sandra. "My tips were incredible. Because I had just had a baby, my breasts were pretty big, and the guys liked that. Plus, they liked to smack my ass, and I let them, I didn't get upset. So even fifty per cent was good money. My room was fine, and I ate either at the bar or else I went to the grocery store and got something there.

"I was smoking by then, so that kept me thin. Every payday I gave Patrice a blow job, he was the owner, all the girls got paid on different days so he could get regular service. He only came to my room once, just to try me out he said, and he was so fat that I had to do all the work.

"So, I worked my shifts, saved my money, and on my day off I walked around Halifax. I got to know all of the city, from the docks and the naval base all the way out to Bedford, and even across the harbour to Dartmouth. It was a good five years. And every day I thought about Keith, which is the name I gave to my little boy. I made up stories in my head, where he was, what he was doing, what he looked like.

"One day I was on the ferry, crossing back from Dartmouth, and this fellow started chatting me up. He was a nice guy, so I let him, and when we were getting ready to dock, he asked me if I'd like to go out to dinner. I said yes, and we went to this really nice little place down by the harbour and told stories and enjoyed ourselves. That night I went back to his place. It was the first time since I arrived in Halifax that I didn't sleep in my room above the bar. I told him that I was a waitress and worked shifts with long hours, so we made a date for my next day off, to go to the movies.

"And that went on for a few months, over most of the winter. Then in the spring, he said he was going home, to Prince Edward Island, to help with his family farm, and did I want to go with him. I said yes and gave my notice to Patrice. He said if I'd stayed another three weeks then he'd have given me a five-year anniversary fuck and a bonus, but he wished me good luck anyway. So, I left, and went to PEI."

She paused. Roxanne looked at Rashford, then back at her mother.

"Let's have something to eat," she said.

When Rashford got back to the police house, he found that they had been joined by Bettina and Cicily.

"We'll just eat and run," said Bettina. "Cicily wants to get on the road early tomorrow, she has to drive back to Thompson."

"But I'll be back soon, I promise," said Cicily. She looked across at Rashford and laughed. "Now that I know where the junction is!"

Rashford laid out the assortment of Chinese dishes that Roxanne had ordered over the phone, including some that were not on the menu but were apparently designed specifically to her instructions. The next hour passed quickly, with lots of laughter, and soon it was time for Bettina and Cicily to leave.

"See you again, soon" said Cicily, giving each of them a hug. "It's been lovely getting to know you all."

She linked her arm in Bettina's, and they walked out into the evening.

Once they had left, Roxanne made another pot of tea, this time selecting a caffeine-free Chamomile. They retired to the comfortable chairs, and Sandra continued her story.

"Phillip and I were together on the farm for two years, and then the most awful thing happened. He was doing something to a soybean harvester and the engine slipped into gear, he got pulled into the conveyor. The knives cut up his arm and shoulder, he lost a lot of blood. Another fellow was there and turned off the machine, but it was too late. He was dead before they even got him to hospital. His mom had never liked me, so as soon as Phillip was buried, she told me to leave the farm.

"I went into Charlottetown and found a small apartment down behind Province House. I got a job at one of the bars, when they heard I had worked for Patrice they just laughed and said that the Island didn't work like that. I had good shifts, some weeks I would work lunch and afternoons and other times I would work nights, so I started to actually have a social life. I was nearly twenty-five years old.

"One night I was at a party, and I met this fellow, we got on really well. He walked me back to my apartment building but didn't try to come in, he just asked me if he could see me again, for a date. We went out together three more times before he even tried to kiss me. That was your dad, of course. Marc Gaudet. We had you two years later and got married six months after that. And I've lived on the Island ever since."

"What, you've never left?" said Rashford.

"Not until now, no. Well, I do make runs across the bridge to Moncton, to do a Costco shop, and sometimes to Dartmouth if I need stuff from Ikea. But otherwise, no. I've not even gone back to Eskasoni."

"But where does my brother come into this story?" said Roxanne. "Keith, or whatever his name is."

Sandra took a deep breath, then a sip of water.

"Now it gets interesting," she said. "About a year ago, maybe fourteen months, I got this letter from the government. Social Services. It seemed that my son had used the new provincial disclosure rules and had tracked me down. He wanted to meet me.

"Marc knew nothing about him, of course, so that was my first problem. What should I tell him? I worried about that for days, then eventually I just told him, I just blurted it out. He looked at me and said, 'cool, I've always wanted a boy as well.' I said I was sorry for keeping it from him all these years and he said he knew I'd had a life before, so had he, and I didn't know half his stories either.

"So, then I had to decide what to do about my son, who apparently was called Xavier Ballantyne. His address had been kept secret in the letter I got, and he didn't know where I was, only that I existed and was still alive. So, the next question was, if I did meet him, then where? The Island is a pretty small place and if we met in Charlottetown, everyone would soon know.

"I decided to be a bit strategic and suggested we meet at the Tim Horton's in Sackville. It's on the main highway and kind of at the junction of New Brunswick, Nova Scotia, and the Island, but not exactly. He wouldn't know which way I had travelled to get there. It was a bonus that I could go to Costco first, in Moncton, and stop at the Tim's on my way home.

"So, that's what happened. We agreed to meet at one thirty and I got there a bit early, so I grabbed a coffee and sat down in a quiet corner. I waited until about five to two and was about to leave when this fellow who had been sitting near the window got up. He had been there the whole time I was there. He just came into the chair on the other side of my table and said, 'hello mom.' I looked at him and burst into tears."

Chapter 14

"Chief, we're looking for a fellow called Xavier Ballantyne. Although he might be calling himself Keith now."

"Really?"

"Yes, Ma'am. He is originally from Nova Scotia but was adopted by a family in the eastern townships around Montreal. He grew up there. He joined the army in about two thousand and five, then served three tours in Afghanistan between oh-six and twenty-ten. He saw some serious action. He was at the battle of Kandahar, in that village near Panjwai where that woman artillery officer got killed."

"Captain Goddard?" said Chief Superintendent Pollard. "She was the first Canadian female soldier to die in combat. Ever. That was a big deal at the time."

"Yes, Ma'am. He said that people were more than upset, they were so angry, the officers really had to work hard to keep things under control. But even so, he said they made sure she was avenged.

"Later, on a different tour, he was in the vehicle behind one that got destroyed by a roadside bomb. Three of his friends were killed. After that he apparently got posted to some special unit that did all sorts of crazy things that he won't talk about. He came back after the last tour and stayed in Canada, doing some instructional work at Gagetown, that's a training base in New Brunswick. From there he was sent to Haiti after the big earthquake.

"His last tour was some special operations support work in Mali. I didn't even know we had soldiers in Mali. Anyway, he came back from there and left the army after his twenty years. Then things fell apart.

"He tried working for a bit but had what his work assessment report called 'anger management issues,' so he got fired. He drifted around and then ended up in Calgary, on the street.

"He said he fell in with some other guys, one fellow in particular who was also from Nova Scotia. A Cape Bretoner, from the Cheticamp side. They had both developed some serious issues around alcohol and drugs, but he was saved by this woman he met. He used to go around collecting empty cans and bottles from trash cans and putting them into the recycle depot for money.

"There was this one house where the lady saw him and came out. She said he didn't have to dig in the trash, she would keep them for him and leave them in a bag by the back gate. Which she did. Sometimes she would leave a sandwich as well, or a plastic container with some cooked meat or whatever. There was always a note saying something like a friend hadn't arrived and she didn't want to waste good food.

"One day she came out and they got chatting. She told him about having a bit of a drinking problem herself, but she drank white wine and gin and tonic, so it wasn't noticed by most people. They laughed about that.

"Another time she told him about a friend she had known at college, they had always been very close. One day the friend was walking home from work when a drunk driver came up on the curb from behind and killed her. She talked about how hard it was, when you lost someone suddenly, with no chance to say goodbye.

"'It's just as hard when you know,' he told her, and spoke about a couple of his friends who had been badly wounded and who he knew wouldn't make it. 'What do you say to them?' he said.

Rashford stopped for a breath and the Chief Superintendent interrupted him.

"Sergeant, how do you know all this?"

Rashford had been expecting this question and had discussed it with Roxanne.

"Just tell her the truth," she had said, "and let things happen."

"Well, Ma'am," he said, "I was speaking with his mother."

"His mother?"

"Yes, Ma'am."

"I see. And how, exactly, did you come to be speaking with his mother?"

Rashford told Sandra's story about being contacted by her long-lost son, and then explained the connection to Roxanne.

"After he and Sandra met that first time, they kept in touch. He told her that the lady in Calgary helped him to get an appointment with a doctor, and he got some medications that really helped calm him down. He was doing pretty well. In fact, things were so good, the lady and her husband asked him to look after their house when they went away on holiday.

"That was fine until the day the Americans bombed Calgary. He had a flashback and knew he had to get out, so he buried his medications up on Nose Hill and took off. He said that he couldn't remember everything, but he had done what he needed to do in order not to get caught.

"One time a policeman did catch him, but he managed to escape. He got across the border back into Canada and made his way back to the townships where he had grown up. He stayed back at home for a while but knew something was wrong. He talked to the guy he thought was his dad about it, and that's when he was told he was adopted.

"Of course, this surprised him. He started looking up records online, 'how to find your birth parents' and things like that. His dad told him they had adopted him from the nuns in Antigonish, so that was a good place to start. The fact that a few years ago, Nova Scotia brought in the Act to Open Adoption Records, that was a real help. It didn't take long for him to track down his mom.

"As I said, they met the first time at a coffee shop, then they spoke on the phone a few times. A few months later he actually visited her in Charlottetown. There he saw a photograph of Roxanne, although she's called Anne at home, it was hanging on the wall. Sandra told him that Anne had just moved, from Toronto to Calgary, and was staying with her cousin. His cousin.

"He then said he was going to be going back out west himself, so if he got to Calgary again he would try and look her up. He took the cousin's address and telephone number, and that was the last time she saw him.

"A few weeks ago, the scarf arrived in the mail. There was no letter, just a note that read 'found her'. Then Sandra heard from Roxanne about the bar, and the chase, and how she had ended up in Maple Creek. She thinks she has figured it out, that Xavier was just too shy to approach Roxanne in the bar, so came up with this hare-brained scheme of buying her from the bikers to rescue her and show her she was important to him.

"I think that's BS, though. He may have been looking for her, but he was really looking for his mementoes, his medicine bundle or whatever. That's why he went to Maple Creek, to get them from the truck. He had no idea that Roxanne was there. It was only when he went inside, and saw her, that he got excited. When he burst into the police house, he wasn't shouting 'Cis! Cis!' he was shouting 'Sis! Sis!' But of course, none of them knew that.

"Sandra knew she had to tell Roxanne what was going on, but she wanted to tell her directly. So, she got the bus. And she arrived earlier today."

There was a silence. Eventually, Rashford heard the Chief Superintendent cough quietly.

"Well done, Sergeant," she said. "Now we have a name to go with this case. We still do not have a person, though, do we?"

"No, Ma'am."

"Right, well leave this with me. We shall discuss next steps here at Headquarters. Remember, you are supposed to be on leave. You have your FILTER examination next Monday, so focus on that. And I shall still expect you in my office next Tuesday, as planned. *Kinisitihten?*"

"Yes, Ma'am. I understand."

Rashford kept the rental car for the whole week, and each day they took Sandra out to different destinations.

The first day, they drove north to the Great Sandhills Park, and were disappointed with Sandra's reaction.

"We've got lots of sand dunes on PEI," she said, dismissively. Not even the museum at Sceptre was of much interest to her, although she found the name a strange one for a town. She was bemused by what was described as the world's largest metal wheat sculpture, which they passed as they headed out to Leader.

"There's got to be more to fame than a metal stalk of wheat grass," said Sandra.

"Not only that," said Roxanne, who was busy with her phone. "But according to Google, it's not really the biggest one either. There is one is Rosthern that's ten feet taller!"

"Only Saskatchewan would have duelling wheat stalk statues," said Rashford, bringing laughter from the two women. They arrived in Leader about fifteen minutes later.

"We'll just pop in and see if Gayle is home," said Roxanne.

Both she and Rashford were surprised to see a bright yellow Volkswagen parked outside the police house. They looked at each other, then simultaneously nodded, and Rashford drove away.

"I wonder if Bettina knows," said Roxanne.

"Absolutely none of our business," said Rashford, and Sandra agreed with him.

"They will work it out together," she said. "It is not a good idea to get mixed up in the relationships of others."

There were a few moments of silence, then Roxanne cleared her throat.

"Talking of relationships, what's happened to dad? You've hardly mentioned him."

Sandra looked down at her lap.

"I was waiting for a good time to tell you," she said. "I guess this is it."

"Tell me what?"

"Your dad has left me."

"Because you had a child when you were young?"

"Perhaps, but he says not. He says that my story made him realize that we both have separate life stories, and that the past is just as important as the present. So, he left to go and be with a woman who was his first girlfriend, when he was young."

"What?"

"Yes. She has two children, one is a young woman about your age, the other is a bit older. Not from Marc, of course, from her husband. But she left him as well."

"Where are they? I'll kill him!"

Sandra laughed.

"They're in western PEI somewhere, back in Acadian country. Every second person up west is a Gaudet, if they're not a Gallant that is. Ach, it's alright. I'm glad he's happy."

"But what about you?" said Roxanne.

"Oh, I'm fine, I was able to get my old apartment back, it had even been renovated while I was with Marc. So, I'm right downtown, near to everywhere I want to be. I've got a good job as the floor manager of a little restaurant that gets busy in the summer with the tourists but otherwise is just a nice steady job. I'm happy."

The following day, Bettina and Kôhkum Christine came with them when they went down to the Cypress Hills and showed them some of the sites that were special to their people.

"The tourists don't know about half of these places," Bettina said, "and to be honest, I quite like it that way."

Kôhkum Christine stayed in the car while the others walked around, but she was excited to tell stories once they were driving to the next location.

On the way back to Maple Creek she asked if she could sit in the front passenger seat. She then proceeded to grill Rashford about the history of the Nekaneet, and the cultural, economic, and sociopolitical implications of them signing Treaty Four. In Cree. He participated as well as he could, although he lost track of some of her threads of thoughts. When that happened, she carefully explained what she had been saying, and then continued on with her stories.

The rest of the week passed quickly, and on Sunday afternoon it was time for Rashford to go into Regina to sit the FILTER examination. Roxanne was conflicted, she felt she ought to stay with her mother, but Bettina waved her away.

"You go with him" she said. "He needs your support tonight, before the big examination tomorrow, and then he will need your congratulations afterwards, when he passes."

"Or her commiserations," said Rashford, glumly.

"Don't be silly," said Bettina. "Your Cree is excellent, and you will have no problems with this examination. Go, the pair of you. Enjoy Regina! Sandra and I will be fine. We will see you back here on Tuesday afternoon. My *nôhkom* is already planning the feast we shall have."

"Yes," said Sandra, looking up from her magazine. "Let me have some fun by myself, without you looking over my shoulder the whole time."

"Mom!"

Bettina laughed.

"Don't worry, I'll make sure she doesn't get into trouble."

"Spoil sport," said Sandra, pouting.

Rashford shook his head, then took Roxanne by the arm and pulled her away.

"Come on," he said. "I don't want to be late."

As they drove across the prairies, Roxanne looked out of the window and mused.

"It always reminds me of the ocean," she said. "The long horizons, the always changing light. At home, I used to love going out to this place called Brackley, especially in the winter. The ocean would freeze, it would be white as far as you could see, but the tides would still come in and out. These big blocks of ice would be lifting up and down, even though they were strong enough that you could walk on them."

She turned in the seat and faced Rashford.

"We should go out to the east coast one day," she said.

"Sure," said Rashford, smiling. He reached over and squeezed her hand. "We would probably need to buy a car first, though. That way we can make a proper holiday."

"You want to drive out? Not fly?"

"I'm a prairie boy. I've never been outside Alsama. I'd love to drive around Lake Superior, see Montreal, those kind of things."

"Maybe that's what I'll do tomorrow, then, when you're doing your exam."

"What?"

"I'll look at cars!"

"Just look, though," he said, laughing.

Roxanne flounced back into her seat and spent the next half an hour happily describing the merits of sedans, trucks, four-wheel drive SUVs and other vehicles. Rashford listened and smiled, only interjecting once.

"I didn't realize you were such a petrol-head," he said.

"Yeah. My dad had a garage, just a small place in Charlottetown. He used to fix all sorts of cars, and I used to hang around the place when I was a kid. You just kind of pick it up, don't you?"

"Does he still run it?"

"I don't know, if he's left mom and moved up west. He used to still fiddle about with it. There is another fellow, Jean, who does most of the work now. Dad would just go in now and then and get in the way, I think. Anyway, what about your folks? What do they do?"

Rashford told her about growing up in a small hamlet south of Saskatoon, and how his parents both commuted to work. When he got back from school he would take his dog for walks around the local lake, sometimes he would fish for perch or jackfish. In the fall the lake would be full of geese and ducks, and in the winter months he could skate all the way across.

"It can be cold on the prairies," he said, "but I love it. As long as you dress for the weather, you're okay. It's the people who are too scared to go outside who end up going crazy. Cabin fever, they call it."

They chatted until they saw the high-rise towers of Regina rise up on the horizon. The skyline changed imperceptibly, slowly growing closer, and it was nearly half an hour later before they actually entered the outskirts of the city. They found the Holiday Inn and checked in, then walked around the neighbourhood to find the university.

Once he had his bearings, Rashford suggested they have dinner at the hotel, followed by an early night. Roxanne said she agreed, especially with the early night.

When Rashford woke up, Roxanne already had the coffee pot spluttering away. She handed him a cup, sitting next to him on the bed.

"Wake up, sleepy head," she said. "Time for you to go and be brilliant."

"I must confess that I'm a bit nervous," he said.

"Well, of course, that's natural. But you're going to be fine. I heard you chattering with Kôhkum Christine, all the way back from Cypress Hills. Just try and relax, they're people, they're not trying to trick you. They're only doing their job."

Rashford kissed her.

"Thank you," he said. "I'd better get organized."

"I'll just go downstairs and pick up a couple of muffins," said Roxanne. "You can have one before you leave."

Rashford got up, showered, and put on his dress uniform. He had wondered whether that was appropriate, but the lady at Human Resources had ensured him that he was taking the examination as part of his responsibilities as a police officer, and so he was considered to be on duty.

After taking only a small bite from the bran muffin that Roxanne had brought up to the room, Rashford finished his coffee. He kissed her on the head.

"Right then," he said. "I'll see you around noon."

She reached up and kissed him properly.

"Good luck," she said, smiling. "Break a leg or whatever that saying is."

"I think that's for actors," he said.

"Well, then it applies to you. You're going on a stage, aren't you?"

"I guess I am, yes. Thank you," he said, and left the room.

Rashford walked across the university and found the room where the examination was going to take place. He got lost twice, but with the help of nearby students who didn't run away when he approached, he eventually got there. He was ten minutes early, so he went around a corner to where he smelled smoke.

A young man with a vape looked up from his phone when the policeman approached.

"I know it's against the rules, but you're not going to arrest me, are you," he said, nervously.

"Actually, I thought I'd join you," said Rashford, taking out and lighting a cigarette.

"You can't smoke on campus," said the young man, blowing a large gust from his vape.

"Right," said Rashford. "And what, vapes don't count?"

"No, they're not proper tobacco."

"Correct. And you think it is better to stick to the chemicals, do you?"

"Well, that's what they say. Doctors and people like that."

"People like salespeople, you mean. Of course, tobacco is bad for you. I know that and you know that. If I make a decision to have a cigarette, I know that I'm taking a risk. But I also know what the risk is. With vapes, nobody has figured that out yet. You're just the guinea pig."

Rashford finished his cigarette and stubbed it out. He picked up the butt and wrapped it in a tissue. Nodding goodbye to the student, he went back around the corner and dropped the tissue into a nearby waste bin. Then he straightened his jacket and walked into the building.

There were three people in the room, sitting at a table. When Rashford entered, they stood up, and he went across and shook hands.

"*Tansi*," he said.

"*M'on ana'tow,*" said the man in the middle of the three, gesturing to the empty chair in front of the table. Rashford sat down.

"First, the rules. In English," said the man, although he was not smiling. "That is the protocol."

Rashford nodded. The man introduced himself and the other two members of the panel. One was a woman, a professor from the First Nations University. The second was another man, a researcher from the Saskatchewan Indian Languages Institute. The chairperson, Rashford discovered, was from the Federation of Saskatchewan Indigenous Nations, a major political organization in the province.

Rashford was starting to wish that he had worn civilian clothes. He had not asked Bettina for her opinion, but he could hear her voice in his head. He was pretty sure that, to the eyes of the panel, he was a member of the oppressive racist patriarchy. He decided to just do the best he could, and to avoid getting into any arguments if possible. He focused back on what the chairperson was saying.

"Everything from this point will be in the Cree language. You can use English to ask for clarifications, if you don't understand, but you will lose points each time you do so. We have a list of prepared questions, and we will start with those. Then we will have a more general conversation. There are also written and reading comprehension components. The full examination will take three hours. Do you have any questions?"

"*Namoya*," said Rashford.

"Very well, let us begin. First, *awina kiya*?"

"*Niya* Gavin Rashford," he said. And so began a very intense three hours.

At noon, the three examiners stood and thanked Rashford for sharing the morning with them. He shook their hands, then went outside into the cool Regina air. As always, a strong wind was blowing across the campus. He ducked behind the building again, and to his surprise the young man with the vape was also there.

"Do you live here?" said Rashford.

"Class break," muttered the student. "What about you?"

"Exam finished," said Rashford, lighting a cigarette.

"Since this morning? One exam?"

"Yes.

"Holy shit, what course are you taking? I don't want to take that one."

Rashford laughed.

"It was my FILTER. That is the Focused Indigenous Language

Training for Emergency Responders program. We have to pass it to keep our jobs."

"Holy shit. Really?"

"Yes, really."

"So, what, they make you sit in a room and write for three hours. That can't be right, man."

"No, it's not like that. You go in a room and there is a panel, three examiners. They ask you a series of prepared questions, and then they give you a short story to read. Then you talk about the story, and they ask more questions.

"Then they ask you to write a letter, where you talk about the good things you enjoy about your job, and what you think might be done differently. I had to write mine to my Chief Superintendent. I don't know if she actually sees it, I wasn't clear about that.

"Finally, you read your letter back to them, and they talk about what you had said. That's like a real conversation, it doesn't feel like an exam at all. When that was finished, so was the exam."

"Did you have to learn Sioux or Cree?"

"Yes. You can learn any Indigenous language, I chose Cree."

"Which bits of the exam were in Cree?"

"All of it."

The young man stared at him.

"All of it? Like, reading, writing, speaking?"

"Yes."

"Holy shit. Respect, man, respect."

The man took a last drag on his vape and put the tube into his pocket, raised his forefinger to his eyebrow, and then sauntered off back to his class. Rashford finished the cigarette, thought for a moment, then lit another one. He smoked that more slowly, then set off back to the hotel.

Roxanne was already back. She had been to three different car showrooms, and seen a couple of vehicles she liked, but none that had jumped out and said, 'buy me'.

"That will come," she said. "I'll know our car as soon as I see it. Now, let's have lunch, and you can tell me about your morning."

They ate in the hotel restaurant again, and Rashford told her about the examination. He also noted that the service was noticeably better than it had been the night before.

"It must be the uniform," said Roxanne. "They're all jealous of me and trying to impress you."

Once they had finished lunch, Rashford said he should go back to the room and change, before they decided on what to do for the afternoon. He came out of the bathroom to find Roxanne in bed, her clothes piled on the chair.

"I've decided what to do this afternoon," she said, throwing back the sheet. Rashford stood looking at her until she felt uncomfortable.

"What?" she said, pulling the sheet back over her chest.

"You're just so beautiful," he said.

"That's alright then," she said, pushing the sheet away again. Rashford undressed and got into the bed.

"I'm exhausted," he said. "I think I'll just have a little nap."

"Don't you dare," she said. "You can rest your eyes, and I'll do all the work, but if you go to sleep then you'll wake up missing parts, Gavin Rashford. Clear?"

"Yes, Ma'am," he said.

They took a taxi into downtown, walking around the grounds of the legislative building and watching the ducks on Wascana Lake. Later, they spent the evening at the Regina Casino, playing the slot machines and wandering around the poker tables, watching the action. They had a nice dinner in the Union Station restaurant, and Roxanne clutched his arm as they looked at the old schedule board high on a wall in the main concourse.

"Isn't this romantic," she said. "We met in an old railway station, remember?"

"Oh yes, I remember," said Rashford. "Will you still be here in the morning?"

Roxanne gave him a big hug and a deep kiss, her arms around his neck.

"Get a room," muttered a passing waiter, in Cree, who then turned beet red when Rashford replied in the same language and told him they already had one booked.

"Sorry," said the waiter, "not many *môniyâw* speak our language."

"It's OK," said Rashford, laughing. "Tell me, is it true that half the people who work here are First Nations?"

"Pretty much," said the waiter, proudly. "There are many Métis, of course, and even a few Inuit, but it's mainly Treaty 4 people, and some other people, from outside our land."

Having lost the twenty dollars each had decided would be their limit for the evening, they walked outside and stood looking up at the stars.

"It would be an hour to walk back," said Rashford, "or we can take a cab."

"Cab," said Roxanne, "I've been on my feet all day."

The next morning, Rashford left Roxanne by the hot tub and pool.

"We're supposed to check out by eleven," he said, "but I've asked at the desk, and they've given us an extension until two this afternoon. I should be back by noon, I hope."

"I'll just stay down here for an hour or so," she said, "then I'll go back up to the room and get ready. See you soon. Say hello to the Chief Superintendent from me."

"Will do."

He gave her a kiss on the head and walked briskly out of the hotel. It was only twenty past nine, but he did not want to be late, so he took a taxi to the NWMP headquarters building. The traffic was moderate, and the journey took twenty minutes instead of the usual ten.

By the time he had signed into the front desk, and passed through the security checks, he just had time to use the washroom before taking the elevator up to the Chief Superintendent's office suite on the second floor. He nodded to the receptionist, a serving officer he knew whom he had met a few times before, and vaguely noted that she looked attractive in her uniform.

"My face is up here, Sergeant," she said, then burst into laughter when he turned bright red.

"No, sorry, no, I didn't, sorry, I ..." he said, stuttering.

"It's alright," she said. "I'm not going to report you. But you owe me a beer."

His blush subsiding, Rashford readily agreed. A few moments later, the inner door opened.

"Good, you are here," said Chief Superintendent Pollard. "Please, come in. Sarah, can you get us coffee, please. And hold my calls, unless they are from the Commissioner."

"Yes, Ma'am," said the receptionist.

Rashford followed Pollard into her office and stood quietly while she described the view from her windows. Sarah came in and placed a tray on the table. Rashford saw that the tray held two coffee cups, both emblazoned with the NWMP logo, a medium size French press, a small jug of cream, and a bowl of sugar cubes.

After Sarah had left, Pollard indicated that they should sit down. It was only after they had each prepared their coffee that she started to speak.

Chapter 15

"First, let me congratulate you," said Tracey Pollard, reaching over the table to shake Rashford's hand. "I hear that you passed your FILTER examination with flying colours."

Rashford coloured slightly.

"Thank you, Ma'am. I haven't heard anything."

"No, and you won't, not for at least two weeks. The results have to be tabulated, approved by the university, and then signed off by me. No, this is just me giving you a heads up. I play squash with Professor Helen Tootoosis, who was on your panel. She said she has never heard a *môniyâw* who was so fluent in Cree.

"Helen told me you were so good, Chief Whitecalf, the FSIN guy, was so impressed he made up that letter assignment. Normally you just have to write a piece to introduce yourself to a meeting, fifty or sixty words. So truly, Sergeant Rashford, congratulations."

"Thank you, Ma'am."

"The second thing I have to say is that we have been talking to the military and there is no record of anyone called Xavier Ballantyne ever having served in the Canadian Armed Forces. Any of them, Army, Navy, Air Force. Nobody with a name that even comes close. I think it's another clue."

"What do you mean?" said Rashford. "Ma'am."

"Sandra told you that she had her child at the hospital in Antigonish. The University there is called St. Frances Xavier University. I spoke to a woman at my squash club, she wears an X ring. Apparently, you only get one if you're a graduate, and they wear it like a secret symbol. Anyway, she told me that there is a very pretty road that loops around Cape George, which is near Antigonish. The road goes through a place called Ballantyne's Cove. I think he picked names that would subconsciously make her believe that he was from that area."

Rashford sat straighter in his chair. He looked at the Chief Inspector.

"So, if he doesn't exist, then perhaps neither do his stories. But why would he make that all up, for Sandra?"

"People do strange things to impress their mothers," said Pollard.

"If she is in fact his mother," said Rashford.

"I was going to get to that," said Pollard. "Do you think you can persuade Roxanne and her mother to give us DNA samples, which we can check against the samples we know came from Ballantyne. Or Dallas. Or whomever he is."

"I can certainly ask, Ma'am. I don't think there will be a problem."

"Thank you."

Chief Inspector Pollard paused, tapping her pencil gently on the desk. Rashford remained silent. After a few minutes, she looked straight at him, her face grim.

"Now this is where I would normally say, you have passed your FILTER and so you are now ready for your next assignment. Unfortunately, I am not able to say that in this case."

Rashford felt a jolt of surprise but kept his face expressionless.

"Ma'am?"

"The three-strike rule has caught up with you, Sergeant. I'm sorry."

"I'm not sure I understand, Ma'am."

"Remember Samuel Augustine Samson, Sergeant? Up in Black Rapids? The fellow who accused you of harassment and racial profiling, not to mention making him a laughingstock of his community by encouraging everyone to call him 'Snowdrop'. Well, he has rejected my letter of explanation and demanded a formal inquiry by the Civilian Review and Complaints Commission. They have agreed to hear the case. That was strike one, especially given the context of why you were posted to Black Rapids in the first place.

"Second, there was the business in Saskatoon, when you were robbed in your hotel room by a woman with whom you had spent the night. I know that your relationship is different now, and that she repaid the money, but at the time you were at best fleeting acquaintances. You were fortunate indeed that all she took was cash, you were carrying formal identification and other official documents with you, it could have been most embarrassing. That was almost strike two, but I think I'm going to call that foul.

"Then, of course, there was all the mess at the beginning of this operation. From my inquiries, it seems that you knowingly misrepresented how you met Ms. Gaudet the second time. You wilfully failed to record the details of her vehicle in your report, even when the same vehicle was mentioned during your regional meeting. And you colluded with a civilian, Mr. Alf Robertson, to defraud the Prairie Lily Insurance Company. Any one of those would be strike two."

Rashford sat as rigidly upright in the chair as he could manage.

"Finally, I have received an official complaint from a Mrs. Suzanne Stordy. She alleges that you publicly shamed her and her friend, Paul, by accusing them of having extra-marital sex in a public place. An accusation you levied, apparently, in front of Mrs. Stordy's sister-in-law and her best friend."

"Her sister-in-law?"

"Yes. Apparently, the husband isn't into bears, but his sister is."

"Oh."

"'Oh' indeed, Sergeant. Could you not have been a bit more discreet?"

Rashford looked at her, spreading out his arms, palms raised.

"I assumed that they all knew but just pretended it wasn't happening. 'Don't ask don't tell' or whatever that saying is. But I mean, surely someone would twig, them always being there first, at the lake?"

Pollard shrugged.

"Perhaps. But the official line is that they all thought Missus Stordy and her friend were there early to make sure they could set up the spotting scope in the best place. Not everyone has your sort of mind,

Sergeant. Or the imagination to dream up that accusation, for that matter."

"It wasn't really an accusation, Ma'am. I was just checking a theory and trying to make sure that I was dealing with the truth."

"No matter. It seems that Mrs. Stordy basically now blames you both for the break-up of her marriage and for the substantial financial damage that will come as a result of her being the wandering party in the relationship. So, that, indeed, is strike three."

Pollard sat back in her chair and steepled her hands in front of her. Rashford looked across the table.

"What happens now, Ma'am?" he said.

"Well, one of two things. The most logical one is that you will be placed on a full-time leave, with pay, while a full investigation against you is conducted. This will focus particularly on the items in strike two and three, although they will have to review strike one as well. Once that is complete, the report will be submitted to the CRCC, as will be a report from Saskatoon City Police. The CRCC will then come to a conclusion.

"I hesitate to predict such things, Sergeant Rashford, but one outcome would be that they will terminate your employment as an officer with the force."

"How long might such an inquiry take, Ma'am?"

"It's hard to say. Three weeks to a month at least, perhaps more."

Rashford thought for a moment.

"What is the second thing, please, Ma'am?"

"The second thing would be that you retire from your position now, claiming that the stress of the case has had a negative impact on your health. You can elicit sympathy by talking about how Mr. Ballantyne came so close to your girlfriend and her friends. You have twenty years in the force, your pension will be quite reasonable."

"What about the other things, Ma'am. The strike things."

"Well, if you retire and leave the force, I'm sure that CRCC can be persuaded to quash the complaint from Mr. Samson. The Saskatoon Police Service would only produce a report if they were asked to do so, by me. Apart from myself, only Staff Sergeant Miller and Corporal

Morgan know any of strike two, and they each only know bits. I am the only one who has the full picture."

"Which is why you are the Chief Superintendent, Ma'am," said Rashford.

"Indeed, Sergeant, indeed. Then there is strike three. I'm not quite sure what to make of Mrs. Stordy, it may require a full and suitably abject apology on your behalf, claiming stress, and so forth. She is obviously upset at being caught, although from all indications this was a regular event for the two of them. Honesty in the family court might be all that is required."

The two sat in silence for a few minutes.

"You do not need to make an immediate decision, Sergeant," said Pollard. "Drive back to Maple Creek and call me in the morning. Before ten, if you would be so kind. I have a media event at ten thirty."

She stood and held out her arm. Rashford stood as well and shook her hand.

"Thank you, Ma'am," he said.

"You're welcome, Sergeant," she said. "And truly, congratulations on that FILTER result. Quite incredible."

He nodded, turned, and went towards the door. From the corner of his eye he saw Pollard pause, then lean over her desk and pick up the phone.

"Sarah, come and clean away these coffee things, would you," she said. "Thank you."

Rashford left the office, passing the uniformed receptionist in the doorway. They nodded to each other, and then he was gone.

Roxanne spent the drive back to Maple Creek alternatively laughing and crying, cursing and congratulating, whispering and shouting. At first, she raged at the Chief Superintendent, accusing her of being a 'backstabbing evil traitor bitch', and at other times she thanked her for opening a door to allow Rashford an exit from the backwater of Maple Creek. Rashford drove steadily, keeping his eyes on the road even when Roxanne started throwing her arms around in a tantrum.

It was only as they pulled into the parking spot by the detachment building that he got her to calm down. She promised not to tell anyone about his predicament, at least not until he had had a chance to think about the consequences of both decisions. Roxanne composed herself in the car, using the mirror to repair her makeup before they went into the police house.

The house was empty, with a note on the table informing them that Sandra had gone over to help Kôhkum Christine and Bettina make the dinner. Rashford and Roxanne were expected to join them at five thirty or as soon as they got home, whichever was the latest. Rashford looked at his phone.

"It's only four thirty," he said. "Let's have a shower."

"Together?" said Roxanne, grinning.

"I bags the soap," said Rashford, pushing past her to the bathroom.

Later, as they were getting dressed, they talked about what life could be like, without the police force. The conversation went around in circles, and eventually Rashford suggested that they leave things until the next day. Roxanne agreed, and they walked out into the soft late afternoon air of a prairie summer day. The magpies in the trees were chuntering at each other, and a group of goldfinches still in their summer plumage flitted through the lilac bushes. The steady breeze stirred the leaves of the trembling aspen, providing an aural backdrop as they walked the quiet streets.

They were surprised to see the bright yellow Volkswagen parked outside the small house, and even more surprised to see a police car. Walking up the steps, Rashford felt a pang of regret that Fox Woman was no longer there to bark at him. He knocked on the door and they walked into the house.

The front room appeared to be full of people, all of whom suddenly shouted "surprise!" A large banner hung along one wall, with 'Congratulations Gavin' written in black felt-tip marker pen. Looking round, Rashford saw that in addition to those whom he had expected, plus Cicily and Gayle, there was also Alf the mechanic, and a younger man who Rashford assumed was Brian the helper.

Roxanne clapped her hands in delight, running over to greet Kôhkum Christine with a hug. The elder sat in her chair, a huge smile across her face, and laughed at something Roxanne said. Bettina and Cicily were standing together near the door into the kitchen. Rashford went over to them.

"Congratulations, Gavin," said Cicily, giving him a hug.

"*Ka mamihcimowehk*," said Bettina, "I hear you did well."

"I thought the examination results were not going to be made public for two weeks," said Rashford. "How come you know already? Did Gayle find out?"

Bettina laughed.

"Don't be silly," she said. "Alvin Whitecalf is my second cousin, because his father was married to *Nôhkum's* younger sister. He called to congratulate her on her teaching. Gayle was surprised."

"Yes," said Cicily, laughing. "Gayle thought we were here for a different celebration."

"Oh, and what was that?" said Rashford.

Bettina held out her hand wiggled her fingers. There was a large ring on her engagement finger, with a pale-yellow stone set in a band of silver.

"That's beautiful," said Rashford. "What kind of stone is that?"

"It's called Chemawinite," said Cicily, "but it's more commonly known as Cedar Lake amber. It's only found in northern Manitoba, and I found some during one of my walks in the bush."

"Didn't Gayle do a great job," said Bettina, admiring the ring again.

"Gayle?" said Rashford.

"Yes," said Cicily. "Didn't you know? She's a lovely silversmith, makes all sorts of jewelry. When I came down last time, a couple of weeks ago, I brought it with me and dropped it off to Gayle on my way home. Betts had told me about her work, she made those earrings she has, and so I asked her to make this ring for me. For us."

She smiled and squeezed Bettina's hand.

The memory of the yellow Volkswagen parked outside Morgan's police house sprang into Rashford's mind, and he smiled ruefully at Roxanne, who was listening from across the room. She just shook her head, warning him not to say anything stupid. So, he didn't.

"It really is a work of art," he said, then turned away to speak to Alf, who had appeared beside him.

"Nice jacket, Alf," he said, looking at the yellow and purple tartan sports coat that Alf was wearing like a badge of accomplishment. "Very jazzy."

"Isn't it?" said Alf, doing a slow pirouette. "I bought it with some of the insurance payout."

He gave Rashford a big wink, then nodded across the room to where Brian was leaning against a wall, deeply engaged in conversation with Gayle Morgan.

"I reckon someone might get a ride in a police car tonight," Alf said, chuckling. "I suppose I'll have to walk myself home."

The two men stood quietly together for a few minutes, watching the hubbub around them. Then Alf turned to Rashford.

"Fancy a bit of fresh air?" he said.

"Sure," said Rashford, and they slipped quietly out of the back door.

After the party, the garden was an oasis of calm. It had grown dark, and a full moon swelled above the trees in the adjacent garden, providing enough light for them to see each other.

"The Cree say that's a Flying Up Moon," said Alf, spitting a wad of something out onto the grass.

"Why? What does that mean?"

"It's the time of year when all the ducks have got their feathers back, after the summer moult, and they come out of the reeds and start flying again. I thought everyone knew that."

Rashford just shook his head.

Alf pulled out a package of cigarettes and offered one.

"Here you go," he said.

Rashford took it automatically and leaned forward into the flame of the lighter Alf cupped in his hand. It was only as he exhaled the first drag that he realized.

"Hang on," he said. "How did you know I smoke?"

Alf squinted at him through the smoke of his own cigarette.

"You remember my nephew's girlfriend's brother, the one who sold me the chainsaw?"

"Yes," said Rashford, wondering what was coming next.

"Well, he takes some classes over at the University, in Regina like, and he was having a fresh-air break when you ducked into his hiding space and had a smoke. Twice."

"So, he phoned you?"

"Well, not exactly. He phoned me because he heard two of the examiners talking, when they were leaving the building, and he called to tell me that he thought you'd done okay on your exam. Then he mentioned the smoke bit, to explain how he knew who they was talking about."

"Right," said Rashford, gazing up at the sky in disbelief.

"How come everyone knows what I've said or done, almost as soon as I've said or done it?" he said.

"Small town life," said Alf. "No escaping it. Unless you don't do or say anything, of course. Then they'll talk about that."

Cackling, he stubbed out his cigarette, and walked back into the house. Rashford smoked his for a moment longer, then followed suit.

The party was a great success. Bettina had somehow managed to source some moose meat, which her grandmother had made into what she called Trapper's Pie. The meat had been ground and mixed together with some minced pork. Four rashers of bacon were cut up into small squares, using scissors to snip them off, then sauteed in pan with onions, wild garlic, and the dried leaves of prairie sage. Once the bacon was sizzling, the ground meat was added and cooked.

"Keep stirring it," admonished Kôhkum Christine. "Don't let it stick or it will burn."

While this was turning brown in the pan, a dozen large, peeled potatoes were being boiled to within an inch of their lives. Once they were cooked, the water was drained away, and the potatoes were mashed together with butter and salt, and a small dash of cream.

"My secret ingredient," said Kôhkum Christine, laughing.

The meat mixture was then turned into a large baking dish, and the mashed potato spread on top. A thick layer of orange cheddar cheese was then grated over the top, and the pie was baked for thirty minutes in a medium oven.

Sandra had heated a bag of frozen peas, which formed the vegetable, and everyone received a large bowl of Trapper's Pie with a small mound of green peas sitting in the middle like a cenotaph. In the centre of the table was another bowl, this one filled with chunks of Bannock, which were used to mop up the sauce.

Once the meal was finished, Bettina stood up.

"I have a couple of things to say," she said. "First, let us thank the Creator for this meal, and for our friendship here tonight."

They all bowed their heads, and a few murmured a short prayer.

"Second," said Bettina, "I want to unofficially congratulate Gavin on his examination today. He made us all proud."

Everyone clapped, and Rashford bowed his head again, acknowledging the applause.

"Third, I want to thank my friend and partner, Cicily, for gifting me this beautiful ring."

She held out her hand and waggled her fingers again, the stone catching the light and sparkling in the room. Everyone applauded again, and this time Cicily bowed her head.

"Finally," said Bettina, "I want to thank my *Nôhkum,* who the world knows as *Kôhkum Christine*, for raising me, for helping me become the person I have become, and for hosting our gathering here tonight."

She raised her glass of fruit juice up in front of her. The others stood up from the table, also raising their glasses. Everyone turned and looked at the old lady, who sat at the head of the table, smiling.

"To *Nôhkum*," said Bettina.

"To *Kôhkum Christine*," said the rest of the group.

They all took a drink, then replaced the glasses on the table and clapped until the elder waved for them to stop. They all sat down again, except Sandra. She waited until everyone had noticed her, and stopped talking, then spoke.

"I am a guest on this land," she said, "and I bring you greetings from the People of the Dawn. I would like to thank you for welcoming me, and for making me feel at home. Thank you also for looking after my daughter and providing her with a strong circle of friendship. As we say in my language, *wela'lin.*"

She nodded to each person in turn, repeating the word, and then sat down.

Rashford looked around, then stood.

"If I may," he said, looking at Bettina. She nodded.

"I would also like to say a couple of things," Rashford said.

"First, to *Kôhkum Christine*, for her patience and her expertise and her teaching. Without her, I may still have passed the FILTER. With her, because of her, I was certain to pass. I truly thank you for all you have done for me."

The elder nodded in appreciation.

"Second, to all of you here, thank you for the contributions you have made to making my life in Maple Creek such a wonderful experience. I am truly grateful for all you have done for me."

"But." said Gayle Morgan, looking up from the middle of the table. Cicily looked at her.

"I can hear a 'but' coming a mile away," said Morgan. "So would you, if you'd had my life."

Alf chuckled, and Brian patted Morgan's arm tenderly.

Rashford nodded.

"Correct. But, even with all that help and support, I am not going to stay here. In fact, I am not even sure if I'm going to stay in the North-West Mounted Police."

There was a stunned silence. Even Roxanne was looking wary, wondering what was coming next.

"It will take some weeks, until the end of September or later, for this case to be wrapped up. When it is finished, though, then I will be put on administrative leave. It seems that there are some things the higher-ups didn't like about the way I do things. Anyway, I won't be able to stay here. I'm going to ask the Chief Superintendent if I can take my accumulated holiday time, during the leave. There are some who say that the fall is the best time to see this country. Or should I say, these countries, Alsama and Canada. It will be a good time to travel.

"I am hoping that Roxanne will join me, to drive across the prairie, through the forests of the lake country, to the far ocean, to her place, to the land of the People of the Dawn. If she agrees, then we shall buy a car. I don't know which one, but we will know it when we see it.

"And then we will drive, following the road that seems right for that day, until we get to our destination. Once we are there, then we will see what happens. We might be able to get to places that I don't even know exist."

He turned and looked to his right, where Roxanne sat, looking up at him with wonder in her eyes.

"Roxanne, will you make this journey with me?" he said.

She jumped up and hugged him, kissing him madly around the face, tears streaming down her own.

"I think we can take that as a yes," said Gayle Morgan, leading the clapping and the laughter.

As he had predicted, Alf walked home alone from the party. Morgan took Brian for a drive in her police car, and it was four days before he returned to work. Cicily took a leave from her job and stayed with Bettina and Kôhkum Christine, helping to train the new puppy on the days when Bettina was away at the college.

Roxanne and Rashford walked home hand in hand, talking with Sandra about the places they hoped to see on their drive to Prince Edward Island. She had a bus ticket for the next day, and refused to change it, saying that she needed to get home and prepare a welcome feast, no matter how long it took them to get there.

Once they were back at the police house, Rashford raised the question of them providing a DNA sample, to help the investigation. Sandra was unsure at first, but he explained that the sample would not be kept any longer than needed.

"It's not going to be put in the data bank," he said. "They will just run your sample against the data bank and see if there is a match. It might help us to figure out who this fellow really is, the one we've been chasing."

"What do we have to do?" said Roxanne.

"It's pretty easy. You can get DNA from pretty much any biological material. Dried blood stains, saliva, hair, teeth, body fluids, whatever. But the quickest and best way is an oral swab."

"What's that?"

"I have some in the office. They're like a Q-tip, but only have the lump at one end. You roll it around inside your mouth, and then we put it in a special sealed plastic bag, and then it goes to be tested."

"And they won't keep my results on file?" said Sandra.

"No. There's a paper you have to sign, that says you will only agree to them using the sample for comparative purposes related to this specific investigation. And the police sign it as well. So then everybody is clear on the rules."

The two women looked at each other.

"I guess I can do that," said Roxanne.

"Me too," said Sandra, after a short pause. "You said hair as well?"

"Hair works, yes, as long as it's got the roots attached. You can't just cut off a lock or anything. But we don't need both. The swab will be enough."

"No, not from me. How about from Xavier?"

"Xavier? You have his hair?"

"Well, some of it. When he was over visiting me, in Charlottetown, he gave me a locket. Here."

She opened the top button of her shirt, revealing a thin gold chain hanging around her neck. She carefully lifted it over her head and showed the oval silver pendant hanging from the end. She unclipped the clasp and opened the lid, revealing the strands of hair inside. She proffered the locket to Rashford.

"Don't touch it," he said. "Quick, let me get a bag. Don't move."

He almost ran out of the house and round to the main office. When he got back, he found Roxanne and Sandra frozen in place. He carefully opened the evidence bag and asked Sandra to tip the hair inside.

"Can I keep some?" she said, her eyes starting to tear.

"Of course," he said. "I need about ten strands, that's all."

She shook the locket lightly and some of the strands fell into the plastic bag.

"How did he get this, the hair?" said Rashford, as he carefully sealed the bag, then wrote the time and date on the outside.

"He kind of combed his hair with his fingers and some fell out, then he put it in the locket," said Sandra.

"That might work, then," said Rashford. "Fantastic. This is very helpful. Now, here are the swabs."

He brought out two more evidence bags, each containing a single one-ended swab, and carefully rotated the end in Roxanne's mouth. When he had finished, he put the swab back in the bag and labelled it carefully. He then repeated the test with Sandra.

"Thank you both," he said. "I'll go and put these in the fridge for now, and make sure that they get to Regina tomorrow."

"Will it help catch him?" said Roxanne. "Fancy Boots, I mean?"

"I don't know," said Rashford. "But it gives us more chance than we had before."

Rashford telephoned to the Chief Superintendent at nine forty-five and told her his decision. She responded that she wasn't sure that it was a wise thing to do, given the circumstances.

"I've got no idea which way the CRCC Inquiry will go," she said. "You're taking a bit of a risk."

"I think it's worth it, Ma'am. I am hoping that I can apply for a month's leave, Ma'am, my accumulated leave."

"Put in the forms, Sergeant, put in the forms. I think we can manage that, though."

"Thank you, Ma'am."

Pollard was silent for a moment. Then she cleared her throat.

"Inspector Whitehead will be happy, though," she said.

"Why? Because now he can keep chasing me to fill in his darn forms?"

Pollard laughed.

"Perhaps. But mainly because he doesn't think you should leave the investigation, not just yet."

"Why not, Ma'am?"

"He says you sometimes fudge the rules but you're generally a good detective," she said.

"Thank you, Ma'am. By the way, Sandra and Roxanne agreed to give DNA samples, for comparison purposes only of course."

"Of course. That's excellent. I'll send someone over ..."

"I already took them, Ma'am. They're in the fridge here. And Ma'am ...?"

"Yes?"

"Sandra has a locket, she said her son gave it to her, the fellow who visited her. It has a lock of his hair. She agreed to give me some of that as well."

"Really? Well done indeed, Sergeant. Thank you. I shall send a car from Swift Current right away; they should be there later this morning."

"Thank you, Ma'am."

"It will help us to confirm or eliminate a few things. We got some confirmation DNA from the rooms at the Mountain View house. The samples from the lockable rooms don't match anyone in our system. But the ones from the other room belong to out guy. So, we know he was there.

"Inspector Whitehead is convinced that Dallas slash Ballantyne was running some sort of high-class brothel, keeping women captive and making them available to his guests."

"The rich people in the fancy cars?" said Rashford.

"Exactly. Whitehead and his men found traces of some kind of rope ingrained in the wood of those bed posts, and also on the hook that supported the chandelier. They looked there because it wouldn't switch on, then they realized it was purely decorative, it wasn't even wired in."

"So, these women were tied up? Or hung up?"

"It seems both scenarios are possible. But we need to find one of the girls, first, before we can be sure."

"Was it yellow rope?"

"It was. How on earth did you know that?"

"There was some in the tool-box on the back of his pick-up truck," said Rashford.

"I don't recall that from the report."

"Sorry, Ma'am. That might have slipped my mind."

Chief Superintendent Pollard put on her most unctuous and ingratiating voice, the tone of which had terrified police officers for the past two decades.

"Tell me, Sergeant," she said, sweetly. "Is there anything else that might have slipped your mind?"

Rashford did not speak for a few seconds. Then he cleared his throat.

"There are a couple of things that are not in any report because I just thought of them, Ma'am," he said.

"Yes?"

"Missus Toews, the neighbour, she told us that one visitor drove a fancy Rolls Royce car. A Phantom 3, I think she said it was, from the thirties. They must be really expensive and there can't be that many around, even in Alberta. Perhaps the Inspector would be able to check with a dealer, or a classic car club, and see if they know of anyone who might own such a car."

"Good idea, Sergeant. Thank you. And the other point?"

"Tell Whitehead to look in the slough," said Rashford.

The Chief Superintendent took a deep breath.

"Oh, dear," she said. "I hope you're wrong this time."

That evening, Rashford and Roxanne watched the Saskatchewan six o'clock newscast. They heard Pollard commend Rashford for his work on a very difficult case and describe him as a talented and enthusiastic officer whose many skills were well known.

She failed to mention the CRCC investigation or the possibility that he might get fired at the end of it.

Roxanne clicked off the television and went over to sit in Rashford's lap.

"Why don't you show me some of those many skills," she said, biting his ear lobe.

It was a bright cool morning in early October when they bade farewell to Maple Creek. The previous night they had taken Kôhkum Christine, Bettina and Cicily out to dinner at the Bel-Air restaurant.

"It's not goodbye," said Bettina. "Our people don't believe in saying that. We say, 'see you later', because we know that we will."

The chef herself had come out, to thank Roxanne for talking her into making General Tsao chicken.

"All our customers just love it," she said. "Every night we almost sell out. So, thank you and, please, accept this meal tonight with our thanks."

They each had a bottle of Tiger beer, which they raised in acknowledgment, and then the eating continued. Cicily was the one who asked the question on everyone's mind.

"How long will this road trip take, do you think? Do you have a planned itinerary?"

"Not really," said Rashford. "We'll head across the prairies on the slow road, to the south, through the short grass prairie. I've always wanted to see Weyburn, my great-grandfather homesteaded there when he first immigrated to Canada."

"Then we'll stop near Brandon," said Roxanne. "One of my cousins is stationed at the army base at Shilo, just south of there, and he said he could take us out to the range for a ride in a LAV, a light armoured vehicle. How cool is that?"

"We'll cross the border into Canada at Falcon Lake," said Rashford, "then drive through the northern forest, through places like Kenora and Ignace, until we get to Lake Superior. There's a place near Thunder Bay where you can go and collect your own gemstones, it's an amethyst mine."

"Yes," said Roxanne, "and then there is the giant goose at Wawa, the petroglyphs at Agawa rock, and the locks at Sault Ste. Marie. There will be so much to see!"

"After that," said Rashford, "it will depend on how much time and money we have left. If we can, I would like to go and visit my aunt Lenora, in Chatham. That's down in southern Ontario. She's in her eighties and I've not seen her in years. After that, I would like to go to Ottawa, and to Quebec City, and then to drive along the Saint Lawrence valley to New Brunswick."

"Once we're in New Brunswick, it's only a five-hour drive to the Confederation Bridge, and then less than an hour to Charlottetown. So, after we leave Riviere-de-Loup, we'll call mom and tell her to start getting dinner ready."

"That sounds like quite the adventure," said Bettina, laughing. "Send us lots of pictures from your phone!"

"Of course," said Roxanne, "in fact I'm going to set up a vlog and send videos and reports every day. Kôhkum, make sure that Bettina shows you how to log in on the computer."

"No problem," said Kôhkum Christine, "I have my iPad."

They had been driving for eleven days and had just driven over the bridge from Quebec City when Rashford's cell phone rang. He pulled over to the side of the highway and answered it. It was Chief Superintendent Pollard.

"There have been a couple of developments that I thought you should know about," she said.

"What might those be?" said Rashford, intrigued.

"Well, first, Inspector Whitehead says to tell you that he had already thought of the car dealer angle and might have a lead on the owner of a Rolls Royce Phantom 3. It's a fellow in Calgary but they're going very slowly with the investigation, they don't want to spook him. Also, he had a couple of officers search the slough. It's only a couple of feet deep, apparently. They found lots of muck and mud, but nothing else."

"Thank you. What was the second thing?"

"I thought you might like to know this," she said. "We have the results back from the DNA comparisons. I am sorry, but there is no match between the samples we took from Sandra Sylliboy and Roxanne and those we have of the man who called himself Xavier Ballantyne."

There was a pause.

"I see. Well, thank you for calling," said Rashford.

"Wait, please," said Chief Superintendent Pollard. "There was a positive match on the other sample, though. The hair from the locket, it's a ninety-nine-point-nine per cent match with the samples we have from Claude Dallas."

"It is him," said Rashford, softly, ignoring the questioning look he was getting from Roxanne.

"Yes, it seems that Claude Dallas and Fancy Boots are actually one and the same. Your intuition was right, and now you have some evidence to support it."

"Thank you, Ma'am."

"You should also know, the DNA samples we took from Roxanne and her mother did trigger a match in the system, just not with Mr. Dallas-Ballantyne."

Despite himself, Rashford was intrigued.

"With whom, then?"

The Chief Superintendent paused again, for longer this time. Eventually, she spoke.

"With a homeless man who the Calgary police found frozen behind a dumpster last winter," she said. "Again, there is a ninety-nine-point-nine per cent correlation between the samples."

"Holy fuck," said Rashford.

"What is it?" said Roxanne, reaching out her hand and grasping his sleeve.

"One moment, Ma'am," he said. "This is an old car so we don't have a hands-free system, but I'll put you on speaker phone so Roxanne can hear."

He clicked the button, and Pollard's voice became audible in the car.

"Hello, Roxanne. Are you having a good trip?"

"Yes, thank you."

"Excellent. I have been following your vlog, it certainly looks very interesting."

"Thank you, ummm ..."

"Call me Tracey, you don't work for me."

"Thank you, Tracey."

"As I was saying to Sergeant Rashford, it looks like your brother did exist, but has passed away. I am sorry to be the bearer of bad news. My condolences on your loss."

"Oh. Right. Thank you. I never knew I had a brother, of course, so it's hard to get emotional. But I know that mom will be sad."

"Are you okay with telling her, or should I ask the local police to go around to her house?"

"I can tell her. Are there any more details?"

"Not really. It seems that he was living on the streets of Calgary, and had been for some time, at least five years. Nobody knew where he came from, before Calgary, but one outreach counsellor said that sometimes he talked of being fostered, and of running away from an abusive home. But no details, I'm afraid."

"That is sad news."

"Yes. The outreach worker did say that he called himself Xavier, or sometimes Mister X, but when they found his body there was no identification with him. He was buried as a John Doe, in a Calgary churchyard."

"Can I tell mom that she will be able to get a proper stone for him, with his name?"

"Oh yes, I'm sure that will be possible. Let me make a note and I'll try to find out the protocols."

There was a short silence. They could hear the Chief Superintendent tapping on her tablet.

"Done. There was another thing. One of the volunteers from the downtown soup kitchen said that about a year ago, he seemed to get happier. Apparently, a new guy moved into town and became his friend. The volunteer said she didn't like him, this so-called friend, he always seemed a bit creepy, and he was the one who kept buying their booze."

"Do you think that was our guy?" said Rashford.

"Probably. I think he befriended Roxanne's brother, or half-brother I suppose, and got to know his story. Then he basically took on his identity, at least for the past six or eight months. When did your mom say he first contacted her?"

"Earlier this year, so the timeline fits," said Roxanne.

"None of this makes any sense," said Rashford. "Who is this guy?"

"That's a very good question," said Chief Superintendent Pollard. "And we really have no idea. We have his DNA now, so if he shows up on the system a red flag should be raised. But we have no name, and he seems to have disappeared. There has been no sighting of him since he left the police house in Maple Creek, and only one thing even related to him since we found the truck at Saskatchewan Crossing Provincial Park."

"What thing was that Ma'am?"

"A Saskatchewan Roughriders cap, Sergeant."

"How do we know that it is, or was, his?"

"Well, because sewn into the lining of the cap was a wig. A wig of white hair, plaited into a ponytail."

"No way!"

"I'm afraid so, yes. Basically, the one stand-out feature in all the descriptions turns out to have been false."

"Another misdirection," said Rashford. "Although that also explains one thing for me."

"What's that?"

"When Ms. Stordy described him, out at Cameron Lake, she said she didn't think he was wearing a hat. But she didn't say anything about long white hair in a ponytail."

"I see. Well, that's where we are, anyway," said Pollard.

"Is there still an active search?"

"No," said Pollard, gently. "Sorry, but we have enough live people running around doing bad things, I can't waste resources on a ghost. As I said, if he trips a red flag, then of course I will go after him. But not until then."

"So, he gets away again, even though he left tracks all over the country?"

"Yes, I'm afraid he does. And remember, Sergeant, you are on holiday. Just forget about this. If we get him before you get back, then you will read about it in the papers."

"Yes, Ma'am."

"You did an incredible job, tracking him all across Alberta and Saskatchewan. But now you're going to be spending some time on your little island, so worry about other things. The price of lobster, stuff like that."

"Yes, Ma'am."

Rashford said a few more words, then ended the call. He looked across at Roxanne.

"I won't be able to just forget him, you know," he said. "I can't turn off like that."

She reached over and patted his arm.

"I know. But Tracey is right, you can't do anything right now."

Rashford put the car in gear, indicated, then pulled out and merged with the traffic heading up the highway past Saint-Jean-Port-Joly to

Rivière-de-Loup. From there he planned to turn right, to Edmundston, before crossing New Brunswick to the Confederation Bridge.

"He's made a fool of me twice," he said, "so it will be third time lucky for me. I don't know what I'm going to do on this island of yours for the rest of our holiday, but I'm going to be keeping part of my mind on Albert Johnson or Claude Dallas or Xavier Ballantyne or whatever he is calling himself now. That's a promise. Everyone leaves traces and tracks of their passing; hunters call it the spoor. But if you follow the spoor long enough, you get to understand their habits. Then one day they get caught in the snare. You just have to know where to set it."

Chapter 16

Rashford and Roxanne drove over the Confederation Bridge on a mild mid-October afternoon, the Northumberland Strait calm a hundred feet beneath them. Ring-billed and herring gulls floated effortlessly on the updraft, flying parallel to the top of the concrete barriers that lined the bridge. The tall lampposts with the security cameras and the lights were crowned with spike belts, to discourage the birds from using them as an observation post or a roost. Instead, every few hundred metres a large black-backed gull would be resting, imperiously, on the balustrade, gazing balefully at the cars passing less than two metres away.

Once they were on the island they saw fields still bright green from recent rain, interspersed with acres of red soil that showed where the potato harvest had taken place. The stands of poplar were drifting masses of yellow, and a few swamp maples had started to turn red, harbingers of the fall to come. They were startled by a large heron which suddenly flew up from a narrow river they crossed, and then laughed as they drove by the concrete replica of a stegosaurus, emerging from a yard of smaller sculptures.

Sandra greeted them with enthusiasm and delight, ecstatic at having her daughter in her home again. Rashford spent most of their first evening nodding and smiling as the other two laughed and chattered. As the evening wound down, Roxanne started to yawn, and her mother was quick to take the cue.

"I'm sorry, I've only got a small place," she said. "So, I'll sleep out here on the couch tonight, you guys have my bed."

Rashford protested but Sandra was adamant.

"I already changed the sheets," she said. "And anyways, I'll be up before you in the morning, I'm always up with the sun."

The next morning, however, she was still snoring gently as Roxanne tiptoed around her, making coffee. It was only when the pot bubbled and hissed that she jerked awake, sitting up and rubbing her eyes. She pulled the sleeping bag up around her and gratefully took the proffered cup from her daughter.

"Lovely, thank you," she said, sipping and blowing at the same time. "Sorry, I woke up a few times in the night, this old apartment building creaks in strange places and I'm not used to the noises out here."

"You should have stayed in your bed, mom," said Roxanne, rubbing Sandra's shoulder. "I could have had the couch, and Gavin would have been fine on the floor. Wouldn't you?"

"Yes, of course," said Rashford, rolling his eyes when he was sure Sandra couldn't see him.

"Anyway, you can have your bed back tonight. We're going to Cape Breton."

"We are?" said Rashford.

"Yes, I've been thinking. We only have a couple of weeks before we have to head back. The weather is perfect right now, let's go and see the colours."

"Don't you want to stay here for a while?" said Sandra, disappointment in her voice.

Rashford looked at Roxanne.

"Maybe another night, anyway," he said. "We should see at least a bit of Charlottetown. We can leave early in the morning."

He turned to Sandra.

"But Roxanne's right. You have to sleep in your own bed. We'll manage out here."

Sandra nodded.

"Okay, that's a deal," she said.

They all drank their coffee. Sandra looked at Rashford, then back to Roxanne.

"What else do you need to tell me?" she said.

Roxanne put her coffee mug down on the table.

"They found my brother," she said. "Half-brother. I'm sorry, mom."

Sandra stared at her.

"Sorry? Why? That's good news ... oh."

Her face crumpled as she took in the meaning of what Roxanne had said. Rashford watched as the two women embraced, then both began to cry quietly.

"He passed last winter," said Roxanne, gently.

"Where?"

"In Calgary. He was on the street, mom, and nobody knew who he was. It was only when they took our DNA that they realized who he was. It didn't match with that psychopath they were looking for, but they had taken a sample from Xavier to try and identify him, earlier. That meant he was in the system and our DNA was a match. I'm so sorry, mom."

Rashford cleared his throat.

"I'm sorry for your loss, Sandra. But just so you know, the Chief Superintendent is looking into the protocols for how we can put a marker on his grave."

"We can do that?"

"Of course. Now that he has been identified, he can have a proper headstone. The Chief said she would be in touch as soon as she has the details."

Sandra nodded.

"Do you have any more information about him? How he lived his life?"

Rashford was unsure how much to share. He looked towards Roxanne. She shook her head.

"Not really," she said. "It seems he was on the street there for quite a while, at least five years. Nobody knew where he came from, before Calgary, but he called himself Xavier, or sometimes Mister X. It looks like he didn't make it to the shelter one evening, and when they found his body there was no identification with him.

"How sad," said Sandra.

"Yes," said Rashford. "The other thing we learned, though, is that about a year ago some new guy turned up and became his friend. There's no proof, but it looks like this might have been the guy we've chasing. The one who I tracked across country but who then escaped my custody. The one who then tried to kidnap Roxanne and use her in in a sex-slave operation, and who killed Fox Woman, Bettina's dog. The one who met you and pretended to be your son, Xavier. I think this fellow befriended your son and learned all about him, his life story, and then stole his identity."

"Why would he do such a thing?"

"I have absolutely no idea. I don't think we'll ever find out, at least not until we catch him. And that might be a while. As the Chief Superintendent said, they have enough live people running around doing bad things, they can't waste resources on hunting for a ghost. So, we have to hope that he somehow gets his DNA taken again, for something, and then that will send up a red flag."

Sandra nodded. She thought for a moment.

"My son. You said he was using the name Xavier?"

"Yes."

"So, can I put that on his stone? Xavier Sylliboy?"

"Yes, of course."

"Can I call him Keith as well?"

"You can put whatever you like on the stone," said Rashford.

"Thank you. I'll put something like, 'Here lies Xavier 'Keith' Sylliboy. Born 5 May 1987.' They will have the date of his passing, won't they?"

"It should be in the records, yes," said Rashford.

Sandra wiped her eyes.

"I wish I knew his story," she said.

In the end they stayed with Sandra for three nights and promised to stop-over again on their way back from Cape Breton. On the day of departure, they left early, driving into the sunrise as they traversed the island to get to the wharf. Rashford spent most of the drive complaining that they had to pay for the ferry, whereas the bridge had been free.

"When we return, we'll come back the other way, then the ferry will be free. When we drive back over the bridge to the mainland, we will have to pay a toll for the bridge," said Roxanne.

"That's crazy," said Rashford. "Surely it should be the same cost each way?"

"Well, perhaps in a normal world. People here say it's because they want to make it easy for tourists to get to the Island, and hard for them to leave."

Rashford laughed.

"Madness," he said.

As they drove through the mixed wood and farmland, with glimpses of the Northumberland Strait off to their right, Rashford pointed at an older-looking house.

"What's with the stars?" he said. "I've seen a few of them. Are they putting their Christmas decorations up early?"

"No, that's an Acadian signal. After the deportations, when the British expelled all the Acadians back in the seventeen fifties, some people made their way back here. People put up a star to show that this was a safe house, if you spoke French."

"And they still need to show that?"

"It's just in case, you know. That was a pretty traumatic time for the Acadians, you know. Ten thousand people thrown off their land at gunpoint, half of them died in shipwreck or exile. We have long memories."

"Right," said Rashford, and kept driving, wondering why he couldn't remember learning about this at school.

They had paid an extra fee and made a reservation for the nine-thirty ferry, but it turned out that there were very few cars in the line-up. The traffic was mostly semi-trailer units and logging trucks laden with softwood for the pulp and paper mills on the mainland. On the ferry they had to leave their car on the lower deck, and Roxanne rushed up the stairs so she could reserve seats at a window table. It was only when she had established her space that she let Rashford join the queue at the cafeteria.

"Make mine the Islander breakfast, please," she said, "with coffee. It's the best deal going!"

Once they had eaten and cleared away the plates, Roxanne told Rashford to go out on the deck.

"Enjoy the view," she said. "I'll stay here and hold the table. If it's not too cold, then maybe I'll go out later."

Rashford walked around the side of the cabin, then up the rickety metal stairs to the top deck. Some people, well wrapped in scarves and coats, toques pulled down over their foreheads, were sitting on the molded plastic benches.

"Grand day," said one, nodding to Rashford as he walked past.

Smoking was no longer allowed on the ferry, not even outside, and some passengers were starting to twitch. Rashford noted with amusement how they were chain-chewing sticks of gum and checking their watches to see how many of the seventy-five crossing minutes had elapsed. He looked for whales but didn't see anything except a couple of prehistoric looking cormorants, known locally as Shags, sitting low in the water and watching the ferry as it sailed past.

Going back into the main cabin, Rashford picked up two more coffees then went and sat down next to Roxanne.

"So, what's our plan, then?" he said. "I don't believe we're just going to look at trees, there are plenty of those on the Island."

Roxanne leaned her shoulder into him.

"There are two things you must remember," she said. "First, the autumn leaves in Cape Breton are the best in the world, it says so in all the tourist brochures, so that has to be true. They even call it the Celtic Colours festival, so many people come to look. As soon as we get to a tourist place, we need to book places where we can stay, it will be very busy."

"Okay," said Rashford. "What's the second thing?"

"People over there don't like you calling PEI 'the Island' because that's what they call Cape Breton. Mind you, people in Newfoundland don't like either of those, because that's what they call the Rock! But

Capers can be pretty sensitive, so just be careful about that, especially if we're in a bar."

Rashford laughed.

"I'll behave, I promise," he said. "Anyway, what is the plan?"

Roxanne took a sip of her coffee, then tapped the plastic spoon against her lip.

"This might sound silly," she said, "but I would really like to go to Eskasoni, where mom is from. I've never been there. I spoke to mom about it and she has called a cousin, who said we can stay with her for a couple of days if we would like. Is that alright?"

"Of course," said Rashford, "no problem. What else?"

"Well, do you remember mom telling us about having her first baby in Antigonish? My brother, who called himself Xavier. I was thinking that we could stop in there, we have to drive right past the town anyway, and see if the nuns are still around. I wonder if they have any old paper records, that they would let us see?"

"I guess we can only ask," said Rashford.

"And then, yes, I think we should drive the Cabot Trail, not just to see the leaves but also because it is one of the most beautiful drives in the world."

"We seem to have a lot of those in Canada," said Rashford. "Someone once told me that the Icefields Parkway in Alberta was one of the most beautiful drives in the world."

Roxanne laughed.

"That's in Alsama now," she said. "Not Canada. And anyway, this one has mountains and the ocean. Not just mountains."

"Fair enough," said Rashford, wondering again why people were so competitive and possessive about the landscapes in which they happened to live, or which they perceived as home. He remembered how he had once met a policeman on exchange from New Zealand, who introduced himself by stating 'this is my river, this is my mountain, this is my iwi.'

"'Your iwi is your tribe,' he had said, 'but the others place you in the land. Only then do you give your name. It's the Māori way, and all of us Pāhekā or European people, the settlers, we follow that now as well.'"

They left the ferry at Pictou, then took the Sunrise Trail along the north shore. It was a calming drive, with long views over the Northumberland Strait, and they enjoyed a break when they reached the lighthouse at the end of Cape George. They pulled into the small, gravelled parking area and walked, hand-in-hand, to the lighthouse itself. The area around the tower was cleared, with two wooden benches placed to provide commanding views of the sea.

"Gosh, it's beautiful," said Roxanne, putting her arm around Rashford's waist. She squeezed lightly.

"There's nobody else here," she said. "Give me a kiss."

Rashford obliged, and they embraced for an extended time. Then he pulled away.

"I bet there's a small beach down there," he said. "Shall we go and look?"

Roxanne looked at him with a slight smile.

"Sure," she said. "Lead on."

Rashford guided her down through the scrubby Labrador tea bushes until they reached the treeline, then followed a small game path that cut through the spruce.

"It looks like a fox or rabbits use this trail a lot," he said, showing her the compressed grasses on the trail. The path continued steeply down and sometimes they had to hold onto a tree bole or a low branch, but neither slipped as they navigated the slope.

After five or six minutes they reached the edge of the trees. There was a small lip where the ground finished, then a drop of about a metre down to a small beach. Rashford sat on the edge of the lip, then pushed himself off. He landed lightly on the gravel below, then turned to Roxanne.

"Come on, I'll catch you," he said.

She sat down on the edge as well, pushing back with her arms so that she more or less slid off the earth platform. Rashford reached up and caught her under her arms, guiding her down to the beach. As she stood and looked around, a few pebbles and chunks of dirt continued to splatter down around her.

"It's glorious," she said, then turned and reached up to embrace Rashford again.

"Are you thinking what I'm thinking?" she said.

"What? That it's going to be a long climb back up to the lighthouse?"

She punched him slightly.

"No, silly."

"Well, what, then? That it's going to be hard even getting off the beach back onto the trail?"

She punched him again, harder this time.

"Ow."

"Perhaps, now that we're here, we should have a quickie?"

She undid her jeans and slid them down over her hips.

"Not too quick, I hope," she said.

Rashford waited until she had kicked off her shoes and jeans, placing them on a flat rock near the bank, then took her by the hand and walked along the beach.

"Over here," he said, leading her to where a fallen spruce tree lay horizontal to the gravel. The side branches were embedded in the beach, and the ones on the top of the bole had been crushed flat by wind and storms. Rashford took her in behind the tree and leaned her against the fallen trunk, then kissed her.

She responded, hurriedly undoing his belt and murmuring into his throat. Suddenly he stopped and turned her around, then pushed gently on her back so she folded face forward over the tree, her stomach resting on the bole. She spread out her arms, her fingers caressing the rough bark.

"No reason we can't both enjoy the view," he said, his own jeans falling to his feet as he held her by the hips.

As they emerged from the trees into the scrubby bushes that led up to the grassy slope, they noticed a grey saloon car parked next to their Jeep. There was an older couple sitting on one of the benches. The lady waved at them.

"Ah, you found the beach, did ya? I used to love going down there, when I was a girl. Didn't I, Harry?"

The older gentleman harrumphed a little, then turned surprisingly clear eyes on Rashford and Roxanne.

"The gulls are noisy today," he said. "Did you notice?"

They looked at each other.

"Or maybe it was the geese."

His partner slapped his arm.

"Don't be cheeky, Harry," she said. "You were young once."

She winked at Roxanne.

"Not that you'd know it now, mind," she said, laughing.

Roxanne blushed, and Rashford smiled to himself as he led her back to the car. They drove down the hill in a companiable silence, exclaiming as they entered the cluster of houses at Ballantyne's Cove.

"This is the place he used for his name!" said Roxanne.

They slowed down and drove out onto the wharf. Looking around, they could see a few houses perched on the side of the cliff, but it was obviously only a small community. They bought an ice cream from a stall set up in an old caravan but decided not to visit the tuna interpretive centre. Back on the road, they made good time on the drive into Antigonish.

After checking in to a hotel located just off the highway and conveniently close to a mall and a liquor store, they drove along the shop-lined main street and over a rusting metal bridge. The hospital reared above them as they travelled up the hill, but Roxanne was checking the house numbers on the other side of the road.

"That's the one," she said suddenly, pointing to an older looking home half hidden behind some trees. The window sashes were painted a dark green that looked peaceful against the grey siding. Rashford pulled up to the curb, just behind a simple metal gate with a traditional clasp handle.

Roxanne took a deep breath.

"Ready?" he said.

"Yes," she replied, "let's do it."

Roxanne climbed out of the passenger seat and stood on the sidewalk, looking down the path towards the house. The garden itself was encircled by a low stone wall, from which stood metal posts with chain iron fencing forming a sturdy barrier. A hedge of mixed bushes, mainly honeysuckle and ironbark with a smattering of lilacs, formed a hedge behind the wall and prevented a casual observer from looking into the garden.

Rashford came round the front of the car and took her hand.

"Ready?" he said, again.

She shook off his hand and tossed back her hair.

"Yes," she said, then opened the gate and walked down the garden path.

"If I have this right," said the nun, "you wish to look at our birth and adoption records for the spring of 1987. Is that correct?"

"Yes please, Sister," said Roxanne.

"And why should I share such information with you, young lady?" said the nun.

Rashford cut into the conversation, pulling Roxanne by the arm so she was forced to take a step back.

"Excuse me, Sister, perhaps I can elaborate," he said, placing himself squarely in front of the nun.

"Ms. Sylliboy Gaudet here is my client. She is trying to find the details of her brother, whom she never met but who contacted their mother a few months ago. He accessed information under the Adoptions Act. Their mother, Sandra Sylliboy, was brought here from Cape Breton to have her first child. We are simply looking for details, to help put everyone's mind at rest."

The nun looked at him, her head to one side.

"And who are you, exactly?"

"My apologies, Sister. My name is Gavin Rashford, and I am a private investigator who has been retained by the family."

Roxanne suddenly started to cough, covering her mouth with her hand as her cheeks reddened. The nun glanced at her, then back at Rashford.

"Are you indeed? And do you have any identification, Mr. Rashford?"

"Of course, Sister," he said, pulling his wallet out of his pocket and searching through the many cards.

"I do apologize, Sister. It seems that I can't buy anything anymore unless I first join a club of some sort. Ah, here we are."

Rashford handed over a small, laminated card, which the nun examined and then returned.

"My photograph makes it look like I just got out of prison," said Rashford.

"Have you?"

"No, Sister! Not at all."

"Very well," she said. "Come along to the office."

As they walked down the hallway, Roxanne cast a questioning look across at Rashford. He just shook his head and kept walking. The nun led them through a battered looking door, the white paint flaking to reveal the panel board beneath, and into a room cluttered with filing cabinets. She pointed to two wooden chairs, the type found in small rural museums showcasing an old one room school, then went over to a large grey cabinet which was secured with a large new padlock.

Rashford and Roxanne sat down and looked around. The walls were painted a pale green colour, with old posters tacked along one side above a wheezing radiator. The windows were closed, and the room was hot and oppressive. After a few minutes, the nun turned from the cabinet and came over to the table. She placed a brown manilla file in front of them, then stood back.

"These are our records from January until June, nineteen eighty-seven," she said. "You may look at these, but you can take nothing from this room. Is that clear."

"Yes, sister," said Roxanne.

Rashford held up his hand.

"May I take photographs of any pertinent information?" he said. "With you here to check the image, of course, to make sure I don't have anything confidential or private."

The nun, seemingly mollified, nodded.

"Perhaps," she said. "Let me wait and see what you might want to photograph."

Rashford agreed, then turned the file towards him, and opened the cover. Roxanne leaned in so she could see clearly.

They quickly flipped past the entries for January and February, slowing down as they read the pages for March and then stopping altogether at April.

"There she is," said Roxanne, pointing. Rashford nodded.

There were five names on the page. The first two were of girls who had left the home, giving the type of transport arranged and the destination. There were also details of the child they had borne, notations as to length, sex, weight, colour of eyes, and so forth. The final line indicated that in both cases, the child had been adopted, but no details were provided.

The other three entries were the names and home addresses of girls who had arrived that month. Sandra Sylliboy from Eskasoni was the second on the list. They turned over the page to May.

Here there were more details. Joannie Carruthers, from Glace Bay, had apparently suffered a miscarriage and gone home. Sandra had given birth to a boy, recorded as being christened Xavier Breton. He had been eighteen and a half inches long, seven pounds three ounces in weight, with brown eyes and black hair. The report noted that "the mother discharged herself on the second day after the birth", and that the boy was subsequently adopted.

Sylvie Cheverie, from Grand Étang, was recorded as also having given birth to a boy, recorded as being christened Simon Spring. He had been born the day after Xavier, an inch or so longer and about six ounces heavier, but otherwise they were identical. Sylvie had stayed at the house for four days after the birth, and then her mother had arrived to drive her home.

"May I photograph these two pages, please," said Rashford. "This one and the one before?"

The nun looked, then nodded, so Rashford brought out his phone and took two careful pictures.

"Thank you for showing us this," said Roxanne, tears appearing at the edge of her eyes. The nun handed her a tissue; the box obviously placed in the room for moments like this.

"Is it possible to look at the actual adoption record?" said Rashford.

The nun shook her head.

"No, that would be breaking confidentiality," she said.

Roxanne started to cry again, proper tears now.

"But perhaps I can help a little," said the nun, going to a different drawer of the filing cabinet and pulling out a large green binder. She brought it to the table, and they saw 1987 on the cover, written in a neat hand. She opened it to a tab marked 'May.'

"Let me see. Ah, yes. So, Xavier Breton was adopted by a good Catholic family from the eastern townships around Montreal. They were of Scottish descent, their name was Sinclair, and they decided to keep Xavier as they quite liked the name. But they gave him theirs as well, of course."

"Of course," said Rashford. He looked across, trying to see under the nun's finger.

"Is that what happened to Simon?" he said, nodding at the other line. The nun nodded, sadly.

"Yes. He was a difficult boy, Simon. As you can see, he was sent to three different places in his first five years, but nobody would keep him more than a month. They said he would cry, not like a baby but like a banshee, real wailing and screaming. He spat out his food, he didn't sleep, oh my dear, there were horror stories.

"Eventually, when he was six, we had to give him to the government. They made a donation to support the costs we had incurred, and some fellow arrived to take him away. Kicking and screaming, he was."

The nun seemed to close her eyes for a moment.

"I had to go to confession, later," she said. "I was so happy to see the back of him. Isn't that awful?"

"Where did he go?" said Rashford.

"I'm not sure. They were talking of taking him to the residential school, him being Indian and all, but it won't have been the one at Shubenacadie, that had been knocked down the year before. Somewhere out west, perhaps. I wasn't that interested, to be honest, we just needed him gone. It was the early nineties by then and things had changed, people didn't like us taking their babies. 'Our services were no longer required,'" she said, putting air quotes around the statement.

The three of them were quiet for a moment, then the nun stood upright and slammed the binder closed.

"Enough nostalgia," she said. "We have enough to do in the here and now. I hope that the information was useful, but I really cannot share anything else."

She returned the files to the cabinet, carefully locking the padlock.

"That looks new," said Rashford.

"Yes," said the nun. "We had two break-ins a few months ago, just a week or so apart, and each time someone rummaged through the files. Nothing was taken but we want to try to maintain confidentiality."

"We appreciate what you've told us," Rashford said.

He and Roxanne stood up and followed the nun out to the front door. On the step they stopped and shook hands.

"I hope that information will help you and your mother, dear," said the nun.

"So do I," said Roxanne, "so do I."

As they were driving back to the hotel, Roxanne could not hold back any longer.

"Come on, then," she said, "show it to me!"

"Show you what?" said Rashford, innocently.

"That ID card thing. Where on earth did you get that?"

Rashford laughed, then drove with one hand as he reached into his pocket with the other. He pulled out his wallet.

"Top left-hand side," he said, "at the back."

Roxanne took out the laminated card and looked at it. There was a photograph of Rashford, his name, and the name of a company.

"Private Investigators of Southern Saskatchewan," she read. "Open. Fair. Flexible."

She turned it over a couple of times, but the back was blank.

"When did you become a private investigator?" she said.

"Keep looking at the card," he said, "there's a secret code."

They had driven along main street, past the riverside trailer park and the crenellated towers of the university, when she made a loud pout of disgust. As Rashford turned onto the highway, she looked across at him.

"I give up," she said. "I can't figure it out."

"Neither could the nun, fortunately," he said, looking back at her. "Here's a clue."

"A clue?"

"Yes. This was a gift from Gayle Morgan. To mark my passing the FILTER exam. Does that help?"

Roxanne looked at the card again.

"Not really, no," she said.

"Remember, she has that twisted British sense of humour," said Rashford.

"Still not helping."

"Just look at the initials, not the words. And only the capital letters."

Roxanne mouthed the words to herself.

"P for Private, I for Investigators, S for Southern ..."

Suddenly she burst out laughing, then slapped Rashford on the arm.

"Oh, piss off," she said.

"Exactly," said Rashford.

Chapter 17

They left for Cape Breton the next morning, after a hearty breakfast described as 'The full Gaelic'.

"I've never had black pudding before," said Roxanne.

"I don't think we need the recipe," said Rashford, using his fingernail to pick at a piece that was stuck in his teeth.

As they merged onto the divided highway that headed east to Cape Breton, Roxanne pointed at the large cemetery extending up the hill on the far side of the road.

"Mom was right," she said, laughing.

"What do you mean?"

"She once told me that people said there were only two ways out of this town, and they ran next to each other. The highway or the grave."

"That's a terrible thing to say!" said Rashford.

The highway was almost empty of traffic, and they made good time. As they dropped down to the jewel of Tracadie Bay, Roxanne fiddled with the buttons of her jacket and then spoke.

"Have you figured out, what kind of work do you want? For when we get back, I mean."

"Funny you should say that" said Rashford. "Yesterday was fun, and sort of crystallized something I've been thinking about for a while. I've been thinking about becoming a private eye. A proper one, with a licence and everything."

"How easy is that to make happen?"

"I'm not sure, I figured we could have a look when we get back. Right now, let's just see where this road takes us."

It took them first to Auld's Cove, where they stopped for coffee and mid-morning donuts at the busy Tim Horton's restaurant, then over the causeway. The waves were lapping at the edge of the stone barriers placed to minimize storm damage, and the gulls were screeching as they flew the length of the causeway and back.

"I wonder if the water ever comes over the road," said Roxanne. "I'll have to ask somebody."

They drove alongside the railway and then onto the bridge, travelling under the large sign that read, "Welcome to Cape Breton," in English, Gaelic, and Mi'kmaq.

"This bridge must open up to let ships through," said Roxanne. "Look, there's the wheelhouse for the controller guy."

As they left the bridge and drove up the hill towards the rotary, Rashford indicated to the right.

"Look, a travel information place," he said, pulling into the large car park. "We can get maps and stuff here and see about accommodations."

The Tourist Centre was a long low building, a single-story structure crammed with brochures and maps. There were also revolving metal kiosks filled with CDs, postcards, personalized name plates, and other souvenirs.

"There's enough tartan here to blanket the province," said Rashford, under his breath. Roxanne kicked him on the ankle. He hobbled over to a desk where a young woman with a tartan neck scarf, tartan earrings, tartan waistcoat and a tartan skirt sat smiling.

"Good morning, dear," she said. "How can I help you today?"

Rashford explained their route, and the lady made a few suggestions, and then a few telephone calls. She pulled out some documents, which Rashford studied. After fifteen minutes, he went back over to Roxanne, who was looking at the CDs of Cape Breton music.

"Okay," he said. "I have a bunch of maps, and detailed information on the must-see things, like hikes and waterfalls and so on. I asked about a park pass so we can go straight in there, as many times as we like, but you can only get those at the park gate. We've only got a week, so I booked us for two nights in Cheticamp, two nights in Sydney, and I left two nights for us to visit with your cousin in Eskasoni. I've got an updated list of restaurants that are open, and of events related to this Celtic Colours Festival. For lunch today we're going to stop in Mabou, and I've got tickets to a concert by Natalie MacMaster for when we're in Sydney. I've also got weather-permitting tickets for us to go whale watching at Pleasant Bay. We'll pick up any other information we need along the way."

"And does it?" she said.

"Does what, what?" said Rashford.

"Does the sea ever wash over the causeway?" she said, patiently.

Rashford looked at her, then turned and walked back over to the desk.

They went nearly all the way around the rotary and then followed the coast road through Judique and the spruce forests to Mabou. Rashford pulled to the side of the road in front of what looked like an old house, with white vinyl walls and an asphalt shingle roof. Roxanne looked at him with a question in her eyes, but he put a finger to her lips.

"Pub lunch," he said. "Trust me."

Two hours later they were still singing as they pulled out of Mabou.

"And then we rise again," said Rashford, coming with a flourish to the end of the song.

"What an amazing pub," said Roxanne. "How did you find that place?"

"The tartan lady told me about it. It's quite famous because the family than run it were a big-name musical band back in the day."

"Do you think it was one of them who was singing?"

"I've no idea. There was so much noise I couldn't hear half of what they were saying. The music was good, though, and those songs sure were catchy."

"The food was great as well!"

"Well, my fish and chips were brilliant. I'm not sure about your spinach and kale salad, though. Are they even foods?"

Roxanne punched his arm.

"Philistine," she said. "Right, what's next on this magical mystery tour your tartan lady friend made especially for you?"

"We drive up the coast to Cheticamp, looking out for whales along the way."

"Whales?"

"Yes. Oh, and moose. Apparently, there are a lot of those around, and they're on the road."

"Right. So how about, I look for whales, and you look for moose?"

"Sounds good," said Rashford, laughing.

The road wound its way along the western edge of the Island, affording them magnificent views of cliffs and coves, and endless miles of rolling sea. They saw no whales, though, and no moose either, although as they crossed the bridge at Margaree Harbour a large flock of birds caught their attention. Rashford pulled over and they got out, the wind buffeting them as they looked at the river.

"Some have reddish heads and grey bodies," said Roxanne, who had grabbed the binoculars. "Others have white bodies and dark green heads. They all have the same red colour beak, though."

"I think they're mergansers," said Rashford, trying to hold the bird identification book open. "Let's look in the car."

They managed to get back inside without losing a door to the wind, and Roxanne exhaled with relief.

"That was a bit blowy," she said. "Now, what did you think they were?"

Rashford found the page and showed it to her.

"Yes, that's them," she said. "And look, the females are the ones with the red heads. Like me!"

She laughed, running her fingers through her hair as she tried to smooth it down.

"Maybe I should call you Merg," said Rashford.

"Don't you dare," she said, folding her arms and pouting theatrically.

Rashford grinned, then pulled back onto the road. As they travelled north the hills started to get more pronounced, and the Cabot Trail curved around them in a serpentine fashion. On one straight stretch Roxanne suddenly shouted for him to stop. He immediately pulled over.

"What's the matter?"

"Back there," she said. "You drove straight past them."

"Past who?"

"The people. Sitting in the field. Go back."

He looked at her.

"Please."

Rashford checked the road and then made a u-turn before driving back a hundred metres. He saw the people, sitting in a circle, and the open gate that led into the field. He indicated and turned in.

"That's Margaret Thatcher," he said, suddenly realizing that the 'people' were in fact all scarecrows, wooden poles with cross staves for arms, wearing a miscellany of old clothes and realistic Halloween masks.

Roxanne clapped her hands together.

"And that's Pierre Trudeau," she said. "Come on, let's have a look."

They pulled to the edge of the field and parked on a narrow strip of gravel, recognizing this as the correct place by a piece of wood on which the word 'parking' had been hand painted. They got out of the car and walked around the circle, laughing at the different people whom they recognized. One did not look at all famous.

"Who's that?" said Roxanne.

"That's Joe, the guy who founded this place," said Rashford, reading from the small plaque that was nailed to a stake hammered into the ground next to a man in a baseball cap and a plaid shirt.

"Yeah, it seems he built this in 1984 and it ran until 2011, after he died. It wasn't exactly here, though, it was just down the road in Cap LeMoine. It was called Joe's Scarecrow Village. When everything was closed and the display taken apart, some people kept some of the scarecrows.

"Then, during COVID, in the early twenties, one of Joe's cousins decided his Pandemic Project would be to rebuild it as used to be. So, he put out the call and some of the people who had kept the scarecrows brought them back, and he also made some new ones, and this is the result."

"It's brilliant," said Roxanne, clapping her hands. "Come on, let's take a selfie with the astronaut!"

They walked over to the scarecrow who was wearing a glass-fronted bubble-head mask, his 'body' covered with a white jump suit. On the chest a hand-lettered sign read, 'Can you hear me Major Chris?' Roxanne stood on one side, her arm around the scarecrow. Rashford stood on the other side, arm extended.

"Smile," he said, and clicked his phone.

Twenty minutes later they were driving down the long main street of Cheticamp, looking for their bed and breakfast house. There was a lighthouse to their right, which as they approached became recognizable as a restaurant, then a row of older houses and a small garage and gas station. The houses were all painted in bright colours.

"My mom told me there are two reasons for that," said Roxanne. "First, when the fishermen painted their boats, they needed one-and-a-quarter cans of paint, but the salesmen only sold it in full cans. So, they had to buy two cans, and they then used the rest on their house. This led to the second reason. Because the house and the boat were the same colour, they could find their way home at night, even if they were drunk."

Rashford just shook his head, not sure whether she was simply making this up.

"Your mom sure told you a lot of stuff," he said.

"At least she didn't tell me it was okay to lie to a nun. I still can't believe you did that."

"It didn't hurt, and it got us what we wanted."

"But, still, a nun!"

"Under all that religious stuff, they're just normal people," said Rashford.

On the harbour side of the road there was a row of smaller shacks, each decorated with bunting and multicoloured flags. Signs outside indicated whether they sold souvenirs, local pottery, arts and crafts, ice cream, or postcards.

If the smell and the raucous calls of a hundred gulls were not clue enough, a large commercially produced sign identified the long grey building at the wharf as the community fish plant. The tide was high, and a line of boats were tied up three deep and tight to the harbour wall. Men walked across the decks from vessel to vessel, carrying buckets and ropes, calling out to each other in a mix of English and French.

"There's a sign," said Roxanne, pointing, and Rashford turned off away from the water, down a lane which ran at a right angle to Main Street. They drove into a low valley and then partway up the other side, turning there into the driveway of a bright yellow house. They got out of their car and stretched, looking back the way they had come. The road went down and back across the valley, but they were high enough that they could see the ocean beyond the line of shops and houses. The front door of the house opened, and a woman stepped out, drying her hands on a tea towel.

"Hello bonjour," she said. "Welcome to Seaview House. My name is Chiasson. Marguarite Chiasson."

She looked to be about sixty years old, wearing a blue and grey coloured cardigan over a white turtlenecked shirt. Her long skirt was black, and her grey hair tied back in a severe bun.

Roxanne stepped forward.

"Hello, Madame Chiasson, I'm Roxanne," she said, shaking hands, "and this is Gavin. Pleased to meet you."

Rashford nodded.

"You will be here for two nights, I think, yes?" said the older lady. "Let me show you around and to your room."

Rashford picked up their two small bags and followed Roxanne as she walked alongside Madame Chiasson. He could hear their conversation but could not really participate.

"Breakfast is from eight until ten in the morning. There will be toast or cereal, not both. Also, tea or coffee. No double dipping, you must choose one. There is a card in your room. If you fill it during the evening and leave it on the table here, that will help me make the right time for your food."

The woman pointed at a varnished round wooded table with three interlocking legs which stood in the middle of the entrance hall. She gestured to a door opposite the one through which they had entered.

"Breakfast is in there," she said, "and in the evening the room can be used as a lounge, if you wish to sit and read, or watch television. During the day I would prefer you are out of the house between ten o'clock and five thirty."

She led the way up a flight of stairs to a small hallway with three doors. She opened the first door, on the left. The bedroom was square, with a queen-sized bed covered in cushions, an old armchair with worn looking fabric on the arms, and a small chest of drawers. Above the bed was a crucifix, and on one wall was a sepia photograph of a good-looking man with a long ponytail and a cowboy hat, sitting at a desk in a room filled with records and CDs. There was a window at the far end of the room, looking back the way they had driven from the town.

"This is your room," she said. "It is the one with a view of the sea, and the sunset. Room number one. Here is the key, and that small key will open the outside door when you come back."

She passed over a keyring with a large old fashioned metal key and a smaller gold one, then stepped back into the hallway.

"The middle door is the bathroom, normally you would share it, but I have nobody staying in room number two right now. So now it will be your private bathroom, but I shall not make an extra charge."

Rashford looked at Roxanne, but she ignored him.

"You can leave your bags now," said Chiasson, "and then perhaps you would like to find somewhere for your dinner. Many places will close at seven. When you come back, please make sure the car is on the left side of the gravel, for parking, my car prefers the right side. And also, please lock the door when you are inside the house. Any question for me?"

Rashford shook his head, bemused.

"Where is the card, for breakfast?" said Roxanne.

Marguarite Chiasson walked to the bed and lifted a small card from the pillow. She handed it across, and Roxanne passed it to Rashford. He saw that the card had Room 1 written at the top, and then four times, listed in a column with a small line at the end of each row.

"Eight to eight thirty, eight thirty to nine, nine to nine thirty, and nine thirty to ten," he said. "Those are our options?"

"Oui, monsieur."

"What if I'm ready for breakfast at eight-fifteen?"

"It depends how you marked the card," she said. "It will be waiting for you, and perhaps cold, or you can wait for it, and perhaps read the newspaper."

Roxanne put her hand to her mouth to stifle a giggle. Marguarite stared at Rashford.

"Any other question?"

He shook his head.

"No, madam," he said. "Thank you."

She inclined her head in appreciation, then turned away. At the top of the stairs she hesitated, then looked back.

"If you like Acadian food, Le Gabriel c'est tres bonne. Aussi, L'abri Café, mais it is more Canadian."

She continued down the stairs.

"Merci," said Roxanne, to the woman's back, then followed Rashford into the room. He was sitting on the bed, looking at her, his elbows on his knees and his hands to his head.

"What?" he said.

"Nothing. You picked it," said Roxanne, bouncing down next to him and kissing him on the cheek. "Come on, this will be fun!"

"As long as I park in the right place and my breakfast isn't cold," said Rashford.

Roxanne dug her elbow into his side.

"Don't be grumpy," she said. "I bet she used to be a nun; she is used to everyone doing exactly as she tells them. And anyway, we don't have to pay extra for our private bathroom! Come on, let's go and find some food, I'm starving."

At the restaurant, Rashford was surprised when the waitress asked him if he would prefer home-cut or pre-packaged frozen French fries with his fish. He looked at her in amazement.

"Who would choose pre-packaged frozen ones?" he said.

"You'd be surprised," she said. "A lot of people do. Especially tourists. I think that some people don't understand that French fries are originally potatoes, they think they are somehow made all crinkled and ready to eat. Donc. Pour vous?"

"Pour moi, 'home-cut' s'il vous plait."

"Okay. Et madam?"

"I'll have the fish cakes, please, with beans."

"Okay. Anything else?"

"Can we start with a soup, please?" said Rashford. "I would like to try a bowl of the Andre's meat fricot."

"And I shall have a cup of the chowder, please," said Roxanne, handing her menu back to the waitress.

"And to drink?"

"I'll have a glass of wine, please. What's your house white?"

"We have pinot grigio or sauvignon blanc."

"A glass of the pinot, please."

"Large or small?"

"Large."

"Monsieur?"

"What local beers do you carry?"

"Nothing from Cheticamp, there's no brewery here yet, but we've got the 1497 IPA and the Celtic Shores Trail Ale from the Route 19 Brewery, that's down in Inverness. And we've got the Red Coat Irish Red and the Sons of Hector Brown Ale from Breton Brewery, over in Sydney."

"I'll try one of those Sons of Hector, please."

The waitress left them alone and they looked around the small restaurant. There were only a few other diners, with another group of young men playing pool in an adjacent room. Their voices and laughter, a mixture of English and French, provided a gentle background rhythm.

The waitress returned with their drinks and a large bowl of mixed breads. When she had left, Rashford raised his glass.

"To our holiday," he said, and they chinked their glasses together.

"You have that look," said Roxanne. "What are you thinking about?"

"I've been thinking about what the Chief told us, about the DNA results. I've been trying to figure out why Claude Dallas would pretend to be Sandra's son, and how he would know so much about her. I know we've been more worried about why he was after you, when we thought of him as Fancy Boots, but I think the story must go back before then."

"I don't think she knew him from anywhere else," said Roxanne.

"No, I don't think so either. But let's think this through. Go back to the beginning, when Sandra had her baby, and then left him with the nuns. Who else was there?"

"That girl who had the miscarriage, and the one who gave birth a day later."

"Right."

Rashford took out his phone and scrolled through the photographs.

"Here, this is the page from the book. That girl's name was Sylvie Cheverie, and she was from Cheticamp."

"Which is here," said Roxanne, smiling.

"Exactly. I think we should ask around, see if we can find her, and then ask her what she knows about her son, Simon. There has to be a link somewhere."

Just then the waitress returned with their soups, and they ate hungrily, dunking roughly torn pieces of bread as they enjoyed their meal. Their conversation moved on to what sights they would see in the National Park, and which hikes they might attempt. They had a second drink each, then paid the bill and left the restaurant.

"It's a beautiful evening," said Roxanne. "Let's walk a while."

They strolled along the boardwalk that skirted the harbour, looking in the windows of the small booths selling tourist wares, watching the boats rocking gently at their berths, listening to the gulls crying mournfully from the light posts. Roxanne took Rashford's arm.

"Look at the moon," she said, pointing off to the hills behind the town.

The moon was just clearing the treeline. It was nearly full and illuminated the water in the harbour to a silver sheen.

"What a beautiful place," said Roxanne. "I'm glad we came here."

"Me too," said Rashford. "Come on, let's get back to the guest house."

The next morning, they got to the dining room at eight fifty-five. There were two tables, one of which was set with plates, cutlery, cups, and glasses. Their breakfasts arrived at nine o'clock exactly. They enjoyed the scrambled eggs and bacon, accompanied by toast and raspberry jam, all washed down with a large pot of tea. Marguarite was very cordial and brought them extra orange juice when requested and smiled when Rashford complimented her on the crispness of the bacon.

"Crunchy but not blackened," he said. "Just perfect!"

As they poured the last of the tea into their cups, Marguarite appeared again, this time carrying a cup of coffee. She stood by the table, looking pensively around, then turned to Roxanne.

"May I join you for a moment?" she said.

Roxanne looked at Rashford, who nodded.

"Of course," she said. "Gavin, can you bring her a chair, please."

Rashford stood but Marguarite waved him back down. She placed her coffee on the table then turned and pulled over an adjacent chair. After sitting down, she looked at them each in turn.

"I wish to apologize for yesterday," she said.

"Apologize for what," said Roxanne.

"For my rudeness. Yesterday was a hard day, the fifth anniversary since I lost my husband, and when you arrived, I was very sad."

"We are sorry for your loss," said Roxanne, and Rashford nodded. Marguarite lowered her head in appreciation.

"Thank you," she said.

There was silence for a few moments.

"Thank you for parking to the left when you came back," said Marguarite. "It's silly, but my husband always used to park to the right, and yesterday, it just, it just seemed important that it was left free for him."

"It was no problem," said Rashford. "There was lots of room."

"Yes, it is a big driveway."

They sat quietly again. Roxanne cleared her throat.

"The photograph?" she said. "The one in our room. Is that your husband?"

"Oh, no, no. That is Charlie. My brother. He used to run the music store, maybe you saw it, on your way into town yesterday? He passed away nearly twenty years ago."

She abruptly changed the subject.

"Where did you eat last night?"

"We went to Le Gabriel, like you suggested. It was lovely. We both had the soup, Gavin had the meat fricot and I had the chowder, then I had the fish cakes and Gavin had the fish and chips."

"With home cut fries," said Rashford, laughing. "It was great."

"Good, I am glad you enjoyed your meal. And today? What is your plan?"

Rashford put down his teacup, then looked across at Marguarite. He pulled a map out of his pocket and glanced at it.

"Well, we're going to go into the national park, of course, just this end today. I thought we could try the Skyline Trail hike, as well as the Bog Walk and Le Buttereau. We'll do those in the morning, then come back to town for lunch, and afterwards we might go for a drive to see what is on Cheticamp Island. Then this evening we'll wander along the boardwalk by the harbour and try to find that L'abri Café you mentioned."

"That sounds like a good day," said Marguarite. "The Skyline will take you a couple of hours if you go all the way to the end, the other two are pretty short. Watch out for moose, and even bear and coyote. Lots of animals around here."

She peered over at the map and pointed at a place where the road split.

"If you go here, to get to the Island, you'll see Charlie's store on the other side of the road. It's not his anymore, of course, but it still has his name. They have lots of Cape Breton music there."

"There is one other thing we might do," said Rashford. He looked to Roxanne for support, and she nodded.

"What is that?" said Marguarite.

"Well, we're trying to find someone, if she is still here, if she is still alive."

Marguarite seemed to straighten her back and hold her coffee cup a little more tightly.

"Who is that?" she said.

"Sylvie Cheverie," said Rashford, "originally from Grand Étang."

The handle of the coffee cup in Marguarite's hand broke, the cup falling to the floor and the remaining dregs of the coffee staining out across her skirt.

"Oh," she said.

It took a few minutes for them to clean up the spilled coffee. Roxanne grabbed a handful of paper towels which she used to dab up the liquid. Rashford collected the bits of broken cup off the floor. Marguarite wrung her hands and apologized, over and over again, for her clumsiness. Eventually things calmed down and the three were sat facing each other.

"I didn't mean to upset you," said Rashford, reaching over and patting Marguarite's wrist.

She shook her head, then used her other hand to wipe a tear from her cheek.

"No. It's alright. It is just, just, I haven't heard her name for so long."

She spoke so softly it was almost a whisper. Roxanne had to lean forward to hear what was said.

"Would you like to tell us about her?" said Rashford.

Marguarite looked at him, then across at Roxanne.

"It's nothing, really. Just a small-town story."

She paused, then stood and walked over to the window. Looking out, gazing down the driveway to the main road and the sea, she began to speak.

"When I was a girl, Sylvie was my best friend. I grew up in Point Crosse, and she was from the next community down the shore, Grand Étang. Every morning the school bus came along, picking us up along the way. She was already on the bus, and she always kept me a seat, next to her. We were like sisters.

"In high school, she was a good student, I was a bit of a crazy one. Not like now, eh?"

Marguarite choked back something that was halfway between a laugh and a sob, then turned to face the table.

"When we were sixteen, we were picked to go to Youth Camp down near Baddeck. Two kids from each school across Cape Breton were invited. I don't know why they picked us, but we were happy. We took our bags and went off for our weekend adventure.

"There was a lad there from the east side. He was loud and rough, you know, a bit of a bad boy. I quite liked him and tried to sit next to him round the bonfire, but he only had eyes for Sylvie. He kept ignoring me and eventually I got so mad, I left the fire and went to bed. It was all my fault. I shouldn't have left her alone."

"What happened?" said Roxanne.

"In the morning, she wasn't in our room. I went looking for her, but nobody seemed to know where she'd gone. We told the camp workers, and they checked all the rooms, even in the boys' dorm. Nothing. Then they realized that the boy had gone as well.

"Someone called the police, and two of them came round and talked to us all. They seemed to know the boy, at least by reputation, and said they would let us know when they found them. That was the Saturday morning, and so they cancelled the camp, and the bus took me home.

"Her parents were worried sick, of course, and came to our house to ask me what had happened. But I didn't know anything. Then the next day, the police brought her back. They had found her over in town, in Whitney Pier. She was all messed up on drugs of some sort, pills this boy had given her. She didn't even know his name! Then a month or so later, she realized she was pregnant."

Marguarite came and sat back down at the table.

"She had pretty much stopped talking to me by then. She started missing school, and even when she was there, I sat somewhere else on the bus. When she started to show, she stopped going to school altogether, her parents would not allow it. I heard she went to the mainland to have the baby, and the nuns took it. She came back to the shore for a while, but only for a couple of weeks. She didn't come to school, I only heard this from other people.

"One day she hitched a ride with some tourists, she went up into the park. They said she walked nearly all the Skyline Trail, almost to the end. Then she just slipped off. Or maybe she stepped."

Rashford looked down at his hands. Roxanne leaned over and embraced the older woman, patting her gently on the back.

"You say the nuns took the child," said Rashford. "Do you know where?"

Marguarite shook her head.

"Not really. There was gossip, of course, people heard stories. Some said that he was messed up because of the drugs she'd been taking when he was conceived. Others said he had a vicious temper, like his dad, and that no foster home would keep him. After a while people just sort of stopped talking about him, it was like he never existed.

"I met her mom once. It was six years after Sylvie had passed, I was home from college with my teaching diploma. We bumped into each other in the boulangerie, and I just started crying. She told me not to blame myself, I hadn't done anything wrong. Then she said that Simon, that was the boy's name, he had been taken to a school out in Saskatchewan, a special school for Indian kids. That was when I discovered that Sylvie's mum was Mi'kmaq, I had never known. They were just people, y'know?"

The rest of their holiday was uneventful. They explored the national park, hiking the trails and enjoying the spectacular scenery. They were mesmerised by the Lone Shieling, a crofter's cottage relocated from the Scottish Highlands and plunked down in the middle of a red oak forest. The leaves were spectacular, even more so as they returned from an otherwise fruitless whale watching trip off Pleasant Bay. The sun had been setting behind them and the richness of the colours seemed to vibrate as they approached the shore.

At the northern end of the Island, they took a detour up to Meat Cove, a small hamlet perched on the edge of the cliffs. Here they did see whales, a pod of pilot whales cavorting in the bay below. They bought coffee from the entrepreneurial café, to fortify themselves before facing the return drive down the hairpin bends of the dirt road.

Once back on the highway they made good time through Neils Harbour and Ingonish. As they drove over the crest of Cape Smokey,

Rashford was pleased they were on the inside lane. Cars driving towards them, coming the other way around the Cabot Trail, were squeezed perilously close to the edge of what seemed like a very long drop off.

"I'd rather risk a scrape from the cliffs," he said.

"Prairie boy," chided Roxanne, laughing.

They took the little chain link ferry at Englishtown and then dropped over Kelly's Mountain to the Seal Island bridge on their way into Sydney. They spent a couple of days exploring the city and the rest of the industrial heartland of Cape Breton, and in the evenings wandered along Charlotte Street. In an Irish bar they met a group of local men, who had obviously been drinking for a while, and started chatting to them.

"We used to be miners," said one, "but now they closed the pits, and we look for pogey, not coal."

"Where's youse from, then?" said the loudest and largest of the group.

"We're from the Island," said Rashford, adding "ow" as Roxanne kicked his ankle.

The large man got slowly to his feet; his fists clenched.

"He means we've been travelling around the Island," said Roxanne, quickly. "He's from the prairies, I'm from Charlottetown."

"I used to work in Alberta once," said the big man, nodding, then wandered off to the washroom, and the moment was gone.

The next day they travelled out to Eskasoni and visited with Sandra's cousin, who showed them all around that community and introduced Roxanne to a hundred second- and third cousins she never knew existed. After two nights they said their farewells, and were gifted some moose meat and smoked fish before they retraced their steps back across the causeway.

It was late afternoon as the ferry crossed the Northumberland Strait, the sea burning under the setting sun, the bright white plumage of gannets shining like beacons against the darkening sky. Roxanne stood next to Rashford on the top deck, enveloped in his arms, her head against his chest.

"That was a lovely holiday," she said. "Thank you."

Rashford watched the long low profile of Prince Edward Island start to emerge from the horizon.

"And now back to paradise, at least for a few days," he said, squeezing Roxanne tightly.

She squeezed back but didn't say anything.

"What's the matter?" he said.

"Oh, nothing. Just thinking about mom. Here on her own, trying to cope with losing her son. Me all the way out west. Worrying."

"What are you saying? Do you want to stay here?"

Roxanne shrugged, then shook her head.

"I don't know what I want," she said.

Chapter 18

Sandra was delighted to see them return safely from the mainland and cooked some of the moose for their supper.

"This is Mi'kmaq Trapper's Pie," she said, laughing. "Just like Kôhkum Christine makes. Except my sage comes from Sobeys', not the prairie!"

As they ate, they answered her questions about their trip. She was pleased to hear that Roxanne had met some of her numerous cousins, and that they had found Eskasoni to be as beautiful as she remembered.

"Auntie Jean wants you to go over and visit," said Roxanne. "You should think about that."

"I will," said Sandra, "maybe next spring."

It was only once the dishes were cleared and they were sitting drinking tea that Rashford cleared his throat.

"Simon Spring," he said.

Sandra looked at him.

"Who?"

"Simon Spring. We think that's the name of the fellow who contacted you, who pretended to be your son."

"Who is he? Why would he do that?"

"I'm not sure about the why," said Rashford. "The who is a bit easier. He was the son of Sylvie Cheverie, who was the Cape Breton girl who had her baby at the same time as you, in Antigonish. He was taken away from her, for adoption, but she did not deal with the situation as calmly as you did. I'm afraid she seems to have taken her own life."

"Like Nancy, in the song."

"Yes. There's no proof of that, it could be that her death was an accident, but I think suicide is more likely. Anyway, Simon was adopted at about the same time as Xavier. But he was a difficult child, it sounds like maybe he had some issues to do with Fetal Alcohol Syndrome, although this was before they had diagnosed that as an illness.

"So far, we have found that he was moved between foster homes but did not settle anywhere, and when he was six, he was taken out west to one of the residential schools. I think I know which one, because most of them were closed by the early nineties. There were only one or two still operating. I've asked Gayle Morgan to make some inquiries, see what she can find out. Until then, we're stuck."

"How did you find this out?" said Sandra, looking across at him.

"Oh, he's practising for his new career," said Roxanne, laughing.

"New career? What new career?"

"When he retires, he wants to be a private eye."

The next morning was going to be their last full day on the Island. Rashford pulled on his boots.

"I think I'll just go for a walk," he said.

Roxanne looked up from her book.

"Okay," she said. "Will you be long?"

"Maybe half an hour or so," said Rashford. "I'll just go down to the harbour and back."

"I'm going over to see mom. She went to work but said she thought it would be a quiet day, so I'll go and visit. Then, I thought we could take her out for lunch, being our last day and all."

"Sure," said Rashford. "Good idea. See you shortly."

Once out on the street he turned right and walked down the hill. He passed a number of shops, mainly smaller independent businesses, and some older houses, with round brass plaques indicating the names of the merchants who had built them, back in the early 1800s. The plaques were painted brown, with the names and dates in raised metal painted yellow. The street ended with a turning circle, and a bench that looked out across the harbour. A police car was parked at the edge of the circle.

Rashford walked over and saw the policeman watch him approach. He stood to the side of the driver's window, slightly in front of the car, with his hands by his sides. The officer wound down his window.

"Can I help you, sir?" he said.

Rashford introduced himself, explaining that he was a police officer himself and was visiting Charlottetown on holiday. The one he was talking to nodded.

"Are you hoping to join the force here, sir?"

Rashford shook his head.

"Not right now, thanks," he said. "But I have been thinking of private work, once I retire. Is there much of that around here?"

The officer shrugged.

"A bit, I guess. But it's all small scale. Errant husbands and wandering wives, lost kids and lawyer assists, that sort of thing. There are a few guys who do the job, but it's not like in the books. We don't have much in the way of murders or international crime rings around here."

"Nothing to laugh at, at all," said Rashford.

"Excuse me?"

"Oh, just something a colleague likes to say."

"Right. So, have you applied, then?"

"No, I'm not ready yet. I might decide to leave the force next month or not for another couple of years. Do you know, how long does the process take?"

"It depends. Would you apply to a firm or direct?"

"Probably direct. I wouldn't want to lock into any existing company, you know. Think I'd want to test the waters first."

"Fair enough," the officer said, "There's only really one mob here in town, and there's a fellow up west who works independently. The rest are all off-Island firms. It'll probably take a few weeks, though, maybe even a month."

The radio in the police cruiser crackled and the officer picked up his handset. He listened a moment, then waved at Rashford as he started the car.

"Good luck!" he said, the window winding up as he drove away.

Rashford watched him go past the hotel, turning on the flashing lights as he went. As he approached the four-way stop the siren blipped, and the cruiser went through without slowing down. A pedestrian hurriedly stepped back from the curb, and a car with right of way jerked to a halt in the intersection.

Rashford shook his head, then turned and walked out to the edge of the harbour. He went past the bright red metal sculpture that consisted of four large numbers displaying the current year and made his way to the wooden bench. Pulling his coat closer around his body, he sat down.

Rashford lit a cigarette and contemplated the view. The wind was ruffling the water of the harbour. On the far shore he could see the lighthouses that marked the site of the first French settlement, a fort which overlooked the passage out to the Northumberland Strait.

To the right were the starter mansions of the nouveau rich, designer homes that marched down to the shore, a non-edible rotation which had taken over acres of arable land. These were empty most of the day, he knew, the owners busy at work in town, but lit up every evening and threw shimmering reflections across the harbour.

To his left he saw the creamy grey and soft brown bulk of an apartment building, rearing up from the water's edge. An attempt to evoke visions of the Adriatic coast, he thought, spoiled only by the large golden arches of the fast food court next to the adjacent gas station.

A small boat eased across his line a vision, the man at the tiller hunched over. Two long poles laying across the gunnels showed that this was one of the inshore oyster fishermen, coming back after spending a few hours turning the molluscs on the seabed. Rashford waved and the man raised a laconic hand in response. The sound of the outboard motor reached him, and a vague smell of fuel, then the boat was gone and all he could see were the waves.

He stubbed out his cigarette, then picked up the butt and placed it in his pocket as he made ready to stand up.

"Still smoking real cigarettes, then?" said a voice behind him.

Rashford swivelled on the bench and looked up into the face of a vaguely familiar young man. He scanned the albums of his mind, flipping past mental photographs of the many criminals with whom he had had interactions over his career. He found no matches.

"Do I know you?" he said, eventually.

"Not really," said the young man. "I mean, we met once, but you don't know me, like."

Rashford stared at him. The young man came round and gestured to the bench.

"May I sit down? Bum a smoke?"

Rashford nodded and edged over to the end of the seat. The young man sat down and gave a loud sigh. Rashford took out his cigarettes but did not offer them.

"First, where did we meet?"

The young man laughed.

"University of Regina. You gave me a hard time for vaping."

Rashford looked at him in disbelief.

"You're Alf's nephew's girlfriend's brother?"

"Yup. Pete Eastman."

The young man held out his hand and Rashford shook it. Then he extended the cigarette pack. Eastman deftly extracted one and waited while Rashford took his own.

Rashford snapped his lighter and lit Eastman's cigarette first, then his own. He leaned back against the slats of the bench and exhaled.

"First question, why did you phone Alf, about my exam?"

Pete Eastman looked down at the gravel by his feet.

"Well, I figured he would want to know, you know? He had told me all about you being super smart and everything, and I thought you'd find out who I was and then get me into trouble for the chainsaw."

Rashford laughed.

"Why? You covered for him on the insurance, that was nothing to do with me."

"Well, I didn't know. And when those two profs started raving about your exam, I thought I should let Uncle Alf know. He always says there is no such thing as too much information, you know?"

"I bet he does," said Rashford, nodding. "OK, second question. What the hell are you doing here?"

Eastman looked at him.

"Here on PEI generally, or here by the harbour specifically?"

"Both."

"Promise you won't laugh?"

Rashford nodded.

"Cows," said Eastman, tapping off the ash from his cigarette and then taking another long drag.

"Cows?"

"Yeah. It's a weird story, and it's all Uncle Alf's fault."

"Of course, it would be. Is he really your uncle?"

"Nah, I just call him that."

"Okay. Go on, then. Tell me."

"You know it's been a dry year out west? Well, some rancher out near Maple Creek decided he couldn't keep all his herd, he didn't have enough feed for the winter. So, he decided to get rid of a few cattle."

Rashford nodded that he understood.

"But they're not regular cattle, like. They're special, a heritage breed called Kerry cows. They're smaller than those black and white ones ..."

"Holsteins," said Rashford.

"Yeah, that's them. These are smaller, and they all have horns, male and female. They're originally from Europe and are one of the oldest types of dairy cow around, apparently. Anyway, this rancher guy had a whole herd of them."

"Which he couldn't feed," said Rashford.

"Right. But he didn't want to just butcher them, you know, on account of them being rare, like. So, he advertised in some cow rancher magazine or blog or something, that he would give them away to a good home. And some feller here on PEI decided he'd take a couple."

"What's Alf got to do with this?"

"I guess the rancher was in the shop getting his truck fixed and asked Alf if he knew anyone who'd like a trip to the east coast. He'd organized a fellow to drive a trailer down, but the guy was scared of cows, so he needed an offsider to go with him. Alf knew I wasn't doing much so he gave him my name."

"I thought you were at university?"

"Well, I was, but I'm taking a bit of a break."

"Oh, I see. A Thanksgiving graduate."

"No, I didn't graduate, I'm just not going to classes right now."

"No, I meant ... ah, never mind. So, you got hired to cow-sit?"

"Pretty much. We drove down last week. Rusty would drive until he maxed his hours for the day and then we'd pull into a truck stop for the night. He had two bunks in the back of his cab, so I got the top one. We got here and dropped the cows off at their new home, a farm about half-way in from the bridge, then came into town to have a look around. We thought we'd stay here for a couple of days before heading home."

Eastman dropped the end of his cigarette onto the ground and stubbed it out with his boot. He sat back on the bench, looking out across the water.

Rashford opened his packet again and offered a second cigarette, which Pete took. Once they were both smoking, Rashford spoke again.

"Alright, so that explains why you're here on the Island. But why are you here now, meeting me down here by the harbour?"

"That's where Uncle Alf comes in."

Eastman paused, and Rashford noted that he had coloured slightly.

"This next bit's a bit embarrassing."

"Go on."

"We came into town two days ago, me and Rusty, the driver. We got a room in a cheap hotel on the edge of downtown, separate beds of course."

"Of course."

"Then we went out to a couple of bars. We listened to some music and had some beer, just had a good time, you know? Some of the talent here is just brilliant. There was a fiddle player at one of the pubs, Richard Wood I think was his name, he was incredible. Long haired guy with a beard. Looked and played like a madman, and then he started step-dancing as well! While he played! I've never seen anything like it. The crowd went nuts."

Eastman shook his head at the memory.

"Anyway, at one of the pubs I met someone, and went back with them to their place. I told Rusty I'd see him at breakfast, so we could get ready to head home.

"But when I got back to the hotel, yesterday morning, he was already packed. He was waiting for me and he told me that he was leaving me here. I guess he hadn't realized I was gay and got all freaked out that I had danced with and then gone home with another guy. 'I'm not letting a poof sleep in my cab,' he yelled as he left."

"A 'poof'?" said Rashford, raising an eyebrow. "I didn't think anyone said that anymore."

Eastman smiled, ruefully.

"Only truckers from the prairies, I guess," he said.

"Anyway, we'd booked the hotel for two nights so I phoned Uncle Alf, to ask him what I should do. And to see if he'd send me some money for the bus, I don't have enough cash. He told me that he thought you were around here somewhere, and he'd try and find out, then he'd call me back. Which he did about an hour ago. He said he'd heard you were likely going to be down here by the sign."

Rashford thought it through and laughed.

"Right," he said. "I get it. Alf probably phoned Bettina, who gave him Sandra's number, so he called her last night. We weren't there so he left a message. Sandra picked it up this morning, waited until she knew we'd be awake, then talked to Roxanne. I'd already left by then, so they phoned Alf back, and told him where I was likely to be, and he phoned you with the information. And here you are."

Eastman nodded.

"I am," he said. "Here, I mean."

"Hang on," said Rashford.

He took out his phone and called Roxanne, who confirmed his deduction.

"You'll be a great PI," said, laughing.

She also told him that Sandra had decided to take the day off work and they were both heading back to the apartment.

"I'll see you there," said Rashford, ending the call. He stubbed out his cigarette and picked up the butt.

"Pick up yours as well," he said, pointing to the floor. "Don't litter. Then come with me."

They walked back up Queen Street, dropping the cigarette ends into a metal garbage container standing outside the door to one of the pubs. After crossing the four-way they made their way past the theatre and art gallery complex, then turned right and walked down past the tarpaulin-covered province house, erstwhile centre of the provincial government. As Sandra kept muttering, the stone masons responsible for renovating this heritage building appeared to have found a job for life.

Crossing at the traffic light by the small theatre, they looped up past the cafes and boutiques to the Irish pub, then turned left and walked along until they were back at Queen Street, stopping again to browse the windows of the second-hand bookstores. Rashford made his way to Sandra's apartment, buzzing up from the lobby so that Sandra or Roxanne could automatically open the door. They took the elevator to her floor and walked down the carpeted corridor. The door was latched open, so Rashford held it, allowing Eastman to join him in the small vestibule. They took off their boots and walked into the main room.

Roxanne and Sandra were sitting curled up next to each other on the small couch, mugs of coffee on the small side table beside them. They looked up as he walked in.

"Nice walk?" Roxanne said. "Coffee is fresh."

"Yes thanks," said Rashford, then gestured behind him.

"Look what I found. Or should I say, look what found me."

Pete walked in behind him and nodded at the two women.

"Hello," he said, quietly.

"You must be the boy Alf was telling us about," said Sandra. "The one who got stuck here?"

"Yes," said Eastman, "Yes, I am."

"Would you like coffee?"

"Yes please."

Rashford walked into the small galley kitchen and poured two cups.

He walked back around and gave one to Pete, then indicated he should sit in the chair opposite.

Roxanne looked over at Rashford.

"So, what do you think of Charlottetown?" she said.

Rashford shrugged.

"Not much. It seems like a nice town. Kinda small, though."

Roxanne laughed.

"After Maple Creek, you mean?"

"No, but as a place to live, if you really want to come here."

"Oh, I do, eventually. This is home, Gavin, this is where I need to be. But we don't need to make a decision now. Do we, mom?"

Sandra shook her head.

"The path will be clear when you decide to take it," she said. "Let's have our coffee and find out what this young man has to say for himself. Then we can go for lunch. There's a great Korean place just across the street."

Everyone looked expectantly at Pete, who cleared his throat nervously.

"Well," he said. "Here's the thing ..."

As Pete retold his story, Rashford's phone started to vibrate. He picked it up and looked at the display.

"Gayle Morgan," he mouthed at Roxanne, who nodded.

"Hi, Gayle, just a second," said Rashford, covering the phone with his hand. He spoke to the group.

"Keep talking, Pete, tell them what you told me. Then you guys go to the restaurant, and I'll meet you there. This call might take some time."

Sandra and Roxanne nodded.

"Tell us as we walk," said Sandra, getting to her feet. Rashford saw them all out of the door then turned his attention back to his phone.

"Sorry, Gayle, just trying to get people organized here. What's happening? Do you have any news?"

When he got to the restaurant, Sandra and Roxanne were already there, with Pete stuck in the middle at the back of the booth. They told him that they had ordered, not being sure how long he would take. He slid into the booth next to Sandra and grabbed a menu. When the young woman came over, he ordered the bulgogi, and some green tea. She bowed and moved back to the counter next to the sushi station.

"That was Gayle Morgan," he said. "She sends her regards to everyone."

"Oh, yes?" said Roxanne. "And what did she say about her investigations. Did she have any news?"

Rashford took a small notebook from his pocket. He flipped through the pages, then stopped.

"I wanted to make sure that I got this right," he said, waving the notebook around the table.

Roxanne and Sandra nodded. Pete took a sip of his water and looked on, nonplussed. Rashford scanned his notes, then summarized.

"Well, basically, yes. There is some news. Gayle was able to locate this Simon Spring guy in the records. Ever since the feds turned all the school documents and things over to the Truth and Reconciliation Commission, people are not so scared to let you see the real truth anymore.

"Gayle found that he was enrolled at the Gordon Indian Residential School in Saskatchewan from 1993 until 1996, when it closed. Then he bounced around in foster care for a few years and was at a group home in Regina for a while, but it sounds like he was pretty much out of control. His juvenile records are sealed, of course, but Gayle said people who knew him then didn't seem to have much good to say for him. One described Simon as just a normal punk, robbing what he could, stealing cars, beating people up.

"Then he disappeared. Suddenly he wasn't hanging out in North Central anymore. Gayle found a fellow who used to be with a group called the Eagle Walkers, they would patrol the streets and try to offer help to people who needed it. Girls who seemed too young to be out on the street, people who'd overdosed, folks with mental health issues, the normal forgotten ones. This fellow said he'd heard that one day Simon walked into the downtown recruiting office and joined the army. Around 2004 or 2005, he thought."

"How on earth did Gayle find the Eagle Walker?" said Roxanne.

"Ah, well that is one of those strange-world coincidences. It turns out that the Nekaneet First Nation has established an urban reserve in Regina. Gayle talked to Kôhkum Christine and got some names from her, then she and Bettina went down and did some visits. It seems that people who wouldn't normally speak to the police were happy to chat with the granddaughter of Kôhkum Christine and her friend.

"So, that's where we are. Gayle wrote this up and gave the information to Chief Superintendent Pollard, who said she would check with the Army. But to be honest, she expects it to take a while. The Forces aren't very good at sharing information with outsiders. But at least we have a name now."

"If he used the same one when he joined up," said Sandra.

Roxanne made much the same point.

"At least we know what he was called when he was at school, before he joined the Army," she said. "We don't know what name he used there, though."

"I think you would have to show some sort of proof of identity," said Rashford. "I don't think you can just walk in and say 'hi, I'm Fred Smith, I want to join up'."

"Maybe not now, but back then, who knows?"

"That's true," said Rashford. "Things in Afghanistan were starting to heat up, I bet they were desperate for recruits."

"Have you checked Google?"

"Google? What for?"

"Well, you know he's been using all these names of outlaws and criminals, it seems like each time he starts a new life he takes a new name. Maybe he started doing that when he was looking to leave Regina."

"That's an interesting thought," said Rashford.

He took out his phone.

"Let's see. What happens if I type in 'notorious Regina gangsters 2000s'?"

Roxanne slid out of her side of the booth, then came and leaned over his shoulder.

"Daniel Wolfe," she said, softly. "The Indian Posse guy. Look, it says that he ran Regina in the early 2000s. He would have been the big name in town when Simon was hanging around north central."

Rashford leaned back and she kissed him on the head.

"No harm no foul," he said. "I'll get in touch with Gayle later today, tell her to add Daniel Wolfe to the list."

From the back of the booth, Pete waved his hand.

"He won't have just used that name," he said. "It would have been too obvious. He would have mixed it up somehow."

Rashford nodded in agreement.

"You're right. I'll get Gayle to suggest to the Chief Superintendent that she ask the Army to look for four names: Simon Spring, Daniel Wolfe, Simon Wolfe, and Daniel Spring. That covers most of the bases. There might be some news before we get back."

"Perhaps," said Roxanne quietly, then returned to her seat. The waitress arrived with the four lunches, and talk changed to the weird white saddle colouration that Pete had seen on the otherwise black Kerry cows.

Chapter 19

That night when they were in bed, Roxanne nudged Rashford with her hip.

"I've had an idea," she said.

Rashford rolled over and put his arm over her side, running his fingers over her breast. She batted his hand away.

"Not that," she said. "Something serious."

Rashford sat up and looked at her.

"What's the matter?"

"Nothing, silly. But I think this might be win-win."

"What are you talking about? Who's going to win what?"

Roxanne sat up next to him and leaned her head on his shoulder.

"Just let me finish, okay?" she said.

"Okay. Go on," said Rashford, putting his arm over her shoulder.

"Well, you know how Pete needs to get back to Saskatchewan but doesn't have any money?"

"Yes."

"And you know how I was thinking that mom might need someone to stay with her for a bit?"

"Yes," said Rashford, slowly, realizing what was coming.

"Well, why don't you let Pete drive back with you, in the Jeep, and I'll stay here for a bit, then fly back later. That way you have company, maybe he can even share the driving, and I don't leave mom on her own."

Rashford was silent.

After a few moments, Roxanne sat forward, then turned to look at him.

"Say something."

"How long would you stay here?"

"I don't know. Just as long as mom needs me, I guess."

"While I go back to Maple Creek?"

"Yes. You're going to have to deal with this inquiry thing and I know you, you'll want to follow-up on finding this fellow. You're obsessed with him."

"Well, duh, he tried to make you one of his sex slaves! Yes, of course I want to catch him."

"No," said Roxanne, quietly. "This goes back a lot further, since before you met me. You've been after him since he beat you up in that border crossing."

"He didn't beat me up! He sucker-punched me."

"Whatever. The thing is, he got away, and everyone thinks it's your fault."

She leaned over and kissed him, then sat back.

"And so do you."

The next morning after breakfast, Roxanne called Pete's hotel and invited him to come over to the apartment. When he arrived, she told him to sit at the table.

"Right, here's the deal," she said. "Gavin has to return to Regina for work, but he's going to stay here an extra day. He'll be leaving tomorrow morning. You are on your own today and tonight, but as long as you're here with your bag at eight tomorrow morning, you can ride with him. Okay?"

Pete looked from one to the other.

"Okay, I guess," he said. "But what about you?"

"I'm fine, I have some stuff to do here, I'll fly back to Saskatchewan later."

Rashford coughed gently, then spoke to Eastman.

"Do you have any money, to help share the gas?"

"No. Sorry, but I'm broke. Uncle Alf will have to send his credit card to the hotel again, so I can stay tonight."

"I see."

There was a pause.

"Can you drive, to share the driving?"

"Is it automatic? I've never driven shift."

"I see. No, it's a proper car. It's manual."

"Then sorry, no."

There was another pause.

"Can you be quiet for long periods of time, just looking at the scenery?"

"Yes. Yes, I can do that."

"Well, that will be a pleasant change."

"Gavin!" said Roxanne, indignantly.

Sandra laughed.

"Well, you could talk for Canada, you," she said.

"Oh, and no smoking in the car," said Rashford. "Only when we stop. And that goes for vaping as well."

"I told you, I don't vape anymore," said Pete, indignantly.

They left shortly after nine o'clock the next morning, leaving Roxanne tearful on the street, clutching to Sandra's arm. Rashford stared straight ahead, ignoring Pete's open window and waving arm until they turned at the traffic light.

"You can close that now," he said.

Eastman clicked the button and the window whirred smoothly closed. It was silent in the Jeep.

"Do you want to ..." he started.

"No" said Rashford.

Pete settled back in his seat and looked out of the window.

They drove up past the University and the mall, then turned left past a modern church with a large sign outside.

"No strangers here, just friends you haven't met yet", said Eastman, laughing. "That must really pull them in."

"Quiet and peaceful, remember," said Rashford, and Eastman settled back into his seat again.

They joined the highway at a roundabout and then drove steadily for forty minutes. A number of smaller roads led off into what were no doubt even smaller communities, and at one Pete pointed excitedly.

"Shamrock. That's where we took the cows," he said.

Rashford harumphed and kept driving.

They were almost at the bridge when he pulled into a gas station which had a coffee shop attached.

"Bathroom break," he said. "We're not going to stop for the next two hours."

He filled the Jeep with gas and went inside to pay, then met Pete as he exited the washroom.

"Get in line and order yourself a coffee and a donut," he said. "Mine's a double double with a honey crueller, please. Here's ten bucks."

He used the washroom and came out just as Pete was paying for the order.

"Keep it," he said, when Pete proffered the change. "We'll work the money out later."

They got back into the Jeep and drove up to the toll booths that guarded the exit to the Island. There were five or six vehicles in each line, so Rashford joined the one which had no camper trailers. The other lines moved steadily forward but theirs remained static.

"This always happens," said Rashford, drumming the steering wheel. "I always pick the wrong line. Some dingbat arguing the toss about the fee, I guess."

He looked around but another car was in line behind him, so he could not pull out and try a different booth. Eventually a car pulled over from the truck weigh scales behind them and drove to the front of the booth, where it stopped. A policeman got out. He leaned into the window of the car at the front of the line, then pointed at a pull-over area to the side. The driver slowly left the booth and pulled up on the verge, the officer walking after him.

The cars moved forward quickly then. When Rashford got to the booth he flashed his police identification and gestured over to the errant car.

"What was all that about?" he said.

The toll collector barely glanced at the identification card.

"Oh, some tourist who's got no cash but whose credit card must be maxed out. He couldn't pay the toll. The cops'll sort it out."

Rashford grunted, then pulled away from the toll booth, merging behind a large tractor trailer as the four lanes came together and funnelled all the traffic onto the Confederation Bridge.

Once across the bridge they made good time, skirting past Moncton and stopping at a truck stop near the big Canadian Forces Base at Gagetown for lunch. Most of the other diners were in camouflage green battle dress and cast interested glances their way, but nobody spoke to them.

It was only when they were outside, standing in the lee of the restaurant and having a cigarette, that two soldiers joined them in the designated smoking area. They nodded at each other.

"Are you based here all the time?" said Rashford.

"No, we're from Shilo, Manitoba," said the taller of the two. "We're here for a training course, four weeks in beautiful New Brunswick!"

"It's nice to see the trees, though," said his companion. "And the hills. Manitoba is kind of flat."

"Hot, dry and dusty," said his companion. "Afghanistan without the mud huts."

"Yeah, we're driving back to Saskatchewan," said Pete.

The soldiers nodded.

"Were you in Afghanistan?" said Rashford.

The taller soldier looked at him.

"Yes. And before you ask, it was a beautiful country and most people were nice. But then there were the bad guys, and that wasn't very nice at all."

Rashford looked at him.

"I'm a police officer," he said. "Sometimes it seems like we're dealing with the same crap every day, and no matter what you do, it just doesn't make a difference."

"Yeah, well imagine doing what you do but everyone has guns and knows how to use them. Imagine driving to work always wondering which car is going to blow up next to you. Imagine losing your buddies and not being able to do anything about it. And then ten years after we leave, everything goes sideways again and you have to ask yourself, why were we there?"

"Because we were asked to go, Dave," said the shorter soldier, gently.

"I'm sorry," said Rashford. "I didn't mean to upset you."

"It's okay," said the second soldier. "It's impossible for people who weren't there to understand. The stuff we saw, and did, it never goes away."

They stubbed out their cigarettes in the metal can that served as an ashtray.

"Happy trails," said Dave, and the other waved as they walked away. Rashford and Pete watched as they clambered on to a large military vehicle bristling with antenna and displaying a short-barrelled cannon extending from the turret. The engine started with a cloud of blue exhaust smoke.

"Is that a tank?" said Pete. "I've never seen one up close before."

"No, it's a LAV, a Light Armored Vehicle," said Rashford. "Look at the wheels. They're individual tires, not tracked like a tank. Roxanne has a cousin in the army, and we stopped at his base, on our way out here. They're really tight and cramped inside, and noisy as hell."

Pete watched as the vehicle moved slowly away, then followed Rashford as he returned to their own vehicle.

Once they were back on the road, driving through the indeterminable spruce forest and small towns of northern New Brunswick, Pete ventured to speak.

"So, how long do you think this trip will take us, then?" he said.

Rashford glanced at him.

"Well, seeing as how I'm the only one driving, I figure we'll be six days to Regina."

"Six days? Yeah, that sounds about right. We took seven in the truck but Danny, my driver, he was only allowed up to eleven hours a day and then had to take a break. We were limited to speed, though, so we tried to get in a nine- or ten-hour day of driving. It was really slow in northern Ontario!"

"Yeah, it would be. Which way did you come, north or south?"

"I'm not sure."

"Did you see the giant Canada goose at Wawa?"

Pete thought for a moment.

"No, I don't remember that. But we stuck to the highway, we didn't go off looking at things."

"No, this is right on the highway. If you'd come that way, you'd have seen it. You must have gone the northern route, though Hearst and Cochrane."

Pete nodded excitedly.

"That's right. Cochrane. There was a sign for a polar bear park there, but we didn't have time to stop. I remember that."

Rashford grunted.

"Well, we won't stop this trip either, we're going the other route. When we stop this evening, I'll show you on the map."

They settled into a companiable silence. The radio picked up a country music station from somewhere and they listened to old Patsy Cline songs for a while, then turned it off when the static got too bad. They gained back an hour just before crossing into Quebec, then made good time down the highway which ran parallel to the St. Lawrence River.

They had started seeing the road signs for Montreal when Rashford pulled off the road at Drummondville and found a Comfort Inn.

"This'll do for tonight," he said, once he had checked in and parked outside their room. "I'm just going to go for a run, to get the kinks out, then we'll have dinner."

"I don't want a run, but I wouldn't mind a beer," said Pete, laughing.

Rashford pointed across the parking lot.

"There's a St. Hubert restaurant and bar just over there. I'll come back and grab a quick shower, then I'll meet you in the bar in about an hour. Okay?"

"Sounds like a plan," said Pete, as they entered the room.

Rashford pointed to the bed nearest the far wall.

"That one's mine," he said. "You can have the one by the window."

The chicken was superb, as expected, although both took the safe option of a chicken dinner, ignoring the comments of the waiter that the poutine was really good. Once they had eaten and were sipping their beer, Rashford pulled out and unfolded a paper map.

"I know we can see this on our phones," he said, "but I'm old school. And this is a basic road map of Canada, so you can see where we're going."

He angled the map so Pete could see it, then placed his finger on the red line that ran through eastern Quebec.

"We're here," he said. "You can see how far it is from Charlottetown. But we've got a long way to go."

He traced his finger along the route, explaining each day of the journey to come.

"Tomorrow we should get to Ottawa, we'll find a place somewhere near Arnprior for the night. Then we cut across to Sault Ste. Marie, and then follow the north shore of Lake Superior round to Thunder Bay. That'll take us past the Wawa Goose, here. From Thunder Bay we'll go up through the boreal forest to the border with Alsama. Once we're through there, it's a quick run into Winnipeg, and then the next day will see us back in Regina. Okay?"

"You're the driver," said Pete. "But that sounds good to me."

Rashford looked across the table, then pulled out his wallet.

"I'm going to pay for dinner tonight," he said, "but that's it. You're on your own from now on."

Eastman looked at him and his face started to flush. He began to protest but Rashford held up his hand.

"It's okay. I understand you don't have any money. I'll pick the hotel each night and pay for the room, so don't worry about that. But for food and stuff, here, take this."

He pulled a folded over bunch of notes from his wallet and handed them to Pete.

"There's five hundred bucks there. Consider it a loan. I expect you to pay it back when you can, or else persuade Alf to assume your debt. But I don't want you hanging on my pocket for every nickel or dime you want to spend. So, use this as you want. But remember, we've got another five days on the road, and there's no more on the tree."

Eastman took the cash and held it carefully, as though it might break.

"Thank you," he said, eventually. "I really appreciate this."

Rashford nodded.

"Right then. Let's finish this beer and then get an early night, tomorrow is going to be a long day."

They got away early the next morning and the first part of the drive was quiet. It was raining and there was a light fog, but that did not seem to slow down the traffic. Unfortunately, Rashford missed the junction with Highway A-30, which would have bypassed Montreal, and kept on the Trans Canada Highway. It was still rush hour as they went through the tunnel under the river and emerged onto the Île de Montréal. The cacophony reverberated around them, increasing in volume when they realized they were in the wrong lane and had to cut across three lanes of traffic in order to keep on the autoroute heading towards Ottawa.

As soon as they had crossed the Pont de l'Île-au-Tourtes, Rashford took the first exit. He pulled into the parking lot of a fast-food restaurant and stopped the Jeep, then sat back with a loud sigh.

"What a manic bunch of drivers," he said. "I need a cigarette."

They both got out and stood next to the vehicle as they smoked, huddled against the rain and the wind. Once they had finished Rashford locked the car and they ran into the building, used the washroom, and then bought coffees to go. They stood outside in the shelter of a large metal box attached to the wall restaurant and had a second smoke. Suddenly a young woman walked up to them. She snatched the cigarette out of Rashford's mouth and threw it to the ground, stomping on it with her boot. Eastman reared back, holding his cigarette high above his head.

"Pas de fumer ici," she said, glaring at them both. "C'est la règle du neuf mètres."

She pointed at the metal structure next to which they were sheltering. Rashford suddenly realized that it was an air intake fan for the restaurant.

"Oh, sorry," he said. "We didn't ..."

"Pah!" she said, then stood, waiting.

"Kill the smoke, Pete," said Rashford. "It's illegal here."

Eastman dropped his cigarette and stubbed it with his shoe, then bent to pick up the butt. The woman nodded, curtly, then turned and walked back into the building. They watched her go, then walked back to their vehicle.

"I thought everyone in Quebec smoked," said Eastman, shaking his head.

"Not everyone," said Rashford, laughing. "Sorry about that. I'd forgotten the nine-metre rule. We're okay here by the Jeep but they are strict on the proximity issue."

The rain had stopped so they leaned against the door and lit new cigarettes. Rashford nodded towards the restaurant.

"See. She's watching."

They drove along the cracked four-lane highway towards Ottawa, the road flanked by trees or fields as it cut across eastern Ontario. Rashford kept a steady five kilometers above the speed limit, and they made good progress. After about an hour, Eastman cleared his throat.

"Can I ask a question?" he said.

Rashford looked sideways at him, then turned back to face the road.

"Sure," he said.

"I didn't really understand that conversation in the restaurant, with

Sandra and Roxanne," said Pete. "Who is this guy you're trying to find? What's the story?"

"That's two questions," said Rashford. "But in a way, they go together. It's quite a long story, though."

"We're not doing anything else," said Pete, "so go for it."

They were nearly in Ottawa by the time Rashford had finished recounting the story of Claude Dallas, as he still called him. He spoke about the way he had tracked him across Alberta, from Red Deer to Hannah, and then through Saskatchewan to Prince Albert. He described the North Saskatchewan River, and the bays and islands of Lake Winnipeg, and all the traces he had found and used to follow the trail.

When he got to the part where Dallas had headbutted him and escaped, taking his official sidearm in the process, Rashford broke his own rule and lit a cigarette. He offered one to Eastman, and at the same time opened the window a crack. The noise of the wind meant he had to raise his voice a little.

"So, then I was sent to do penance, in the north," he said. "I was up there for a year and a half. It was after that when I got posted to Maple Creek, where I met Alf."

"Where does Roxanne come into this?" said Eastman.

Rashford skipped over the incident in Saskatoon and spoke of being stopped beside the highway in Consul, Saskatchewan, during a prairie storm. He recounted how Roxanne had been escaping from someone who had been chasing her, someone who they came to call Fancy Boots, because of the highly decorated cowboy boots he was wearing. He made Pete laugh out loud as he described tracking Fancy Boots to Mountain View, Alberta, and then to Waterton National Park, but grew serious again when he spoke of the death of Fox Woman, Bettina's dog.

"This is where it gets a bit confusing," he said. "Roxanne's mum, Sandra, turned up around then, and talked about being contacted by the child she'd given up for adoption years ago. A lot of that didn't make sense to me, but it was only as we talked that things kind of clicked into place. I still don't have evidence, but now I think I know what happened."

"What?" said Eastman.

"Later," said Rashford. "We're past Ottawa now, let's find a hotel for the night."

They had finished dinner at the hotel's restaurant and walked down to a secluded copse of trees at the edge of the lawn. A gravelled path ran along parallel to the water and there was a fine view of the Madawaska River. The hotel was officially a smoke free property and they moved round to the river side of the trees, then backed in under the canopy, before lighting their cigarettes.

"What was all that Indian Posse stuff?" said Eastman, looking out over the river. "I remember hearing about them, they were pretty big back in the day."

"Yeah. That was another connection, and might be the last link in the chain," said Rashford.

"What do you mean?"

"Well, we've got Claude Dallas, and Fancy Boots, and then we've got this fellow who was pretending to be Sandra's son, calling himself Xavier Ballantyne. But he wasn't, because we know Sandra's son is dead. We have proof of that. Then we've got Simon Spring, who was born at the same time as Sandra had her boy, maybe a day later. With me so far?"

"Not at all," said Eastman, shaking his head.

"Well, here's what I think happened," said Rashford, bending down to stub out his cigarette. Just then an angry-sounding voice called out.

"Oi! You! Yes, you!"

Rashford turned and saw an older man walking towards them, waving a cane in the air. He was marching rather than striding, and from his bearing Rashford thought he was probably a veteran.

"This is a no smoking property, you know! That means everywhere. Including out here on the lawns."

The man halted about ten metres away. Rashford saw he had a hotel name badge pinned to the breast pocket of his jacket.

Eastman stepped forward from the edge of the trees.

"There's nobody around here," he said, reasonably. "And the wind is blowing the smoke towards the river."

The man stopped and glared at him.

"So what? Why does that negate the rule? It's a no smoking property, and that means no smoking on the property. Anywhere on the property."

Eastman riled at the man's tone.

"Are you in charge of rule enforcement, then?" he said, using a sarcastic tone.

The man indicated his name badge.

"Yes, I bloody well am," he said, his voice rising even further.

Rashford intervened.

"It's alright, Pete. The gentleman is quite right. We were in the wrong."

He turned to the man.

"My apologies. We thought we had managed to actually leave the hotel grounds, I thought this was a public footpath, you see."

The man stood his ground.

"It is," he said. "But that's there and you're here. On the hotel side."

He gave a loud harumph, as if to say, 'bloody idiots.'

Eastman looked at him, incredulous.

"Hang on. So, you're saying, if we stand on the other side of the path, it's okay to smoke?"

The man shook his head.

"Not at all. But it would not be a hotel issue. That side is ruled by the municipal bylaws, so you can smoke there as long as there is nobody else around. As soon as other people are present you must stop. And I am present."

"But you are concerned about the hotel rules," said Rashford. "Not the municipal ones."

"Young man, I am concerned about ALL rules," said the man, drawing himself up to his full height. "It's because people think they can pick and choose which rules to follow that this country is in the mess it's in."

Rashford was more and more convinced the man was a military veteran.

"Thank you for your service, sir," he said, delighted to note from the man's response that he had been correct. "Where did you serve?"

If anything, the man stood taller and straighter.

"Balkans, mainly. Croatia and B-H."

"Nobody following the rules?" said Rashford, gently.

"No damn rules to follow," said the man. "Have you heard of the Medak Pocket? Canada's first significant military action since Korea and it got ignored back home. Pshaw!"

"I've heard of it," said Rashford. "Were you there?"

"Bloody disaster area. Everybody ethnic cleansing each other. Colonel Calvin had to shame them to let us in. So, come on you two, clear off. I want to get back to my tea."

Rashford nodded.

"Come on, Pete," he said. "We'll walk along the path a way, until there's nobody around, and then we'll have our smoke on the other side of the grass, by the riverbank."

The man nodded, then turned on his heel and marched back across the lawn towards the hotel.

"How ridiculous can you get," said Eastman, shaking his head. "Pompous little man."

"Just doing his job," said Rashford, leading the way down the path.

It was not until the next morning, as they were driving the long monotony of Highway 17 as it ran between Algonquin Park and the Ottawa River, that Rashford picked up the story again.

"So, this is what I think happened," he said, turning off the radio.

Eastman looked at him in surprise.

"Hang on," he said. "Let me check."

"Check for what?" said Rashford.

"Whatever's going to interrupt you this time. This is the third go you've had at telling me what this is all about."

Rashford laughed.

"Fair enough," he said. "Let's have a smoke and I'll try to finish the story this time."

Eastman lit the cigarettes and cracked open his window. The wind whistled in but the smoke blew out. Rashford sighed, noisily.

"Right. Okay, well you know the middle bit of the story. I told you about Claude Dallas, Fancy Boots, Xavier Ballantyne, and Simon Spring, and that I think they're all the same bloke. And there are other aliases that he's used as well. I'm not quite sure of the why of all this yet, but this is what I think is the who. This is the beginning of the story.

"I think that Simon Spring was born in Antigonish and taken away from his mum by the nuns. He probably had a case of Fetal Alcohol Syndrome, but they didn't know how to diagnose that then. He had a pretty hard childhood, lots of foster homes and group homes, and a three-year spell in a residential school. Eventually he ended up on the streets of Regina, where he was your typical inner city thuggie.

"Then something happened. I'm not sure what, but it scared him enough that he had to get out of town. So, he joined the army. They channelled his energy and taught him how to use it efficiently. They taught him to live off the land, and probably how to kill people. And off he went to Afghanistan and other places, to practice what they had preached.

"When he left the army, he got a job for a while. Made friends, lived with a buddy. But then things started to go wrong. I don't know what. Bad dreams? Bad temper? A feeling of being lost, isolated from the people he'd been with for years? Who knows? He lost his job. Perhaps he left home, perhaps his buddy threw him out. He ended up on the street. Somehow, he got to Calgary.

"A woman connected with him there and persuaded him to see a doctor, to get medicines, to take his tablets. He started to get better. She even let him live in her house while she and her husband were away. Then the western troubles started, and the Americans bombed Calgary. It seems like that brought all his fears back and he quit taking his medicine. He left the city and started travelling east, going overland. I told you all about that already."

"Yes, I remember that," said Eastman, nodding.

"So, here we are now, and I still don't know the why of it all. Why did he pretend to be all those different people? Why did he take on those different identities? Why did he befriend the real Xavier and present himself as him, to Sandra of all people? Why did he have

Roxanne kidnapped from the bar? That's what I don't understand. He was doing okay and then he just sort of lost it."

"Well, that's easy," said Eastman. "PTSD."

"What?"

"PTSD. Post-Traumatic Stress Syndrome. It's a classic case. From what you've told me, this all started when he witnessed the bombing in Calgary. PTSD usually starts with major emotional stress or even a major physical reaction triggered by something that reminds you of the traumatic event, and I'm guessing that reminded him of stuff he saw when he was in the Army.

"Some people can control it with drugs and counselling, but in severe cases you see things like angry and aggressive behaviour, loss of trust in other people, self-isolation, irritability, anxiety, self-distrust and self-harm, those sorts of things. The symptoms can also include self-delusion, negative thinking, and paranoia."

Rashford looked across at him with amazement.

"How do you know all that?" he said.

"I'm majoring in psychology, at university."

"But hang on, you said you'd dropped out."

"No, I didn't. I said I was taking a break. You're the one who said I was a Thanksgiving Graduate or whatever you called me. I couldn't be bothered to correct you."

"So ..."

"So, I know this stuff. I've been interested in psychology for years, since grade ten. I've read pretty much all the main textbooks. My prof recognized this and told me I could challenge the exams without attending classes, which is why I had time to be a cow sitter."

"Right," said Rashford. "I'm sorry. I didn't mean to insult you."

"No biggie. It was kind of fun, you thinking I was a lazy drop-out."

"So, what do you think he's doing now?"

"I've no idea," said Eastman. "This is purely speculative, but I would imagine he's gone somewhere he feels safe. It sounds like you got pretty close to him, and he's probably scared."

Chapter 20

They arrived back in Regina early in the afternoon of day six, as planned. It was a Thursday. Pete Eastman had been delighted to see the giant Canada Goose at Wawa and had thirty-eight photographs on his phone to prove that he had been there. In the university carpark he shook hands with Rashford.

"Thanks for the ride. I appreciate it. Are you going back to Maple Creek?"

"In a day or so. I've got to check in at headquarters here first."

"Right. Well, I'll talk to Uncle Alf and get him the money I owe you, so just drop in and see him when you get there."

"Sure."

"And tell him I'm doing okay, for a drop-out!"

Rashford laughed.

"I'll do that."

He got back into the Jeep and drove down the Wascana Parkway, crossed the bridge over the lake and merged onto Broad Street. Traffic was light and in ten minutes he was parked outside the police headquarters. He walked to the red brick building and checked his reflection in the dark glass of the main door. Taking a deep breath, he opened the door and walked inside, then crossed to the reception desk.

"Sergeant Rashford to see Chief Superintendent Pollard," he said, opening his wallet to show his identification card.

The uniformed receptionist ran his finger down a list of names on the desk.

"I don't see you here, Sergeant," he said.

"I don't have an appointment, but I think she'll want to see me," said Rashford.

The duty officer raised his eyebrows but picked up the phone. He spoke briefly, then listened. After a few moments, he put the receiver down.

"The CS has someone with her at the moment," he said. "Please take a seat and someone will be down in a minute."

Rashford looked around and saw a row of pink plastic chairs arranged in a straight line against the wall. As he walked across, he noted that there were eight of them. He sat on the one that was third from the left, folded his hands in his lap, and waited.

Sarah laughed as she walked across from the elevator, her heels clicking on the tiled floor.

"I figured you'd be in that chair, Gavin" she said, shaking his hand. "You've got your back to the wall so nobody can creep up on you. You can see the elevator and the front door, and also keep an eye on young Stephen there."

She nodded across to the officer at the reception desk, who waved back.

"Come on," she said, "I'll take you up. You've intrigued the boss, and I figure you've got about an hour. She's asked me to cancel her next two appointments and get coffee for you both. So, well done you, whatever it is you've been doing."

"It's a long story, Sarah," said Rashford. "We'll have to catch up later."

"Promises, promises, just like the beer you owe me," she said, laughing, then led him into the suite. She knocked softly on the inner door and then opened it, ushering Rashford inside.

"Sergeant Rashford, Ma'am," she said. "I'll get the coffee."

The Chief Superintendent stood up and shook hands with Rashford, then indicated he sit in the chair opposite her desk. He did so. She studied him quietly.

"How was your drive back?"

"It was fine, thank you. Long but okay."

"Your ride-along couldn't drive, then?"

"Not a standard, sadly. But that's okay, I like driving."

"And how is Roxanne?"

"She's fine, Ma'am, as far as I know. I've not spoken to her today yet."

"Right. Ah, here we are. Thank you, Sarah."

Her administrative assistant placed the tray on the desk and then withdrew, closing the door quietly behind her. Pollard poured the coffee.

"Help yourself to cream and sugar," she said, sitting back in her chair and taking a sip from her own drink.

"It's freshly made," she said, putting the cup back on the desk. "Quite hot."

Rashford nodded. He left his cup on the desk.

"So, six days of driving," said the Chief Superintendent. "If I know you, that's the same as six days of thinking. What have you come up with?"

"Well, Ma'am, this is all about Claude Dallas, or at least the person who called himself that name. We already knew the what, where, and how, but now I think I know the who as well. I've also got a bit of an idea about the why."

"Intriguing. Do proceed, Sergeant."

Rashford repeated the story he had told Eastman, fleshing in the details of his enquiries in Antigonish and Cheticamp. He finished by raising the possibility of PTSD as the underlying reason for everything that had happened.

Pollard listened carefully, sometimes jotting a note on the pad in front of her, sometimes taking a sip from her coffee. When he was done, she nodded her head.

"That certainly all fits together, Sergeant," she said. "Now, let me add one other piece of information to the puzzle."

She tapped at the keyboard of her desktop computer, then scrolled through a number of screens.

"Here we are. This information was supplied by Corporal Morgan, but I understand you made the initial request."

"Yes, Ma'am."

"She's not your personal assistant, you know," said Pollard.

"No, Ma'am."

Pollard looked at him, sharply, as if to check that he wasn't making fun of her.

"I mean it. She has her own job to do. First the residential school business and now this."

"Yes, Ma'am. Sorry, Ma'am."

"You owe her a dinner at least."

"Yes, Ma'am."

Pollard turned her attention back to the screen.

"Where were we. Yes, right, Corporal Morgan's research. She has discovered that someone called Simon Wolfe enlisted in Regina in October 2004."

"Got him!"

"Well, not quite. But yes, it looks promising. Now we are waiting to hear back from the Army. We've asked for a career summary, date of discharge, and last known address, plus any other information they think might be useful."

"Where do they send his pension?"

"Exactly. Although most of that is online now and could be going anywhere. So, now we wait. Again."

She tapped her pen against her bottom lip.

"Meanwhile, what are we to do with you, hmmm?"

Rashford sat straight in his chair, looking ahead.

"You are still on suspension, you know. The Civilian Review and Complaints Commission is due to present its report on Monday afternoon, so why don't you take the weekend off and come back here first thing on Tuesday. Let's say, eight o'clock. Then we'll go from there."

"Yes, Ma'am. Thank you, Ma'am."

Rashford got to his feet, saluted, and walked out of the office. He nodded at Sarah as he passed, then stopped as he reached the door. Looking back, he saw that she had gone into Pollard's office and was picking up the coffee cups.

He waited until she had brought the tray back and closed Pollard's office door behind her. He held the door open for her and then followed her down to the small kitchen. Leaning against the wall, he watched her as she rinsed out the cups. Eventually she turned and looked at him.

"What?"

"I was wondering, can you recommend a hotel where I can stay for the weekend? The Holiday Inn will be full of families, I want somewhere a bit quieter."

"How much do you want to spend?"

"I don't know, whatever's reasonable, I guess. Why?"

"Well, the Stone Hall Castle is pretty cool but it's four hundred bucks a night," she said, laughing.

Rashford shook his head.

"Why don't you get out of town? The BraeBurn Inn is nice, up in the Qu'appelle Valley. It's less than an hour from town, very quiet and peaceful."

"Thanks."

"You're welcome. Enjoy your weekend."

Rashford nodded, then left the kitchen and walked back to the elevator. Once outside he got in his car, thought for a moment, then called the BraeBurn Inn.

The BraeBurn Inn was open year-round and, at the beginning of November, not terribly busy. He was able to get the Tiki room, so called because of the indeterminate motif on a large wall-hanging which dominated the room. The only Tiki he had seen was a gift given to him by a New Zealand police officer who was on a six-month exchange to the old Canada. It had been small and curved, made from some sort of jade, and he had kept it for a while and then gifted it to a woman he was seeing at the time. This looked nothing like that.

The wall-hanging was a stylized portrait with a Maōri-influenced face, a Polynesian tapa background, some Melanesian bamboo sticks arrayed as a head-dress, and an applique representation of the hull of a war canoe. Rashford had no idea of what actual culture the design was meant to represent. But it was hanging over a king-sized bed, which he preferred.

The room was small but neatly furnished, with an electric fireplace, an easy chair, a mini-fridge, and a microwave. It also had high-speed wireless internet and an HD television with satellite connection, although he wasn't sure he would need either of those. The door opened onto a narrow hacienda-type porch which extended the length of the building. A wooden slat boardwalk and grey wooded arches were backed by whitewashed walls and completed the Albuquerque effect. Outside each room were two plastic wicker armchairs and a round glass table, on which reposed a black molded ashtray.

Rashford emptied the few clothes in his backpack into the various drawers of the small dresser, put his toothbrush into a water glass on the side of the bathroom sink, and stored a six-pack of Red Ale in the minifridge. He preferred the smooth ale, brewed by Pile O' Bones brewery in Regina, to their stronger Space Cadet IPA. Domestic duties completed, he changed into his running gear and followed the trail that ran alongside the north shore of Echo Lake.

He ran five kilometres, past Fort San, then turned and returned along the same trail back to Fort Qu'Appelle. Showered and changed, he sat in one of armchairs and watched the sunset. Sipping on his beer, and smoking a cigarette, he found himself feeling relaxed for the first time in weeks.

He pulled out his phone and checked the time, mentally adding in the two hours difference before calling Roxanne. He told her about dropping Pete off at the university and described his meeting with the Chief Superintendent.

"So, what are you going to do until Monday?" she said.

"Nothing, much," he said, explaining about booking the room in Fort Qu'Appelle for three nights.

"I've found a couple of running trails, and there are two or three restaurants which seem okay. I'm just going to hang out here until

Sunday, then go back into Regina and get organized for Monday morning."

"Why not go back to Maple Creek?" said Roxanne.

"Well, it's a bit far, and someone is billeted in the police house, so I'd have to stay at the motel anyway."

"You could stay with Bettina and Kôhkum Christine," she said, "or even Alf!"

"Perhaps, but I'm actually looking forward to some quiet time. I've just had six days in the Jeep with Pete, you know."

Roxanne laughed.

"What, he didn't follow your rule and keep quiet the whole way?"

"Sadly, no. You should have heard him when we saw the Wawa Goose. I had to drag him away."

"I know, he posted photographs," she said.

"What have you been up to?"

"Not a lot, really. Mom and I have been out for coffee a couple of times, there are some new places in town that do really a nice latte or cappuccino. We've wandered around the shops and met a few people who I haven't seen for years. Just hanging out, you know."

"How long are you going to stay?"

"I told you, I don't know. Not until you've got this case sorted out, anyway. Mom thinks I can get a temporary job for the next few weeks, until Christmas."

"Christmas? That's two months away!"

"Well, I am going to have to contribute to being with mom. I can't just eat all her food. There's a little consignment boutique that's looking for someone with retail experience, I'm going to talk to them tomorrow."

There was silence.

"Gavin, are you still there?"

"Yes."

"What's the matter?"

"I guess, I was expecting you back here before Christmas. You said it was only going to be for as long as your mom needed you."

"It will be. But she needs me now, can't you see? And especially this

Christmas, what with finding and then losing Keith, it's really upset her."

"I won't get leave to come out at Christmas, you know. I've used it all up for this year, even if I keep my job."

"That's alright, we can talk."

Rashford was silent again. Then he cleared his throat.

"Well, we can talk more tomorrow evening. I'll call you about this time, you can tell me about your visit to the boutique."

Roxanne hesitated before answering.

"Not tomorrow, okay? I'm meeting an old friend, we bumped into them today and got chatting. They just came back to the Island as well. We're going to go out to Hunter's for dinner and drink."

"Saturday, then."

Roxanne hesitated again.

"Look, why don't we wait until next week, after you've had your meeting with Tracey?"

"Why, where are you going for the weekend?"

"Mom and I are going to go up to Lennox Island, to the Mi'kmaq community there. A healer from Eskasoni is going to be over and mom wants to see him. So, we're going to be staying up there, and I don't know when I'll be free to talk."

"Right," said Rashford. "I'll call next week."

"Thank you. I knew you'd understand."

"Does this old friend have a name?"

"What?"

"This person you're meeting tomorrow, do they have a name?"

"Of course! Their name is Darryl."

"Darryl."

"Yes, we were at school together and used to hang out, back when we were young. It will be good to catch up."

Rashford did not comment for a moment, biting off some responses that he knew he would quickly regret. Eventually, he suggested they end the call.

"I'm not sure what time the restaurants here close," he said, "and I need to get my dinner. I'll call you next week."

"Great," said Roxanne. "Talk soon."

That evening he drove around the small community and found a family restaurant where he decided to avoid the Indian food special dinner but treated himself to a full rack of baby back ribs instead. Afterwards, he drove out along the south side of the lake and parked in a small area just up from the beach. He turned off the engine and let his eyes adjust to the dark, then stepped out of the Jeep, cursing as the interior light came on and startled him. He lit a cigarette and leaned against the front radiator, looking out over the water.

The new moon was in the waxing crescent phase, less than a quarter full and the arms reaching out to his left. The stars glittered above him. He could recognize the Big Dipper, and also Orion, and thought the planet rising to the east-northeast was probably Jupiter, but the others were a mystery to him. He was hoping for the northern lights but on this evening was disappointed.

Returning to his motel, Rashford cracked open another beer, then sat and watched the news. When he had enough of the chaos and havoc of the day, he took the last of the can outside and smoked another cigarette. Stretching, he stubbed it out in the ashtray, threw his can into the small blue recycling tub, and went back inside. He locked the door, got undressed, and went to bed.

It took him a while to get to sleep, his mind racing with images of Darryl. Why had Roxanne tried to hide that he was a guy, he wondered. Was he an old boyfriend? How come his name had never come up before? Why was she not wanting to talk to him until next week?

He recalled the last two times that he had called her during the journey back west, once from Ottawa and the second time from just across the border, in Winnipeg. For each call she had seemed distracted, cutting off his descriptions of the various sights he had seen along the road, ignoring his accounts of the funny comments made by Pete in response to a new food or a strange tourist attraction. She had said that things were fine with her mom, and she was fine, but that was all. There were no long and engaged conversations, no extended companiable silences. No communication, he thought now, just the exchange of information.

With that thought, he turned on his side, pulled the quilt up over his shoulder, and went to sleep.

The next morning, he slept late, then went for a long and meandering walk around the town. He picked up a coffee and blueberry muffin from the first Tim Horton's he saw and was given directions to the Treaty 4 governance centre, on the edge of town opposite the PowWow grounds. It was a leisurely thirty-minute walk, and after admiring the teepee shaped structure he made his way back into town.

In truth, there was not much to see, and after admiring the brick and stone facade of the Hudson's Bay Company Store, proudly emblazoned with 1897 to signify the year of construction, and the similarly inscribed 1911 Grand Trunk Pacific Railway Station, he found himself at the town museum. This displayed the original trading post building, abandoned when the new retail store was constructed, and a variety of interesting artefacts from the area.

Leaving the museum, he wandered back through town, stopping at a fast-food place for lunch. He sat inside to eat his burger, fries, and onion rings, deciding to avoid the root beer float and stick to coffee, then continued to walk down Bay Avenue until he saw the driveway to the motel. He sat on the verandah and had a cigarette, then decided to go for a drive.

Rashford consulted the town and area map he had picked up at the museum and followed the road which ran along the south side of Echo Lake. At B-Say-Tah he parked and wandered along the sandy beach, which although it was the weekend was empty on this cool November day. He continued around Echo Lake, crossing the bridge over the narrow channel that linked to Pasqua Lake and then turning east to return back along the north shore of Echo Lake.

He pulled off the road again at Fort San, following a driveway up to what turned out to be a ramshackle two-story building. The bottom row of windows were all boarded up with sheets of plywood, and weeds were growing in the cracks of the concrete steps. As he returned to his car a large black dog came bounding up to him.

"It's alright, she's friendly," shouted the elderly man who came walking out of the trees, shaking the long red leash he grasped in one hand and leaning on the cane he held in the other.

"Kula, come here," he called, to which the dog responded by sitting down next to Rashford, who scratched her ears. The dog's tail wagged furiously as the man arrived, breathing heavily from his exertions.

"I'm so sorry," he said, panting and leaning forward so he could put his hands on his knees. "We don't normally see people up here, so I let her run off-leash. She got away before I saw you."

"It's no problem," said Rashford, still scratching the dog's ears. "She's fine."

"Well, yes, thank you," said the man. "But she's young and I have to train her properly, not everyone is as decent as you."

Rashford laughed.

"Oh, this one's a beauty," he said.

"Yes, and she knows it," said the man, having got his breath back and straightened up. "Where's yours, then?"

"My what?"

"Your dog. That's the only reason people come up here, to walk their dogs. At this time of the year, anyway."

"No, not me. I came to have a look at the Sanitorium, but there's not much to see."

"Not anymore, sadly," said the man. "Damned government. It used to be a special place, this, and they let it go."

"Really?" said Rashford. "How?"

"It was a beautiful building, constructed late in the First World War as a sanitorium for people with tuberculosis. The warm dry air of southern Saskatchewan, you know? Then in the sixties they stopped treating people by hospitalization and the government made it a Summer School of Arts. Fabulous, those years, just fabulous. All sorts of interesting people coming here to visit.

"Then after twenty years or so, that stopped, and it became a summer school for Sea Cadets. Can you imagine? Is there anywhere in Canada further from the ocean than here? It's a thousand kilometers to Churchill and that's the nearest salt water!"

Rashford figured that he was supposed to laugh at this information, so he did. The old man nodded.

"That only lasted for a decade and the government decided to sell it to a private company. They were supposed to be socialists, the government, but they got scared in the oh three election and were trying to get back the rural vote. Fat lot of good that's done them. Anyway, the private company has done bugger all and the building is nearly derelict, as you can see. So that's where we are. Nice place for the dog, though."

He clipped the leash onto the collar and walked off down towards the road.

Rashford got into his car and followed. He pulled alongside the man, keeping some distance so as to protect the dog, and opened his window.

"Would you like a lift anywhere?" he said.

"No thanks, my car is just down the road. We have a regular route. Cheers now."

He kept walking, his dog on a short leash by his side, and Rashford pulled onto the main road and continued back towards the town. He passed a dark Audi Q5 pulled into a layby a hundred metres down the road and assumed that was the man's vehicle.

Ten minutes later, he pulled into the golf course on the edge of Fort Qu'Appelle and parked near the entrance, pulling to the side of the driveway. He got out of his car and walked over to the kiosk situated just off the drive, stopping to look at some foundation stones and a post marker on the way. It was as he had been told at the museum, the small stone structure was all that remained of the first North-West Mounted Police post in Saskatchewan.

At the kiosk Rashford paid his respects to the memory of Superintendent James Walsh, a hero of the force, who in 1880 had expanded this outpost to become a divisional headquarters. The post itself had been a relatively quiet place, with none of the excitement Walsh had experienced in his interactions with Chief Sitting Bull and the Sioux, who had moved north after the Battle of the Little Big Horn. The only visitors of note, Rashford observed, had been the North-West Field Force led by General Middleton, who stopped at Fort Qu'Appelle on their way north to face Louis Riel at the Battle of Batoche.

Rashford returned to his car and drove back to the motel in a pensive mood. He poured himself a glass of water, then sat outside on the veranda and smoked a cigarette. He had only been there a few minutes when a car pulled into the parking lot and drove up towards him, stopping in the bay next to the Jeep. The afternoon sun was behind the car, and he could not see the driver. As the car door opened, Rashford tensed but did not move.

He relaxed when he realized that it was a woman who climbed out of the vehicle. She was quite tall and wearing a dress, which he thought odd for November. Rashford shielded his eyes with his hand and got to his feet.

"Can I help you?" he said.

The woman laughed.

"I was out for a drive and thought I'd check and see if you'd come here," she said. "I figured you could catch me up on that long story you mentioned. I've brought coffee."

As she stepped up onto the veranda and placed the two paper cups on the round table, her face became visible and he realized it was Sarah, the administrative assistant for Chief Superintendent Pollard. He reached out and shook her hand, still warm from the coffee cup, and indicated that she should sit down. She did so, taking a packet of cigarettes out of her purse before placing it on the floor next to her chair.

"Do you mind?" she said, waving the packet.

"Not at all," said Rashford, "I just had one."

He reached over and lit her cigarette, then sat back in his chair and sipped his coffee.

"Well, this is a surprise," he said.

"Yes, sorry for the no warning," said Sarah. "I tend to go for long drives on Saturday afternoons, just cruising the prairies, you know, it reminds me that there is a world outside the office. Today I went to see the art gallery in Yorkton, so I thought I'd stop in here on the way back, see if you took my advice. I hope you don't mind."

"No, not at all. Was it any good? The gallery?"

"It was okay. I've not been before. It prides itself on representing local artists, so there's no Gaugin or Picasso or anything. And you know what they say, 'it might be local, but is it art?' A bit like that, I'm afraid."

Rashford laughed.

"Well, yes, I did take your advice, and I've been exploring the pleasures of Fort Qu'Appelle."

"And ...?"

"Well, that's it, really. It's a small town and I think I've seen it all now."

They drank their coffee and smoked some more cigarettes as the afternoon light started to fade. Rashford told her about the old sanitarium and the NWMP memorial kiosk, and then answered her questions about his pursuit of Claude Dallas. It was nearly dark when he excused himself to go to the washroom.

Coming out, he crouched down next to the mini-fridge and opened the door. He saw that he had four beers left, plus some cans of soda water and two small bottles of orange juice.

"Would you like a beer?" he said, calling out through the door. He heard Sarah push her chair back and then footsteps as she entered the room. She came and stood next to him.

"That depends," she said.

"On what?" he said, looking up. He realized that he was staring down the front of her dress, the neckline of which had hung down as she leaned forward. It was apparent that she was not wearing a bra.

"On whether I'm driving anywhere tonight," she said.

Chapter 21

Rashford presented himself to the reception desk at the police headquarters at seven forty-five on Monday morning. He had driven in from Fort Qu'Appelle the afternoon before, taken a room at the Holiday Inn, and retrieved his dress uniform from the storage lockers. It was a grey Regina morning, with the wind whipped clouds scudding across the sky.

He dashed inside the building, carrying his hat, and smoothed out his uniform in the foyer. He then identified himself to the young constable on duty, who as expected called up to the Chief Superintendent's office. This time, however, when he had put the phone down, he gestured to the elevator.

"The CS says you're to go on up," he said. "She says you know the way."

Rashford nodded, then took the elevator to the second floor. The outside door to Pollard's suite was open, so he went inside and crossed the empty administrative office. He knocked on the inner door.

"Come in then close the door," said Tracey Pollard, and he did.

The Chief Superintendent stood up and reached across her desk to shake his hand.

"Sit down," she said, passing a paper coffee cup across the desk.

"Sarah's not in yet, I'm afraid, so I picked some up. From seeing you here I figured you for a double double man."

"Yes, Ma'am," said Rashford, bemused.

"Did you have a good weekend?"

"Yes, Ma'am. Thank you. I went out to Fort Qu'Appelle and looked around the valley."

"Excellent," said Pollard.

She sipped her coffee and looked down at the papers on her desk, having obviously met her quota of irrelevant chit-chat for the day.

"Right, let's start with the CRCC Report, shall we?"

Rashford straightened himself in the chair. He heard the smattering of rain and focused on the rapidly intensifying smears of moisture across the window.

"As you know, there were three major elements to the investigation," said Pollard, putting the papers back on her desk and looking straight at him.

"The first was the complaint by Mr. Samuel Augustine Samson, formerly of Black Rapids but now resident of Flin Flon, that you racially profiled and harassed him, simply because he is Métis. He claimed that you made his life such a misery, he lost a significant business investment and had to leave his community.

"The investigation showed that the intercept of the aircraft chartered by Mr. Samson was initiated by the Lac La Ronge detachment, and that you and Special Constable Toutsaint were responding as lawfully directed, and in line with the search warrant provided to you by La Ronge. Further, Special Constable Toutsaint has testified under oath that you never uttered the name 'Snowdrop' in his hearing and that you appeared surprised when he told you that this nickname had been applied to Mr. Samson. 'Surprised and amused' were his exact words. The CRCC has concluded that the complaint is completely unfounded and that no sanctions against you are justified or will be applied."

Rashford nodded.

"Thank you, Ma'am," he said.

"Element two, the errors and omissions in your formal log concerning the situation in Consul, when you reacquainted yourself with Ms. Anne Sylliboy Gaudet, and your subsequent attempts to set the record straight. Attempts, I might say, that were driven by circumstance rather than by any altruistic motive on your part. The investigation upheld the complaint that your record keeping was insufficient and unbecoming of an officer with your rank and experience. The CRCC has issued a letter of censure which will be included in your personnel file, as a permanent record of this misdemeanour."

Pollard slapped the desk with her hand, making Rashford flinch.

"I've told you before," she said. "You have to tighten up and play by the rules. Stop being such a loose cannon. There is no place for maverick officers in the force."

"Yes, Ma'am. Sorry, Ma'am."

"Don't be sorry. Just do it. Now, where was I?"

The Chief Superintendent regained her composure.

"Right, element three. The Stordy affair. Again, the investigation found that you displayed a singular lack of judgement by confronting her and her paramour in public but have accepted your argument about the stress of the case.

"The CRCC has issued a letter of apology to Missus Stordy, on behalf of the Force, but did note that you only presented facts for verification, and that those facts are not in dispute, whatever the consequences. She may come after you in civil court, of course, but I doubt it. If she does, my earlier advice that you offer a full and abject apology remains, but I do believe that the CRCC finding absolves you of any culpability, professional or civil."

"Thank you, Ma'am."

Pollard tapped the papers into a neat pile and placed it on the corner of her desk. Rashford continued to watch the rain. There was almost a full minute of silence before the Chief Superintendent spoke again.

"So here we are, Sergeant. There will be a letter of censure on your file, but otherwise you are now clear of the complaints against you. So now we are back to where we were a month ago."

She got to her feet and walked around the desk, indicating that Rashford should also stand. He did so and was surprised when the Chief Superintendent held out her hand, passing him an envelope.

"Congratulations, Sergeant Rashford," she said. "You have passed your FILTER examination with flying colours and so you are now ready for your next assignment."

They shook hands, and then Pollard urged him to sit in one of the two comfortable chairs that flanked a low glass table. As he did so, she went to the door and opened it before calling into the outer office.

"Sarah, could we have two coffees, please. This commercial stuff is dishwater."

While they waited for the coffee, Pollard suggested that Rashford open the envelope she had given him. He did so and was delighted to see that he had passed the FILTER examination with a score of 98 per cent. Pollard looked aggrieved.

"Which part did you screw up?" she said.

Rashford was saved from replying by the entrance of Sarah, with a tray of coffee. She smiled and nodded at Rashford, who smiled back. She put the tray on the glass table and then withdrew, lightly touching his shoulder as she left.

"Congratulations on the exam result," she said.

"Thank you," said Rashford, then turned back to look at Pollard, who was staring at him intently.

"Ready?" she said.

"Yes, Ma'am."

"With respect to your next assignment. You should know that I am not sending you back to Maple Creek, at least not yet. You have the rest of today and tomorrow to move your stuff out from the police house there, and into your new accommodation. Which is at the Depot."

She saw the look on his face and the barracuda smile appeared.

"Don't worry, you won't be in with the recruits. We have a few special rooms at the barracks that we hold for visitors and other dignitaries. Check in at the Guardroom and they'll send you to the Security and Facilities Coordinator, who will sort you out.

"Yes, Ma'am."

"Now, on Wednesday morning we'll have a team meeting. You are going to tasked with finding this Simon Wolfe fellow."

"Team, Ma'am?"

"Yes. Don't get your knickers in a twist. I know you like doing everything on your own but you're going to need help, and that's what the team will give you. Understand?"

"Yes, Ma'am."

"And don't get too excited, it's only going to be a small team."

Rashford nodded, then looked at the window to see what was causing a scratching noise. The rain was falling steadily now, but there were no branches knocking against the glass. Pollard noticed his look.

"Oh, don't worry, that's just Sarah. She must have got lucky this weekend."

Rashford stared at her. The Chief Superintendent smiled.

"She thinks I don't know, but it's quite common knowledge. If you look at the little wooden rail that goes around the edge of her desk, you'll see some small notches. Each one signifies one of her conquests."

Rashford opened his mouth, but no sound came out.

"It's alright, Sergeant. No concern of yours. Wednesday, oh nine hundred. Be here."

She stood up, indicating that the meeting was over.

"Yes, Ma'am."

He took a quick swig of coffee as he stood, saluted, and left the room. In the outer office he saw Sarah, sitting primly at her desk. She saw him glancing at the neat row of four vee-shapes carved into the desk rail, one of them looking noticeably fresh. He raised an eyebrow.

She grinned at him.

"I stopped at that Chinese restaurant in Balgonie," she said. "Met a young farmer. Still, there's always room for one more if you change your mind."

Rashford shook his head, and walked out of the office, the sound of her laughter ringing in his ears.

That afternoon he drove out to Maple Creek and spent the Monday night seeing his friends and catching up on the gossip.

Bettina informed him that Kôhkum Christine was in the hospital, although it was only for tests, and she was expected to return home in a few days. Bettina was still working at the college in Swift Current but was thinking of taking a sabbatical year.

"My nôhkum won't live forever," she said. "We all know that. This is going to be her ninety-seventh winter. When she passes, then it will be lonely here. Cicily is transferring to a new job, at the University of Toronto, and she has invited me to join her there. It will be a good place to honour nôhkum Christine and decide what I want to do with the rest of my life."

Rashford gave her a hug, then scratched the ears of the new puppy, who seemed to be growing rapidly.

"What is he?" he asked.

"She. She's a Bernese Shepherd."

The dog rolled over onto her back and waved her large paws in the air. Rashford bent over and gave her a belly rub.

"What on earth's that?"

"She's a cross, she had a Belgian Shepherd mum and a Bernese Mountain Dog dad."

"Holy crow. She's going to be big."

"Yeah. Big and smart."

"What's her name?"

"Pollard."

Rashford was still laughing as he drove the short distance to the Alf's car service. The old man looked up when he opened the door, then called out to his assistant.

"Brian, watch the shop for a minute, I've got to go out back."

He led Rashford to the side door behind the counter and they stepped outside into the yard. Alf lit a cigarette, offering one to Rashford.

"How's that woman of yours, then?"

"She's okay, thanks. Staying with her mother for a bit, while I get this case finished."

"Aye. We don't need gangsters and bikers coming around here."

"I'll do my best to prevent that," said Rashford.

Alf shuffled his feet from side to side, then reached into his inside pocket. He passed Rashford an envelope.

"Open it," he said. "Make sure it's all there."

Rashford pulled the flap away from the back of the envelope and looked inside. There were five brown one hundred-dollar bills, the unsmiling face of Prime Minister Sir Robert Borden looking up at him. They were crisp and looked new.

"Just off the press, Alf?" said Rashford.

Alf spat on the floor.

"Straight from the hole-in-the-wall," he said. "Thanks for looking after young Pete."

"No problem. Glad to help."

"Aye, well it was good you were there. That truck driver better not come here looking for service, I'll tell you that. I'll serve him good and proper."

"Maybe you don't want to be telling me that, Alf."

"Telling you what?"

Alf cackled, stubbed out his cigarette, then walked back towards the building.

"See yourself out," he said, pointing at the large gate. "You know the way."

Rashford closed the gate behind himself, then drove down to the police detachment. The new duty officer, a young Constable, was sitting at the desk doing paperwork. He jumped to his feet and saluted as Rashford walked in.

"I just need to go to the house and get my stuff," said Rashford. "You can come along if you want, make sure I don't take anything else."

"Oh, no sir, it's alright," said the Constable, flustered.

"No, I'd like you to. I know you assume you can trust me, but this way there's no room for error or misinterpretation. Never assume, Constable."

"Yes, sir. I mean, no, sir."

"Lock the door behind you," said Rashford, and walked down the path. The constable caught up to him and opened the door, standing aside so that Rashford could enter. He picked up the two bags that had been packed and left behind when he went on his administrative leave and looked around to make sure he had not missed anything.

"I think that's it, Constable. Thank you for your assistance."

Rashford took his bags and locked them into his vehicle, then walked next door to the Aspen Motor Inn. He checked in, then crossed the street to have dinner and a drink at the Jasper Hotel. Some of the regulars nodded at him, and one even said hello, but nobody engaged him in conversation.

As he sipped his beer he smiled at the memory of Sarah, and the look on her face when he had risen from the minifridge with a can of soda water in his hand.

"I'm sorry," she had said, her faced reddening. "I didn't mean to be forward ..."

"No, that's okay," said Rashford. "It's just that I'm in a relationship right now."

"Oh, I thought that was over. You know, when she didn't come back with you."

"Roxanne's spending some time with her mom, that's all," said Rashford.

"Maybe in another life, eh?" said Sarah.

"Maybe," he said, and had given her a chaste kiss before she left.

He was back in the office on Wednesday morning, having spent the Tuesday driving back and then getting himself settled into the visitor's room at the Depot barracks. It was a large single room, much like those found in a medium-class hotel, and he was delighted to find that his rate included both a pass to the gym and a meal plan from the cafeteria.

He had slept well, gone for a run around the sports fields, and had breakfast, all before showering and getting changed ready for his meeting. Now, he sat outside the Chief Superintendent's office, waiting for Sarah to invite him in. The elevator door opened, and Gayle Morgan appeared, her face flushed as though she had been running. Rashford stood to meet her.

"Gayle," he said. "I didn't expect you to be here."

She smiled and came over, shaking his hand and then giving him a light hug.

"I've been put on some poxy task force," she said. "What about you? What have you done now?"

Rashford was saved from a response by the door opening. Sarah came out and nodded at Gayle.

"Good morning, constable," she said. "Hello, Gavin. Would you both follow me, please."

She walked off down the corridor, her heels clicking on the tiled floor. Morgan raised an eyebrow.

"Gavin?" she said, whispering as they moved to follow her. "First names, is it? Are you on her ledge of fame?"

"Shush," he said.

Morgan grinned and raised her voice.

"What's happening, Sarah?"

Their guide looked back over her shoulder.

"Conference room for both of you, that's all I know," she said.

"Bull," said Morgan, "you know everything that happens around here."

Sarah just shook her head, then stopped at an unmarked door, tapped lightly, and opened it for them. They entered and found Chief Superintendent Pollard standing in front of a large white board. A variety of coloured marker pens were arrayed on the table in front of her.

"Come in," she said. "Thank you, Sarah. Coffee in half an hour, please."

Sarah nodded, then left the room, quietly closing the door behind her.

Pollard cleared her throat.

"I see you've met," she said, her barracuda smile appearing to signify she was making a joke. "Welcome to my special task force."

Rashford looked around the room.

"You two are it," said Pollard. "We only have limited resources, you know."

"What are we actually tasked with, Ma'am?" said Morgan.

The Chief Superintendent picked up a black marker and turned to the board. In the centre, in large capital letters, she wrote: SIMON WOLFE. She turned back to face them.

"It's easy," she said. "Find him. Arrest him."

Rashford and Morgan looked at each other.

"I've had enough," said Pollard. "This has been going on far too long. I want him in custody, or I want a good reason why not. I'm giving you two weeks and then we'll reassess."

"Two weeks?" said Rashford, his voice rising. "Ma'am."

"Well, two more weeks, really. You've already had over two years."

"Ouch," said Morgan, earning a glare from the Chief Superintendent, who then proceeded to give them each a marker.

"Let's start with what we know. Facts on this side," she said, drawing a vertical line and indicating the left of the board. "Suppositions on this side. Get to it."

Rashford wrote on the board first.

"He was born in 1987, in Antigonish, Nova Scotia. His mother was a young girl from Grand Étang in Cape Breton, Sylvie Cheverie. He was taken away from her at birth, by the nuns. Later, she took her own life."

"He grew up in care," said Morgan, "and ended up at the Gordon Indian Residential School, where he stayed until it closed in 1996. Then he was in different foster homes but kept getting kicked out because he was always causing trouble. He hung out in north-central Regina for a while, just a typical street punk. Then something happened and he joined the Army in 2004."

"I think I know what happened," said Rashford. "But this goes on the supposition side of the board. I think he upset the Indian Posse somehow. Maybe he skimmed something from them, money or drugs, whatever. But they were after him and he had to get out."

"What makes you think that?" said Morgan.

"A thing I read at the museum in Fort Qu'Appelle last week. There was a shooting there in 2007, a rival gang thing. Now that was after he joined up, of course, but apparently in the early two thousand's there were feuds between Indian Posse, Native Syndicate, and a couple of other gangs. People got hunted down and beaten badly for the slightest indiscretion, sometimes killed. If he was running wild in Regina at the time, he must have been connected with one of the gangs, even just peripherally."

"That's all very interesting," said Pollard. "And it tells us where he was. It doesn't tell us where he is."

"Well, it is relevant," said Morgan. "If we fast-forward to a couple of years ago, Lance Corporal Simon Wolfe leaves the army. He had served with an armoured regiment, tanks and stuff. He was married and had two kids. Things were fine for the first year and then he lost it. According to his ex-wife, he got depressed, angry, moody, violent. He lost his sense of humour, had anger-management issues. He lost his job and started drinking. He started to scare her, so she told him to leave. He ended up on the street."

"Where?" said Rashford.

"Calgary."

"So," said Rashford, "we have an Afghanistan veteran, on the streets in Calgary, probably with undiagnosed PTSD. Somehow, he starts to recover, gets friendly with the professor's wife, gets medications, all is going well. And then the Americans stage their intervention, and everything goes sideways. And he reinvents himself as Claude Dallas."

"The hero outlaw," said Pollard, nodding.

"You catch him and have him in custody," said Morgan, "but he sucker-punches you and escapes. Then what?"

"Again, supposition," said Rashford. "I think he goes back to Nova Scotia, trying to find his birth mother. Someone broke into the house where the young women stayed when the nuns looked after them, before they had their babies. I think he found his file, then went to Cheticamp. But his mother was long gone, she had committed suicide after he was born. He went back to the house of the nuns, broke in again, who knows why, and this time saw that another boy had been born at almost the same time. Perhaps he saw the name, Xavier, it's not that common, and made a connection to the guy he'd met on the streets in Calgary. He went back there, and stayed for a year, hanging out and learning all about the real Xavier. Then, when he froze to death, he thought it would be fun to assume his identity."

Pollard shook her head.

"That's all a bit nebulous, Sergeant."

"Perhaps. But bear with me. He assumes the name Xavier Ballantyne and knows the real Xavier is dead, so he contacts Sandra. He makes her believe that he is her son. More importantly, he now has a mother."

"And a sister," said Morgan, nodding.

"And a sister. And he knows she is in Calgary. So, he goes back to find her."

"How he is paying for all these cross-continent jaunts, may I ask?" said Pollard.

Rashford shook his head.

"I'm not sure," he said. "Perhaps he hitch-hiked or took the bus."

"Or perhaps he had a job," said Morgan, slowly. "One that paid well."

Rashford nodded, comprehension dawning on his face.

"A job managing the sex place at Waterton," he said, excitedly. "Yes, that makes sense."

He strode to the board and wrote the key names on the board.

"And then he paid the bikers to abduct Roxanne!" he said.

"Just a minute," said Pollard. "You're mixing things up. Was the abduction of Roxanne because he was looking for new blood for the brothel, or was it because he had tracked down the woman who he was pretending to be his sister? I'm confused."

"You and me both," said Morgan, scratching her head. "Let's forget all the abduction stuff for a minute. What's the common feature in these stories?"

They all looked at the board.

"Calgary," she said. "I think we should look for him there."

Pollard and Rashford turned to look at her.

"According to the report I got from Veteran's Affairs, that's where his pension goes as well. It's a direct deposit to a bank, so he doesn't have to be there to access the money, but it's another link. And maybe the bank will have a contact address."

Pollard nodded, slowly.

"Yes, we can liaise with ..."

"With respect, Ma'am," said Rashford, interrupting her. "Can we do this without any local liaison?"

"Why?"

"Well, it's just this thought I've had. Not a thought, really, more of a niggle."

"A niggle? About what?"

"It might not be anything, Ma'am. But when we tracked him to Waterton, it seemed like he knew we were coming. The false IED on the gate, the pre-planned escape route. And then the bikers who found the truck, how on earth did they know to cruise through Maple Creek? They must have had some information. Even going back to the abduction of Roxanne from the bar, how did he know she would be there? I think there's an Alberta connection."

Pollard was incredulous.

"To the Force? Don't be ridiculous."

"Remember he's weird, Ma'am," said Morgan. "Sergeant Rashford, I mean. He's always making these connections that don't make sense, and then they do. Perhaps we should listen to him."

Rashford nodded, gratefully.

"All I'm asking is that we go on our own. No liaison. I realize you'll have to tell someone, but can that be kept at a high level? At your level?"

Pollard thought for a moment.

"I could mention this to Superintendent Toews, he and I go way back. Someone over there has to know that you're in Alberta, and working in the province, even if you are undercover."

"Thank you, Ma'am," said Rashford.

Chapter 22

They drove over to Calgary on Thursday and stayed at the Comfort Inn by the University because it had good parking and had easy access to the commuter train system that ran across the city. It was also close to the Shaganappi Mall, which was where they went first.

Annie Smith, the young woman who managed the ArtsChic Boutique, was pleased to answer their questions. She had heard what had happened to Roxanne at the Barrel Races club and was appalled that there was a connection to her store. Neither she nor her staff remembered who had actually bought the scarf, but they confirmed that Roxanne had often taken her lunch, alone, at the Food Court.

"She was hit on a couple of times," said another of the shop attendants. "Some older guy was leching her."

"Can you remember what she said about that?" said Morgan.

"Not really. Just that he was old, a bit fat, limped. Just icky, you know. Thought a lot of himself. Tried to pretend he was a cowboy. 'Saddle up with me and we can have some fun,' that kind of thing."

"Thank you," said Rashford.

They left the mall and drove down Crowchild Trail, crossing the river and then turning off into the Military Museums complex. After showing their identification at the main door, they were led across the wide atrium. The stopped in front of the Mural of Honour, a huge collage of two hundred and forty individual panels that collectively made up a mosaic that commemorated Canadian service personnel from each of the three branches of the Armed Forces.

"That's amazing," said Morgan.

"Yes, isn't it?" said their guide, himself an older veteran. "People come from all over just to see that. And the other exhibits, of course."

"Of course," said Morgan.

After a few moments of reflective silence, they continued through a door marked 'Private' and found themselves in a small windowless office. Some regimental banners hung on the wall, together with a selection of old recruitment posters. A middle-aged man in civilian clothes sat at the desk. He stood when they entered and came around to shake hands, then ushered them into the two chairs placed for visitors.

"My name is Friesen," he said, returning to his side of the desk. "Lieutenant Colonel, retired. How might I help you?"

They had previously agreed that Morgan would take the lead and she did so now, explaining what she knew about Simon Wolfe and asking if the Lieutenant Colonel could help fill in the blanks. He listened patiently until she had finished, then sat back in his chair. He folded his hands behind his head and looked up at the ceiling.

"You will understand that I cannot make any official comment," he said. "I am simply not authorized to do so."

"We understand," said Morgan.

"However, I can give you some background, unofficially. If you take the information outside this room then I will deny that I ever said it. I will also deny that you were ever here, and our CCTV cameras will uphold that denial. Are we clear?"

"Yes, sir," said Morgan.

Friesen rocked himself forward and brought his hands down. He looked at Rashford and raised an eyebrow.

"Yes, sir, understood," said Rashford.

Friesen nodded.

"Lance Corporal Wolfe," he said, pensively. "A somewhat troubled young man. What do you need to know about him?"

"Anything you believe might be relevant to our case, sir."

"And what is the case, exactly, young lady?"

"The case," said Rashford, interrupting, "is that we have a suspect whom we believe to be Wolfe who has been involved in numerous illegal activities. Robbery, abduction, assault, living off the avails of prostitution, impersonation, possibly drug offences and even murder. We are trying to find him."

Friesen just looked at him.

"And," said Morgan, gently, "we would like to know about his mental state. We worry that he might be suffering from PTSD. We would really appreciate your advice."

Friesen nodded.

"Very well," he said, ignoring Rashford and focusing all his attention on Gayle Morgan. "As I said, a somewhat troubled young man."

He consulted some papers on the desk before him.

"He enlisted in 2004, and completed basic training, then was posted to a tank regiment, the Lord Strathcona's Horse, also known as the Royal Canadians. He did three tours in Afghanistan."

"We understand that he might have served in other theatres as well, sir."

"That would be classified, I'm afraid. All I can tell you is what is in the official record."

"Right."

"He left the CAF with an honourable discharge and then, I'm afraid, things rather went sideways. He did not handle the transition to civilian life well. Many veterans don't, you know. They miss the camaraderie of their unit, the routines of army life. It's a systemic problem, I believe."

"Did he keep in touch with anyone? From his army days?"

"A few people. He was here a couple of times. The Strats are headquartered in Edmonton, of course, but there is a bit of a memorial to them here at the Museums. Once they had a sort of reunion event and I think he came for that, met up with some of his pals."

"When was that, sir?" said Rashford.

"Oh, eighteen months or so ago. Maybe two years. Ask at the desk on your way out, they can tell you exactly. I just remember that he got in a bit of a ruckus and one of his officers had to sort it out, quieten him down."

"An officer, sir?" said Morgan. "Do you recall who that might have been?"

"No, just some retired Captain, he must have been his tank commander or something. It was just the drink, nothing really to note."

"Except that you did note it, sir," said Rashford.

"Yes, well. Most chaps can control themselves in public, you know. He looked a little worse for wear, I think he'd had a few before he got here."

"What was the ruckus about, do you recall?"

"Money, I believe. It usually is. That or a woman. Pardon me miss."

Friesen nodded his head towards Morgan, who inclined hers in return.

"I think he felt he was owed money for some work he'd done, but I really didn't hear the details. And as I said, his Captain sorted it out pretty quickly and got them both to stand down."

Friesen spoke for a few more minutes, giving them some general information about the role of the Military Families Resource Centres but observing that Wolfe had never registered with the one in Calgary. He also spoke about the mental health problems experienced by many veterans.

"Every battalion that served has lost six or seven people to suicide," he said. "We give people years of training, place them in the pressure cooker of combat for months on end, and when they return after their tour, they get two weeks at somewhere like Wainwright or Gagetown before being redeployed, and it starts all over. There's just no time to decompress. We've had more people come back from Afghanistan and take their own lives than were killed over there."

He looked ready to speak about this issue at some length and so, eventually, Morgan glanced at Rashford. He nodded and rose to his feet.

"Thank you, sir, you've been very helpful," he said, extending his arm. Friesen stopped talking and shook his hand.

"Sorry. Old soap box of mine. And don't even let me get started on the delays in paying pensions or transitioning people to provincial health care. It's absolutely shocking."

"Yes, sir," said Morgan, also standing and shaking his hand. "Thank you for your time."

"You're quite welcome," said Friesen. "Good luck with your case. Do you know the way out?"

"Yes, sir, thank you," said Rashford. "We might have a quick look at some of the displays as we go."

"So you should, so you should," said the Lieutenant Colonel, sitting back down at his desk. "So you should, indeed."

They left the office, Morgan closing the door softly behind her. Rashford led them back across the atrium and into the display areas, first to the Memorial Hall of Honour for the Princess Patricia's Canadian Light Infantry.

"My uncle served with the Princess Pat's," he said, as they walked around the display, marvelling at the large room with the names of the fallen etched into the granite panels. "Luckily he came back, so his name's not here."

"Were you ever tempted to join up?" said Morgan.

"Nope. I always wanted to be a police officer," said Rashford. "I wanted to try to make justice, not fight for peace."

They walked back past the scale dioramas depicting scenes from various wars, illustrating everything from the PPCLI being Canada's first regiment to deploy overseas, during the First World War, to their achievements in Afghanistan.

Across the hall they entered the Regimental Museum and Archives of the Lord Strathcona's Horse and were greeted by a serving officer in uniform.

"Good afternoon, sir, Ma'am," he said, "welcome to the home of the Strats. Is there anything particular you are looking for?"

Rashford looked around.

"Do you work here?" he said.

Yes, sir. Captain Johnson. Sergeant Peters over there and I are serving as staff here at the moment. We try and help people with requests."

"What sort of requests?"

"Oh, you know. Identifying old photographs, finding lost service records, that sort of thing."

Morgan looked interested.

"If we gave you a name of someone who served, could you find their photograph?"

"It depends. When and where did they serve? If we have something, we can probably find it on the data base."

She smiled at him.

"Lance Corporal Simon Wolfe, Afghanistan," she said.

"Sergeant?"

Rashford turned around, but then realized that the captain was speaking to his sergeant. Peters clicked on the keyboard, manipulated the mouse, and then pressed a button. There was a whirr and Peters reached behind his chair, then pulled a sheet of paper from a printer.

"Here you go," he said, passing over the photograph. Morgan studied it, with Rashford looking over her shoulder.

"Is that him?" she said, quietly.

"Hell, yes," said Rashford. He turned to the captain.

"Were you here for the reunion?" he said.

The captain shook his head.

"No. We started our rotation a month ago, so we were still in the field and missed that one."

"I heard that this fellow got into a bit of an argument, at the reunion," said Rashford.

The captain shrugged.

"Happens all the time," he said. "People have a few bevvies and then remember something that someone said twenty years ago, it all spills out. Can't do much about it. Just have to try and calm things down, really."

Rashford nodded.

"Thanks for your time," he said. "And thank you for your service."

They left the office and walked back through the atrium, pausing again to look in awe at the mosaic mural.

"It's quite something, isn't it?" said Morgan.

Rashford agreed, then led them both outside and back to the car. He unlocked the door and they got inside, but he didn't turn on the ignition. The shadow from the CF-5 fighter jet mounted on a pedestal fell across the lawn in front of them.

"Today's Thursday, right?"

"All day," said Morgan, agreeably. "Why?"

"I've just had an idea," said Rashford. "I'll tell you about it over a beer. Let's head back to the hotel."

The next morning, they were back at the Shaganappi Mall at eleven o'clock. The operators at the food court were just opening up, and Rashford found one who was willing to let him stand at the back of the booth.

"Just stay out of the way, mind," she said.

"You won't know I'm here," said Rashford.

He and Gayle Morgan had a quick stroll around the mall, noting the exits, and then returned to the food court. At eleven thirty he stepped into the shadows behind the large menu board. From his vantage point he could see the whole of the food court but, he hoped, nobody would see him. Morgan sat in the centre of the tables scattered around the eating area, nursing a cup of coffee. They had set up a closed circuit on their radios.

"Remember, if he comes up to you, just chat him up and let him buy you lunch. Nothing else!"

"I'm not very good at being picked up by strange men," said Morgan. "You should have brought Sarah."

"Meow."

"I'm not being catty. Have you seen her desk? It's famous!"

"I think that's a bit mean. There are only four notches on the rail."

"Ha! So, you did look! What you don't know is, that's her second desk. The rail on the first one fell apart."

"Meow, meow."

Morgan just laughed.

"Calm down," said Rashford. "Everyone will think you're one of the crazy people, talking to yourself, and nobody will approach you."

"Suits me," said Morgan, but she stopped talking.

Rashford stood behind the menu board, watching intently. The food court started to fill up as families and couples took a break from their shopping, and shop workers took a break from their work. Every time a single male entered the seating area, his senses tingled, but most of them went and joined someone already sitting at another table.

At ten past twelve, Rashford was starting to think he had made mistake. Then he saw a familiar figure enter from the main corridor, pausing to scan the seating area.

"Stand by, eyes on target" he said, and watched Morgan as she scratched her eyebrow, the agreed sign that she had heard him. He looked back and for a panicked moment could not see the man, then located him making his way between the tables, sometimes catching an outstretched leg with his walking cane. He found his way to Morgan's table, where he stopped. She looked up at him.

"Is anyone going to be sitting here?" he said, his voice sounding electronically altered as it came across the speaker in Rashford's ear.

Morgan just looked at the man, her face an obvious inquiry.

"It's just, I don't like to faff about when I'm carrying a tray, you see. So, if I could sit here, then I can go and get some lunch and just come straight back. I don't have to try and find an empty table and risk dropping everything!"

Morgan nodded.

"I've only got a half hour break," she said. "But you can sit here if you like."

"Thank you. Are you eating?"

"No, just coffee."

"Not hungry?"

"Well, a bit, but it's a new job and I haven't been paid yet."

"Well, perhaps I can get you a sandwich or something? As a thank you."

"Really? Are you sure?"

"Positive."

The man was oozing charm in a way that made Rashford realize how he had fooled everyone for so long.

Morgan said that she would have a chicken wrap and salad, and then stood up.

"Why don't you sit down, I can get the food," she said. "I promise I won't run away with your money."

He laughed.

"I'm sure you wouldn't but no, I need to make sure that I get the right things. Just wait here."

He made his way over to the side of the food court opposite and bought two chicken wraps, with salad on the side, plus two bottles of water. He managed the tray with ease as he returned to the table. Rashford listened and watched as Morgan chatted with him.

"How did you hurt your leg?" she said, between bites of her sandwich.

"Oh, it was a long time ago. An old war wound, you might say. I come in every Friday to get it checked and receive an injection, for the pain."

"Can't you just take tablets, at home?"

"The doctor says not. But anyway, it's OK. This gets me out of the house. I lost my wife a few years ago and live on my own now, so it's good to talk to other human beings once a week."

They chatted for another fifteen minutes, while Morgan ate her food, and then said she had to go.

"Thank you for lunch," she said. "It was a pleasure to meet you."

"And you, young lady. If you're here on another Friday, perhaps I shall see you again?"

"Perhaps. Shall I clear the tray?"

"No, it's alright. My driver will be here in a few minutes, to pick me up. He will clear it, thank you. I hope you will excuse me not getting up."

He extended his hand and Morgan shook it, then walked away. As Rashford watched, the man swivelled in his chair, then nodded at someone across the food court. A younger man moved away from the wall on which he had been leaning, then melted into the crowd in the hallway, walking some fifteen yards behind Morgan.

"Gayle," said Rashford, whispering urgently. "You've got company. It's Wolfe. He's following you. Lose him, for god's sake."

"Copy that," said Morgan. "You keep on our man."

Thirty minutes later, Morgan drove their car around to the Shaganappi Drive exit of the mall and pulled up in front of the door. Rashford ran out and slid into the passenger seat, pointing towards one of the exits from the car park.

"Black Nissan Qashqai," he said, "just leaving over there."

"Eyes on," said Morgan, accelerating away then having to brake for a woman with a stroller, who simply walked out in front of their car. The woman glared at them.

"It's called a road for a reason," said Morgan, under her breath. "Stupid pillock."

Rashford decided not to ask what a pillock was.

Morgan must have read his mind.

"Baby goldfish," she said.

"Oh," said Rashford, wondering again what language she spoke at home.

"Was everything okay in there?" he said.

"Yeah. I went into the ladies' room and then phoned Annie Smith, at the boutique. She said she would play along so I went there and pretended I was just back from my shift. She threw a fit and fired me, shouting that I was a slack piece of humanity and would have to buck up if I wanted to hold a job. I stomped out and saw our friend looking in the window, he'd obviously heard all of it. He turned the other way and didn't follow me, I'm sure."

"No, he came back and met our friend in the food court, then they left and went to their car. I followed them. I'm not sure what his role is. Sometimes he acts like a personal assistant but at other times he walks like a bodyguard."

"There they are," said Morgan. "Shall I call in the plates?"

"Yes, let's see who we're dealing with."

Morgan used the police radio and asked for a check on a set of Alberta number plates.

"They're personalized," she said. "India Whisky twenty two."

"India Whisky two two," confirmed the officer at the detachment. There were a few minutes of silence, then a burst of static.

"Late model Nissan Qashqai," said the officer on the radio, "registered owner is ..."

"Ian Whitehead," said Rashford.

"Umm, yes," said the officer. "That's correct. Excuse me, but it says here that he is also a police officer."

"Yes, I know," said Rashford. "Thank you for confirming this information. Out."

Morgan clicked off the radio. She looked briefly across at Rashford.

"Do you want to tell me what's going on?"

Rashford shook his head.

"I'm not sure myself, not exactly. I have a hunch but no proof yet. What I do know is that the man we know as Simon Wolfe, also known as Xavier Ballantyne, Claude Dallas, and many other aliases, a wanted fugitive, is the general henchman and driver for Inspector Ian Whitehead of the North-West Mounted Police, Pincher Creek detachment."

"Oh," said Morgan. "Just another day in the life, then."

Rashford laughed.

"Yup. Well, let's follow them and see what happens next. How are we for gas?"

"We're good. They're up there, about ten cars ahead. Luckily, we're not in a cruiser. There are lots of Jeeps in Alberta, we won't stand out."

"Not in town. It might be more difficult later on, when traffic thins."

They followed the Nissan down Crowchild Trail, once again passing the Military Museums with the iconic fighter jet still reaching for the sky, then crossed the southern suburban wasteland of the city and merged onto the McLeod Trail. As Rashford had predicted, the traffic was lighter as they headed south, and Morgan dropped back, keeping a steady distance so as to maintain visual contact.

The landscape opened up, with fewer housing developments and wider tracts of rolling ranch land dotted with groves of trees. An hour later, they had just passed the small town of Nanton when the Qashqai indicated right and turned off the highway, heading west. Rashford looked at his map.

"They're heading across to the twenty-two, I bet. Then straight down to Pincher Creek."

"Shall I keep following them? There's nobody else turning."

"Well, let's turn off and follow for a while, maybe ten minutes. If they keep going straight, we'll figure out what to do."

"Okay, you're in charge of this task force."

Morgan indicated and moved into the right-hand lane, preparing to exit on to the smaller two-lane paved road.

"No, stay in this lane, same speed," said Rashford, suddenly, surprising Morgan with the vehemence of his tone. "Don't turn off."

She switched off the indicator and kept driving. Rashford turned in his seat and leaned over into the back of the Jeep, scrabbling his hand on the floor.

"Coming down the ramp," he said.

Morgan glanced over and saw a Nissan Qashqai driving down the ramp back onto the highway. It was still high and to her right. She kept to a steady speed and the Nissan merged in three cars behind.

"Do you think he sussed us?"

"Maybe," said Rashford. "But more likely it's just force of habit, to see if anyone followed them up the ramp and off again."

"He's following us now," Morgan said, laughing.

"That's okay. We're just tourists going down to Fort Macleod. Just hold your speed. Tell me if they start to overtake. They know me. I'll look in the back seat again, hide my face."

"Yeah, well he knows me as well. What do I do?"

"Here," said Rashford, handing her a baseball cap. "Put this on. That'll hide your hair at least."

They continued for another forty-five minutes, both cars maintaining their position, until they were approaching Fort Macleod. As they crossed the bridge over the Old Man River, Rashford pointed down to the right.

"Look, a rest stop area. Let's pull in there, see what they do."

Morgan indicated and took the narrow exit road that led into the parking lot. There were numerous bays dotted around, interspersed with clumps of brush willow and the occasional poplar tree.

"Go the back, as though we're looking for a private area," said Rashford.

"Copy that."

Morgan drove through the parking lot, which was empty on this Friday afternoon in late November. The incessant southern Alberta wind ruffled the leaves on the willows and blew the fallen poplar leaves across the tarmac. She checked her rear-view mirror.

"Shit. They've turned off as well."

"Interesting," said Rashford. "Okay, pull up over there. Then prepare your weapon but keep it out of sight. Let them make the play."

Morgan parked. Rashford opened the windows of the Jeep slightly and lit two cigarettes. He gave one to Morgan, then put his arm around her shoulders.

"Just another sex-mad couple," he said, looking behind through the rear-view mirror.

"Yup," said Morgan, blowing out smoke and watching though the side mirror.

The Nissan parked about fifty metres away, behind them and to their left, next to a large entanglement of scrub willow. The doors opened and the two men got out. They looked at the Jeep, then the older man nodded towards the willow bushes. They split up and both stepped out of sight, one to each side of the shrubs. Morgan stiffened, and brought her handgun into sight, resting it on her lap.

"They're going to come at us from both sides," she said. "Classic ambush."

Rashford removed his arm from her shoulders, then stubbed the cigarette on the floor in front of his seat. He took Morgan's from her hand and did the same, then picked up the two stubs.

"Nah," he said. "They're just having a pee."

Rashford and Morgan watched as the two men returned to their car and drove back onto the highway. Morgan started their vehicle.

"Not too close," said Rashford. "They'll remember the Jeep for sure now."

"It's not my first rodeo," said Morgan, easing out into the traffic a dozen car lengths behind the Nissan.

"Sorry," said Rashford, settling back into his seat.

A few minutes later a large green highway sign indicated that the road was about to divide into three routes.

"They're going right," said Rashford, "the road to Pincher Creek and Crowsnest Pass."

"Copy that," said Morgan, indicating and merging smoothly into the correct lane. The majority of the traffic had taken the central lane, towards Lethbridge, and as they merged onto the highway, they were only four cars behind their quarry. The road straightened out, a long line of power generating windmills stretching to their left.

They drove for another twenty minutes, through the small town of Brocket. The snow-capped Rockies loomed on the horizon in front of them, the windmills now replaced by a line of utility pylons that ran parallel to the highway but on their right.

"He's turning," said Morgan. "What shall I do?"

"Keep on the highway until we're out of sight, then pull over," said Rashford.

The Nissan indicated and turned off to the right. As the Jeep passed the intersection, Rashford saw that it was a gravelled road leading towards a campground. Morgan drove a few hundred metres and then pulled onto the verge of the highway.

"We'll give it a couple of minutes," said Rashford. They got out of the Jeep and leaned against the side of the vehicle. Rashford lit them both cigarettes.

There was not much traffic, mainly trucks hauling produce to or from British Columbia. A trick of the light made the mountains appear very close, the snowy peaks glistening under a grey sky. In front of them, under the pylons, three strands of barbed wire were stretched taut between fence posts. A cluster of white towers in the middle distance indicated another windfarm, and a low line of bare brown hills marked the horizon.

"How are we going to play this?" said Morgan.

"I think we're getting close to the end," said Rashford, meditatively. "We'll follow them to their destination, and then call it in. I think we will need back up for this one."

"Really? Maverick Rashford is playing by the rules and not going rogue? I'm impressed!"

Morgan laughed, then stubbed out her cigarette.

"Come on then, time to rock and roll."

She walked back to the driver's side of the vehicle, waited until a large semi-trailer went past, then opened the door and got into her seat. Rashford climbed in next to her. She started the Jeep and pulled across the highway, executing a U-turn and driving back to the intersection. There was no traffic approaching so she indicated as she crossed the highway and they bumped onto the firmly compressed gravel road.

Chapter 23

The gravel road went straight for about five kilometres. Ahead of them, the low hills came closer. They passed a collection of trailers and farm vehicles collected around a derelict building, the roof caved in and the exposed beams charred by fire.

"Someone's dream of a country life isn't working out too well," said Morgan, under her breath.

Two kilometres further on, Rashford told her to slow down.

"Look," he said, pointing up to the left. A driveway curved up the side of a small hillock, leading up to a large house situated just beneath the crest. The Nissan was visible, parked on the forecourt in front of the building.

As they approached the driveway, Rashford saw a sign with a name and civic number. He jotted them down in his notebook as they passed.

"'Perseverance'," said Morgan. "That's a strange name for a house.

"It's the regimental motto for the Strathcona's," said Rashford, nodding to himself. "I saw that at the museum. I think we've got them."

They continued along the road and crested another small rise, pulling over to the side of the road once they were over the hill. A wide valley extended across their field of view, with the Old Man River snaking its way along the bottom, bunches of cottonwood trees marking its path.

"Wow," said Morgan. "Some view."

Rashford looked back over his shoulder.

"I bet the house sees this from the side," he said. "And then the Rockies from the front. How the hell does a police inspector afford a house like that?"

He pulled out his phone and called the Chief Superintendent. Sarah answered.

"Hello Sergeant. The Chief is here. She was hoping to hear from you. I'll put you through now."

"Can you hear the sound of wood being carved?" said Morgan, grinning. He elbowed her in the ribs.

"Thank you," he said to Sarah while glaring at Morgan, who just laughed.

Chief Superintendent Pollard came on the phone and Rashford reported what had happened, and where they were presently located.

"It's a bit late right now," said Pollard. "This is going to take some time to get organized. Why don't you two find a place to stay in Pincher Creek overnight. I'll call you later this evening, once I've had a chance to talk to Mike Toews."

"Copy that, Ma'am," said Rashford.

Morgan turned the Jeep around and drove back past the house on the hill, the Nissan still parked outside. They got to the highway and turned right, then drove into Pincher Creek.

"This will do," said Rashford, as they turned into the Stardust Motel. "It's got a restaurant and a bar, what more do we need?"

The rooms in the chalet-style buildings were clean and comfortable, and they settled in quickly. They had just finished dinner when Rashford heard his phone buzz. He excused himself from the table and went outside onto the terrace to take the call. A few minutes later, Morgan joined him. She leaned on a nearby balustrade.

"Thank you. Ma'am," said Rashford. "We'll be there. Good night."

He closed his phone and turned to Morgan.

"We're on for the morning," he said. "Dawn raid. Rendezvous is 0630 at the intersection with the highway."

"We should leave here at six, then," said Morgan. "That'll work. Get an early night and a good sleep."

"First, a beer and a game of darts," said Rashford. "I saw a couple of boards in the pub."

"Darts?" said Morgan. "You play darts?"

"Yes, of course," said Rashford. "I used to be pretty good, back at the Depot during training. Why, don't you?"

Morgan looked at him steadily.

"I've chucked a few arrers in me time," she said, her Mancunian accent suddenly stronger. "Tha' gets the beer in and I'll book a board. Five oh one at a buck a game, open start and double finish."

Rashford looked at her.

"I don't think I understood any of that," he said.

"Don't thee mind, luv," she said. "I'll show yer."

The next morning, his wallet twenty dollars lighter, Rashford was still moaning about her cheating.

"You can't cheat at darts, Gavin," she said, patiently. "You're either in between the lines or you're not. The numbers go down depending on how many points you score, and the first one to get from five hundred and one to zero, ending on a double score, wins. I told you all this last night."

"It was embarrassing," he said. "All those other people taking side bets on whether I'd actually get what I was aiming at."

Morgan just laughed and shook her head.

"Here we are," she said, pulling the Jeep up behind four police cruisers that were parked on the side of the highway.

They joined the group gathered around the lead car. A tall, broad-shouldered man stepped towards them.

"You must be Rashford and Morgan," he said, shaking hands. "I'm Mike Toews. Come and meet the lads."

Introductions were made all round and then Chief Superintendent Toews took over the briefing.

"We're not going to be doing anything clever this morning," he said. "I had a drone do a fly-by yesterday evening and there is no way we can sneak up on them. It's a house on a hill, clear approaches all around."

"That means a clear line of fire as well," said Rashford.

"Yes, Sergeant, and we'll be ready for that. But hopefully we can just go in and hammer on the door. Lights and sirens when we get to the bottom of the drive and go up as fast as you can. Everyone clear?"

There was a chorus of "yes, sir" in response.

"Follow me then," he said. "And look after each other."

He got into his cruiser and pulled away down the gravel road, the other cars in convoy behind him. They drove at a steady sixty kilometers an hour and were soon at the driveway. As he passed the 'Perseverance' sign, Toews activated his lights and siren, and accelerated up the hill, some crows and a pair of magpies scattering from the sudden intrusion. The other vehicles followed, and everyone skidded to halt on the gravelled forecourt, hemming in the Nissan.

Police officers spilled out of the cars and rushed at the house with guns drawn. Toews hammered on the front door.

"Armed police," he shouted. "Open up."

There was no response, so he nodded at a constable who was holding a portable battering ram. The man ran forward and powered the ram at the door, which fell back open.

"Armed police," shouted Toews a second time, and then moved inside, Rashford at his shoulder. They found themselves in a large open hallway, with paintings lining the walls. Doors were spaced every few metres and officers ran into each room on the ground floor, covering their colleagues. One by one they shouted 'clear' and then stood waiting for instructions.

"You two stay here," said Toews, pointing. "The rest, upstairs."

Rashford ran up first, stopping on a small landing. Two corridors led away, similar to those in an upmarket hotel, one to each wing of the house. Toews paused next to him.

"Left or right?"

Rashford shrugged.

"I'll go right," said Toews, heading off down the corridor.

Rashford went left, slamming open the first door and finding an empty bedroom.

"Clear!" he said and moved to the next door. That was clear as well. He reached the end of the corridor and opened the third and final door.

He burst inside and then stopped, waving his hand to the constable behind him. All was quiet.

The room he had entered was a good-sized square and decorated as a living room. There were a pair of two-seat couches along the walls, and a round wooden table set for breakfast. There were three large windows. The one to the right looked down and across the Old Man River valley. The one to the left looked down across rolling hills towards the south and American border. The central window framed a perfect view of the Rockies.

In front of the window, sitting in a large, upholstered armchair, was Inspector Ian Whiteside. He was holding a shotgun, the barrel aimed directly at Rashford. Next to him, his hand hanging down by his side holding a large handgun, stood the man Rashford had last faced on the Alsama border a few years earlier.

"You're a hard man to find, Mr. Dallas," said Rashford. "Or should I say Johnson? Or Smythe? Or Bourque? Or any of the others? Or Wolfe?"

The man sneered.

"Not Smythe," he said. "He was a useless bag of shit."

"Wolfe, then. Let's use that, shall we."

The man shrugged.

"If we've finished introducing ourselves, Sergeant, perhaps we can get on with things?" said Whitehead. "You will escort us to your car, if you please, and then I won't shoot you."

"You know that's not going to happen," said Rashford. "It's over, Inspector."

"Captain, please. And this is Lance Corporal Wolfe. I think we'd prefer those titles."

Rashford nodded. He sensed the Chief Superintendent come up to his shoulder.

"Mister Toews, what a delight to see you," said Whitehead, moving the shotgun slightly. "Please step back, if you don't mind."

Rashford took a step forward.

"Not you, you stay there."

Rashford stopped.

"So, I think I have this right," he said. "Wolfe was part of your crew, in Afghanistan?"

"Indeed. He saved my life. That traffic stop I told you about, the only thing I didn't mention was that it was in Kandahar, just outside the city. The bastard pulled a gun and shot me in the knee, Wolfe here took him out immediately. And his three friends. I couldn't repay that, so I told him that once we got out, he could come for me for help anytime, if he needed it."

"And so you met again, on civvy street?"

"We did indeed. Providence shined on me. I was at the mall for an appointment, and we bumped into each other. Yes, Sergeant, I know that's where you found me as well. You and that stupid policewoman, who tried to pretend she was just a normal working girl. Ha! She stank of being in the job, you know. She'll never make an undercover officer. We both saw her. And you, hiding in the shadows."

"This appointment. It seems odd to me, that you need such regular check-ups for a sore knee."

"Bravo, Sergeant. Bravo! It's not for my knee. I have cancer, it's all through my bones. Terminal, I'm afraid."

"I'm sorry to hear that," said Rashford. "So, what happened when you met? Old buddies again after all those years? Went for coffee, did you? Share war stories?"

"Don't be facetious, Sergeant. Wolfe here was a bit down on his luck. He was trying to find his sister, who by a stroke of fortune was a friend of mine. In fact, he and I reunited when he approached the table where I was having lunch with her. Pretty little thing, she is."

"She's not your friend," said Rashford, his teeth tight.

"But that's where you're wrong, my friend. I know you took advantage of her naiveté but before that she was all over me. Always wearing her tight little sweaters, thrusting those big breasts in my face. And all that cost me was a lunch. Just think what I would have got for a dinner. Oh, that's right. You know, don't you."

"Gavin, stop," said Morgan, who had approached without his knowledge. She placed her hand on his arm and held him back.

"And here's his little sidekick," said Whitehead, indicating with the shotgun that she should step forward. She did, then stopped.

"You probably guessed what a slut she was, didn't you," said Whitehead. "Women know these things."

"What I don't understand is why you had your assistant here kidnap her from the club," said Morgan, ignoring the comment. "If she liked you so much, that is."

"That was business, not pleasure. I needed a new girl for a, for a, aah, for an enterprise I run down near Waterton Park. The Sergeant has been there, haven't you?"

"Which Wolfe managed for you," said Rashford, suddenly realizing the connection.

"Indeed. And it was going well, until you showed up. Very well, in fact."

"The Rolls!"

Rashford snapped his fingers.

"Of course, that's why we never heard anything else about you tracking down the owner of the Phantom 3, the one Carolyn Toews told us about."

He paused, then turned to the Chief Superintendent.

"Toews? Any relation?"

"Henry is my cousin," he said, then spoke to Whitehead. "So, if I understand correctly, you were going to use this lady as a whore?"

"More of a special treat for gentleman with special tastes," said Whitehead. "Gentlemen who are willing to pay good money to have those tastes satiated. She would have oiled up nicely and just glistened, hanging from the chandelier."

"You're disgusting," said Morgan.

It was Rashford's turn to pull her back, and step forward himself.

"What happened to the other girl?" he said.

"What other girl?" said Whitehead, puzzled.

"The one who Roxanne was going to replace. Did you kill her?"

He directed the last question to Wolfe, who just shook his head.

"I've not killed anyone," he said.

Whitehead spoke up.

"I took her for a drive in the Rolls," he said. "She'd gotten silly, developed too much of a liking for the white powder one of the clients was giving her. At first it just helped loosen her inhibitions, if you get my meaning, but then it got so she needed a shot before she would do anything. So we had to lose her."

"Lose her? What do you mean?"

"I took her to Blairmore, just past the Frank slide. Some people I do business with came over from Hope and picked her up. Their clients are not as fastidious as mine."

"So, you just sold her on, like a piece of meat?"

"More like a worn-out piece of furniture. What did you want me to do, Sergeant? Kill her? That wouldn't have been very nice now, would it? Anyway, this way I got at least a bit of my investment back as well."

"What did you do with the car?"

"The Rolls? Oh, it's in one of the garages here, I think. Is that correct, Lance Corporal?"

"Yes, sir. Garage three, sir."

It was the first time that Rashford had clearly heard Wolfe speak, but he knew immediately this was the person he had tracked across Alsama.

"Have I got this right, then?" he said to Whitehead. "You left the Army and became a police officer, but quietly ran a brothel on the side? Surely that alone wouldn't pay for this place, plus the other house, and the Rolls Royce. What other things did you do?"

"It's a quiet corner of the province, down here," said Whitehead. "But we have border crossings both interprovincial and international, and where there are borders, there are always people who want their business, what should I say, expedited. Yes, expedited. For a fee."

"And sometimes people have trouble with some yahoos, and need a hand getting things sorted out?"

"Exactly. Although all I ever took there was the espresso, I assure you. Mind you, Maria was starting to develop into quite the buxom young woman, she might have had promise. And she was desperate for adventure and something different."

"Not that desperate," said Morgan, pushing forward and moving another step past Rashford. "You evil man."

Whitehead laughed.

"That's hardly in the hostage negotiation handbook, Constable. Watch your language."

"But why bother with the bikers?"

"It was easier. We were going to make the Lance Corporal be the hero of the hour, after she'd earned her price back, of course."

"I tracked her down through her cousin," said Wolfe. "I spoke to her on the phone. We had agreed to meet at the mall. When I got there, she was having lunch with the Captain."

"What made you think she was your sister?" said Rashford.

"I saw the papers that the nuns kept," said Wolfe. "They said I was the son of the girl from Cape Breton, but I wasn't. I asked and the family said she died without having a baby. Nobody wanted him, you see. But the nuns mixed up the papers. My mom wanted me, she just wasn't allowed. She told me."

"You're the one who broke into the nuns' house in Antigonish," said Rashford, nodding.

"I did not break in! The window was open, the filing cabinet wasn't locked. And I didn't take anything, I just looked."

"It's alright, Lance Corporal," said Whitehead. "Just calm down."

He looked at Rashford.

"Can you imagine, Sergeant? All your life, people accuse you of everything that goes wrong, stuff you had nothing to do with? All your life, people call you names? Abuse you, physically and mentally?

"Then you join the Army, and things are good. People recognize your skills. You have respect. You have a community. You have comrades. And then it's time to retire, and they just throw you out. They expect you to cope on your own."

"Are you talking about Lance Corporal Wolfe, or yourself?" said Morgan.

Whitehead laughed.

"Both of us, I suppose."

Rashford turned his attention back to Wolfe.

"If I've got this right, you tracked down Roxanne, thinking that she was your sister ..."

"Not thinking! She is my sister!"

"Okay, you tracked down Roxanne, and she agreed to meet you in the food court at the mall. Is that correct?"

"Yes, but when I got there, she was having lunch with another man."

"The Inspector ... sorry, the Captain," said Rashford. "No doubt she wanted a witness when she met you."

"Perhaps. But when I realized that the man she was with was the Captain, I knew I had to speak to him. That was more important. I excused myself, then waited until she had left."

"Then he came back for a chat," said Whitehead. "He told me he was in dire straits. I needed someone to manage the house. And the rest, as they say, is history."

"And you warned him off, when we did the raid?"

"Of course. And delayed things so he had chance to go and steal a vehicle from that nosy bitch across the way. Then, when he was in the park, I gave him the green light to head out, after the bikers found his truck."

"They reported to you?"

"Of course. And once I realized you had the truck, in Maple Creek, that narrowed the search. It didn't take long for them to find it."

"How come she never recognized you?" said Rashford, looking at Wolfe. "Later, I mean. When you had her in your truck, or when you broke into the police house?"

"I'd shaved," he said. "When I got back to Alberta from the east coast, I'd grown a beard. I still had it when I met her the first time."

"I made him shave it off," said Whitehead. "I had nearly not recognized him at the mall. A soldier needs to look clean and tidy. So, now what?"

"Now I am going to arrest Simon Wolfe here, on charges of kidnapping, living off the avails of prostitution, and assault of a police officer. Me. There will be other charges later, of course."

"Of course," said Whitehead, scoffing. "The Mountie always gets his man, eh? What about me?"

"I think the Chief Superintendent would like to arrest you himself, Inspector. You're not my concern."

"What's the point, eh? I've got terminal cancer. They tell me I'm going to be dead in less than three months. I won't even have a court date by then. And the Lance Corporal, here. His is a classic case of post-traumatic stress disorder, he will be given a reduced sentence. Is it worth all the bother?"

"Please put the shotgun down, Inspector."

"Or what? You'll shoot me? Perhaps that's what I need, Sergeant."

He cradled the shotgun higher and pointed it at Rashford.

"I'll get a nice spread from here, Sergeant. Should get all of you."

Rashford stepped forward again, pushing Morgan behind him.

"Simon Wolfe, I am arresting you ..."

"No! I'm not going to prison."

Wolfe raised his hand and placed the gun against his chin.

"Perseverance, sir" he said, then fired.

As Whitehead looked up in horror, Rashford lunged forward and knocked the shotgun to the side, the weapon firing and blowing out one of the windows. The two men and the armchair crashed over to the floor, Rashford pinning Whitehead down. The Chief Superintendent came quickly over.

"Ian Whitehead, I am arresting you on suspicion of running an illegal bawdy house and living off the avails of prostitution. I wish to give you the following warning: You need not say anything. You have nothing to hope from any promise or favor and nothing to fear from any threat whether or not you say anything. Anything you do or say may be used as evidence."

He produced a pair of handcuffs and secured them around Whitehead's wrists.

"Get him out of here," he said to one of the younger officers, who helped Whitehead to his feet. The older man stopped and looked down at the body.

"He served his country well, you know," he said, quietly. "He had an awful life, all the cards stacked against him right from the start, but he did okay. I put him forward for the Military Medal, but they said he was just doing his job, nothing special. I tell you it was special to me! What a waste. That damned war killed a hell of a lot more than the hundred and fifty-eight Canadians they always report, let me tell you, and it's still killing them."

"Come on, sir," said the Constable, and escorted him out of the room.

Rashford and Morgan stood looking down at Wolfe.

"Well, you got him," said Morgan.

"I wanted him alive," said Rashford. "Whitehead was right, this was probably a case of PTSD. He should have been given a chance to explain himself."

"Gavin," she said, gently. "He took that chance away. You gave it to him, but he didn't want it."

He nodded, slowly.

"Come on, she said. "Let's leave this for the medics and the scene of crime folk."

They turned away and went over to the Chief Superintendent.

"Thank you for your help in all this," he said, shaking their hands. "What's next?"

"We'll report to our CS and head back to Saskatchewan," said Morgan.

"Fair enough. I'll be in touch with you both for statements over the next few days."

They nodded, then turned and left the room.

The closing of the case took nearly two months. Whitehead was charged and arraigned, then remanded in custody at the Bowden Institution, some hundred kilometers north of Calgary. When his cancer progressed, he was transferred to a hospice in Okotoks, where he died just before Christmas.

His body was returned to his family, who held a small funeral in Innisfail, where they lived. The NWMP sent an inspector from Red Deer as a representative of the force. He called Rashford, who knew him from his days in that division, and told him that two veterans from the Lord Strathcona's Horse (Royal Canadians) had also been present.

"It was all very quiet," he said. "Because he died before the trial, technically he wasn't guilty of anything. But it wasn't a full-blown police funeral, or even a military one. Just family, really."

Rashford called Marguarite Chiasson in Cheticamp and told her about finding Simon Spring, and what had happened. Two days later she called him back.

"The family would like the ashes returned here," she said. "Then they can bury him in the same grave as Sylvie. The priest has agreed to this. Is that possible?"

It was, and Rashford organized a courier to transport the remains. Nearly two weeks later he received an e-mail from Marguarite, with a link to a story in the Cape Breton Post. When he opened it, he found the headline 'Mother and son reunited.' The story focused on the young mother whose child had been taken from her at birth, her unresolved death soon afterwards, and the difficult life of her son. The father was not mentioned. The reporter managed to write his story in such a way that Sylvie Cheverie was said to have died in a tragic accident, while the text implied that she had taken her own life. The role of the church in this episode was highlighted.

The story of Simon Spring Wolfe, as he was called by the family, focused on the experiences of Indigenous children across Canada in the latter half of the twentieth century. From the sixties scoop to the horrors of the residential schools, no trope was left unturned. The transition from street punk to respected soldier was reported with tact, and the impact of PTSD on veterans gave important background to support the assertion that with better care and resources, the story might have been quite different.

The article ended with a description of the funeral. The extended Cheverie clan, who had previously only heard of Simon as a seldom-discussed family rumour, were present in full force. Five members of 2 CAV, the Canadian Army Veterans motorcycle group, turned up and formed an honour guard. Two distinguished gentlemen represented the local Legion, and a local musician played haunting tunes on the fiddle. The story was illustrated with two photographs: one of Sylvie as a smiling and vivacious sixteen old, and the other a formal military one of a young Simon before his first deployment to Afghanistan. The similarities between the two were striking, and it was obvious that they were related.

"This reporter is probably going to win some sort of award for this," said Rashford, sharing the story with Morgan.

"We've still stuck here and have all the paperwork to do," she grumbled, even though she enjoyed working from Regina instead of the rural community of Leader. Rashford laughed.

"Well, it's a nine-to-five job right now, and that's good," he said. "Plus, we get a healthy walk every morning."

They were still staying in the guest rooms at the Depot, so it was a ten-minute walk to the headquarters building. A lot of the new recruits thought they were mad, but with their winter issue parkas, gloves, and fur hats, they strode through the Regina morning with no regard for the winter wind and sleet howling down the wide avenues.

"You should look to us as your examples," said Rashford one morning as they emerged from the Depot and passed a young recruit in the parking lot.

"Yes, sir," said the recruit, saluting and then getting into his car.

Rashford had spoken a few times to Roxanne but had not yet managed to broach the topic of her meeting Wolfe in Calgary.

"Just ask her straight out," said Morgan. "Get it off your chest."

"I'd rather wait until I see her," he said, but that was seeming less and less likely. Roxanne and Sandra had planned an enjoyable Christmas together, and no mention had been made of her leaving to travel west.

On New Year's Eve, Rashford took the plunge. When he had Roxanne on the line, he asked her if she had any resolutions for the new year.

"I'm going back to calling myself Anne," she said. "I've met up with some old school friends and they still curl, in the Women's Leisure League. I went along a few times as a sub, in case anyone didn't show up, and now they've asked me to join their rink. But I recognized that I'm not as good as I used to be, or as I thought I was, so I think Anne is better right now."

"Are you going back to Calgary, to see your cousin?

"Nope, I don't think so."

"Roxa ... sorry, Anne. I have a question. Wolfe said he met you, at the mall. You were having lunch with Whitehead, the guy you told me glommed on to you. Wolfe said he'd contacted your cousin and she'd told him where you would be."

"Really? I don't remember." There was silence on the phone. "Hang on, yes. A guy did come to the table, once. Weird guy, with a big bushy beard. But he didn't say who he was. He just said hello, then see you later, then he left. I thought he was talking to the man."

Rashford was silent, thinking.

"Is that important?" she said, at last.

"It might have been, but probably not. He shaved the beard off soon afterwards, so your description wouldn't have been any good, anyway."

They were both quiet.

"What are you doing tomorrow," she said.

"Tomorrow? Nothing special. Why?"

"It's New Year's Day, silly. I'm going to the levees."

"The levees? What's that?"

"It's an old Island tradition, dates back hundreds of years. All the big people host a reception. The Lieutenant Governor, the premier, the mayor, the university, the Island Regiment. Lots of businesses do as well. Everyone dresses up. They start at eight and go until early evening, we drink moose milk from morning to night!"

"Moose milk? What the heck's that?"

"Eggnog and rum. The Haviland Club has the best!"

"It sounds disgusting."

"That's just because you're from away," she said, and he could hear the pout in her voice.

"So, you and Sandra are going to spend the whole day drinking?"

"Sandra? No, she only goes to a couple. Darryl has got us tickets on the bus, you get picked up outside the cenotaph and then it goes from place to place. That way nobody is worried about drinking and driving."

"And when might you come back west?"

"Oh, Gavin, I just don't know. Mom loves having me here, and it's been great to have friends around me. I miss you though."

"Yes," he said. "I miss you as well."

There was another protracted pause.

"Well, have a good time tomorrow," he said, and finished the call.

That afternoon he asked Morgan if she had any plans for the evening. She hadn't, so they decided to go out for dinner at the Regina Casino and see in the New Year there. They had an evening full of laughter and got a taxi back to the Depot.

As they walked up the path to the building, Rashford put his arm around her and nuzzled her hair. She laughed, then pulled away.

"Off to bed, you," she said. "Medicine Hat was nice, but I don't want to go back there."

Rashford pouted.

"And don't pout," she said.

He saw her to her room and gave her a kiss on the cheek.

"Good night," she said, going inside. He heard the lock click on the other side of the door.

He spent New Year's Day watching American football on television, thinking about levees and moose milk. The next morning, he went for his scheduled meeting with Chief Superintendent Pollard.

"Happy New Year," she said, standing up in greeting and shaking his hand. "I wonder what excitement this one will bring?"

"I'm not sure, Ma'am."

"Well, let me start it with some good news. You're being promoted. Congratulations, Staff Sergeant."

"Promoted?"

Rashford was more than surprised, he was shocked.

"I didn't realize ..."

"You did a wonderful job on that last case, Gavin. Chief Inspector Toews wrote a glowing report. We cleared up the Dallas case, and also the Fancy Boots case, and you broke up a prostitution ring as well. All in all, not a bad piece of work."

"Thank you, Ma'am."

"Today's Thursday. Take the next week or so to find yourself a place to live. You're going to be based here for the first little while, but you can't stay in the Depot forever."

"Yes, Ma'am."

"There are going to be some movement in the next month. Staff

Sergeant Miller is going to be retiring, so I shall have to fill the vacancy at Swift Current. That won't be for you. It needs someone with a bit more experience. But when the musical chairs stop, you'll have a seat somewhere on my team here. Come back in a week on Monday and we'll decide your first assignment."

"Yes, Ma'am. Umm, what about Gayle Morgan, Ma'am?"

"What about her?"

"Will she be going back to Leader, Ma'am?"

"No, I'm going to transfer her as well. She will be the new Senior Constable at Swift Current. But please don't tell her just yet. I'm meeting with her at eleven."

Rashford saluted and made for the door.

"Oh, and Staff Sergeant Rashford?"

"Yes, Ma'am?"

"After I chat with Constable Morgan, I'm taking a week's vacation, so try not to cause any trouble until I get back."

"Yes, Ma'am."

As he left the office, he nodded a greeting to Sarah, who was sitting behind her desk as usual.

"Still only four notches, I see."

She reddened.

"Oh, that. It was just a joke, a bit of fun to liven up the day."

"A joke?" said Rashford.

She looked at him, still blushing.

"A joke that got out of hand," she said. "I'm sorry."

"How did that happen?"

"Oh, I just got fed up with everyone teasing me, that I worked crazy long hours at the beck and call of the Chief Superintendent, and that I didn't have a social life. So, I made one up."

Rashford paused.

"So, the young farmer?"

She laughed, self-consciously.

"There was no young farmer. I went home and ate perogies with my mom, then we watched a soppy movie on TV. That's what we usually do on a Saturday night."

"Your mom?"

"Yeah. I live with her. Not quite the proper image for a femme fatale, eh?"

She returned to her typing.

Rashford laughed, then said goodbye and left the office.

At the end of the day, Rashford and Morgan met for a late afternoon drink. They congratulated each other on their promotions and stressed that they hoped to be able to work together again soon. Morgan had brought a copy of the Regina Leader Post and they spent time going through the apartments available in the Classifieds section. Morgan found a few possibilities in Swift Current and Rashford ended up with a short-list of six in Regina.

The next morning, he telephoned and found that four of the apartments were still available. He spent the afternoon driving to each and found one that he liked. It was in a four-plex, on the eastern side of Wascana Lake. It was a twenty-five-minute bike ride to the office, which he thought might be good for him in the spring, and meanwhile it was only a fifteen-minute drive. He was also only a few minutes walk from Broadway Avenue, where he could cross the busy Broad Street at a pedestrian light and find himself in Wascana Park. The trails along the lake, he thought, would be perfect for a morning run.

He communicated back and forth with the owner through text and e-mail and by early Friday afternoon he had a lease, starting the following Monday. He used e-transfer to send his deposit, then sat back and thought about how he might spend his weekend. For a few minutes he contemplated going out to Maple Creek, then decided he didn't want to spend the next two days taking about Roxanne. Or rather, Anne.

He called her anyway.

"Hello, Gavin," she said. "I didn't expect you to call today."

"I just thought I'd check how you were, and give you my news," he said.

"Oh, I'm fine," she said. "I'm a big girl, Gavin. I don't need you to look after me or check up on me every two minutes. It's creepy."

"Creepy?"

"Yes. Everything is fine, okay? Mom and I are getting along great. I've reconnected with tons of friends. I have a job. I've got a lead on a small apartment that will be vacant at the end of the month. I'm an Island girl and I'm so happy to be back home. Can't you understand that?"

Rashford was silent.

"What's your news?" she said, at last.

"I've rented an apartment, more of a townhouse really. In Regina."

"You're staying there, then," said Anne.

It wasn't a question.

"Yes. I have been promoted to Staff Sergeant. Pollard says that she'll give me my new posting next week, but it will be based out of Regina."

"Congratulations."

"Thank you."

"No, I mean it. You're good at what you do, Gavin. And you're a prairie boy. You don't really want to come and live here by the ocean, do you?"

"Not really, I suppose," he said. "But you like the prairies!"

"Not that much," said Anne. "It's too dry. And people aren't as friendly as they are here."

"I thought you got on well with Bettina?"

"Yes, but that's just one person, really. Here, I go shopping, I meet someone I knew at school. I go out for a coffee or a drink, people come up and chat with me. I'm not just the policeman's girlfriend, I'm a real person. And I like that."

"So, this is you breaking up with me, is it?" said Rashford.

"We had a good time, Gavin," she said. "I'll always remember that."

Rashford was not sure whether he felt angry or upset, or some weird combination of both.

"How's the new boyfriend?" he said.

"What new boyfriend?"

"Darryl."

To his surprise, Anne laughed. Loudly.

"They're not my boyfriend," she said. "They're not even a boy. They're trans. They're just a friend. Oh, Gavin, is that what's been worrying you, that I have a boyfriend here? Don't be so silly."

"I'm sorry but yes, it upset me, thinking that," he said.

"Don't be jealous, Gavin," she said. "Just live your life. And I'll live mine. Okay?"

"Okay," he said.

They chatted for a few minutes longer, then Anne said she had to go and hung up.

Rashford sat quietly and smoked a cigarette. He realized that he was not surprised by the conversation he had just finished. In fact, it was almost a relief, he had been having similar talks with himself for days.

After reflecting for another few moments, he picked up his phone. He made one call, and then a second. When Sarah answered, she seemed surprised to hear his voice.

"Sorry, Staff Sergeant, I thought you knew. The Chief is out of the office today."

"Yes, I knew that. I had a question for you, actually."

"Yes?"

Rashford cleared his throat.

"I was wondering whether you would like to go out for a drink tonight?"

There was a pause. Rashford thought to himself, geez, I screwed this up. Then Sarah spoke.

"That would be lovely, thank you. What time, and where?"

Rashford exhaled the breath he didn't realize he had been holding.

"Whenever is convenient. I've booked a room at the Stone Hall Castle for the weekend. Just call me when you get there."

"The Castle? Nice."

"Yes, I remembered that you recommended it."

There was another pause, while they listened to each other breathing.

"Is there parking?" said Sarah, eventually.

"I thought you could take a cab over," said Rashford. "That way you can have a drink and still be home for your perogy dinner."

"Perogy dinner is on Saturday," said Sarah. "That's tomorrow night."

"Yes," said Rashford. "I know."

About the Author

J. T. Goddard is a retired professor of education whose career, over 45 years, took him to every province and territory of Canada, and to a dozen countries around the world. He now happily calls the Maritimes home. *Tracks* is his second novel.

For more information, visit www.timgoddard.ca.

Also by J. T. Goddard

Traces (2021)